Needs & Wants

Needs & Wants

RHEA T. JACKSON

Needs & Wants by Rhea T. Jackson

Cover Illustrations from shutterstock.com

ISBN: 978-0578-35618-1

Printed in the United States of America

First printing 2022

Dedication

To the loves of my life who are still here with me, departed from me, and have yet to meet me:
To my grandmother, Ruth Lee, I will see you again one day.
To my husband, Samuel, you ignite a fire within me.
To my niece, auntie is waiting to love on you.
To the child I've prayed for, you may not come from me, but you are already a part of me.
To my family, I love you all.

Acknowledgments

First and foremost, I must give honor and glory to my Lord and Savior, Jesus Christ. Without him, I would not be where I am today. I am so grateful for the love, blessings, and mercy he bestows upon me. Second, I want to thank my husband, Samuel. There is never a moment that he doesn't make me laugh and smile. And when he helps me brainstorm my ideas, he's always there with a listening ear, raised eyebrow, and his beautiful smile. Third, I must thank my family and friends. There are so many of you all out there, so I will try to keep it short and sweet so that you can get to reading. Mom and Dad, I love you both so much. Thank you both for supporting me and raising me to be loving yet tough. To my older brother, Deven, and his wife, and my older sister, Nikia, you guys are beyond awesome. There is never a dull moment with you all. To my aunts, uncles, and cousins, I am not going to name all of you, but you know who you are. I love you all so much. Thank you all for supporting me. To my best friend and second sister, Rosie, the love and support you have and continue to pour into me is nothing but the sunshine itself. And to my brother-in-law, Alex, and his wife, thanks for encouraging me and letting me use your desk. I really appreciate that. Lastly, I want to thank Mr. Tyrone "Tony" Reed Jr. for helping me out when I had questions about the self-publishing process. Your knowledge was invaluable to me. With all that said, thank you all so much. Let's read!

Chapter One

Lobotomy wouldn't get the elusive Elijah Bryson to say he loved her anytime soon, let alone a gunshot to his crooked pinky toe, Breanna Ellis thought. Seven years and a five-year-old later, love waltzed its fairy dust, carrying ass out the door and slammed it shut in her face.

Maybe Leslie was right. He just needed time to reflect on their relationship; Elijah just needed to see the enjoyable moments they shared—that mumbo jumbo reverse psychology shit never worked on him. The man could never decide if he wanted chicken or beef between two hamburger buns whenever he went to Wendy's. Trying to convince him to buy their fish sandwich instead of a hamburger or chicken sandwich resulted in a tear playing at one of his tear ducts and him puckering his lips as if he'd gotten spanked by his fourth-grade teacher, Mrs. Walsh.

Breanna peered into the bathroom mirror and sighed as she combed her raven tresses. This man held her in more horrible confines than she had imagined for the past five years. Well, not all of them were bad. God blessed Mr. Hide and Go Seek beyond measure, and Eros himself touched his tongue. She'd never complained about that. Hell, that's how Isabella got here. But despite the joy their daughter's arrival brought him, it still didn't help him open himself to her about why he felt the need to be so overprotective. Instead, it caused more silence. More arguments.

Whatever was bugging him, Breanna had had enough of it. She was done playing guessing games on whether he loved her more this day or the next. She was done.

Turning on the faucet, she let the cool water run over the back of her hand until steam surrounded it. Breanna loved Elijah. She honestly did. Or did she? She closed her eyes, trying to keep that tear from falling. God! She hated him for making her so empty.

"Babe?"

Breanna jumped from her black flats and turned toward the opened door. Elijah's steel-blue eyes gazed into hers, searing their impressions into each of hers. "You scared me, Eli," she said, wiping the fleeting tear away as fast as she could.

Elijah frowned as he stepped closer to her. He reached his hand toward her face. "What's wrong?"

He wanted to ask this question now. He was five years too late for that.

Breanna stared at the black and white yin-yang-styled tree of life clock hanging above their bedroom door and let her shoulders slump. No matter how much they argued, that clock let her mind escape from the crap flowing from his mouth. Breana gave a half smile, watching the clock strike six-forty pm on the dot. Saved by the time for work.

"Can this wait? My shift is about to start in twenty minutes."

"You do this every time, Bree." Elijah walked out the light blue-colored bathroom, mumbling under his breath as he strode.

Breanna turned toward the shower and scoffed, viewing its white, gray, and blue hexagon-shaped tiles behind the glass. That was the one place she and Elijah loved staying in together when Izzy was fast asleep. Even the white and gray-streaked porcelain floor that resembled wooden planks made her close her eyes. She couldn't keep up with the countless times they stood on that very floor, stroking, caressing, and drying each other off before he whisked her off to bed. She missed that.

Breanna followed his path and stepped into the bedroom. The light sky-blue paint melded perfectly with the color scheme of their bathroom. That was all Elijah's doing. He was an architect and interior designer smashed into one. Too bad he couldn't be a better emotional supporter and communicator.

She watched him kick off his work boots near the foot of the bed and sit down. He pulled off his shirt, exposing a set of roman numerals of Isabella's birthdate on his inner forearm. A bruise sat near the last number, turning that area of warm beige skin into an uneven swatch of blacks, purples, and deep reds.

"You don't talk to me anymore."

2

"Elijah, I just told you I don't have time for this."

"Then, when is the right time for this, Breanna?"

Breanna pulled her hair into a bun, then tied her black apron around her waist. "You talk about me always pulling this stunt. What about you? Every time you come home from work, I've got to go in."

"So, now you're blaming me because I work until seven o'clock most nights."

"You fuckin' flip houses for God's sake, Elijah. Some nights I'm already gone before you get home, which forces me to take Izzy to my momma's house."

He scoffed. "Not your mom again."

"What about her, Elijah?"

"She's part of the problem between us."

Breanna shook her head. "You're mainly the problem because you refuse to talk to me."

Elijah ran his fingers over his beard, then scoffed. He focused his attention on Isabella's picture when she was just an infant and smiled for a moment. "Then why don't you come to me and talk?"

"I've tried. You just don't want to open up to me, Elijah," she said, sliding on her glasses. She made her way to the bedroom door. "Besides, I'm probably a waste of time to talk to, anyway."

"What? Breanna wait," Elijah said. He stood from the bed and walked toward her. He grabbed the back of her arm and pulled her into his embrace as he gazed into her eyes. "You're never a waste of my time. I don't ever want you to think that."

The warmth of his arms around her waist made her close her eyes as she rested her head underneath the crevice between his chin and neck. For that moment, Breanna saw the man who used to dance with her to the croons of Musiq Soulchild before sweeping her off her feet and twirling her around in his arms. She smiled for a moment, remembering how she wobbled whenever he placed her back onto her feet after spinning her around. How in the hell did all that change so quickly?

The man before her used to kiss her from her lips down to her toes whenever he wanted to get her attention, and she loved it when he caressed the small of her back. But the man before her wasn't the person she fell in love with seven years ago. She saw Elijah as the man who wanted her to focus on taking care of their child instead of finishing school. He became the man that wanted complete and utter control of her life. A tear fell. "Please let go of me, Elijah."

He stared at her. "Why are you crying, Bree?"

He wiped the sliding tear away with his thumb, and then pulled her back into his embrace.

3

Breanna let her ear rest on his chest and closed her eyes. The thumping of his heart brought back memories she didn't want to remember; wonderful memories that soured on her taste buds.

"This is what you do, Elijah," she said, pushing him away. "You think taking me into your arms solves every problem, but it doesn't. You choose not to talk to me because sex is your answer for everything."

"What? When have I ever done that to you, Bree?" he asked. He stared into her deep brown eyes and frowned.

Breanna scoffed while shaking her head. "You're going to sit here and lie to me about how you always try to take my clothes off whenever we fight. Maybe that's the way you white folks kiss and make-up, but that's not how this black woman handles shit," she said, pointing to herself.

Elijah ran his hands through his hair and sat on the bed again. Dirt from his blue jeans found its way onto the purple and gray side-striped comforter and clung to it like it was a part of the design. "So, now you're making this a race thing, right?"

Breanna glanced at the clock, then back at Elijah. "When hasn't it not been, Elijah?" she asked.

She grabbed her purse from the cherry oak dresser and glanced inside the bag's massive opening. The notification light danced about on her cellphone as it flashed. Tessa's name followed behind the scroll. Saved yet again, she mused to herself.

If there was anyone who understood what she was going through with Elijah, it was Tessa Chatman. Older, wiser, and a relationship guru in her own right, whether she knew it or not, Tessa was Breanna's relationship connoisseur whenever she needed advice on dealing with Elijah's lack of emotional support, reciprocation of love, and constant whining. Whatever she wanted her to know just wasn't something Breanna could pass up on.

"Did you even hear a word I just said, Bree?"

"Yeah," Breanna replied, folding her arms across her chest. "I heard everything you weren't trying to tell me, Elijah. I'll see you in the morning."

He frowned at her for a moment, then took a deep breath. He stood from the bed and walked into the master bathroom, slamming the door shut behind him.

That was his typical reaction. Elijah always ran from the problem instead of meeting it head-on. Maybe Mama was right. She needed a good, strong black supportive man to keep her afloat, to keep her stable, to give her peace of mind. That was what she needed. Not this bullshit she had been putting up with.

4

Walking out of the bedroom, she pulled the door closed behind her and made her way to the staircase. She rubbed her temple, hoping they weren't loud enough to make Isabella cry. That was the last thing she needed before heading out the door.

"Mommy?"

Breanna stiffened. Please don't let there be any tears. She turned around and smiled at the eye-rubbing child standing beside her bedroom door in her favorite Princess Tianna pajamas. Daisy stood next to her, wagging her tail as she always did whenever she stood around her. She swore if Isabella had never been born, she would have left his ass a long time ago. Their daughter was the only reason she had put up with Elijah for this long.

"What's up, my little Shortcake?" Breanna asked, picking up the small child and planting a kiss on her cheek.

"Do you have to go to work tonight?"

"I do, but Saturday night, I'm off work."

"Can you, me, and Daddy watch a movie Saturday night?" she asked. The smile on her face illuminated her big steel-blue eyes and natural pink lips. Her light caramel skin was an amalgam of her and Elijah. Her dark brown hair was streaked with brownish blonde hues that laid on both her shoulders. Regardless of how Breanna styled Isabella's hair, it refused to stay in curls. That was her genetic fault, for sure.

"Let's see what Daddy wants to do, and we'll catch a movie, okay, Shortcake." Breanna placed the child on her feet and kneeled beside her. She pulled Isabella's soft hair behind her ear and kissed her forehead. It was hard to put on a front before Izzy, yet that child knew just as well when her mommy and daddy were fighting. It was almost like she had an antenna twitching all about her head whenever she and Elijah were standing on shaky ground or trying to mend.

"You promise?"

"I promise, Izzy," Breanna replied. "Mommy's gotta go to work, so she can bring you home some chocolate chip cookies, alright."

Isabella grinned, twisting about where she stood. "Okay."

"See you soon, shortcake. I love you."

The child waved as she yawned. "I love you too, Mommy."

Breanna hurried down the steps, grabbed her car keys off the dining room table, and made her way out the front door. This was going to be the night her life changed, Breanna thought. For the better, in fact. She had to repeat that over and over again for that to sink into her brain. She'd be damned if she let Elijah set her back again.

As she unlocked her car door, her phone blared Raheem DeVaughn's voice throughout her purse. She frowned. Either Tessa had a lot on her plate with overbearing customers, or the boss man was

5

going on one of his rampages again because he didn't know how to separate his at-work boyfriend from his at-home boyfriend. These were the times at Soul Bistro.

"Damn it," Breanna said, missing the call. She got inside the car and closed the door.

Carrying Grandma Isabella's tote wasn't her thing. It wasn't like she was carrying a brick or hammer inside it. Grandma had a bad habit of doing that. But at least nobody fucked with her. If they did, she didn't hesitate to swing it at their head a few times. She smiled. Breanna missed that woman's wisdom and nonchalant demeanor.

God! She wished she was there to give her some advice on how to deal with Elijah's bullshit. If there was one thing she loved about Daddy's mom, it was the fact that the woman never shied away from speaking her mind. Although some called her Big Mama for her cooking, she was always Grandma Isabella to Breanna. And whenever she was in the kitchen, she would give anybody a piece of her mind whether they wanted it or not.

Raheem DeVaughn's voice blared throughout the purse again as she backed out of the driveway. She dug her hand into the satchel and grabbed the device.

"Gotcha," Breanna said, grinning. "What's up, T?"

"Thank God! You finally answered your phone," Tessa spoke. The huskiness of her voice had an alto-like melody that was reminiscent of a singer's vibrato.

"And hello to you, Tessa."

"And all the nice pleasantries to you too, heffa."

Breanna scoffed as she smiled. "Why I gotta be a heffa, though?"

"Cause if you don't get your ass down here and see this piece of artwork that just slow wined his way inside Soul Bistro, you gone be missin' out. That's what."

Breanna arched an eyebrow. "Who are you talking about?"

"I'm talking about the brotha who asked about you before you left early three nights ago."

Breanna's cheeks burned as she smiled. She synced her Bluetooth headset to her phone and gripped the steering wheel with both hands as she stopped at the red light. She had to stay focused so she wouldn't get pulled over. Like that was going to keep her focused if the officer was fine. "Why didn't you tell me somebody was looking for me?"

"That was the night Elijah came to pick you up, remember."

Breanna pursed her lips. "You're right. He made me mad on the way out the door."

"Well, he's here looking for you."

"Stop it, T. I need to focus on the street."

6

"More like you need to focus on keeping your panties dry."

"Tessa! Girl, I'm gonna get you for that one," she replied, giggling.

"Listen to you. You know it's true," Tessa snickered. "Anyway, he's the chocolate brotha with the well-groomed beard, pretty white teeth, and those dramatic cognac eyes. He's tall with that muscular, lean build. And don't let me forget his ass looks good in a pair of black slacks, girl. He sorta looks like Marvin Gaye and Denzel Washington back in the day. He's just sexy as hell."

"Tessa, please stop. I honestly need to focus on the street."

"Sure, sure. I will. But he just sat down at his favorite booth, and today he's serving you with the red button-down shirt with the black and red tie and black slacks to match. And oh! I can't forget that he smells like he's been dipped in honey maple syrup. Ya' ass best hurry," Tessa said. "Cause I ain't getting any younger. And I think he likes them in their early forties."

Breanna laughed. "Okay, okay. I'll be there in the next five minutes."

"You better be."

Breanna ended the call. She made a right turn onto Vickers Street in mid-town toward the East End Estates and drove past mini-mansions on either side of her. Streetlights lit up one by one as she went. Stately trees coming into bloom sat in front of the homes like stage props. She peered at one house, looking directly into the owner's living room through the curtainless windows. She shook her head. They were just inviting trouble to show up at their front door. Then again, they were probably friends with the mayor since he lived in the same area.

Turning onto Plowman Cove, she saw a line of cars heading in the restaurant's direction. She sighed. Friday nights never ceased in bringing in the singles and the drunks. She pulled into Soul Bistro's parking lot and found a spot close to Tessa's car.

There was someone wanting and willing to listen to her and not attempt to make small talk with her. There was someone who wanted to treat her the way she needed to be treated, not treated like the help. He was waiting inside for her, and she couldn't wait for him to grace her presence.

Breanna needed this. She needed to feel that kind of love Elijah used to give her. She needed to feel like the woman she used to be. Breanna needed to be happy.

She took a deep breath and held it for a moment. Breanna needed this, she protested to herself. She couldn't keep waiting for Elijah to change. She just... really wanted him to.

Breanna stopped in mid-step toward the building. If she didn't go after her own happiness, then she would never be happy. She couldn't let Elijah keep pulling her heart in every other direction than the right direction. Pulling the large wooden door handle, she made her way into the building.

Tessa stood near the glass double doors of the second entrance. Pictures of black soul, blues, and jazz legends hung about the rustic bricks before leading into the atmospheric mesh of auburn brown wooden walls and tan ceilings. Globe lights hung from black stems above the patrons' heads as they dined to the sounds of Will Downing's sultry voice.

"Hey, Tessa," Breanna said. She stood beside her, looking for the mystery gentleman her friend spoke of.

Tessa smiled at her, flashing her white teeth. "He's over there."

Breanna moved her head around as she stood on her tippy-toes, searching for him. "I don't see him."

"There he is," Tessa said. She bit her bottom lip and glanced at Breanna.

Breanna swallowed hard. Her lips parted. Watching him sip hot tea from the cup made her spine tingle. No other person could make her spine tingle like that except for... "I know who he is."

Tessa stared at the side of her head. "No shit. Who is he?"

"Nathaniel Morrison. A guy I used to date back in high school."

"Are you serious, Bree?" Tessa said, folding her arms across her chest and rolling her neck from side to side. "Why did you two break up?"

"His parents moved to North Carolina before he had the chance to finish school here."

"Well," Tessa smiled. "There's no time like the present, isn't there."

Breanna smiled. This was what she needed, she thought. "It sure isn't."

Breanna walked over to his booth and sat on his opposite side. She placed her purse on the table and rested her hands on it. She stared at him and smiled. His eyes caught hers; his lips turned upward into a seductive smirk.

"Breanna Ellis," he said. His deep voice reverberated through her vaginal walls. "It's so good to see you again."

"It's good to see you again too, Nathaniel."

8

Chapter Two

"My god," Nathaniel said. He took a long sip of his tea. His eyes never left hers. "I haven't seen you since high school. You look amazing."

Breanna's cheeks flushed. She couldn't contain the smile he'd placed there. That was something Elijah had forgotten how to do, or refused to do, as of late.

She glanced at Tessa, who was all smiles, standing by the door. She didn't even pay attention to the guests walking into the restaurant. Leslie caught her eye too, but the resting bitch face couldn't have been more prominent. That was Leslie. It took her a moment to latch onto new changes. But she did whenever she thought it was justified.

"I don't think I look that great," Breanna said. "I had a little girl about five years ago."

Nathaniel coughed, spitting out some of his tea. "Really?!" He placed the teacup on the table and wiped his mouth and hands with a napkin. "Damn, girl! The radiance never left you."

Breanna smiled. "You're quite the charmer. Just like you were in high school."

"Those were the days, weren't they?"

"They were," she replied. Every word he spoke seemed to have wrapped its hands around every portion of her body and clung to it tightly. "How's your mom and dad?"

"About to celebrate forty-five years of marriage." Nathaniel glanced at her with a wry smile, then chuckled. "Why you changin' the subject?"

"I'm not," Breanna said. Her lips parted slightly. Damn! Time had done him well, too. His lips were so freaking kissable. "I haven't seen or heard from them in like forever."

He nodded, flashing his perfect white teeth as he smiled. "They're good," he replied. "But you ain't gonna ask about how I've been doing? That's just wrong."

Breanna covered her smile with her hand. She giggled, watching him wipe away fake tears and pout. "Oh, I'm so sorry, Nathaniel. How have you been doing?"

"Good," he said, taking another sip of his tea. Placing the cup on the table, he pulled his cellphone from his back pocket, set it on the table, and slid it in her direction. "But I'll be better if I could catch up with you a little more."

Breanna looked at him. Elijah didn't have to know she was talking to Nathaniel. He didn't know who Nathaniel was. "Are you asking for my number?"

"If that's okay with you." He looked at her, then ran his tongue over his lips to catch the last remnants of tea he sipped. "By the way, are you still attached to the white boy I saw pick you up a few days ago?"

Breanna held her breath for a moment, then slowly released it through her nose. If he saw Elijah come inside the restaurant, that meant Nathaniel had already scoped him out. She looked at him, then stared at his phone, still sitting on the table. Things could go sour in a millisecond if the two of them ever came face to face with each other. But that would never happen if she played her cards right. The sudden crashing of dishes hitting the ground made Breanna jump. She had to move her ass before Howard ran from the back in a panic. "He's the father."

"Whoa! You serious, Bree?" Nathaniel blurted out. His eyes were wide.

"We met in college. He was..." Breanna paused, looking away from Nathaniel. A lump swelled in her throat. Elijah was her one back then. No other man could replace him until he changed... for the worse. "One thing led to another, and we brought a little girl into this world."

"Sounds like there's some pain there," he said. "He did you wrong or something?"

"Something like that."

"Come on, girl, you ain't gotta front with me."

Breanna sighed, then gave a slight smile. "I'll tell you when I'm ready, if that's okay with you?"

"My shoulder's always here for you," Nathaniel said, patting it. He smiled. "Your name is right here."

10

Breanna reached for his phone and entered her number into it. For the second time that night, she felt comfortable. She didn't know if it was the fact that Nathaniel made her smile or the fact that he cared about what she had gone through with Elijah. Whatever it was, she felt like she could kick off her shoes and rest her feet on an ottoman. "Text me first before you call, okay."

"Yes, ma'am." Nathaniel grinned.

"I gotta get to work before boss man finds me out here chatting with you."

He nodded. "It's good seeing you again, Breanna. I can't wait to talk to you again."

"It's really good seeing you too, Nathaniel. I can't wait either."

Breanna locked eyes with him one last time, then made her way to the back of the restaurant. She walked through a set of double doors leading toward the kitchen and made her way down the hall and into the break room. She opened her locker and smiled, feeling her cheeks burn from the smoothness that lingered on his every word.

She couldn't contain the butterflies Nathaniel let loose within her, let alone stop thinking about how fine he was. It seemed like he hadn't aged a day in his life. She stuffed her purse inside the locker the best way she could without ripping the material. Big Mama would have emerged from her grave if she knew she'd tore it. That would have been a sight to see, Breanna thought.

It had been a long time since someone had taken the time to listen to her; it had been an even longer time since someone made her feel like she mattered. Her smile faded from her lips. Elijah used to make her feel this way. Whenever he stared at her with his steel-blue eyes and gave her that wry smile with his full yet somewhat thin lips, she'd feel that invisible finger slide down her spine. Even the way his brown tresses sat just at the cusp of his thick eyebrows in loose curls made her feel like someone was pressing their moist lips against the side of her neck. She closed her eyes. She couldn't take too much more of the war between them.

Opening her eyes, a picture of her and Elijah hugging each other stared back at her. Their smiles were evident of the love and happiness they shared. It was just before Izzy was born; it was just before they started attacking and berating each other.

No matter how much she tried to cover it up, Breanna knew Elijah no longer loved her. Sure, he said it, but the emotion, the weight of the word, was gone from their relationship. Breanna stared at the picture once more. Why did she feel so heavy from looking at it? Why did she feel like she had just broken a sacred vow? She didn't need this type of conflict in her life.

If Elijah didn't give two shits about her, then why should she care about him. The man took her back to the forties and fifties and expected her to be okay with it. No, sir. Guilt didn't have a place in her heart. If anyone needed to feel guilty, it should have been Elijah for how he treated her.

"How's Isabella doing?"

Breanna jumped for the third time that night. Why the hell was she so jumpy? "Hey, Leslie. I didn't hear you come in."

Tessa walked inside behind her and blew a kiss at a poster of Prince on his motorcycle that hung on a bland white wall where a cheap black leather, more like pleather, couch sat against. Scuffs and scrapes littered the wall where former and current employees hung posters of their favorite singers. Breanna shook her head. She couldn't understand how a man adorned in a tight purple suit with a white ruffled shirt was the symbol of sexiness. She would have preferred Musiq Soulchild. Now, that man was sexy. She would have hung a poster of him on the wall too, but she and Elijah adored the man's sweet melodies and soulful lyrics. When they first met at the university's library, she remembered hearing "takeyouthere" blast through Elijah's earbuds. How did they grow so far apart yet love some of the same things?

"Leslie, why you got your arms folded like you somebody's mama or something?" Tessa stared at her as she shook her head. Breanna stared at the two of them. This was turning sour fast.

Leslie looked at Tessa for a moment, then rolled her eyes, focusing her attention on Breanna. Her thick black natural coils sat on her shoulders like a spring floral bouquet. Leslie's white chiffon blouse and black pencil skirt accentuated her curvier, pear-shaped figure well. Her dark chocolate skin was mesmerizing. Her almond-shaped eyes and semi-full lips gave her a sex appeal Breanna found herself somewhat jealous of. Had AJ been there, he would have pulled down his glasses and whistled at her. They were cute like that.

"I can fold my arms if I want to, Tessa." Leslie sat on the black pleather sofa and pulled off one of her black pumps, revealing a hole the size of a tangerine in her nude stockings.

"Okay," Tessa said, walking past her. She peered at her, then back at Breanna with a smirk. "I'm just trying to make sure that you're alright over there. You look like you ain't had any for some time now."

"For your information, Tessa." Leslie retorted. "I have a happy ending every time I go to bed, and whether it's intimate or not, I'm never without. You, on the other hand, that's questionable."

12

A frown sat upon Tessa's brow as she stared at Leslie, who only smiled at her reaction. Breanna knew all too well where that was going to lead to.

"To answer your question, Leslie, Isabella is doing better," Breanna said, hoping to cut the tension in the air. She looked at them both. World War II was about to be reenacted in that tiny ass room.

Leslie diverted her attention away from Tessa and smiled at Breanna. "That's good to hear," said Leslie. "I remember you telling me she had another asthma attack about two weeks ago."

"She and Elijah both," Breanna replied.

"Aww damn! I forgot he had asthma too," Tessa said. She caught eyes with Leslie once more, then turned her attention back toward Breanna.

"I need to add him to my insurance so that I can help him pay for his inhalers."

"I thought he had that lucrative ass business flipping houses and bought his own insurance?" Tessa asked. She opened her locker and pulled out her flats. She slid them on one by one. Tessa pulled her semi kinky dark brown hair that rested in between her shoulder blades into a ponytail. She undid one button on her white button-down blouse and pushed up her medium-sized breasts, trying to make them look bigger than they appeared.

Breanna shook her head, watching her smooch at herself in the tiny mirror. Both she and Leslie had more girls than she would ever have. She guessed that was the gift and curse of having more hips than breasts and a slender waist with shapely thighs.

"He and Adrian own that company," Leslie responded.

Tessa stared at Leslie and rolled her eyes. "Oh! I forgot that yo' boo thang was in cahoots with Elijah. I wonder how that's working out."

Breanna looked at Tessa and Leslie and folded her arms. There was no reasoning with these two. No matter how hard she tried, they were always slick with the attacks. But Breanna had to give Leslie some credit. She never allowed Tessa to get under her skin for a moment. That was that thick skin without the nicks and bumps. That was that same skin Grandma Zora had.

That woman practically raised her and Amber when Momma and Daddy were going through their divorce. She always found time for the both of them when Momma and Daddy couldn't force themselves to stay in the same room together and talk for just a second. She always had their best interest in mind when neither of them didn't. Well, that was more of Daddy never having her best interest in mind after he left Momma for Regina. Leslie had that kind of love and fortitude for those who she loved.

13

And like Grandma Zora, Leslie took up for Elijah when he didn't deserve the sympathy. That was the same thing Grandma Zora did for Daddy. Neither of those assholes deserved it.

"So, what's your problem with me anyway, Leslie?"

Leslie smiled. She slid back on her pump and stood from the couch. "I don't mean any harm, Tessa, but I do," she said. "You need to be trying to help your friend salvage and mend her relationship rather than trying to fix her up with brotha man from the fifth floor."

Breanna stared at Leslie and frowned. "Everyone can't have a relationship like you have, Leslie."

"So, you think my relationship is perfect? Well, it isn't, Bree," she retorted. "It's far from it. We, however, know how to talk through the shit. That's something you need to do with Elijah."

"You make this sound so easy, Leslie," Breanna replied. "Elijah won't listen to me. That's the one thing I understand."

"From what I understand, it's the other way around."

"Are you serious with that mess right now, Leslie?"

Leslie tilted her head back and grunted while releasing a deep breath. "You don't wanna listen to me, Breanna. You'd rather mess up something that only needs a little work. A little work that you're not willing to commit to."

"You've got some balls to say that shit to my face." Breanna stepped closer to Leslie and stared into her eyes. Even in heels, Leslie was still a couple of inches taller than she was. Too bad she was short on the knowledge of how to recognize a terrible relationship. She was going to be swimming up the creek if AJ suddenly changed his demeanor toward her.

"And you got some balls for talking to another man instead of trying to work out your relationship."

"Oh my God, Leslie. You need to study your man guide a little more thoroughly, honey. Are you sure you didn't pay AJ to sleep with you?"

"I don't think you understand what men want or need at all, Tessa," Leslie said. "You'd rather cheat than work out a good relationship. Now that's sad."

"What's sad is your goodie, goodie relationship advice, Leslie." Tessa walked to the drink machine and swiped her debit card. Pressing on the Fiji Water, she watched as the machine gathered up her favorite bottled water and dropped it into the dispensary like a prize waiting for her to collect. "You have a solution for everything, don't you?"

"Well, the last time I checked, I didn't run my fiancé away. Remember Ishmael, Tessa? I haven't forgotten him. He was such a nice guy."

14

Tessa pursed her lips. A frown followed suit. "I'll be at the front of the house waiting for you, Bree," she said. "When you get done listening to her tired ass shit."

Breanna watched Tessa walk out of the break room. Though incoherent, she could tell Tessa was cursing under her breath. Leslie was wrong for that one, but at least their bickering stopped.

After Ishmael called off the engagement, Tessa swore off relationships altogether. All she wanted was the casual fling or a little rustle under the covers, and she was over it.

"Leslie—"

"Bree, as much as I love you, sis, I really want you to think about fixing your mess at home before you go creating some more mess with somebody else."

Breanna's brows drew together. "Mess. You honestly think that I caused this?"

"I'm not saying that, Bree."

"Then, what are you saying?" Breanna slammed the locker door shut and gave Leslie her full, undivided attention.

"What I'm saying is that you and Elijah need to talk about forgiveness, responsibility, and trust. Something that both of you shy away from each other about."

"Well, whenever you get pregnant and AJ forces you to stop working because he wants you to focus on taking care of the baby, then tell me how you really feel," Breanna said.

"Breanna... I didn't—"

"Whatever, Leslie." Breanna walked out of the break room and into the front of the house. She stared at Tessa and shook her head. Leslie had overstepped her boundaries. The bitch had no clue what it was like to feel emotionally drained and subverted to be submissive to a man who didn't so much as consider her needs and wants.

Breanna inhaled, holding her breath for a second, then exhaled. Her phone buzzed in her pocket. Hoping that it was Nathaniel sending her his number, it was Elijah. She frowned. Sure, the text said that he loved her and wanted her to have a good night, but his words were no longer authentic to her anymore. They were forced; they were used like a placebo.

There was love there. It honestly was. But two years of bliss was all they had. Still, Elijah was unlike any man she'd met. That's what she loved about him. When she first met him at South Wellington College, he was the guy who attended school full time during the day and worked with his father at the local carpentry shop he owned in downtown Kentfield at night. Back then, he and his former girlfriend,

Morgan Everly, were on the outs. She should have known then what she was getting into.

Yet Morgan wasn't the easiest person to get along with. High standards and attention seeking weren't the only endearing qualities she had. No. If the woman were a car, she would have been a Mercedes Benz. Expensive, hard to maintain, and easy to wreck, Morgan was quite the woman back then. She was probably still the same now.

Breanna could remember the day Morgan cursed Elijah out in the library and stormed out of the place. Everyone watched and chatted quietly amongst themselves from the show she displayed. But Elijah, he just sat at the table, seeming so unbothered by her complaints. He knew she had been messing off with the guy from the art department. He just wanted her to come clean with it.

And not knowing what the commotion was all about, Breanna peered around the bookshelves and dropped every book she'd stacked like a Jenga Tower from her arms. He came in like a knight and helped her pick them up. His music blasted through his earbuds. That was the moment she saw more than just a frustrated man; she saw a man who was patient, who was kind, who had gorgeous steel-blue eyes and damn fine for a white guy.

The man Morgan left for another wasn't the man Breanna saw as demeaning. He was a gentleman. And he always gave her as much time as she needed. Even when they dated, he never rushed her. Wanting to get to know her, Elijah didn't pressure her into having sex. He wanted her experience to be the lasting memory that never escaped her mind and body. He never wanted to give her anything less than elation since he was her first. But when she got pregnant the following year, Breanna had no idea that pregnancy would be that hard on her body. It seemed like it wanted to give out every time she moved. That's when her doctor told her she should have never been pregnant. Isabella was a blessing.

The day she fainted on her way out of Elijah's apartment was the same day he started deciding what was best for her without her consent. The doctor explained she needed to rest more, but it wasn't like she couldn't do anything. She just had to scale back on her usual activities. Elijah saw that as an opportunity to put her down.

Begging her to take some time from school, Breanna agreed, but what was supposed to be a short-term leave became a five-year stint. She sighed. Leslie had no fucking idea what she had gone through. She couldn't pretend even to know what she felt, let alone give her advice.

"Earth to Breanna," Howard said. He stood in front of her, waving his hand. "Are you okay, darling?"

Breanna nodded, then smiled. "Yeah, Howard. I'm fine."

16

"Are you sure?"

"What makes you think that I'm not okay, Howard?"

He wrapped his arm around her waist and walked her to the kitchen. "You haven't been yourself since you and your husband were arguing three days ago."

"We're not married, Howard. You know that."

"Breanna," Howard said. "When I opened this restaurant three years ago, you were the first one I called, and you and your family have been such a vital part of this restaurant."

"But you helped me out when I needed to buy a car, so we're even."

"True," he said, smiling. "But you haven't been the same since I asked you to take on another role besides being a pastry chef."

"Please don't think that I'm mad at you, Howard. When Anna and her BFF, Jessica, quit, I knew you couldn't afford to lose any more money after you found out those two birds were stealing from the cash registers."

"True. But you've put in more time than any other employee here, Breanna. If you weren't at this restaurant right now, I'd be out of business," he said. He took her hands into his and squeezed them tight. "The woman who I know has been a joyful life to be around. Not a woman who seems to have lost everything precious in her life."

Breanna sighed. Howard may have been her boss, but he was more like the brother she never had. Besides, he wouldn't understand what she was going through; he wouldn't understand from her point of view. But she knew he understood why she took on the extra work. With Izzy developing asthma like her father, she knew she couldn't take any chances on not being able to provide for her daughter. That was an ultimate given. But those subtle thoughts of Elijah needing help with his insurance rummaged through her mind as well.

"I'm okay, Howard," Breanna said.

Howard stared at her. He pursed his lips and furrowed one of his eyebrows. "Okay. I'll take your word for it, but I want you to go home at twelve tonight."

"But I thought you needed me until three in the morning."

"Tessa and Leslie can cover you."

"Then who's baking the chocolate-filled beignets?"

Howard gave her a wry smile. "Well, Benny's coming through tonight, and he's pretty crafty in the kitchen, so—"

"But what about Daniel?" Breanna asked.

"He'll be there," Howard replied, whipping his perfectly permed coils in the air as he sashayed in his black fitted trousers and pink and purple striped shirt to the double doors.

17

Breanna felt her phone buzz in her pocket again. She frowned. Oh, God! What did Elijah want now? She stared at her phone. Her frown turned upward into a smile. It was Nathaniel

Chapter Three

One whole hour with no coughing or wheezing. Elijah could breathe now. Isabella was breathing better after he'd given her two pumps from his inhaler. No matter how much he tried to keep himself and Isabella calm during those attacks, the choking, coughing spells, and tears welling in her eyes unnerved him more than it did her.

He blamed himself for passing that horrible trait to their daughter. He didn't want her to suffer the way he had when he was her age. He remembered how Dad used to rush him outdoors and have him force air into his lungs. Sometimes it worked. But there were times Dad had to rush him to the emergency room after he fainted.

Breanna may have hated him for that. Honestly, he couldn't blame her if she did.

As Izzy's small hands loosened from around his neck, Elijah sighed. He stood from the sofa with his daughter in his arms and carried her upstairs to her bedroom. Daisy followed them with a smile and wagging tail. The dog pushed the door open with her paw and invited herself in front of them both. She fluffed her doggy bed with her front paws as she grunted. Daisy turned around several times and kicked the blanket out of the way before lying down. Elijah stared at the Labrador Retriever and smiled. At least he knew she was happy.

"Daddy." Isabella stirred. "I want Mommy."

He kissed her forehead. "She'll be home soon, Izzy."

"You promise." She yawned while Elijah tucked her under the bedsheets.

"I promise," he replied, kissing her forehead one last time for the night. "Close those little eyes, okay."

She smiled while snuggling her pillow as she closed her eyes.

Elijah waited to leave the room, hoping she wouldn't stir again. But her steady breathing gave him the green light. He switched on her night light, then pulled the door up behind him. He ran his fingers through his brown hair and took a deep breath. Elijah knew Isabella could tell something was off with her mommy and daddy. No matter how much they tried to hide it from her, that child knew when something was up. Maybe that came from his mother. That woman would let nothing fly by her head without investigating first. Intuition was strong in his family.

As he made his way down the steps, he heard jangling keys at the doorknob. 12:30 in the morning, and Breanna was already at home? It must have been a low turnout, or Howard finally gave her regular working hours.

He watched her walk into the family room from the foyer. Her face was buried in her phone as she walked past the open concept dining room. She tossed her keys onto the table and passed by Elijah. He closed his eyes and sighed.

"You're not going to speak to me, either?"

Breanna looked up from her phone and stared at him. Her glasses sat on the midpoint of her nose like she was a school librarian. "I was going to speak."

"From the looks of it, you weren't."

"So, now you're getting angry with me for not speaking to you."

"Breanna, I don't want to fight with you."

"Then what are you doing, Elijah?"

"Not now, Bree," he said. "I just put Izzy down about five minutes ago."

Breanna stopped in her steps. "She had another asthma attack?"

"She did," he replied. Elijah paused as he opened his mouth to speak, grazing his teeth against his bottom lip. The last thing he wanted was to wake Isabella with their arguing. "They're getting worse, Bree."

Breanna walked to the sofa and sat down, tossing her phone onto the ottoman in front of them. She stared at the dark television screen. She hesitated, then spoke, "Do you think she'll ever grow out of this?"

"Honestly, I don't know," Elijah said. He looked at Breanna and took her by the hand. "She'll get through this; she's a fighter... like her mommy."

"I know she is," Breanna said. A smile tugged at her lips. "I'm just so afraid she won't."

20

"I know." He gazed into her brown eyes and squeezed her hand tighter, not wanting to let it go. "Breanna... can we talk?"

She turned from him, focusing her attention on the black television screen. "We do this every night, now," she said. "I don't think talking is enough anymore."

Elijah swallowed hard, then let go of her hand. "I love you, Bree. I will always love you."

"Why don't you show it, Eli?"

"I show you every chance I get," he said. Elijah stroked her cheek with the back of his hand, then turned her head with his index and middle fingers to meet his lips. He kissed them, savoring the cherry tanginess.

Breanna wrapped around his neck, giving him the all-clear to pull her closer to his body. He kissed her deeper and then unclipped the hairpin holding her hair in a bun, letting her black wavy tresses fall to her shoulder blades. Breanna's caramel brown skin melded with his warm beige skin as he laid her down on the sofa. Her fingernails slid against his bare arms, then stopped.

"Elijah," she whispered.

He stared into her eyes. "What's wrong?"

"I can't do this." She pushed him off her and sat up. "I can't keep letting you choose when you love me or not."

"Why do you keep thinking I don't love you?"

"When you told me how to run my life."

Elijah stood from the sofa and walked into the kitchen. "I was looking out for the mother of my child."

"You didn't have to stop me from living my life."

"I didn't tell you to stop living. I wanted you to be careful."

"By telling me to stay down and keep me from finishing my degree," Breanna said. She stood from the sofa. "I just wanted you to honor my independence."

"I do, Bree. I've constantly told you that you should open your own bakery, but you won't listen to me."

She scoffed. "And the proverbial tables have turned, didn't they?"

"If you don't love me, Bree, just tell me." Elijah stared at her.

Breanna paused. Tears welled in her eyes. "I love you, Eli. I'm just afraid that you'll hurt me again."

"I've never tried to hurt you, Bree."

Breanna grabbed her phone from the ottoman. "But you did, Eli."

She walked past him, leaving him standing in the kitchen.

Elijah watched her walk up the steps and cursed under his breath. No matter what he said, no matter what he did, nothing seemed to help

21

her understand that he never tried to hurt her. He wanted Breanna to be safe, to be healthy. He didn't think he took away her independence.

He opened one of the counter drawers and pulled out a small black box he'd been hiding from her. Elijah sat the ring on the countertop and sighed. His first thought was just to throw it away. But he couldn't give up. Whatever he had to do to make things right, Elijah was willing to take every bump and bruise for it.

Saturday was finally here. This was the day Isabella would make sure Mommy and Daddy sat down and talked to each other without yelling. This was going to be the day Mommy and Daddy would be happy again. She had to see to that.

Besides, all the other kids in her pre-k class had mommies and daddies that were in love and married. She never understood why her mommy and daddy never got married, though. Didn't they want to be a happy family? Didn't they want to be together forever?

Gigi said that Mommy and Daddy just needed to trust each other more. But why didn't they? Did they not love her enough to want to be married? Did they care about her happiness too? Maybe she made them angry. Or maybe she was the blame for their unhappiness. Still, Isabella didn't want to give up on them; she had to show Mommy and Daddy how much they needed one another—how much they needed her to keep them together. It would be a dream come true if she could stop them from fighting.

If Mommy and Daddy could get married on her sixth birthday, that would be the best birthday gift ever. But how would she get them to see that they needed to be a solid family? Maybe Gigi and Yaya could help her out. Maybe if she begged Auntie Amber enough, she would help, too. Besides, Auntie Amber could never get enough of her rosy cheeks.

This was more than just a fairytale. This was a mission.

Sitting up in her bed, Isabella smiled as she watched Mommy sleeping next to her. Her long hair draped over her shoulders like a

23

blanket. Isabella smiled. She loved to see Mommy sleep. She always worked so hard. Even when Daddy tried to keep her at home that one time she sprang her ankle, Mommy still went to work.

That Mr. Howard man was the reason she couldn't come home like regular mommies did. He changed her hours every chance he got. It was probably because he didn't like the fact Mommy was happier baking and selling pastries from home than when she worked at that restaurant. And he always smelled like cheap bubble gum. The nasty kind that would get stuck in between her teeth, the roof of her mouth, and on the side of her lips every time she tried to blow one lousy bubble. Yuck.

"Good morning, my little shortcake." Mommy stirred as she rolled to her other side.

"Mommy," Isabella scooted close to her back, leaned over her shoulder, and kissed her cheek. "Can we do something fun today?"

Mommy smiled. Her eyes were still closed. "I thought you said you wanted to watch a movie tonight?"

"I do," she replied. "I was just hoping that we could all go to the park today, too."

Mommy sat up in Isabella's bed and placed her arm around her small body. "Shortcake, I don't know if Daddy is up to it today."

"But he told me last night that he would be," Isabella said, pouting.

Breanna closed her eyes and sighed. "Then, let's make sure that he's going to keep to his word, okay."

Still pouting, Isabella looked at her and got out of bed. "Okay, Mommy."

"What's with the sad face, Izzy?" Daddy said, opening the door.

Mommy stared at him for a moment, then got up from the bed. "Come on, shortcake. Let's get those teeth brushed and that face washed, okay."

"Okay." Isabella walked to her daddy and wrapped her arms around his waist, squeezing him tight. "I love you, Daddy."

"I love you too, Izzy," he said. He leaned over and kissed her forehead. "March to that bathroom ASAP, Shortcake."

As Isabella made her way to the bathroom, she heard her bedroom door close behind Daddy.

They're fighting again.

She ran to the bathroom and turned on the faucet. She peeped back at her bedroom door as she tiptoed toward it and pressed her ear against the solid slab of wood.

"Just do this for Izzy, Bree. That's all I ask."

"Then, all I ask is that you don't make a big deal about us not talking, Eli."

"Bree, I just wish you would understand that I never tried to hurt you."

"I don't think you've tried hard enough."

The doorknob twisted, alerting Isabella that she needed to get back to the bathroom.

"Bree, I'm tired."

"So am I, Eli."

"Then let's not fight in front of Izzy today. Please."

Isabella tiptoed back to the bathroom and began brushing her teeth before the door opened. Her cheeks burned and reddened from the welling tears in her eyes. She brushed them away before Mommy and Daddy could see her crying.

Why couldn't they just talk to each other? What was so hard about them talking to each other, anyway? Isabella grabbed her face towel from the countertop and wheezed. This couldn't be happening now.

"Izzy," Daddy said, running into the bathroom. Breanna stood behind him as she watched him take an inhaler from the drawer and shake it. "It's okay, Shortcake. Mommy and Daddy are right here."

"Slow your breathing, Izzy," Mommy said, walking inside the bathroom. She lifted her from the floor and sat her on the vanity. "We're not going anywhere."

Tears welled in Isabella's eyes as she felt her chest tighten harder and harder. "It... hurts... Mommy."

"It's okay, Izzy," Daddy said, giving her two pumps of his inhaler. "Just breathe."

Taking the forced cooling air into her lungs, Isabella closed her eyes, trying to force herself to breathe normally again. She prayed. She wanted Mommy and Daddy to be together again, but not to this extent. What if this was God's intention to start them on their way back to each other? She knew God would never hurt her. From what Mommy and Daddy always told her, she was in good hands. Still, the thought lingered in the forefront of her mind. What if this was the way they were meant to come together?

"Isabella, take hold of my hand," Mommy said.

"You're doing good, Izzy," Daddy said, rubbing her back as he smiled at her. "Keep breathing."

The tightness released her chest. She could feel the air push through her lungs like it usually did. Isabella coughed as she stared at her Mommy and Daddy, then pouted. Tears flowed down both her cheeks. She held out both her arms to her daddy.

"It's okay, Izzy," Daddy said, picking her up off the vanity. "It's over now."

Isabella sobbed. "I'm sorry."

"Why are you apologizing, Isabella?" Mommy wiped her tears away with her thumb.

"Because... because..." she stammered. "I have these attacks."

"Izzy, don't you ever apologize for that," Mommy said. "We love you. No matter if you have asthma or not, that won't stop us from loving you."

Isabella nodded her head against her daddy's shoulder.

"How are you feeling, Shortcake?" Daddy asked.

She nodded her head against his shoulder once more. "A little better."

"We should probably give Dr. Ackers a call and let him check her out," Mommy said.

"But Mommy," Isabella pouted. "What about the park?"

"No park today, Shortcake," Daddy said. "We need to see about you first."

She lifted her head from his shoulder and stared into his doppelganger eyes. "But I'm okay, Daddy."

"Well, we just want to make sure that you are okay, Shortcake," Mommy said. She walked out of the bathroom and disappeared down the hall into her own bedroom.

"Let's get you dressed so we can get you a check-up." Daddy placed her feet on the ground and led her to her bedroom by her hand. Daisy rolled over onto her back and wagged her tail as she saw them enter Isabella's bedroom.

This was all her fault. They would have been at the park by now had she not had another asthma attack. Stupid asthma. She wished it would run away from her and never return like the time Daddy scared that old, nosey man away from the house. That man claimed he was selling water hoses, but Daddy said he had seven friends inside a barrel waiting for him inside the house. Who would ever have seven friends in a barrel, anyway? She didn't know, but Daddy sure did.

"Eli," Mommy said, standing in the doorway. "I just called Dr. Ackers. He said he can see Isabella as soon as we arrive."

Daddy pulled out one of her favorite Disney Princess t-shirts and a pair of jeggings and laid them on the bed for Isabella. "Okay."

"I'll go get the truck ready."

Silence took over them both. Isabella didn't understand why Mommy and Daddy never moved, but they seemed lost in each other's eyes. They seemed like they were happy—they were the mommy and daddy she remembered dancing to Twinkle, Twinkle Little Star to help her go to sleep before they started glaring at each other with daggers and swords.

"I'll be in the truck," Mommy said.

"Okay," Daddy responded. "We'll be out there in soon."

Isabella sat on the bed and smiled at Daddy as she tugged on her jeggings and shirt. He was a mountain. She thought Mommy was tall too, but he loomed over them both. And whenever he smiled, his eyebrows reminded her of thick brown bent lines, while Mommy's were more like thinner arched arrows without the heads. The special thing about Mommy and Daddy was their skin. There weren't many kids in her classroom that could say their mommies and daddies were different colors from each other, but hers were. That's what she admired about them. People around them noticed too. Some of them even said rude things and threw finger signs at them, but they were still her mommy and daddy.

Maybe that was the reason they didn't get along anymore. There were too many people trying to pull them apart instead of letting them be happy. Yaya once said that Mommy needed someone who looked like her. Didn't Yaya look like Mommy?

"You ready, Izzy?"

She nodded. "I'm ready, Daddy."

"Watch the house, Daisy," Daddy said, taking Isabella by the hand and leading her out of the bedroom and down the stairs.

The sun peered into her eyes as she stepped outside the door in front of Daddy. Mommy sat in the driver's side of the truck. Her face was buried in her phone while her thumbs tap danced across the touch screen.

"Come on, Shortcake," Daddy said, lifting Isabella off the ground and into the truck. Getting her seated in her booster seat, he locked her in place and then kissed her forehead. She watched him close the door and hop in the front seat with Mommy. They stared at each other again. Still, there were no words shared between them. It was these moments Isabella wanted to scream at the top of her lungs to make them wake up. But the attacks would hinder her even if she tried to make a loud peep.

Silence wouldn't rule the day. Mommy and Daddy were going to talk. Even if she had to ask the "why do you and Mommy make those weird sounds at night" question, they were going to talk.

"Daddy? Mommy?" Isabella inquired, somberly. "Is the doctor going to give me a shot?"

Daddy chuckled. "Dr. Ackers is only going to check you out. No shots."

"But what if he sees the need to give me a shot?"

Mommy smiled. "He shouldn't give you a shot. Not on a Saturday anyway, shortcake."

"Well, there was that one time he gave her a shot on a Saturday, though," Daddy mentioned.

Mommy brought the truck to a stop at a red light and grinned at Isabella in the rearview mirror. "Never mind, Daddy," she smiled, shaking her head. "That was when you were a little baby, and you needed medication to help you breathe."

"Just like now?" She asked. A twinge of butterflies fluttered in her stomach. For one, Mommy and Daddy were talking. Two, there was the real possibility of her getting a shot. Regardless, if that was the price of getting those two to talk, it was worth it. She just had to be a big girl today—a really big girl.

"We're here," Breanna said, parking the trucking and then making her way toward the building

Isabella peered at Dr. Ackers as he stood outside the clinic's door, beckoning them to come inside.

Stupid asthma.

"Alright, Izzy. Let's get you inside so the doc can check you out."

"Okay, Daddy." She waited for him to unbuckle her. As bad as her asthma was, maybe he could help Daddy with his, too. "Can you get a checkup too, Daddy?"

"I'm okay, Izzy," he said. He swept her off her feet and propped her on his shoulder. "Mommy and Daddy just need to make sure your asthma isn't getting worse."

"But you have them too," she replied.

"I know, Shortcake," he sighed. He waited, then asked, "Would it make you feel better if Daddy got checked out too?"

"Yep!" Isabella answered, quickly.

"Okay, I'll ask him," Daddy said.

Once they got to the door, Elijah placed her on her feet and ushered her to walk inside the light yellow and white building to meet Mommy. Breanna took her by the hand and followed the doctor into a small room painted with green fields, a sun, and a rainbow beaming down on kids playing with a dog on the corner of the wall.

"Well, hello, Ms. Isabella," Dr. Ackers smiled. "I'm glad you came by to see me today."

She waved. "Hi, Dr. Ackers." She squeezed Mommy's hand tighter as she approached the examination table.

"Let's get a listen to those lungs, shall we?" Dr. Ackers said, gesturing for Elijah to hoist her onto the table.

He unwrapped his stethoscope from around his neck, placed the earpieces inside his ears, and pressed the diaphragm against Isabella's chest.

"Take a deep breath and hold it for me," he said, moving the chest piece around. "Now, release it."

She looked at her mommy and daddy, noticing they sat apart from each other.

"How's her breathing?" Daddy watched Dr. Ackers's every move.

"It's a little ragged, but it's not labored, which is a good thing," he replied. Dr. Ackers smiled at Isabella. "Can you tell me what happened last night and this morning?"

Isabella nodded. "I had an attack last night, and then, I had one this morning."

"Did your chest hurt during the attacks?"

She nodded. "It hurt pretty bad this morning."

"Did it hurt at all last night?"

She shook her head with a pout. "Not really."

"Well, everything sounds fine, Mom and Dad. She just needs to keep using her inhaler whenever she feels pressure or wheezes."

Both Mommy and Daddy nodded.

"Your mother told me you have a birthday coming up in six months," he said, trying to lighten the mood. "You're turning the big six years old, huh?"

She smiled while nodding her head.

"What do you want for your birthday?" Dr. Ackers asked.

"I don't want to say it out loud," Isabella mumbled.

"Izzy," Mommy said, giving her that mama look. "You're a big girl. You can speak up."

Her bottom lip quivered. A tear splashed onto her cheek and rolled to the side of her jaw.

"What's wrong, Isabella?" Daddy stood from his seat and walked next to her. Planting a kiss on her forehead, he wiped her tear away with his index finger. "Tell Dr. Ackers what you want for your birthday."

Isabella closed her eyes tight and sniffled. It was scary enough that Dr. Ackers was contemplating jabbing a needle in her arm—now she had to share her most precious want to get through this checkup, knowing there'd be no trip to the park. This was a nightmare.

She sobbed. "I want my mommy and daddy to get married."

Mommy and Daddy stared at Dr. Ackers with open mouths. Daddy turned his attention to Mommy and took a deep breath.

With raised brows and wide eyes, Dr. Ackers smiled. "That's some birthday wish, Isabella."

Isabella looked at her mommy and daddy with a pout, hoping she didn't cause a bigger rift than what was already present. She sniffled. "Are you going to give me a shot now?"

Dr. Ackers held his stomach and laughed. "No. I'm not going to give you a shot today, Isabella."

Isabella nodded. "Could you also check my daddy out too?" She asked, still pouting.

Mommy put her phone in her purse and sniffled. She looked at Isabella, tilting her head. "Why are you sad, Shortcake?"

"Because..." she stammered. The tears streamed down her cheeks like a leaking faucet. "I don't want you and Daddy to be mad at me."

"Um..." Dr. Ackers paused. "I'm going to check Elijah out at Isabella's request. Ms. Ellis, you can take your daughter outside and get her a lollipop from the nurse's station. Becky should be at the front desk."

"Sure," Mommy said, gathering her things. Isabella wrapped her little arms around Daddy's neck as he hoisted her from the table and placed her feet on the floor. "We'll be waiting outside for you, okay."

Daddy nodded. "Okay."

Dr. Ackers watched the door close behind them, turned his attention to Elijah, and applied the diaphragm to his chest. "Take a deep breath for me," he said, listening to his lungs. "Now, exhale."

Elijah focused on the drawing of the family playing together on the wall behind the doctor. "I didn't think she was going to say something like that."

"Kids will say the damnedest things, Elijah," he spoke. "In my twenty-five years of medicine plus the four of my own, I've learned that they will tell you how they feel, whether you want to hear it or not."

"Breanna and I—we just need to—"

"Communicate—" Dr. Ackers interrupted. "You can play house all day long, Elijah, but if you don't acknowledge the problem, neither of you will be happy; Isabella especially."

"I did wrong by Breanna, doc."

"You did what you thought was right to save her and Isabella's life," Dr. Ackers spoke, moving the diaphragm to his back. "Breanna reminds me a lot of my wife, Vicki. Independent to a fault and stubborn as hell, they are two of the strongest women that I know."

"Just trying to tell Breanna to stay down for a while is like flipping over the holy grail."

"I know, Eli," Dr. Ackers said. "Women like that change the world for the better, but they let pride consume them too much. They've seen pain or been hurt and never want to experience that sensation again."

Elijah sighed. "I just want her to understand that."

"Then, you two better start communicating before things get worse or possibly have another child," Dr. Ackers stated. "By the way, are you taking your inhaler whenever you need it?"

"Yes, sir."

He nodded. "I know I'm not your doctor, but I would like you to increase your intake to make sure you are getting enough airflow in your lungs."

"Thanks, doc," Elijah said, standing from the table.

"And don't forget what I said, either. Isabella's happiness is at stake here."

Elijah looked at Dr. Ackers and nodded. "I will, doc."

"I'll be sure to meet up with Ms. Ellis so that I can schedule another appointment for Isabella."

Feeling a buzz in his pocket as he made his way out of the room, Elijah saw a tall, beautiful, light brown-skinned woman wearing a blue tank top dress, standing next to Isabella and Breanna. Isabella beamed as she waved at him from a short distance.

"Daddy!" Isabella said, running to him with her arms wide open.

Both Breanna and the woman turned toward him as they walked in his direction.

He raised one of his eyebrows. "Morgan?"

"Hey, Sunshine," she smiled. She bumped Breanna's shoulder to get closer to him.

Breanna stared at him and smiled through clenched teeth.

"You know that pretty lady, Daddy?" Isabella asked.

"Yeah," he said, picking up the small child. "She's an old friend of mine."

A friend who left him with pleasurable memories and unbearable demands.

Chapter Five

"I didn't know you were the father type, Elijah," Morgan grinned.

She stood an inch or two taller than Breanna. She had dark almond-shaped brown eyes he used to love to lose himself in, and her curves were still in all the right places from the last time he saw her. But why the hell was she here? She hated everything about Kentfield, including him.

Elijah smiled. "I've always wanted kids."

Morgan smirked. "Well, that's certainly not the Elijah Christian Bryson I remember, but I guess time changes everyone, doesn't it?"

Breanna took a deep breath. "It does." She smiled at Morgan. "I hate to leave good company, but I need to speak with Izzy's doctor for a moment."

"Oh, don't let me keep you," Morgan replied, placing her hand on her chest. That smirk never left her face.

"Go with Mommy, Izzy," he said, placing the child on her feet. Elijah watched her run in Breanna's direction and then wave at him. He returned her wave as he smiled.

"Wow, Elijah! I honestly never thought I would see you as the family man," she said, rolling her eyes in Breanna's direction. Morgan twirled a strand of her dark hair around her index finger and inspected it for split ends. "This is surprising."

Elijah looked at Breanna and Isabella from afar and sighed, ignoring Morgan's shade. "What brings you back to Kentfield?"

Her teeth flashed against her light brown skin as she grinned. "There's a new subdivision in Kentfield that's booming right now."

Elijah looked at her. "In the Myers District, right?"

"That's the one," Morgan responded. "I bought about eight plots of land over there, and I am looking to build some high-end homes in the next four months."

"You're going to need a talented architect for that." Elijah kept his attention on Breanna and Isabella as they talked to Dr. Ackers.

"Well, AJ already told me you're one of the best in the state of Tennessee."

Elijah stared at her with a raised brow. "When did you talk to AJ?"

Morgan stepped closer to him and propped her elbow on his shoulder. "About two days ago," she said. "He told me you all had drawn some plans, which per his praise, were derived from your expertise in home design."

Elijah nodded. If there was any man he trusted and loved like a brother, it was AJ. When Dad insisted on him joining the baseball team when he was a little boy, Dad paired him with the kid who lived two houses down from them. Knowing that AJ was the best damn pitcher and shortstop in Kentfield, he wanted Elijah to learn from the best. And that he did. Whatever the man touched, magic happened. But what made Elijah see him as a brother was when he took up for him.

Some of the other kids teased him for panting like an English Bulldog on the field when he breathed hard, thanks to the asthma. They used to call him slim fat. It didn't bother him much, but their efforts to get him to quit the team did. That's what called AJ to action. In AJ's eyes, Elijah had more heart than any other so-called talent on the team, and they were only ten years old.

From that moment on, they were the brothers from other mothers. Dad had to have done that on purpose because there weren't many black families in their neighborhood. Some of the uppity white folks in the neighborhood turned their noses up at them. Yet that didn't stop them from hanging out like they were family. AJ would come over whenever Mom made pot roast, and he would invade the Harvey's household whenever Ms. Debbie and Mr. Francis fired up the grill. They were brothers before anything they did, especially when they started their housing and construction business, the Harvey and Bryson Company.

With AJ's knowledge in business and real estate and his expertise in home design and architecture, they were a threat to other big-name construction companies. They just needed a push. A big push.

"I'm looking to invest in a company I can work with and get some excellent results out of it," she said.

"All we're doing right now is flipping houses," Elijah said. "We have very little in our portfolio to show you."

"Well, I'm going to go meet AJ after I pick up my nephew. You know he works here as a phlebotomist, now."

"Wait, Liam is a phlebotomist?" Elijah asked. He folded his arms across his chest and gave Morgan his undivided attention. "How old is he now?"

She smiled, placing her hand on her hip. "Shawna's baby boy is all grown up now. He turned nineteen last month, finished high school at seventeen, and went directly to Concorde after he graduated. My sister and I are so proud of that young man."

Elijah creased his eyebrows and shook his head in amazement. "I can't believe it. He was a twelve-years-old the last time I saw him."

"The last time we were together," Morgan sighed.

"Morgan—"

"—I didn't come here to reminisce," she interrupted. "I came here so I can get my business off the ground here in Tennessee since I've already got something going in North Carolina and Kentucky."

Elijah stared at her. "Sorry."

"You will be if you don't meet me at AJ's house in the next half hour."

"But I've got to make sure Breanna and Isabella get home."

"Do that or bring them along. I don't give a shit. This is money, Elijah. It's something you can use a little more of right now."

Morgan dug into her small cross-body purse, pulled out a business card, and handed it to him.

He took it and glanced over it before stuffing it into his back pants pocket. "I'll see you there shortly," he said.

"Good. I'll see you there, Sunshine." She smiled at him while walking toward her nephew.

He watched Breanna and Isabella move toward him. She was right about one thing. He needed more money than he was making at the moment. Sure, the business was doing well, but only selling two out of every five houses they flipped brought in enough for one year's salary. It was good money, but between him, AJ, Calvin, and Mr. Glenn, a year's salary vanished before his eyes like a Houdini act.

It would be great if he had more money left over—with the cost of his insurance going up and having to cover Isabella on it, too, it would make an enormous difference. And with Breanna adding him to her insurance, the medical issues would be covered.

Though, she would probably want to kill him more so than claim him on her insurance if he and AJ took the deal with Morgan. Breanna wouldn't like it, but he had to take Morgan's offer. At least this way, she

34

wouldn't assume that he was cheating on her. That was the last thing he wanted her to think.

"Has she changed a lot since I last saw her?" Breanna asked, leading Isabella by the hand as they walked to the truck.

"She's changed."

"If you want to say that's change," Breanna said, unlocking the vehicle. "She practically took me down to get to you. Seems like the old Morgan to me."

Elijah parted his lips to speak, then hesitated. This wasn't the best time to mention to Breanna that she had a real estate investment company, but it was now or never. More like never in Breanna's eyes. "Morgan wants to meet with me and AJ in a half hour."

Breanna stopped in her steps. "Why?"

"She wants to talk to us about investing in our company."

"Seriously? That sounds a little farfetched, don't you think?"

"Not really," Elijah said, locking Isabella into her booster seat and closing the door. "You've heard about Greater Port Properties, haven't you?"

Breanna nodded. "Isn't that the company that built the subdivision we stay in now?"

"Yep. That's her company. She runs it."

"You've got to be kidding me right now."

"I'm not, Bree," Elijah said, getting into the driver's seat. "If she invests in our company, that could be a leg up for me and AJ."

"Maybe a leg up for her too," Breanna said, moving her neck from side to side and bending her index and middle fingers in quotations.

Elijah scoffed while shaking his head. "That's not her intention, Bree."

"Then what is?" Breanna asked, frowning.

"Mommy? Daddy? Did I make you angry with me?" Isabella asked, looking into the rearview mirror.

Elijah and Breanna glanced at each other before looking their separate ways. Dr. Ackers was right. Isabella was an innocent bystander in their mess. "You didn't make us angry, Shortcake," Elijah answered. "Mommy and Daddy just didn't agree on something at the moment."

"Is it about the pretty lady?"

Elijah sighed. Isabella was an amalgam of the two of them. On one end, she had his charm, endurance, and his sarcastic quick wit. On the other end, she had Breanna's beauty, grace, and undeniable understanding for shit way beyond her years. This wasn't just a recipe for success; it was a recipe for resentment waiting to happen. "It is, but she did nothing wrong. She's just trying to help Daddy and Uncle AJ's company."

"If you call that help," Breanna muttered under her breath.

Elijah shot her a sharp look. "We'll talk when we get home."

Breanna rolled her eyes and dove into her phone again. What was it with her and that damn thing? Breanna wasn't one for getting lost in the rabbit hole of social media or texting. That was more of Amber's thing. In the back of his mind, Elijah wondered if it were another man she had gotten involved with.

That couldn't have been the case, though. They've had some serious fights over the past five years, but she never stepped out on him. Breanna would typically go to her mother's house and sleep in her old bedroom when she wanted to get away from him from what he remembered.

He glanced at her again while he drove, his eyebrows furrowed. Maybe it was Ms. Gwendolyn. She never liked him the moment he introduced himself to her. She always shrugged her shoulders and gave him the "boy bye" look until Breanna got pregnant. Mrs. Gwendolyn gave her own daughter hell and then some. The woman complained to her every damn day that she was too young to be ruining her chances of having a decent life. Yet Breanna was twenty-three years old then.

He shook his head and sighed. He couldn't forget how she used to tell Breanna that having a white man's baby would be costly, considering the child would want the finer things in life. Hell, Ms. Gwendolyn lived better than him, Breanna, and his parents combined. After her divorce, the woman went on a shopping spree like no other. She was, what Breanna called it, releasing anger through spending Marvin's money.

As much as he didn't want to admit it, Elijah didn't want Isabella to spend a millisecond with the woman, let alone spend a night with her. The next thing he would know, she would come back throwing her teddy bears at him and screaming her heart away at him because he was white. Goose pimples rose from the hairs on his arms. That was Elijah's worst nightmare.

His cellphone buzzed again, seducing his eyes to peep at it. Morgan's number flashed onto the screen as it continued its undulation. It was like her to remind him of the hour, the minute, and the second, about an event she wanted to go to. That never changed about her. In the back of his mind, though, Elijah wondered what life would have been like if they'd stayed together. Would they have argued as bad as he and Breanna had? Would they have been madly in love with each other?

He wouldn't go down that road. Regardless of how bad the fights were between him and Breanna, he knew they would eventually work things out—Isabella needed her mommy and daddy—they had to work it out.

Looking in the rearview mirror, he saw Isabella bobbing her head and singing along with Jill Scott. He smiled. "Hey, Shortcake. Do you want anything to eat before I take you and Mommy back home?"

She nodded as she sang along with the music. "May I have some fruit salad with extra strawberries, and a ham and cheese sandwich from Miranda's Deli."

Breanna stopped texting and glanced at Elijah. A smile pulled her lips. "You may wanna go easy on the strawberries, Shortcake."

"But they're healthy, Mommy," the child pleaded.

He stared at Breanna for a second, admiring how beautiful she was whenever she smiled. They just had to work through this. "Mommy's right," he said, watching her little smile fade into a pout. "But since you've been such a good patient at the doctor's office, you can get extra strawberries on your fruit salad."

"Thank you," she smiled. "What about Mommy? Aren't you hungry?"

Elijah glanced at Breanna while making a right turn at an intersection. "How about it, Mommy? Do you want anything to eat?"

She pulled off her glasses and stared at him. Her brown eyes made him shift in his seat a little, hoping junior wouldn't get too happy in the seam of his pants.

She looked back at Isabella and smiled. "Sure," she said, turning her attention back to Elijah. "I'll have the same thing she's having. Besides, you owe me that anyway."

Elijah sighed. He knew this would take time, but he nursed the little moments like that as long as he could.

Elijah pulled into AJ's driveway. Morgan stood beside her silver Lexus LS 500 with her arms folded. Her foot tapped to an imaginary beat. It was a good thing the sun was out. Had she kept that up, she would have turned blue skies and flying birds into black clouds and clawed missiles ready to destroy the first house they loomed over.

"You're late," Morgan said. "Time is money."

"Time is time the last time I checked," Elijah said, closing the door to his truck. He glanced at AJ's house and smiled. When AJ said he would use one of their designs to construct his first home, he meant it.

The way it stood amongst the pink and white flowers blooming on the dogwood trees was exquisite. The choice to cover the house in red brick and accent it with creamy white stones at the entryway and garage gave the house more than curb appeal. It stole the eyes of every oh and neck rolling mmm-hmm neighbor. Either way, it was the right kind of attention they needed for the market they worked in.

"I think I rubbed off on you too much, Eli," AJ said, walking toward him. Shaking his hand, he pulled Elijah into a hug and patted his back. "I'm glad you made it."

"Enough with the man hugs, fellas. We've got business to conduct." Morgan walked toward the house. Her hips swayed from side to side in the blue tank top dress she wore, daring their eyes to watch her ass in action.

Elijah took a deep breath. He needed the Lord to give him strength. Temptation was acting like a real bitch right now. "I had to take Breanna and Isabella back home."

AJ raised an eyebrow as they walked into his house. "How's everything between you two?"

"She fucking hates me, man," Elijah sighed. "It's like I can't talk to her without stepping on her toes or something."

"Breanna's headstrong to a fault," AJ stated.

"I know she is, AJ, but she won't let me in. It's like she's ready to go her separate way."

"Maybe you two should try counseling."

"Maybe," Elijah responded. "But she's going to throw that shit back in my face."

"Leslie and I went through counseling about a year ago."

"Really."

"Yeah," he answered. "After her father passed away, she wanted nothing to do with me. She dropped my ass like a pepperoni hot pocket."

Elijah sighed. "And the counseling worked?"

"At first, it didn't. I wasn't as supportive as I should have been, but after the counselor brought it to my attention, I had to change how I responded to her during her quiet moments."

Elijah nodded. When Dad used to tell him that faith without work was dead, he used to ask him if he had faith. Breanna was refreshing air to his lungs. She was the medicine for his headaches. Breanna was his life. "You still got the doctor's number?"

"Sure do," AJ replied. "I can refer y'all too, if you like."

"That I would, AJ."

Walking through the long foyer, Elijah entered the spacious cream-colored dining room. Morgan sat at the elongated wooden table, popping corn chips into her mouth. Leslie sat beside her, sipping lemonade.

"Hey, stranger," Leslie smiled. She got up from the table and walked toward Elijah with her arms open wide. With wide eyes and raised eyebrows, she mouthed the words, "She's intense," as she neared him.

He smiled. Morgan wasn't one for subtlety. Everything always had to be her way, and if it weren't, she'd make sure the person who didn't follow her strict set of rules felt her sting, more like a kick to the balls. That was the main reason they broke up. When Elijah couldn't afford a gift for her birthday, she nearly lost her mind. Hell, she lost her mind when he refused to take her to dine at a restaurant where two pieces of shrimp and some freaking cocktail sauce topped with golden truffles cost damn near two hundred dollars.

Well, she found the fool who could afford it; she probably broke his bank within the week too. Elijah was glad it wasn't him. Or was it about to be him? Sure, she'd changed, but he didn't want to find himself

39

broke on the side of the road dancing for his food and water. For once, though, he had to trust her, especially if he wanted to keep Isabella's inhalers paid for without worrying about how he was going to afford the next month's supply.

"It's been a minute since I've seen you too," Elijah said, pulling her into a hug. He felt Morgan's stare nearly turn him into stone. All she needed were the dancing, hissing snakes for hair and slits for pupils.

AJ walked into the room with a glass of lemonade in one hand and his iPad in the other. Taking a seat at the table, he scoffed with a smile while shaking his head. "You two are so overdramatic. It's only been three weeks."

Leslie whipped her head in his direction, narrowed her eyes, and pointed at AJ with a smirk. "Okay, mister. Keep playing."

Morgan cleared her throat. "Shall we get started with this meeting, good people?"

Elijah, AJ, and Leslie stared at one another, trying to keep their smiles from fading into scowls. Leslie held up an index finger and tip-toed out of the room. "I'll be right back," she sang on her way out of the room.

Elijah sighed. He sat across from AJ and turned his attention to her. "The floor is yours, Morgan," he said.

She smiled. "Well, gentlemen, I sought you two out because you've got floor plans I've heard can create million-dollar homes."

"I wouldn't call it million-dollar, but I would call it efficiently extravagant," AJ replied.

Elijah glanced at him and nodded with a smile. "That's right. We're not going for complete luxury. We're going for luxury, tech, and eco-efficiency."

"Hmm," Morgan hummed. "I like the sound of that." She stared into Elijah's eyes. A smirk pulled at the corners of her thick, rosy lips.

"This home you're in now is from one of the floor plans Elijah drew up for me as a birthday gift," AJ said.

Morgan's eyes widened. "Is it really?"

"Yep." AJ nodded.

"I was in awe when I first saw this house," Morgan responded. "I didn't think this was one of the floor plans you guys have in your arsenal. How many square feet is it?"

"3200 square feet," AJ replied. "It has four bedrooms, three and a half bathrooms, and a theater room made for about ten people."

Morgan looked at Elijah. The smirk on her face widened into a grin. "Impressive. Can I look around? I would love to see the place."

AJ nodded. "That's fine." He stood from his chair and gestured for her to follow him.

"Are you coming with us, Elijah?" Morgan stood from her chair.

"AJ knows this place like the back of his hand," Elijah stated. "I'm going to pull up the other floor plans and the homes we've flipped recently."

Morgan pursed her lips. "Okay," she replied. "Don't run away from me."

Elijah chuckled. "I ain't running yet." He watched the two leave out the room. Leslie stepped inside the area and took a seat next to him.

"What's up with her?"

Elijah sighed. "Morgan's always been like that."

"Like a stick up somebody's ass crack."

Elijah laughed. "That she can be."

Leslie twirled her thumbs. Her smile faded from her lips. "You know Breanna and I got into a bit of a spat Friday night."

"Really?" He raised an eyebrow. "She mentioned nothing to me about that. What happened?"

She sighed. "I... just think we're not seeing eye to eye at that moment."

Elijah straightened his posture in his seat. "Leslie," he hesitated. He knew Leslie and Breanna were like sisters, and they had an honor code like no other. Regardless of if they were beefing or not, what happened between them was sealed up like gold locked away in Fort Knox. "Would you tell me if she was seeing somebody else?"

Leslie bit her bottom lip. "I wouldn't," she replied. "If she were, I think that would be something she should go to you about. Not me."

"I understand," Elijah said. "But if it's detrimental to Isabella, would you please tell me?"

"It's not my place, Elijah," she paused. "I can't be the one to tell you about what she's doing. But if it meant that Isabella would be in harm's way, I would tell you without hesitation. I would just really hate myself in the morning, though."

"I know I'm putting you in a hard spot, but I want to make sure she and I won't put Isabella in a terrible place. She's too young to see that kind of shit."

"Then make sure you don't let Morgan get too close," Leslie said. "She's... oh my God... high off her own shit."

"Like Cat Grant doped up on too much Botox."

"Damn, Bree," Nathaniel said. His voice was soothing, like a saxophone as it hummed over the phone. "Sounds like ole dude trying to keep you under him. I hate to hear that."

Breanna sighed. "That's what he's good for," she remarked. "Keeping me down and then trying to apologize for his fuck up like it never happened."

Hearing the front door unlock, Breanna jumped off the sofa and ran upstairs. "Nathaniel, I've got to go. I don't want him to hear me talking to you."

"Do you need me to come over? I can show him what I'm working with," he boasted.

A smile graced Breanna's lips as she shook her head. "No, Nathaniel. I'm good right now."

"Better be."

"I'll call you tomorrow when I head out for work."

"I'll do you one even better," he said. "I can meet you there. You know, like an unofficial date after your shift."

Breanna closed her eyes and placed the phone close to her heart. Elijah wouldn't change anytime soon and he damn sure wouldn't open up to her. With everything she wanted from him—what she needed him to do for their relationship—she wouldn't get the man back she fell in love with seven years ago. It was now or never. It was—what if Elijah tried to change? What if he tried to make things right between them? Would he have been quicker to fuck it up or make it right? "I would like that, but could you give me a little time to think about it?"

"You got all the time you need, beautiful."

"Thanks." She smiled.

"Don't wait too long, girl," Nathaniel laughed. "This offer might not last long."

Breanna giggled. "I won't. Goodnight, Nathaniel."

"Goodnight, beautiful."

Breanna set the phone on the dresser and walked into the master bathroom. She looked in the mirror and smiled. She didn't know whether to be afraid or excited. The man she shared a bed with was nothing compared to the man who listened to her every word. Momma would be proud of her for even considering Nathaniel's proposal. But what about Isabella? What about if things got serious between them? How would Breanna tell her daughter she wouldn't be able to fulfill her birthday wish?

She turned on the shower and let the water warm to her liking before stepping inside. Pulling off her t-shirt, Breanna looked at the necklace that rested on her collarbone. Elijah knew how much she loved butterflies. She touched the chain with her fingertips. Its smoothness pressed against her digit.

On the day of their two-year anniversary, Breanna was nine months pregnant and ready to pop. Yet, Izzy wasn't due for another week so her doctor proclaimed. That baby had other plans.

Once Elijah had helped Breanna get into his truck to take her to her doctor's appointment, her water gushed onto the seat and floor. How funny was it that the one blessing that occurred on the day they met couldn't keep them from trying to rip each other apart?

"Bree," Elijah stood in the bathroom's entranceway. He gave a half smile. "AJ and I comprised a deal with Morgan. She's going to invest in our company."

"That's good." Breanna glanced at him and then back to the mirror as she pulled her hair into a bun.

"Bree," he hesitated. "I... I want to... tell you I'm sorry."

She stared at him; her eyebrows creased. "What are you sorry about, Eli?"

"The one thing we can never see eye to eye about anymore."

"Elijah, I don't want to do this anymore."

"Then just listen to me." Elijah walked into the bathroom and closed the door behind him. Steam filled the room, forcing him to take off his long sleeve flannel shirt. The white t-shirt he wore pressed against his skin, revealing the taut muscles underneath it. "I know you hate me for what I did to you when you were pregnant."

Breanna folded her arms. "Elijah—"

"—Please let me finish," he interrupted. He stepped closer to her and stroked her cheek with his index finger. "I want to do right by you and Isabella. I don't want to lose the woman I love."

Breanna's eyes widened. "Elijah—"

"I love you, Breanna," he said. He pulled her into his arms and held her tight. "I love you and Isabella more than anything in this world."

Breanna rested her head on his chest and closed her eyes. His heart thumped against her ear. Its calm beating nearly buckled her knees. Had she moved too quickly with Nathaniel? Or was Elijah playing games with her again? "Why now, Eli?"

"Why not now?"

"That doesn't answer the question."

Elijah sighed. "Because I can't go back to the past and undo what I did, but I can fix what's in the present. I want us to go to couples' counseling; I want us to work through this."

Breanna pushed away from him and frowned. "Let me guess, Morgan put you up to this, didn't she?"

Elijah ran his fingers through his hair. "She had nothing to do with this, Breanna."

"I'm supposed to believe that."

"AJ recommended it to me," he retorted. "He and Leslie went there about a year ago."

Breanna looked away from him and closed her eyes as she sighed. Leslie never told her anything like that. She knew Leslie was still grieving after her father's passing, but she never knew it was that bad. She always made it seem she was okay, that nothing bothered her. Leslie lied to her. "So, my best friend can't tell me how she felt, but she wants to impart her and AJ's two cents onto our relationship now? Some fucking friend she is."

"Breanna," Elijah said. "She's more of a friend than Tessa has ever been to you."

"Oh! Now you want to talk about Tessa." Breanna snapped.

"The woman has tried to break us up several times, Bree," he argued. "And every time she comes around me, she's flirting with me. Even Leslie has told me that."

"Mommy! Daddy!" Isabella sang outside their bathroom door. "Are we going to watch a movie tonight like you promised?"

They stiffened, staring at each other in silence.

"Let's not fight in front of Isabella, Bree. Please," he whispered.

Breanna nodded with a frown. "Get the movie started. I'll be down there shortly after my shower."

He sighed. "Sure."

Opening the door, he picked up the smiling child and threw her over his shoulder. "I gotcha now, Shortcake."

Breanna listened to them laugh as they left out of the bedroom. She took off the rest of her clothes, then stepped inside the shower, allowing the steamy water to run over her neck and back. First, Elijah apologized, then he wanted them to go to counseling, all because AJ mentioned it. That was complete and utter bullshit.

And the nerve he had to talk about Tessa like she wanted him. Of all the times Elijah visited the restaurant, Breanna never saw her push up on him. Instead, Tessa always caught him eyeing every beautiful black woman who walked inside the joint.

Breanna scoffed. A white man who had a sheer fondness for black women and a distaste for white women who dyed their hair unnatural colors. She knew there were other white men like Elijah, but he made it known he didn't want to date within his race. Morgan was a great example of his testament.

Breanna closed her eyes and sighed. She hated the mixed feelings he made her feel. She hated how he would give her an apology, then later start an argument with her.

She lathered her body with the soap Elijah normally used. Its chamomile and lemon scent wafted up her nose, making her body remember the quiet moments they shared with the bar of soap between them. She pressed her hand against the hexagon-shaped tiles and cursed under her breath. This was the last time he would make her feel this way.

Washing off the soap, she turned off the water, grabbed her towel from the door, and wrapped it around her body as she stepped out of the shower. She walked into their bedroom, grabbed her phone, and pecked at her screen.

Breanna: I'll see you tomorrow night.

The phone chirped in her hand.

Nathaniel: Good. I can't wait. Goodnight, beautiful.

Breanna smiled. She held the phone close to her heart.

"Mommy," Isabella yelled. "The movie's starting. Daddy made the yellow popcorn too."

"Okay, Shortcake," Breanna replied. The smile faded from her lips. She couldn't end things too suddenly with Elijah. That was going to crush Izzy. She couldn't let them find out about Nathaniel. She had to keep him as her little secret.

Chapter Eight

"So, Mr. Morrison is going to be here any minute now, huh?" Tessa grinned at Breanna like a schoolgirl on a playground.

Breanna opened her locker door and looked in the mirror. A picture of her and Elijah stared back at her. She ripped it from the tape and set it down inside the locker. The last thing she needed was to see his face staring back at her. She pulled her hair from its bun and pulled it into a princess ponytail.

"You know I envy this hair of yours," Tessa said, twirling her thick hair between her index and middle fingers. "I see why Elijah likes it so much. But that's bout to be Nathaniel's hair now," she laughed, dancing in her seat.

Breanna smiled at her. "Anyway, Tessa. It's not that serious yet. Besides, we're just taking things slow right now."

Tessa stood from her seat and peeped out the door's small rectangular window. "Goodie Two Shoes is on her way back to the break room. You better clear the deck fast."

"She ain't my momma the last time I checked." Breanna closed her locker door and straightened out her white blouse.

"Look who done grew a pair," Tessa laughed. "She rubbed you the wrong way, I see."

"Leslie's cool and all, but she flaunts herself like there isn't anything wrong with her, and she knows it is."

Tessa leaned closer to Breanna. "Oh, girl! She and her perfect boyfriend got problems?"

"If you call going to see a counselor a solution to fix what's broken, then I would call those problems. Shit, she even tried to talk Elijah into that mess by sending AJ to tell him."

"Elijah don't need no counselor," Tessa said, rolling her neck. "He needs a swift kick to the ass."

"I couldn't agree more."

Leslie walked into the break room and opened her locker without speaking to them.

Breanna folded her arms, keeping her eyes attached to her every move. She cocked her head to the side and pursed her lips as she sat next to Tessa. This wasn't Leslie's demeanor. Even when she was mad, she still spoke. That was something she got from her father—to be the bigger person, no matter the issue. Well, she wasn't so big today.

Leslie closed her locker and made her way to the door.

"So, now you ain't gonna speak like you don't see two people sitting in here," Tessa ranted. She rolled her neck in Breanna's direction, then turned her attention back to Leslie, whose back was still facing them.

Leslie turned to meet their narrowed eyes. She took a deep breath and exhaled. "I expect this kind of childishness from you, Tessa," Leslie stated. "But you, Breanna, the same person who I called sister the very first day we met in first grade, I didn't expect this kind of act from you."

"You got some fucking—"

Breanna tapped Tessa's shoulder as she stood to her feet and stepped toward Leslie, folding her arms over her chest. "Act? Really, Leslie?" She shook her head with a frown. "While you're sitting here judging me, you need to keep your crappy ass advice to yourself."

"I see," Leslie said. "You're not trying to save your relationship like Elijah is."

"Elijah caused this shit we're going through."

"You blame Elijah for everything, Breanna. The last time I checked, it took two to tango. Isn't that how Isabella got here."

"Don't you dare bring Isabella into this."

"You've done that on your own, Bree," Leslie snapped. "Honestly, you act like you're the saint when you're not."

"What's that supposed to mean, Leslie?"

Leslie shook her head as she smiled. "It means exactly what it sounds like, Breanna," she said. "You created your unhappiness, and that's something you've got to deal with."

"I'm dealing with my problems, Leslie," Breanna retorted.

"More like causing them," Leslie stated.

"Are you serious with this shit right now, Leslie—"

"Nathaniel's out there waiting for you," Leslie interrupted. She opened the door, still holding onto the nob. "I'm not trying to be petty, but I wish I could be the fly on the wall when Elijah finally sees you for who you are."

Breanna watched the door close behind Leslie. It should have smacked her on the way out of it. This was what she wanted. No, this was what she needed. Who was Leslie to judge her on her relationship problems? She wasn't the one seeing a therapist because she couldn't stop grieving. She wasn't the one pushing her man away because she couldn't cope. Or was she?

Silence filled the air after Leslie left the room. It swallowed Breanna whole like a shark gulping down smaller fish with one chump. She could hear Tessa's voice in the background, but all she heard were horns and saxophones in place of her talking.

Had Elijah still been the same man she met in college seven years ago, there still would have been love there. Even when Izzy was born, love was there, but it wasn't toward her. Leslie would never understand that. She was too busy trying to beat an alligator with a stick instead of shooting it between the eyes. Momma surely knew best whenever she gave advice.

"Breanna," Tessa said, standing to her feet and walking toward her. She wrapped her arm around Breanna's shoulders. "Are you okay?"

"Yeah. I'm good," she lied.

"Listen," Tessa said, leading her out the break room. "You can't let bitches like that impede on your life. If she knew half the shit you've been through with Elijah, she would be like me and try to help a sista out."

Breanna smiled. "I do appreciate you, Tessa. You don't know how much you help me."

"That's what sistas are for, girl," Tessa said. She spotted Nathaniel sitting at his favorite booth and waved. "Besides, there's someone here who can do a better job at what I'm doing right now, anyway."

Breanna hugged Tessa and turned her attention to Nathaniel. "I better get over there."

"You better, girl."

She walked toward the booth while taking off her apron and sat across from him.

"Damn, girl." Nathaniel smiled. "Every time I see you, you get sexier. That baby put some curves on you."

She giggled. "Now, you're just gassin' me up."

He shook his head with a wider grin. "Ole dude don't know what he got on his hands."

"I don't want to talk about him right now."

"I feel ya". Nathaniel leaned closer to her. "I'm glad you didn't leave me hanging."

48

"I wouldn't do that to you."

He stared out the window. One by one, raindrops pelted against the glass. Noticing a big red truck, Nathaniel turned his attention back to Breanna. A frown graced his eyebrows. "Ole dude ain't picking you up tonight, is he?"

"No," she said. She stared out of the window, spotting the truck. Thank God it wasn't Elijah. Had he seen them together, Elijah would have lost every fiber of his being. Her eyebrows creased. It was what he deserved had he seen them, though. She stared into Nathaniel's eyes, then looked away from him. "We got into an argument before I left home."

Nathaniel placed his hand on top of hers, grabbing it reassuringly. "You shouldn't have to put up with his shit, Breanna," he said. "That man ain't trying to love you like the way you should be loved."

She sighed. "He's Izzy's father. We've got to try to see eye to eye on some things at least, you know."

"I get it, but you shouldn't waste another breath on ole dude."

Breanna smiled. Nathaniel was right about one thing. She shouldn't have been wasting her breath on Elijah. But deep down, she wanted to see if he would ever work toward fixing his mistakes before trying to force her to go to counseling with him. "I guess I just hold on too tight."

"Or you haven't held on tight enough," a woman's melodic yet raspy voice said from behind her.

Breanna closed her eyes and exhaled. She covered her face like she was shielding the sun from her eyes. There wasn't any way possible that Amber could have come to Soul Bistro. There just wasn't. Of all the restaurants she could have taken her girlfriend to, she had to come to this one. Leslie had something to do with this.

"Who are you?" Nathaniel frowned.

"You don't remember me, Nathaniel," Amber said with a smirk. "I was the math tutor Mrs. Palmer assigned to you and another jock buddy of yours."

"Amber." He smiled wryly. "It's good to see you."

"I thought you moved."

"And I came back."

"Well." Amber pursed her lips. "It's good to see you again, I guess."

Spotting her holding Leilani's hand, he grinned. "I didn't know you were... into... you know... swinging in that direction."

Amber nodded. Her smirk turned into a wide smile. "I didn't know you were into affairs."

He frowned. "Come again."

"That's enough."

49

"Breanna," Amber said, touching her on the shoulder. "Can I talk to you for a moment?"

"Anything you want to say to her in private can be stated openly."

"This isn't your business."

Nathaniel smirked. "Just like your sexual preference isn't my business, but it's staring me right in the face, isn't it?"

Amber frowned, then sucked her tooth. "I don't feel like trying to out dick you tonight, Nathan."

"It's Nathaniel—"

"Nathan," Amber said, cutting him off. "Who I love isn't any of your business, but if you want to share my love life with the world, then maybe you need to tell my baby sister how I took your girlfriend at the football game years ago."

Breanna stood from the table. "Excuse us," she said, grabbing Amber by the arm and pulling her into the restaurant's small lobby. "What is your problem, Amber?"

"What the fuck is your problem, Breanna?" Amber folded her arms across her chest. Her loose blue denim shirt wrinkled under the weight of them. The blue denim jeans she wore hugged her hips like a second skin as she leaned against the wall. "I came here to treat my lady to an early birthday gift, hoping I could get you to make her your salted caramel brownies and vanilla ice cream, and yo' ass look like you bout' to suck face with Nathaniel Morrison."

"First of all, you don't have the right to judge me, Amber," Breanna said, stepping toward her.

"Judge you," Amber snapped. "Girl, you're over there telling this man that Elijah treats you like shit when yo' ass knows that is far from the truth."

"Have you come over to the house lately? Have you heard the arguments we've had?" Breanna said, rolling her neck. "No. You haven't. You would feel like I would if you did."

Amber shook her head. "You act like Momma sometimes. You know that, right?"

"At least Momma's got common sense, Amber. Where did your common sense come from? Daddy?"

The sting of Amber's hand radiated on her cheek as she stumbled backward from its force. Breanna glared at Amber with narrowed eyes. The sting still surged over the softness of her flesh. "You crazy bitch!"

"This crazy bitch got left and right hooks too, if you want em'," Amber warned, getting in Breanna's face.

Leslie and Leilani ran into the lobby and stood in between them. "Let's go home, Amber," Leilani said, taking her by the hand.

"You started this," Breanna hissed, trying to move past Leslie.

"I started this, Breanna," Amber fumed. "You're dumber than I thought you were."

"Shut the hell up, Amber."

"Both of you shut up," Leslie yelled. "You two need to stop this."

Breanna pushed Leslie away from her. "You probably orchestrated this shit, anyway."

Leslie frowned, then placed her hand on her hip. "I never called her Breanna."

Breanna tightened her lips. "Like hell, you didn't."

"I never called Amber, Breanna," Leslie retorted. She trudged toward the restaurant's entrance and stopped. "I took up for you when Elijah asked if you were seeing somebody else. How stupid was I to think you would have ended things the right way?"

"What did you tell him?"

"Nothing."

"What did you tell him, Leslie?"

Leslie scoffed. "In due time, you'll tell him everything yourself." She walked out of the restaurant and ripped off her apron as she walked to her car.

Breanna looked around at the open-mouthed restaurant goers. Praise Jesus for Howard being out on vacation. The last thing she needed was to lose her job when Elijah and Adrian's company weren't bringing in much money, to begin with.

She watched Amber and Leilani walk out of the restaurant. Lightning struck in the near distance, illuminating the night sky. Nathaniel walked beside her and took Breanna by the hand.

"I'm sorry that had to happen to you, Beautiful."

"It's okay, Nathaniel," she sighed. No telling what Amber or Leslie could have told Elijah. They were wrong for defending Elijah. They had no clue of the kind of person he was. Amber and Leslie chose to see a man who tried to protect his family; not the man who took away her choices.

"Are you going to be okay going home tonight?" Nathaniel sat in one of the chairs and pulled her close to him. "I've got extra space at my townhouse if you need a place to crash for the night."

"I don't know if I should," she replied. Breanna exhaled. She watched the people turn around and return to their normal. She wished she could do the same. Breanna wanted to return to her normal with Elijah, but he had driven them so far apart she didn't want to return to him anymore.

And why the hell was everybody team Elijah? They didn't think her feelings mattered at all. They didn't think about her at all. Well, if her sister and so-called best friend wouldn't acknowledge the problems he caused, she knew Nathaniel would be there for her.

"Are you sure?"

Breanna sat next to him and stared into his eyes. She sighed. "On second thought, I could use that room tonight."

Nathaniel smiled, flashing his white teeth. "Don't worry. I'll be the perfect gentleman."

Chapter Nine

The front door should have squealed open by now. It was way past Mommy's bedtime. Isabella sat up in her bed and looked at the clock, watching the big red 6:59 am flash to 7:00 am. Mommy's boss was a horrible man. He always made her work late, and he didn't care. She couldn't stand him, the musty skunk scent he wore, and the too-tight pants he pranced around in.

Isabella scooted out the bed and slid on her pink and white bunny slippers that matched her pink and white bunny nightgown. She and Mommy had the same set so they could look like twins on Saturday mornings.

"Good morning, Daisy," she said, rubbing the sleeping dog on her head. The dog wagged her tail and yawned. She licked Isabella on the nose as she stood.

Isabella giggled as she wiped her nose with the back of her hand. "You gotta help me find Mommy, Daisy."

She tiptoed to her bedroom door and peeped out of it. The faint sound of Daddy's wheezy snoring graced her ears. He must have had another asthma attack. Daisy nudged her with her nose, encouraging Isabella to walk into the hallway.

She stepped into the quiet space. The cherry oak wood floors embraced her slippers' light touch as she walked toward Mommy and Daddy's room. Daisy's wagging tail generated cool air as she walked beside her.

"Don't wake Daddy, Daisy. He's exhausted," Isabella said, placing her index finger on her lips.

She peeped her head into the opened door. He must have forgotten to close it after he put her down for bed. Daddy was sprawled on the bed with the same clothes he wore from the previous day. His arms lay about his head. His inhaler rested in the palm of his hand.

Mommy's arm would have been around him, and her hair would have draped the bottom of his chin had she been in bed with him. She would have heard Mommy coaching him through his asthma attack. But he must have coughed and fought to breathe on his own after he kissed her goodnight. Why wasn't Mommy here to kiss his pain away?

Daddy coughed as he stirred a bit. Isabella hid outside the door, hoping he didn't see her.

"Good morning, Izzy," he said groggily.

Her little eyes widened. Daddy had to have superpowers or something because he always saw her with his eyes closed. He was like one of those mutants from the comic books he loved reading whenever they visited Granddaddy Marvin and Mrs. Regina.

She peeped from behind the door and waved at him. Daddy never moved from that spot. Daisy ran into the room and jumped on the bed beside him. She rested her head on his stomach once she had gotten comfortable. Her head flowed up and down as Daddy breathed.

"Daddy?" Isabella climbed onto the bed and laid next to him and Daisy. Her brownish blonde streaked hair was scattered across Mommy's pillow. "Did that mean man make Mommy work late again?"

"Probably, Shortcake," he answered.

"But she would have called and told you that, right?"

Daddy opened his eyes and turned his attention to her. "She would have," he replied. "Maybe she just forgot to call because she was so busy."

"But doesn't the restaurant close at four in the morning?"

He sighed, then coughed a little. "Sometimes, well-known people ask for special things at the restaurant. You know, like when your favorite Disney Princess came to the library, and you got to take a picture with her."

Isabella nodded as she smiled. "Tianna is my favorite."

"Well, sometimes, people like that can request special things because they're so well-known to people like you and me."

"But Mommy would still come home, Daddy."

"I know, Shortcake." He paused. "She'll be home soon."

Isabella watched Daddy fall back to sleep. She noticed a tear slide down the side of his face and roll onto his pillow. Daddy never cried. Even when his attacks were too painful for him to stand on his own two feet at times, he never shed a tear. Mommy had to come home. Daddy needed her. She needed her.

Chapter Ten

Amber pulled up in Momma's circular driveway and took a deep breath. Seeing Momma's two-door BMW parked outside the front door spelled more than just trouble for her. A downright genocide of her very being was about to ensue. She exhaled. Amber understood why Momma loved Breanna so much. Two bitches of the same fucking feather flocked together.

As she got out the car, her cellphone vibrated against her backside, making her drop her keys. They bounced out of sight underneath her Dodge Challenger. "Shit," she grumbled to herself. "Give me a second, whoever's calling?"

Amber laid on the ground and reached for them. She felt the phone vibrate in her back pants pocket again.

"Why are you all on the ground, girl?" Momma yelled, hanging her head outside the door. "I didn't raise you to roll around in the dirt."

God! She if she could slap the fake teeth from the woman's mouth. "I'm trying to get my keys, Momma."

"Oh, okay," Momma yelled. She closed the door, still watching her every move.

If there was one thing Momma was good at, it was criticizing her looks, mannerisms, tone of voice, who she dated, and even how and where she worked. The phone rang again, making her bump her head on the side of the car door as she grabbed her keys.

She winced then cursed under her breath. A dirt stain smeared across her white t-shirt. At least she got her keys. She pulled her phone out of her pocket and answered it. "It's your dime—"

"—Auntie Amber," Isabella sobbed, cutting her off. "Mommy hasn't come home, and Daddy's having another asthma attack. He can't breathe."

"Okay, baby," Amber said, standing to her feet and jumping in her car. "Auntie's on the way."

Amber cranked up the car and revved the engine, making the V8 HEMI engine roar.

Momma ran outside. "Amber! What is your problem?"

Amber frowned. This bitch right here. "Isabella needs me, Momma."

"Breanna should be at home by now."

"Well, her ass ain't there, Momma." She backed over Momma's tulips and Tiger Lilies.

"Watch what the hell you're doing, girl!"

Amber pointed to her ear and shook her head. "Sorry, Momma. I can't hear you over the engine." She pushed the red Dodge Challenger out of the driveway and jumped the curve as she hit the pavement. Smoke emitted from her tires as she drove. Her frown deepened. Breanna had done some stupid shit, but this took the cake. Whatever she was looking for, she had gotten it. Yet, she should have been pimped slapped with the hand and the glove at a cost like this.

The man she had at home didn't deserve the mess she was putting him through. Sure, he made a mistake, but he apologized for it over and over to her. She only wanted a pity party like Momma.

Amber zoomed through the yellow light, driving past a woman about to make a right into a store's parking lot and cut her off.

"Watch how you drive, bitch!" The woman yelled out of her window.

"Sorry, sweet thang," Amber said, making another right turn toward the park and speeding toward the intersection toward Elijah and Breanna's home. "I'll catch you another day."

Amber abruptly turned left into sister and brother-in-law's neighborhood and zoomed down the street. What would have taken ten minutes to get to their house seemed only like four.

Her little sister had a lot of explaining to do for this one. A lot of it. Amber pulled into their driveway, parked the car, and jumped out the vehicle, closing the door behind her. She ran to their front door and banged on it. She looked down at her stonewashed skinny jeans and scoffed. A blot of mud hugged her thigh like it was a handshake. She didn't want to see Leilani like this tonight.

"Auntie Amber," Isabella cried, opening the door.

Hearing Elijah coughing and choking in the bathroom, she immediately ran into the kitchen, opened their spice drawer, and pulled out some ginger root. Thank God, Breanna listened to her about buying this stuff. "Okay, Izzy," Amber said, grabbing a pot from their dish rack. "Does your papa have another inhaler?"

She nodded as she wiped away tears from her eyes.

"Do you know where it is?"

The child shook her head.

"Okay. You've got to be a big girl and find it for me." Amber placed the pot on the stove and turned the dial to high. She grabbed an empty jar off the island and ran some cold water into it.

Isabella watched Amber's every move, then nodded.

"That's my munchkin." Amber ran inside the bathroom and stared at Elijah. He barely stood to his feet as he held his chest and he gasped raggedly. He slumped over the vanity's countertop as he tried to talk to Amber and nearly fell to his knees. She grabbed his inhaler from the sink and shook it, hoping to hear its response. Amber scoffed. The damn thing had to be empty.

"Come on, Elijah. You gotta stay with me, brother-in-law," she said as she helped him sit against the vanity's cabinet doors.

He glanced at her with dim eyes and nodded. His breathing labored through the wheezing.

"Breathe, Elijah," she said, holding his hand. His eyes fluttered shut. "No! No! No! Stay awake, brother-in-law."

Amber placed her hand on his chest and rubbed it in a slow, circular motion. "Keep your eyes on mine, okay."

He nodded, still fighting to breathe.

"Auntie Amber," Isabella yelled. She and Daisy ran into the bathroom. "I found Daddy's other inhaler."

Amber took the inhaler from her little hand and shook it. Thank God, it was full.

"Thanks, munchkin," Amber said, kissing the child on her cheek. "Go check on the pot of water for me. But don't touch it, you understand."

"Yes, Auntie Amber," the child nodded.

"Tell me if you see steam or not."

"Okay." She hurried into the kitchen. Daisy wasn't too far behind her.

"Okay, Elijah. Let's get some medicine into your lungs." She administered the puffs and kept her hand on his chest. "Take my hand and squeeze it tight."

Elijah took her hand and squeezed it as much as he could.

She smiled, feeling his fingers tighten around her hand. "Keep breathing, Elijah. You've got this."

He nodded. "Amber," he breathed. "Thanks for coming here."

She smiled while nodding her head. "Less talk, more breathing, brother-in-law."

"There's steam coming from the pot, Auntie Amber," Isabella yelled.

"Thanks, munchkin. Your papa is feeling better now," Amber replied. Feeling his chest rise and fall normally again, she sat against the wall.

"Amber," Elijah coughed. "Have you heard from Breanna?"

She shrugged. "I haven't, brother-in-law. She hasn't called or texted you?"

"No. I don't know where she is, and she won't answer her phone."

Amber frowned. It was 12:30 in the afternoon, and the heffa never came home. She knew it wasn't her place, but something had to be said. This was going to get nasty quick if she said something, though. "Elijah—"

"Who is he?" Elijah cut her off.

She closed her eyes. And Momma thought Elijah was just some dumb jock boy who only wanted his dick to be stroked whenever and wherever he went. "What makes you suspect it's another man?"

"I already called your mother," he replied. "She wasn't too happy I called."

"Let me guess. She accused you of hurting Breanna, right?"

"Yep." He coughed again before clearing his throat. "She called me every name under the sun."

"That's Momma," Amber said. She heard Daisy barking at the front door. Hearing it open, she looked at Elijah. "It's best if she told you. Not me."

"Thanks, Amber." He squeezed her hand once again.

"Mommy's home!" Isabella sang.

Elijah sighed. "I don't know what else to do, Amber."

"Put her ass on CS."

Elijah lifted a brow. "What's CS?"

"Child support," Amber replied. "Her ass will straighten up then."

He chuckled. "You may have a point there, but I think I may need to get full custody of her, instead."

"What happened?" Breanna said, walking into the bathroom. A frown sat upon her brows, seeing Amber's face.

Amber stood from the floor. "I'm going to steep you some ginger root tea, brother-in-law."

"Mommy," Isabella said, hugging her waist. "I missed you."

"Mommy missed you too, Shortcake," Breanna said. She kissed the child on the forehead.

Elijah stared at her from the corner of his eye and shook his head. A frown sat upon his brow. "Go help Auntie Amber with the tea, Izzy."

She smiled. "Okay, Daddy."

Breanna walked into the bathroom and sat on the floor next to him. "Are you okay?"

"I'm better," he stated.

"Did Izzy call Amber?"

"Yeah," he responded. "I couldn't breathe."

"Do you want to go to the doctor?"

"I want to know where you've been."

She turned away from him. "I was at Tessa's place last night. I figured I give you some space."

He scoffed. "You sure about that?"

"Yes. I'm sure," Breanna retorted.

"Then, tell me the truth, Breanna."

"I was with Tessa, Eli. Momma was in Nashville last night."

He nodded with tightened lips. "Who is he, Breanna?"

"I can't believe you're accusing me of cheating on you."

"Just tell me who he is, Bree. I won't get angry."

"I can't believe you, Elijah."

"Just tell me, Bree."

"There isn't anyone else, Elijah," she hissed. "Just stop fucking accusing me of shit and look in the mirror."

He nodded. "Okay, Breanna. But if I find out there is another man, I will seek full custody of Isabella."

Breanna's eyes widened. "Are you threatening me?"

"No, Bree. I'm making you a promise."

Elijah got up from the floor and walked out the bathroom, leaving Breanna still sitting on the floor with her mouth agape.

Elijah walked into the kitchen and sat at the island. He ran his hand through his hair, then rested his chin on the palm of his hand.

"Is Mommy coming for tea, Daddy?" Isabella looked back at him with a wide smile.

Amber stared at him. She pursed her lips and raised an eyebrow. Her little sister needed to grow the fuck up. But then again, this was Momma's fault. Thank God she was gay. Had she not been, she would have been more monstrous than her little sister and momma.

Amber sat a mug in front of Elijah and poured the hot tea into the blue painted porcelain cup.

"I really appreciate you for helping me, Amber." He took a sip of the hot tea and smiled. "I'm in your debt."

"You're good, brother-in-law. You don't owe me a thing."

Breanna walked into the kitchen and walked toward the refrigerator. "Hey Amber, can I speak with you just for a moment?"

Amber stared at her with a smile. "Sure, little sis."

"Auntie Amber," Isabella sat next to her daddy. "Can I have the rest of your grapes?"

"Go for em' munchkin."

She followed Breanna out the kitchen and back into the bathroom. Breanna stared at her with narrowed eyes. "What did you tell him, Amber?"

"Like I told you last night. Nothing."

"Then, why the hell did he threaten me to take full custody of Isabella."

Amber scoffed as she shook her head. "That's your problem, Bree. Not mine."

Breanna frowned. "You and Leslie think I caused my own problems, and neither of you has no clue what I've been through."

"We may not understand, but we both know you and Isabella would have died if Elijah didn't find you bleeding all over the bathroom floor. Oh! Need I remind you, you were passed out when that happened."

"That still didn't give him the right to constitute my life, Amber."

"Well, I'm just thankful my little sister and niece are doing well," Amber said. "Yet, you don't seem to appreciate a damn thing he's done for you, don't you?"

"I love Elijah."

"Mmm-hmm."

"I do, Amber," Breanna sighed. "But it's been hard to look at him the same lately. It's hard knowing that he got his business off the ground, and I was stuck with nothing."

"When he suggested you sell your pastries from the house, you seemed happy with what you were doing."

Breanna folded her arms across her chest. "But that didn't allow me to get out of the house or promote my talents."

Amber shook her head. "You've got an excuse for everything, don't you?"

"No. I don't, Amber. I'm finally doing something that makes me happy."

Amber nodded, then smiled wryly. "Best of luck with that." She glanced at her watch. Amber had to get back to Momma's house before she put out an APB on her for not bringing home her Perennials. "I'm going to let you handle this little situation you've gotten yourself into."

"I've got me," Breanna retorted.

"That you do, little sis."

Amber walked out the bathroom and returned to the kitchen. She kissed Isabella on the forehead, then snuck a grape out of Isabella's bowl. She threw it in the air and caught it with her teeth. "Love you, munchkin."

"I love you too, Auntie Amber."

She patted Elijah on the shoulder and smiled while making her way to the refrigerator. "I've got to go. Momma's gonna kill me if I don't take those flowers to her house."

He nodded. "You don't want to make her mad then."

"What you said."

He chuckled. "Thanks again, Amber."

She nodded, grabbing her keys off the island. "No problem, brother-in-law."

Amber saw Breanna in the background, made her way out the front door, and closed it behind her. She closed her eyes and sighed. Breanna was doing the exact thing Momma had done to Dad some years ago. All he did was support her for coming out as a lesbian, and Momma nearly sliced her entire head and neck clean from her body, thanks to Aunt Pauline.

That woman was the devil herself. Aunt Pauline had it out for Dad. She just never understood why she hated him so much. The only plausible thing she knew was how the woman infested Momma's mind with that demonic bull crap about how gays and lesbians were doomed to burn in eternal damnation. Amber understood two things: God loved her—point number one. She loved who he made her to be—point number two. That was enough said. But Aunt Pauline refused to accept her. She, instead, turned Momma into the homo-hating mother who wanted to throw her daughter at the stakes to be burned at the Salem Witch Trials.

Hopping inside her car and cranking the engine, Amber backed out of their driveway. A part of her didn't understand why she was even going to Momma's house. The woman couldn't stand the air she breathed, let alone the ground she stepped upon. She was still her momma regardless of how much she hated the validity of that fact. Amber sighed. Gwendolyn was still her momma.

Chapter Eleven

"How's your mom, Amber," Leslie took a sip of her Arnold Palmer. Amber took a bite of her Chicken Parmesan, then shrugged her shoulders. "I know she loves Breanna more than me. That's how she's doing." Leilani stared at her with narrowed eyes while chewing on her Chicken Alfredo. "I'm sorry, Leslie. I meant to say she's doing well."

Leilani's eyebrows creased; her lips were pursed. "You got one mama, Amber," she said. Her Alabamian drawl lingered at the end of each word she spoke. "You best do right by her."

Amber laughed. "Do right by her? The woman almost gave herself a hernia when she saw me on the ground earlier today trying to get my keys." She laughed before taking a sip of her wine. "My momma was about to come and drill her foot off in my ass."

Leslie smiled, shaking her head. "Sounds like she's doing fine to me."

Amber paused, then took a deep breath. "Thanks for coming out tonight, Leslie. Breanna was supposed to be here with me to celebrate Leilani's birthday, but I guess her new man got all her attention now."

"He must be better than her boyfriend of seven years," Leslie said.

"Wait!" Leilani put down her fork. "They've been together for seven years, and he ain't put a ring on that."

"Elijah has a ring," Leslie said.

Amber's eyes widened. "Well, fuck me sideways. He bought her a ring?"

"He showed AJ the ring about four months ago." She took another bite of her lasagna. "But honestly, I think he's wasting his time."

Amber scoffed. "I second that. The bitch has everything she needs and then some. Yet, she complains."

"I get why she complains, though," Leslie stated.

Amber cleared her throat. "Then, you better tell me how you get it."

"There were times when he wouldn't let Breanna get out the house," Leslie said. "There were even times he didn't want her to so much as make a move because of all the pain she was in. But he realized he was wrong."

"And did he apologize for it?" Leilani took another large bite of Chicken Alfredo.

"Countless times," Leslie and Amber both answered.

"Breanna's just," Amber hesitated, staring into Leslie and Leilani's eyes. "Somebody who I shouldn't be dwelling on right now."

"But she hurt you, darlin'," Leilani spoke. "She wounded both of you in ways that have ripped apart your relationship with her."

"Well, I won't spend another minute thinking about my little sis. She got problems, and I got my own."

Taking another bite of her Chicken Parmesan, Amber noticed a tall, handsome black man leading a woman in a red and black pencil dress by the hand to a table close to the window not too far from them. She squinted. The dim lighting made it hard for her to see the woman's face. But those waves in his hair. That neatly shaped beard. That statuesque body. That was none other than Nathaniel Morrison in the flesh.

"Do you see who I see?" Leilani said, gulping her wine down in one take.

"That's Nathaniel, alright," Amber said, keeping her eyes focused on him.

"Then who's the floozy with him?" Leilani asked, gesturing for their waiter to come her way.

"She doesn't look like Breanna," Leslie said, squinting. "Then again, that maybe her."

"What makes you say that?" Amber stared at Leslie, then directed her attention back to Nathaniel.

"I had a shift at the restaurant earlier today, and I overheard Tessa talking to her on the phone about going on a date tonight."

"I'm tempted to text Elijah," Amber said, holding her phone in her hand. She placed it face-first onto the table and pushed it away. "But I'm not trying to start any mess."

"You know Elijah already knows about him." Leslie drank the last remnant of her Arnold Palmer.

"I never told him about Nathaniel," Amber said, pointing to her chest. "Did he ask you?"

Leslie nodded. "But I didn't tell him anything either."

"So, how did he find out about Nathaniel?" Leilani watched the waiter fill her wine glass with more Moscato, then motioned for him to stop.

"AJ told me Elijah saw Nathaniel jogging in the park after he left our house on Saturday. He recognized him when he came to pick Breanna up from work one night. And Nathaniel waved at him too."

Amber scoffed. "That bastard got some fucking balls."

"Humungous balls, sugar bee," Leilani said.

"He can do whatever he wants," Leslie said. "I'm not wasting my time with Breanna anymore. She acts like I have my shit altogether when I'm still trying to put pieces of the puzzle in place."

"I feel ya' on that, honey." Leilani sipped her wine, trying to savor it.

As they watched the woman walk to the ladies' room, they all saw her long wavy hair bounce off her shoulders as she strode. Like Breanna, she was curvy in the hips and had a small waist. They swayed as she walked. Her breasts barely peeped through the near skin-fitting dress. The way she pushed her glasses up on her nose was a dead giveaway.

Amber closed her eyes and looked away. "I've got to get out of here. Are you all ready to go?"

Leilani placed her hand on top of Amber's. "It's okay, darlin'."

"It's not," she said, gesturing for the waiter to come back their way. "But once I leave this place, it will be."

"Just pray for her, Amber," Leslie said, handing her thirty-five dollars.

"That's a tall order, Leslie, but I'll try." Amber sighed, watching her sister return to the table. A frown creased her eyebrows as she watched Nathaniel pull her sister closer to him and shove his tongue down Breanna's throat as they kissed. His hand slithered its way toward her sister's ass, and the heffa allowed him to do it. Yeah. That was going to be hard for her to do.

Chapter Twelve

The shrieking sounds of a rooster's crow pierced Elijah's ears. He slapped his phone, causing it to fall off the nightstand. He rolled over and ran his hand over the cold bedsheets to his right. Breanna was gone. Again. This was the third week in a row. She was going for a streak.

Elijah sighed. She didn't love him anymore. That was to be understood. But to put their daughter in the closet and close the door without opening it again was cold. Even for her.

Breanna's beauty may have still been present whenever she was around, but her mind and spirit vacated the premises years ago. Elijah saw this coming. He just thought he could do something about it before it got to this point. He sat up in the bed as he heard Izzy's coughing.

He closed his eyes for a moment and took a deep breath.

I can't let her run out of inhalers.

The sounds of sniffles at his door caught his attention. He noticed a pair of tiny fingers grip the side of the wooden slab and smiled. Izzy peeped inside the bedroom and then rubbed her eye with the back of her hand. "What's wrong, Shortcake?"

"I don't want to go to school today." She walked inside and crawled on the bed next to him. She sniffled once more, wiping away more falling tears.

"You've got to go to school, Shortcake. That's going to make you smart and independent like your mommy."

"But I want my mommy to take me to school and leave a brownie in my lunch box like she used to do. I want to see her smiling at me when

I walk inside the building and wave at her from Mrs. Taylor's window," she pouted. Isabella sobbed. "Does she still love me, Daddy?"

He beckoned for her to come into his embrace and rocked her slowly. Elijah wiped her tears away with his thumb before kissing her forehead. "Your mommy loves you so much, Isabella."

"But she never comes home anymore. Did I do something wrong to make her mad at me?"

"No. Isabella. You are the love of her life," he replied. "Mommy's just going through some things right now. That's all."

She wept. "I want my mommy." Isabella wrapped her arms around his neck and rested her head on his shoulder. Her sniffles and sobs made her small body tremble. Elijah tightened his embrace around her, hoping she didn't feel his tears fall onto her skin.

This shit had to stop. Regardless of what Elijah wanted from Breanna, he needed her to be a mother to Isabella. He needed her to realize that she was destroying this child's life. He couldn't and wouldn't allow her or the other man she was screwing to create a rift in their daughter's life.

"Hey, Shortcake," Elijah said, standing up with her still in his arms. "How about we go see Gigi today after school? She'll get you some ice cream."

"She will?"

"All you have to do is tell her what kind you want, and you have it in your hands before you can say hokey pokey."

Isabella giggled, wiping away another tear. "Can we see Granddaddy Marvin too?"

Elijah smiled as he nodded. "We sure can Shortcake." He kissed her on the forehead once more. "Go get those teeth brushed ASAP, and I'll pick up some breakfast from McDonald's, okay."

She flashed him a wide smile and nodded. "Okay, Daddy."

He placed the child on her feet and watched her swing her arms as she walked. She got that from Ms. Zora, he chuckled to himself. Hearing his phone chirp, he picked it up from the floor. Morgan's name displayed on the screen.

Morgan: Morning, Sunshine. Meet me at the sight. We're breaking ground today.

Elijah frowned. Breaking ground meant he wouldn't be home until at least eight or nine o'clock tonight. He couldn't do that to Isabella, not after the three weeks she had been enduring with Breanna missing from her life. He pecked at the screen.

Elijah: I can be there, but I can't stay all day. I've got to pick up my daughter from school today.

Morgan: I promise I won't keep you until the roosters come crowing again.

Elijah chuckled, then pecked away at his phone again.

Elijah: That reminds me I need to change my alarm clock ringtone.

Morgan: Ha! That's too funny. Or too ironic. You haven't changed, Sunshine. See you soon.

Elijah smiled. For once, Morgan sounded like an ordinary woman who wasn't raging out over what color her shoes should be to match her ensemble. It had been a minute since a woman made him smile besides Breanna. Hell, Breanna had kicked him to the curve; he needed to do the same thing to her.

He sighed, raking his fingers through his hair. As much as he wanted to, Elijah couldn't do that to Breanna. No matter who the asshole she was currently screwing was, he wouldn't stoop to her level.

Elijah heard his phone ring as he turned on the shower water. He scoffed, recounting the numerous time he wanted to chuck that damn thing out the window. He couldn't take one freakin' step without hearing the thing go off.

He saw Breanna's name flash on the screen and frowned as he took a deep breath. Elijah wanted her to feel the way he'd felt for the past three weeks. He wanted her to wake up alone in a cold bed. He wanted her to—he answered the phone.

"Elijah?" Breanna said. "Is Isabella okay? I was on my way home, but I got caught up in traffic."

"You know that it's 7:30 in the morning, right?"

She scoffed. "I know what time it is, Elijah."

"And you do remember she has to be at school at nine o'clock."

"Elijah, why are you questioning me?"

He sighed. "Bree," he paused, clearing his throat. "You've forgotten how to be a mother to our daughter."

"What?!" she snapped. "I know you just didn't say that. How dare you even—"

"Breanna," Elijah cut her off. "You haven't been home in three weeks. You only call to pretend like you're concerned, and our daughter believes you don't love her anymore."

"That's not true... I love her—"

"Then act like it, Breanna. I get it if you don't love me anymore. But don't take your anger for me out on Isabella."

"Eli... I... do love—"

"—You don't, Breanna," he retorted. "Just come home for Isabella, please."

"Elijah—"

"—I'll sleep on the couch tonight."

The silence between them deafened his ears. Steam from the running shower water clouded the mirror and his view of the bathroom. The sound of her sucking in a breath made him close his eyes. As much as he wanted her to feel the stings, cuts, and bruises she dished him, Elijah couldn't fathom bringing a tear to her eye.

He cleared his throat once more. "I have to go, Bree. I've got to get Isabella to school."

"Elijah..." she sighed. "I'll see you soon."

He frowned. Breanna should have been awarded the academy award for the many times she said that line. Sure, he didn't want to see her hurt. But the woman needed to endure the same pain he felt. She needed to learn a valuable lesson. "Okay, Breanna."

Elijah ended the call and placed the phone on the vanity before stepping into the shower. Water trickled down his back and chest as he stood underneath the showerhead. Elijah put his hands on the shower wall before him and closed his eyes. It was these moments he used to feel Breanna's hands wrap around his waist or lather his back with his favorite soap. There were even times he'd snatch off her shower cap and pull her underneath the showerhead, soaking her hair after she warned him she'd just pressed her hair.

He smiled. The echoes of her giggles and playful pleas lingered in his ears. His eyes brightened from the smile tugging at his lips. Then, there were those memories of him pulling her into the shower with him when she was fully clothed. It made her fuss at first, but her anger soon gave way to laughs and giggles, which led to moans and pulling the bedsheets from the bed later.

Elijah missed that. No. He longed for that back. Whoever this Nathaniel guy was, he couldn't let him take the one woman who brought joy not only to him but to Mom, Dad, and Katrina.

"Daddy," Isabella yelled. "I can't find my favorite yellow cardigan. Could you help me find it?"

Elijah dragged his wet hand over his face. "Okay, Shortcake. Give Daddy one more minute, and I'll be right there to help you find it."

"Thank you, Daddy," she sang.

Turning off the shower, Elijah heard his phone chirp again. He closed his eyes and sighed. Elijah had to put that thing on vibrate or something before he lost his mind. He smirked. Breanna was right. He was going to get tired of that phone dinging all the time, and he hadn't had it for a year yet. So much for overpriced flashy phones he couldn't quite understand.

Had Breanna been there, she would have fixed the damn thing to his liking, and he would have gone on his merry way. But that wasn't the reality he was living in now. She was... she found love... he had to fix this.

Elijah got out of the shower and wrapped his towel around his waist. Drops of water dripped from the ends of his hair onto his shoulders.

"Daddy!" Isabella yelled.

"I'm coming, Shortcake," he said. The sound of Daisy's barking drowned out the sounds of his chirping phone. Functioning as a single father was tough but doable. He couldn't let Izzy see his frustration, or she would worry herself into an asthma attack, especially with Breanna not coming home anymore. God! All he wanted to do was to have her in his arms again.

"Daddy!" Isabella yelled over Daisy's barking. "That pretty lady is at the front door."

He glanced at the message on his phone and sighed as he closed his eyes. Then again, Morgan hadn't changed too much, he thought. Once she had his house address, he knew her appearances would be frequent if she wanted something and uninviting if he owed her something.

Holding onto his towel with one hand, Elijah ran downstairs, kissed Isabella on the forehead, and opened the door. Morgan's lips turned upward into a smile as she sipped her Mocha Latte through a straw.

"So, this is how you greet your business partner?"

Elijah scoffed. "I just got out of the shower," he said, inviting her inside the house. "Could you give me a minute while I help Izzy find her cardigan?"

"Sure," Morgan replied. She looked at her smartwatch, then turned her attention back to him. "It is 7:50. Would you like me to help you out with anything? I could cook something."

Elijah laughed. The last time she tried to cook something was in a microwave in her dorm room. The woman damn near burned it down because she forgot to remove the aluminum foil from her plate. He didn't need to take out an insurance policy on this house. Mom and Dad would tear him two new ass holes.

"How about you let Daisy outside in the backyard so that she can stretch her legs. You can play with her a bit if you like." He watched her nod her head. The blue jeans she wore accentuated her hips well. The black t-shirt and denim jacket she wore made her look modelesque. He took a deep breath and exhaled. Elijah couldn't understand why he was so tempted by her. He loved admiring the beauty of other women, and he knew to never chase after them because he already had a beauty at home. But for the life of him, he couldn't understand why Morgan lured him the way she did.

69

Maybe this was God's way of keeping him strong. Or perhaps this was his way of telling him to move on. Either way, he could not and would not be unfaithful to Breanna.

"Alright, Sunshine," Morgan said, walking to the back door. She whistled for Daisy and opened the door for her to dash out of.

Isabella looked up at him. "Why does she call you sunshine, Daddy?"

"Like you, I'm bright and warm-hearted, like the sun," he said, tickling her side. "Now, let's go find your yellow cardigan."

She smiled. "Okay, Daddy."

As Elijah followed her up the stairs, he heard the front door creak open. That couldn't have been Breanna. The last thing he needed was for Breanna and Morgan to argue in front of Isabella.

"Eli! Izzy! I'm home," Breanna called.

Elijah closed his eyes again. The real last thing he needed was for Breanna to see him wearing nothing but a towel and Morgan downstairs. Breanna would lose her shit, but it wouldn't be like she didn't deserve it.

Isabella's eyes widened as she turned toward him. "Is that Mommy?"

"It sure is, Shortcake." Elijah spotted her yellow cardigan hanging in the closet and he grabbed it for his daughter. "You're all set, Isabella. Go give Mommy a hug and kiss."

"Okay," she said, smiling.

Elijah watched her run downstairs and then dashed into their bedroom, letting the towel drop to the floor. He opened his dresser drawer, spotting a pair of black boxer shorts and some raggedy jeans he tore about a month ago. Thank God he had those, at least. All his jeans were dirty or shredded because he worked in all of them. It was time he separated work and leisure clothes before he didn't have anymore.

After pulling on his boxers, Elijah grabbed his jeans and held them close to his waist before pulling them on. A pair of new jeans sticking out from Breanna's drawer caught his attention. He opened it, noticing a box of unopened condoms and frowned. They hadn't used condoms in years. After she went on the pill, they stopped using them. That was probably the best decision they made after having Izzy.

Elijah closed his eyes and took a deep breath.

She was fucking Nathaniel.

He coughed, feeling his chest tighten and his breathing labor. He grabbed his inhaler from the dresser and took two puffs. He took another deep breath as the tightness released it. Elijah cleared his throat as he coughed again.

He couldn't let her do this to him anymore. He loved her more than she ever loved him. That was a fact he was going to have to live with. Elijah frowned. Then again, maybe it was time to let her go.

"Elijah," Breanna said, tapping on the door. "I heard you coughing. Are you okay?"

He sighed. "I'm good, Bree." He opened another drawer, pulled out a black t-shirt, and pulled it on. "I've got to get Isabella to school."

"Hey, Sunshine," Morgan yelled from downstairs. "You're going to be late taking your kid to school. Ya' best move your ass."

Breanna lifted a brow and cocked her head to the side. "What is she doing here?"

Elijah chuckled as he shook his head. "She just so happens to be the person investing in my and AJ's business, remember."

Breanna watched him walk past her and folded her arms across her chest. "How long has she been here?"

"Before you got here, Breanna. Which for you, that's been a while."

"Really, Elijah?"

He scoffed. "I don't have time for this, Bree. I've got to get Izzy to school."

"I can take her if you want me to, Elijah. I don't mind."

He stopped in the doorway and hung his head. "Are you sure about that, Breanna?"

"Why are you acting like this?"

"For the past three weeks, Isabella has been crying herself to sleep because she thinks her mommy doesn't love her anymore," he snapped. "You think I'm just supposed to act like everything's okay."

Breanna frowned. "Just because I haven't been home for a couple of nights doesn't mean I don't love Isabella."

"Then what does that mean, Bree. I sure as hell would like to know." Elijah said, walking out the bedroom door. He looked around him, hoping Isabella wasn't around to hear them. The last thing she needed was to hear them fighting, especially since her mommy had just walked through the front door after a three-week sabbatical from them both.

"Eli... wait—"

"I gotta take Izzy to school. I'll see you around; that's if you stay."

Elijah walked down the hall, then made his way down the steps. He frowned. She had some fucking nerve to waltz her ass back home and pretend like nothing ever happened. After three weeks of screwing the shit out of Nathaniel, she must have needed a break to get her vagina back in order. He gripped the stair rail. The blood around his knuckles rushed away, leaving the fleshy white of his skin present.

71

Morgan stared at him with furrowed eyebrows and her hands resting on her hips. Isabella stood next to her, twisting in her brown sandals. The smile on the child's face eased some of his anger away.

"You good?" Morgan watched him grab his keys off the dining room table.

He nodded, smiling slightly. "I'm good, Morgan. Thanks for asking,"

"Where's Mommy?" Isabella asked, looking into his eyes. "Isn't she coming with us?"

Elijah scooped her up from the floor and propped her onto his shoulder. "Not today, Shortcake. Mommy's tired."

"Okay," Isabella pouted. "What about tomorrow?"

"Mommy should be ready to go by then, Shortcake." He tickled her stomach, making her giggle and wiggle against his shoulder as they made their way out the front door. For Izzy's sake, he just hoped that he wasn't lying to their daughter.

Chapter Thirteen

Breanna called him for the third time. But he never answered. She laid on the bed and sighed as she glanced at a framed picture of Elijah cradling Izzy in his arms when she was a baby on the nightstand. She closed her eyes and rested her head on the pillow. A tear streamed down the side of her face. He had some fucking nerve to tell her she didn't love their daughter. Isabella was her everything... she was her— a framed picture of Izzy playing with Daisy when she was three years old demanded her attention.

Perhaps Elijah was right for once. Maybe she was neglecting Isabella. She probably needed to introduce Isabella to Nathaniel since they were getting a bit—no. Breanna couldn't do that. She couldn't drop Izzy in a situation like that and expect her to be okay with it. She would think that Nathaniel would try to replace her daddy. Breanna sighed once more.

God! She should have stayed with Nathaniel for one more day. Maybe she should have—Breanna had to figure out how she could balance this.

The chirping phone demanded her attention, enticing Breanna to picked it up. She glanced at it and smiled, seeing Nathaniel's infamous smiley face emoji coupled with the 100 emoji appear on her screen.

Breanna: How's work?

Nathaniel: When you're the boss, everything's good. What about you?

Breanna: I'm okay. Elijah thinks I'm neglecting our daughter.

Nathaniel: Why don't you just stop dealing with his broke ass?

Breanna: Nathaniel, it's not that simple.

Nathaniel: Sounds simple enough to me. Just tell ole dude he's done for.

Breanna bit her bottom lip as she sat up in the bed.

Breanna: Then, let's wait another month or two before I introduce you to her. I want to make sure she's ready to meet you.

Nathaniel: Sounds like you ain't tryin' to bring her around me. That's low, Bree.

Breanna: I'm not doing that, Nathaniel. It's too soon.

Nathaniel: Ay, I can't text all day. I got clients coming in.

Breanna: Can I call you.

Nathaniel: We'll talk about this later. You swinging by tonight?

Breanna: Not tonight. I need to spend some time with my daughter.

Nathaniel: ... okay. Whatever.

Breanna: Nathaniel, please don't be that way.

Breanna took a deep breath as she held the phone in her hand and waited for Nathaniel's reply. She stood from the bed and walked into the master bathroom. She looked into the mirror, wondering who she wanted to be with more. She ran her fingers over her face, moving the few strands of hair lingering over her eye and then closed her eyes.

The thought of Nathaniel's wrapping themselves around her waist from behind made her smile. But as she opened them, she saw Elijah standing behind her shirtless. She smiled, feeling the remembrance of his warm embrace grace her skin. Images of his hands rubbing her seventh month pregnant belly lingered in her mind as she stared at herself.

Her smile faded. A tear slipped down her cheek. Why was she still thinking about him? Why wouldn't he leave her mind? Nathaniel gave her everything she needed and then some. So why was she still thinking about Elijah when he didn't give a shit about her? She looked away from the mirror. But she still loved him. She still needed—what the hell was she thinking?

Chapter Fourteen

Hoisting the last few plies of wood from the back of his pickup truck onto his shoulder, Elijah guided the wood into the skeleton of the new build where AJ stood inside. The wrath of the spring's sun hammered the back of his neck, causing sweat to trickle down his shirt as he trekked his way inside. His phone vibrated in his back pants pocket for the fourth time. Elijah frowned. Now Breanna wanted to talk.

After the three weeks of no calls and not coming home, he guessed he was the popular flavor again. Sweat rolled down his forehead as he placed the plies of wood on the ground. He took his phone out his pocket and frowned. Breanna's name scrolled across the screen again.

This was the most she tried to talk to him in a while. Perhaps this was a sign of change or another attempt to beat him down with all he had done wrong to her. He sighed, glaring at her name on the screen. Her absence didn't help their daughter. All Isabella wanted was for her mommy to be there to tuck her in at night, kiss her booboos when she hurt herself, and bake with her in the kitchen. Breanna couldn't even do that. Maybe it was time to end the relationship for good. Maybe he was holding on too tight.

"—Hey, bro," AJ said. He placed his hand on his shoulder. "Are you okay? I've been trying to get your attention for a minute."

Elijah stared at AJ and gave a half smile. "Yeah, I'm good, bro."

"Are you sure? You seem distracted."

"I'm more than just distracted," Elijah said. He slid the phone back into his pants pocket. "But I'll make it."

"You probably need to talk to her."

"Breanna?" Elijah took a deep breath, then shook his head. "Whenever she's ready to talk, I'm game."

"But is she trying to talk to you is the question?"

Elijah chuckled to keep from frowning. "She hasn't been coming home, AJ."

AJ's eyes widened. "You serious, Eli?"

"Pigs can't fly, and cows sure as hell can't jump over the moon, bro."

"For how long?"

"Three weeks," Elijah said, wiping the sweat from his head with the back of his hand.

"Damn, man. I'm sorry to hear that. You don't think she's—"

"—Seeing someone else," Elijah interrupted. He noticed Morgan walking toward the other guys near his pickup truck. "And I think I know who he is."

AJ wiped the sweat rolling from his bald head and looked away from him. "What about Izzy? How is she holding up?"

Elijah's phone vibrated in his pocket for the fifth time. She was right on queue. He took a deep breath and stared at AJ for a moment before turning his attention to Morgan. He locked eyes with her for a moment and then looked away. "She believes her mother doesn't love her anymore."

AJ shook his head. "Have you called the therapist yet?"

"I've already made an appointment, but first, I've got to get Breanna on board."

"Onboard for what?" Morgan walked inside the frame of the house. She glanced at AJ and Elijah with a smile and folded arms.

Elijah stared into her brown eyes again. "Nothing, Morgan."

"Come on, Sunshine," Morgan said, standing between him and AJ. "You can tell me anything."

AJ stared at Elijah with a raised eyebrow. "On that note, I'm going to meet the others so we can make plans for phase two."

"I'll be over there in a sec," Elijah said. He watched his friend walk away from them. A cool breeze gave him a little relief from the sun beaming down on him.

Morgan cleared her throat, forcing him to keep his eyes locked with hers. That never changed about Morgan. Her need for constant attention, her need to always be in the know, her need to make everyone bend to her will whenever she pouted. That was the same woman he and AJ knew all too well. That was the same shit that drove him away from her, yet he found himself aching to touch her soft skin. "What's up?"

"I'm concerned about my business partner," she said, standing closer to him.

"And employee, right?" Elijah lifted the bottom end of his shirt to wipe away the sweat rolling down his face. The smell of her lemon and strawberry-infused perfumed enticed his nose.

"Mmm-hmm," she purred, peeping at his abs. A smile settled across her lips. "I'm just trying to make sure you're okay."

His phone vibrated in his pocket again and took another deep breath. Breanna's little games were getting old. He pulled his phone out his pocket and stared at it. Three o'clock stared back at him.

"Fuck, I'm going to be late," Elijah said. As he made his way toward his truck, Elijah felt Morgan's hand grasp his as he walked.

"If there's anything I can do to help, just let me know."

He smiled. "I will."

Elijah made his way toward the others and stepped into the circle as he listened to AJ's briefing on phase two.

"Tomorrow, we'll start on the next build, since we have ten people coming," AJ stated. "So, this means we're going to have some extra help."

"Oh, thank God!" Mr. Glenn exclaimed. His peppered beard glistened from the sweat housed in it as he wiped the remaining perspiration from his forehead. His black and grayish ladened dreads were sprawled over his shoulders, and his chocolate skin appeared smooth under the sun's rays. "Cause at this rate, I'm going to let you young cats have this game."

"I feel ya' on that, Mr. Glenn, but you're the strongest one out here," Calvin said, finishing his bottle of water. His caramel toned hand covered a tattoo of a dragon on the side of his neck as he rubbed it. "You leave, and my skinny ass is done for."

Elijah chuckled. "Well, this is the burning bush we needed. How were we able to hire them?"

"We've got Morgan to thank for that. These are men and women who already work for her, so they're under her payroll."

Elijah smiled as he nodded. "Man, that's good to hear."

"Let's just hope and pray we can have eight houses ready by the midpoint of summer," AJ stated.

"Then, we better pray hard, Adrian," Mr. Glenn said. "Cause we're going to need every bit of it."

"That we will, Mr. Glenn," Elijah replied. He glanced at his phone again. 3:15 pm was here quicker than he wanted it to be. "Hey guys, I gotta go pick up my daughter from school."

Mr. Glenn smiled. "You better cherish those days, son. One day they're small and holding their arms out to ya,' and the next day, they're holding their hands out to you asking for eighty dollars to pay for her and her friends' way to go see a movie."

"Damn, Mr. Glenn. Kayla is that old now?" AJ asked with a chuckle.

"Sixteen and thinks she's grown. That's what my ass got for having four girls at a young age, but I don't regret getting married and having my kids so young," he said, wiping sweat from his forehead again. "I was nineteen years old when I had my first child and twenty-three when me and Shonda got married."

"You hear that, Elijah," Calvin said. The grin on his face exposed all his front and side teeth. "You better snatch that woman up and make an honest woman out of her."

"An honest woman, Calvin?" AJ asked with a cocked eyebrow. He fought hard to keep the smile from tugging at his lips. "How old are you, anyway?"

Calvin shook his head as he laughed. "Shut up, man. You already know my Big Mama raised me. Hadn't been for her, I would have been back in jail."

"Big Mama better not catch you sneaking her Tupperware out of the house, either," Elijah said, getting in his truck.

"Don't rat me out, E. You know she'll roll up on me, man."

AJ and Mr. Glenn looked at each other and broke out in laughter. Elijah chuckled as he pulled off the lot. He needed that happiness, he thought.

He remembered when he and Breanna spent nights talking and laughing with each other in his apartment the night before class. She wasn't the Breanna he remembered anymore. She wasn't the Breanna that used to snuggle his chest and instantly snore within five minutes of laying on him. Breanna was too consumed with pain and hurt. She was too consumed with trying to replace him.

Turning left near the Farmer's Market on Mender Street, he took a deep breath and held it for a moment before releasing it. He never tried to hurt her. But that's what she saw. He couldn't, for one second, bear the thought of losing her and Isabella.

When he learned Breanna had a high-risk pregnancy, he thought about what Mom endured when she carried Katrina. Though Breanna didn't go into labor early like Mom did, she damn near died twice. He took another deep breath as he made a right turn toward Isabella's school. To Breanna, he kept her from living. But to him, he made sure the loves of his life survived.

His phone rang as he pulled into the school's parking lot. Not wanting to look at it again, he let it rattle against the console. He parked his truck behind a line of waiting parents and sighed. All he had to do was just talk to her. Yet, talking to Breanna was like asking how close he needed to stand to the edge before plummeting to his death.

It rang again. That fucking phone was going to make him go insane. Though, it wouldn't have been the phone's fault for his insanity. He sighed again.

"Hello," he huffed, answering the call.

"Hi, Mr. Bryson," a woman's soft voice replied. "This is Dr. Shelby Hampton. Did I catch you at a bad time?"

Elijah glanced at his phone, seeing the doctor's number on display. He swallowed hard. "I'm sorry, Dr. Hampton. I didn't mean to sound so rude."

"No worries, Mr. Bryson," she said. "I wanted to let you know that you and Breanna have a session scheduled with me tomorrow in the afternoon. "Is this still a good time for you?"

He hesitated. "It is, Dr. Hampton."

"Listen, Elijah, the first session is never easy, especially when the other party isn't willing to take part, but I reassure you it will be a quick but thorough process."

"Thanks, Dr. Hampton."

"Please, call me Shelby," Dr. Hampton said. "Indeed, I've gone through a lot to earn this title, but it means nothing if I can't connect with my patients on a level they need me to be at."

Elijah watched Isabella walk outside with her teacher by her side and smiled. He bit his bottom lip for a second. "That would be a little difficult for me to do, but I appreciate you taking the time to see us."

"My pleasure," she stated. "Just... try to keep a level head about what will be said tomorrow, Elijah."

"Thanks, Dr. Shelby," Elijah said. "I look forward to seeing you tomorrow."

"Likewise."

He took another deep breath as he ended the call. He got out of the truck and walked over to meet Ms. Taylor and Isabella.

"Mr. Bryson," Ms. Taylor said, smiling. "It's always good to see you."

"You as well, Ms. Taylor." He smiled as Isabella ran to him and threw her arms around his waist. "How was she today?"

"As always, she was on her best behavior," Ms. Taylor answered. She stared at Elijah with furrowed eyebrows. "But she seemed distracted today."

Elijah looked down at Isabella. "Are you okay, Shortcake?"

The child nodded. "I'm okay. We painted pictures today, Daddy."

"Could you show me what you painted?"

She nodded, setting her backpack on the ground, unzipping it, and pulling out the painting. Isabella held it up to him, flashing a wide smile.

"Is that you and Mommy?" He smiled, examining the work of art Isabella created. For a five-year-old, he had to admit that she was talented. "This is beautiful, Izzy."

Ms. Taylor stared at him once again. "I would like to speak with you just for a moment if you have time."

He nodded. "Sure."

Elijah kneeled next to Isabella and kissed her on the forehead. "Daddy's going to get you settled in the truck. Be a good little shortcake and wait for me, okay."

"Okay," she smiled, nodding her head.

He grabbed her backpack and threw it over his shoulder, then lifted her from the ground. Elijah helped her inside the large pickup truck and strapped her into her booster seat. He tickled her stomach, making her giggle. He handed her the backpack, then closed the door behind him.

"Is there something going on more than her being distracted?" he asked, staring into Ms. Taylor's brown-shaded glasses.

A frown graced her eyebrows. "When I asked the class to write about their favorite things they like to do with their parents, Isabella cried. As a matter of fact, she never completed the assignment."

Elijah looked away from Ms. Taylor. Their little girl had become a casualty of the raging war between him and Breanna. This had to stop. "Is this the first time she's ever done this?" Elijah asked, returning his attention to Ms. Taylor.

"Yes," she stated. "Normally, Isabella is one of the happiest students I have in my class. But today, this question made her drift away from the other students and her studies. So, you know I must ask if there's anything going on that's impacting her emotional state?"

Elijah sighed. "Her mother and I... are going through some things right now."

Ms. Taylor gave a half-smile. She cleared her throat and then glanced at the truck for a moment before focusing her attention on his eyes. "Mr. Bryson, I'm not a psychologist or anything of that nature, but you two may want to talk to Isabella before things get out of hand. She's a big girl now, and she deserves to know the truth."

He nodded. "Yes, Ma'am."

Ms. Taylor placed a hand on Elijah's shoulder. "Now is the time you and Ms. Ellis talk with your daughter. She's a wonderful student, but she's an even better child. Please don't shut her out."

"I understand," Elijah said. He looked away from Ms. Taylor as he nodded. She must have sized him up and readied her game plan for what she would say to him. Women like Ms. Taylor meant well. Hell, they would even question why women like Breanna acted the way they

80

did, but they didn't understand the spectrum of what she was requesting from him to expose their daughter to. Sure, Elijah understood what she wanted him to do, but plugging the image of her parents hating each other was the last thing he needed to add to her already overactive, over-curious mind.

"Mr. Bryson?" Ms. Taylor said.

"Yes."

"I'll see you two bright and early tomorrow, right?"

He smiled. "Yes, ma'am."

As he made his way back to his truck, the phone vibrated in his pants pocket. That damn thing was going in the garbage when he got home. He glanced at it with a frown. A text message scrolled across the screen. It was Breanna. She wanted to talk.

Chapter Fifteen

Watching Isabella run around in the backyard with Dad's construction helmet on her head while Dad ran behind her was the breath of fresh air Elijah needed. He sat at Mom's Island and scooped another spoonful of chocolate ice cream from his bowl and into his mouth.

"Did she say what she wanted to talk to you about, son?" Mom asked, eating a spoonful of vanilla bean ice cream. She closed her eyes and hummed as she smiled.

Elijah shook his head as a smile pulled his lips. Mom never failed to ask a question first and then deviate from it like it never was a genuine issue to begin with.

He watched Mom's grayish blonde streaked hair shimmer in the sun's rays that peeped through the wooden blinds in the kitchen. A cool breeze entered the opened back door. Dad and Isabella's laughter brought back memories of when he and Dad used to play in the same backyard.

"She didn't," said Elijah.

Mom sighed. "You know, I remember when your father and I nearly divorced."

Elijah nodded. Those were times he didn't want to recall. Whenever they fought, Mom and Dad stayed clear from each other. Dinner was so awkward when all he could hear were forks and knives scraping the plates and those two chewing their food. "What happened between you two, Mom?"

"His mother."

"Grandma was a great person."

"To you and Katrina, she was wonderful. To me, she was the absolute devil. That woman hated my guts, God rest her soul."

"Did Dad ever believe what she said about you?" Elijah stared at his mom and scooped up his last spoonful of ice cream, savoring the chocolate goodness teasing his taste buds.

"Son, the woman believed I was out for your father's money. She thought I was stealing every time I went to the shop. Well one day, she made me empty my pockets in front of Jonah and every customer inside. You and Katrina were so young when you saw that happen. Neither of you knew what was going on—" Mom stopped. A frown turned her lips downward. She put the spoon back into the bowl and stood from the stool she sat on. "—That woman made her own son choose between his money and me. And to solve it, we were going to—"

Elijah placed his hand over hers and squeezed it. He noticed the tears flooding her eyes. She refused to let them fall from them. "Your father, being the man he is, told his mother to either get off her high horse or leave Kentfield."

Elijah tightened his lips as he nodded. "She left Kentfield."

Mom placed her bowl in the sink and sat next to him. "Eli, I know how much you love Breanna, and I know how much she loves you."

He chuckled. "You told me I made a slam dunk with her."

Mom laughed. "But you did." She placed her arm around his shoulders and kissed him on the cheek as she squeezed it. "My boy, she was the only young woman I honestly liked. Very articulate. Savvy. Beautiful. Real. She was, and still is, my future daughter-in-law."

Elijah stared at her for a moment with a raised eyebrow. "What did you think about Morgan?"

"Morgan Everly? That crazy-ass coot from East Kentfield. Oh! God no! She makes your Aunt Victoria look like a damn saint."

"Is she still married to the billionaire she met online a few years back?"

Mom shook her head. "Nope. They divorced about three months ago. Now, she's engaged to the guy who created his own tech startup. She said he's worth about a trillion or more, whenever he sells his shares to the right candidate."

Elijah chuckled while staring into his mom's ocean blue eyes. They were his source of comfort. No matter if Mom was distraught or depressed, the calm hue of her eyes never changed. He wished he could have been the same way. He needed her calmness right now. "Mom... I can't do this any—"

"Elijah," Mom said, interrupting him. She turned her attention to Jonah and Isabella playing outside, then stared into his eyes again. "I know it's hard for you right now. The love you have for Breanna seems unrequited, but it isn't. She loves you more than you know."

"How is not, Mom?" Elijah asked. His chest tightened as he breathed. Elijah closed his eyes for a moment, took a deep breath, and released it slowly, averting the asthma attack waiting to punch him hard in the lungs. "Everything I say or do to her sends her one step closer to the edge."

Mom rubbed his shoulder. "Breanna needs to learn how to forgive. That's something she needs to do for herself and you."

"What does forgiveness have to do with what we're going through?"

"When your grandmother decided to come between your father and me, I was ready to take her ass out of this side of the plain." Mom paused. She smiled as she watched Isabella jump around alongside Dad. "We thought the best solution to make her happy was divorce; we even considered it. But we didn't."

"So, you're saying you forgave grandma?"

"I sure am, Elijah," she answered. "Your grandmother was the kind of woman who was used to getting whatever she wanted. And when it came to me, she tried hard to get rid of me until I had you and Katrina."

"But Mom, Breanna thinks I intentionally tried to stop her from living her life—she thinks I got some kinda enjoyment from watching her suffer when I made her stay at home. I didn't."

"Trust me, Elijah." Mom sighed. "I know. I can remember how scared you used to get whenever I walked around the house when I was pregnant with your sister."

"Mom, I thought... I—"

"You only did what you thought was right for Breanna. That's where the forgiveness comes in, my son. Breanna hasn't forgiven you at all, and she hasn't forgiven herself for not being able to stand on her own two feet when she thought she could."

Elijah stared at his mom for a moment and then looked away from her. Spring's winds brushed against his forearms, causing the hairs on his arms to raise. She made it sound so easy. All he needed was to ask for Breanna's forgiveness and have her forgive herself, and things would go back to the way they used to be.

As much as he wanted to believe it, that was a tough one to fathom. Forgiveness. Breanna wouldn't forgive him if he were on fire, let alone forgive herself for something she thought she didn't have a hand in too.

"What's with the solemn faces?" Dad asked, allowing Isabella to lead him inside the house by his hand. "You guys look like you've watched The Imitation of Life and couldn't handle it."

84

"What's the Invitation of Life, Grandpa?" Isabella asked, looking at him.

Elijah shook his head and laughed. "It's the Imitation of Life, Shortcake."

"Oh!" Isabella sang with a wide smile. "Have I ever watched it before, Daddy?"

"You haven't, but if you want to, we can watch it for the next movie night," Elijah said.

Dad raised an eyebrow, then tapped his pursed upper lip. Unlike Mom, his hair was nearly white, except for a few blonde streaks lingering on the sides of his head. His beard was a different story. That thing had been white since Elijah turned twenty-one years old. "Maybe she should watch something a little more up to date. You know, like that new Jumanji movie with the Rock."

Isabella folded her arms across her chest. "I'd rather watch the other one with the guy from Mrs. Doubtfire."

"Robin Williams?" Mom asked. She stared at her granddaughter with an open mouth and then rolled her eyes in Elijah's direction. "My goodness. Do you even watch newer movies, Elijah?"

"I do," he chuckled. "Older movies are better."

"That's my boy," Dad said, flashing his straight pristine teeth in a wide smile. "Still, newer movies aren't bad either. I taught you well, though."

Elijah laughed aloud. He needed the tensionless enjoyment around him. He wasn't ready to face the friction-filled monster lying in wait in his own home.

If only he and Breanna could have a good night without fighting for once, then maybe they could talk without pulling out their weapons of mass destruction. Why wouldn't she just listen and speak to him without readying herself to strike him with her katana? He just wanted the woman he loved back. Why couldn't he have her back?

"Eli?" Dad asked. He walked to the refrigerator, opened it, and pulled out a bottle of water. "How are you and AJ coming along with those houses?"

"So far, so good. Morgan's got some more people coming to help the crew tomorrow."

"Morgan?" Mom frowned. "I didn't know she was in real estate."

Elijah nodded. "Yep. She is, Mom. She's the one who invested in our company."

"Elijah," Mom hesitated to speak. "She's not trying to take your company from you, isn't she?"

"No, Mom. She isn't. She's trying to build her company up and help us along the way."

"Honey, Eli knows what he's doing."

Isabella looked at everyone with puzzlement scattered on her face. "Are you all talking about that pretty lady?"

Elijah looked at his daughter and smiled. "We are Shortcake."

"Well, that pretty lady better watch how she conducts business with my sons' company," Mom stated.

"AJ would appreciate the extra protection, Mom."

"I can't let my boys be taken for a ride."

"Gigi, why would the pretty lady take Daddy and Uncle AJ for a ride?"

Dad laughed aloud as he sat at the island across from Elijah, Mom, and Isabella.

Mom stared at Dad with squinted eyes and scoffed. She covered her mouth with her hand, trying to hide the smile tugging at her lips. "Is this payback for being so inquisitive when I was a little girl?"

"Inquisitiveness is a deep-rooted family trait, Mom." Elijah laughed.

Dad took a swig of his water and held up a finger. "Honey, don't you remember when Katrina stood in our bedroom doorway with her hands on her hips and asked us if we were working with the stork at night?"

Elijah erupted into laughter. "Dad, did Kat really ask you both that?"

Mom nodded as her cheeks reddened. "That girl had the most serious look on her face that night," she said. "How old was she then, Jonah?"

Dad chuckled. "She must have been five or six years old when she asked us that question."

"Gigi? Grandpa? When is Auntie Kat coming back home?" Isabella reached for Elijah to pick her up so she could sit on his lap.

"Hopefully by the end of the month, Busy Izzy," Mom replied.

Elijah stared at the clock above the window next to the sink. Five o'clock was coming faster than he imagined. He tickled Isabella's stomach and then smiled at her. "Hey, Shortcake, are you ready to go see Granddaddy Marvin and Mrs. Regina?"

She nodded. Her bright smile seemed to have made her eyes glow before him. "Do you think Granddaddy Marvin made spaghetti and meatballs for dinner tonight?"

"That's what he promised." Elijah guided the child to her feet and stood from the stool. He looked at the smiles on Mom and Dad's faces. "Go get your backpack so we can go, okay."

She nodded before skipping out of sight down the hallway.

"I'm proud of you for doing that, son." Dad took the last swig of water in his bottle.

Mom paused, examined the recessed lights on the ceiling, and then exhaled. "Does Breanna know Isabella sees her grandparents?"

"She doesn't."

"Son, you need to be upfront with her." Mom stood from the Island again and made her way toward the cabinets. She opened one of the off-white wooden doors and pulled out an old picture of Elijah and Breanna hugging each other when they attended college. Handing it to Elijah, she gave a half smile. "You need to tell her everything."

"Mom, if I told her Izzy saw Mr. Marvin on the regular, she would slice my head clean off my neck."

"Sounds like an excuse to me, Elijah. You've got to tell her the truth because she's not the only person wrong in this situation."

Elijah stiffened. Mom was right. Breanna wasn't solely at fault. Had he told her about Mom's difficult pregnancy and how he never left her side, Breanna would have understood. Then again, she probably would have continued like it was all his fault.

And maybe Dad was right, too. Men were better off staying quiet than speaking the truth. At least that way, feelings wouldn't be hurt, and relationships wouldn't be severed.

"Have they even tried to speak to each other at all, son?" Dad peeled the wrapper off the water bottle and stuffed it through the bottle's opening.

"Dad, she doesn't even know about Amber being your CPA."

"Really?" Dad asked.

Mom sighed. "You two need to talk, and I mean talk, my son. The both of you need to be upfront and honest with each other."

"I know, Mom," Elijah said. He paused for a moment, searching for the best answer to give his mother. "I just hope I'm not too late."

"My boy," Dad said, staring into Elijah's eyes. "It's never too late, especially for a good woman like Breanna."

Elijah took a deep breath, reached inside his other pants pocket, and pulled out a small black box. He opened it and placed it on the island. He slid it toward Mom and Dad and gave a half smile. He watched Mom cover her mouth. A single tear slid down her cheek. "I love Breanna, Mom. And I want to make her my wife."

"Then, you best pray about everything moving forward," she replied. "You best pray like you never have before."

Chapter Sixteen

"That's my big girl," Mr. Marvin said, watching Isabella slurp the last spaghetti string off her plate.

Elijah sat back in his seat and smiled at his daughter. The joy in her eyes was the best thing he got a chance to see every day. He never wanted that to go away, but the way things were between him and Breanna, that joy could be taken away with a single breath.

Regina took a sip of lemonade from her glass and looked at the child dance about in her seat. Her jet-black hair was refined in loose beach curls. The blue and white tie-dye striped shirt and blue jeans she wore made her look like she was in her late thirties or early forties when she was really in her early sixties.

"Did my baby enjoy that spaghetti?" She asked in a soft, husky voice. A smile pulled her lips, flashing her white teeth. Her deep brown eyes seemed to glow from watching Isabella.

Although Mrs. Regina came after Gwendolyn, she was by far sweeter and way more understanding than Gwendolyn wished she could have been. Honestly, Mrs. Regina was more like Grandma Zora than her daughter was. Firm when she needed to be yet soft no matter the situation, she cared about Amber and Breanna as if they were her own, even when Gwendolyn stopped them from spending time with her. Still, Mrs. Regina remained poised. That's what he loved about her so much.

"Do you want to take a to-go plate with you for lunch tomorrow, Eli?" Mrs. Regina asked, directing her attention from Isabella to him.

He smiled as he nodded. "That would be great."

Mr. Marvin stood from the table and gathered everyone's plates. His black and white tracksuit made him look younger than he was. His peppered beard nearly matched his ensemble. Though his skin was darker than Breanna's, Elijah saw where she got her beautiful eyes from. "You know you're more than welcome to come to the barbeque we're having on Sunday," he said, walking out the dining room. "Regina's making her famous peach cobbler, and I got a whole pork shoulder ready for the grill."

Elijah closed his eyes, already savoring the sweet goodness in his mouth. "You're making a hard bargain, Mr. Marvin."

He laughed in the background. "I didn't say it was going to be easy, Eli."

Elijah glanced at the clay-colored wall and looked at the framed pictures of Amber and Breanna hanging on it. He kept his eyes on the one where Breanna stood next to her grandmother in the kitchen. The smiles on their faces were irreplaceable. An apple pie with a trophy sitting next to it sat between the two of them as they smiled at each other.

Mrs. Regina glanced at the picture and smiled. "Breanna was so happy about that apple pie she and Big Mama made together for the state fair."

"How old was she then?"

"I wanna say she was about eleven or twelve," she replied. "Marvin and I had been married for a year by that time."

"Daddy," Isabella asked, tugging on his sleeve. "Can I play Candy Crush? Please?" She placed both her hands together and stared at him with her wide doppelganger eyes as she batted them.

He smiled, taking his phone out of his pocket. Holding on to it, he looked at her with squinted eyes and smiled. "Now, before I give this to you, you need to promise Daddy you won't break it," he said.

Isabella crossed her heart with her index finger. "I'll protect it with all my might, Daddy."

Regina laughed as she took another sip of lemonade. "You and Breanna have done such a good job raising Isabella. She's so articulate and polite. Most kids, now these days, can't even look an adult in the eye, let alone say yes and no ma'am correctly."

Elijah chuckled. "Thanks, Mrs. Regina. It's a process, but we try our hardest."

But for how much longer was Isabella going to have a two-parent household to keep up that process, he wondered. How much longer was it going to be before Nathaniel took his place as a father figure in Isabella's life? Elijah stiffened in his seat and then rubbed his eyes. He wouldn't know what he would do if he had to watch another man play

89

father to his daughter. He cleared his throat. Asthma's tightening, choking fingers gripped his lungs for a moment before releasing it. He took a deep breath. Stress and asthma were like oil and water. They didn't mix.

"Eli?" Mrs. Regina asked. She sucked on a piece of ice from her lemonade. "Have you talked to Breanna about talking to her father? He really wants to talk to her again."

He sighed. "Every time I mention Mr. Marvin's name, she walks away from me. She doesn't want to reach out to him at all."

"Mrs. Regina." Isabella looked up from the phone. "Why come I can't call you Grandma? Aren't you married to Granddaddy Marvin?"

Mrs. Regina placed her elbow on the table, rested her chin on her palm, and smiled. "Your granddaddy and I thought it would be best that way."

"Why?" Isabella set the phone on the table. The music to Candy Crush played aloud.

"Well, that's because we're not related by blood, Izzy."

"But you're still my grandma, and I love you like you're my real grandma," she replied. "So, can I call you Grandma Gina, Mrs. Regina?"

Isabella looked at Elijah and Mrs. Regina with a big smile. "Is it okay I call her grandma, Daddy? Is it?"

Elijah sighed, then nodded. "You sure can, Shortcake. But you got to keep this between you and me, okay."

Elijah held out his pinky finger and wrapped it around Isabella's pinky. They both smiled and then nuzzled their noses together. That was something he and Breanna used to do back in college.

Mr. Marvin walked back into the dining room and sat next to Mrs. Regina. He handed Elijah his to-go plate and looked at his wife. He smiled at her, shaking his head. "I knew this day was coming," he said. "Isabella is very much like her mother. If it doesn't fit, she's going to make it fit in the most logical manner possible."

Elijah nodded. His daughter had the best of both worlds and probably the worst of them, too. While she was inquisitive like Mom, she knew when something wasn't right like Breanna and would address it. But when she pressed to get her way like Breanna did, Isabella would think about how she could get something in a different way like he used to do when he was a kid. Yep. He and Breanna created one hell of a child.

Elijah stared at the time on his phone and sat up in his seat. He moved his neck from side to side, cracking the bones in it. He and Isabella needed to be headed home to turn the lights on for Daisy so she wouldn't be in the dark too long. Knowing Breanna, she was probably laying up with Nathaniel right now. She was probably—at some point, Elijah knew he would have to let go.

Even if the counseling didn't work, he knew he had to be ready to see Nathaniel as the man she chose over him. He just wasn't prepared for that.

Elijah yawned and then rubbed his shoulder.

"Looks like you two need to be getting home," Mrs. Regina said.

"Yeah. That we do," Elijah said, standing from the table. He beckoned for Isabella to take his hand and led her from around the table. "I got a big day ahead of me tomorrow."

"That's right. You and AJ have been working on the new homes in the Myers District. How's that coming along?" Marvin asked.

"Yes, sir." Elijah guided Isabella toward Mrs. Regina and watched her fall into her grandmother's embrace. "Things are coming together pretty well so far."

"That's good." Mr. Marvin rubbed the gruffness of his beard with his thumb and index fingers. "Maybe you can help Amber find a place over there."

"Is she looking for a place to stay?"

Mr. Marvin chuckled. "If you call looking for the worse home that needs more money put on it to fix up rather than finding something turnkey."

"Amber's family. I can help my sister-in-law out."

"If you can help the pickiest person in the world find a place to stay without blowing away her savings, you'll be my favorite child in the world." Mrs. Regina stood from the table and took Isabella's hand.

"But I thought I was your favorite child."

"You are, Isabella," Mrs. Regina said, kissing her on the forehead. "But your daddy is my child too, just like your Auntie Amber and your mommy."

Isabella looked back at Elijah and smiled. "But isn't Gigi your mommy, Daddy?"

"She is, Shortcake, but Grandma Gina can claim me as her child, too," he said. "I get more good food that way."

Mr. Marvin and Mrs. Regina laughed as they led them to the front door. Mr. Marvin smiled, beckoning for Isabella to give him a hug.

"Drive safely, Elijah." Mrs. Regina said. She opened the door and watched them walk out.

"I will, Mrs. Regina. And thanks for dinner."

"You're more than welcome, son." Mr. Marvin waved at them both.

Elijah took Isabella's hand, unlocked his truck, and got her settled inside. He wasn't ready for what was waiting for him at home.

The piercing sound of jingling bells jolted Breanna from her sleep. Daisy rested her head on her leg and closed her eyes. She picked up her phone and stared at it. Neither Nathaniel nor Elijah returned her calls all day. She tossed the device on the ottoman in front of her and scoffed, slumping onto the couch. How in the hell did she piss two men off in one day? First Nathaniel and then Elijah. Perhaps this triangle she got herself into was becoming destabilized. Maybe she needed to rethink some things. Perhaps she needed to stop overthinking.

Breanna heard the garage door groan and hum as it opened. Daisy bolted from Breanna's lap and ran down the hallway. Isabella had always been that dog's favorite human.

"Bree?" Elijah called from the hallway.

She stood from the couch. Her black pajama shorts and black crop top clung to her body. She had to stop sleeping under that thick blanket so much.

"Mommy," Isabella sang. Daisy trotted behind her, wagging her tail. "You're home."

Breanna picked Isabella up and nuzzled her nose into her cheek. The child giggled and squirmed. "For my Shortcake, I would be."

"Go upstairs so you can get ready for bath time," Elijah stated.

His gaze never left hers. Breanna cleared her throat and looked away. In all the years she and Elijah dated, she never seen him look at her like that. The way his steel-blue eyes sat motionless. The way his chest heaved slowly upwards and downwards. The silence between them after his few words were spoken. This wasn't the Elijah she knew. "Are you okay?"

Elijah watched Isabella leave out of their sight, then rolled his eyes in her direction. "Are you Breanna?"

"What? Now you're mad at me for being at home?"

"No, Bree," he said. "I'm just surprised you're home."

She rubbed her throat as she walked past him. "I just needed some time to my—"

"Who's Nathaniel, Breanna?"

Every muscle in her body seized. She sucked in a breath. How the fuck did he know Nathaniel's name? Had he seen him at the restaurant? Even worse, had he seen the two of them together?

"He's a friend of mine. I've known him since high school." It wasn't a lie. That was, in fact, the truth. Breanna just didn't need the two to talk. Ever.

92

Elijah walked past her, nodding his head. "Okay."

Breanna turned her attention to him and narrowed her eyes. "Are you accusing me of cheating on you with Nathaniel?"

"All I want is for you to be honest with me, Bree like I hope you will be tomorrow at the counseling session. That's if you come," he said, making his way toward the steps. "I'm going to give Izzy a bath and put her to bed."

"Counseling session? When did you schedule that?"

"You wouldn't know because you're never here anymore."

"If you wouldn't be so damn difficult to talk to you, Eli—"

"I'm tired, Bree," he said, cutting her off. His eyes nearly burned a hole in her skin from the way he stared at her. "I'll see you in the morning."

Before she could say anything else, he had made his way upstairs. His footsteps echoed in her ears as he walked. Breanna slumped back to the couch. She placed her hand over her heart and swallowed hard as she took a deep breath. What was she doing?

Chapter Seventeen

Breanna pulled up next to Elijah's truck and shifted her car into park. Gripping the steering wheel, she sighed. Why in the hell was she even going through with couples' counseling in the first place? All this was, was just another attempt to make her accept the idea she was feeble and needed a man to rule over her hoopla.

She viewed the height of the Hammond Building, taking in the whitish gray stonework and large Bohemian water fountain in front of it as she got out of her car and walked toward the building. The sun's rays bounced off the flow of water splashing from rock to rock, creating a stair step like design that zig zagged in multiple directions. It was the most peaceful thing she'd ever seen. Too bad that wouldn't be the case for this counseling session.

Breanna pulled open the glass door and walked inside. Hanging lights dangled in between wooden pine beams on the ceiling in their golden luster. The sandstone marble floors coincided with the wooden stair rails on either side of the lobby.

A young woman sat at a massive receptionist's desk, scrolling through her phone. Her blonde hair sat neatly in a flight attendant's bun.

"Excuse me, ma'am." Breanna eyed the painting of a little black boy sitting on his grandpa's lap playing a banjo.

"Yes," she answered in an overly optimistic voice. Her bright hazel brown eyes beamed. "How can I help you today?"

"My name's Breanna Ellis. I'm supposed to meet with Dr. Shelby Hampton today."

She pecked away at her keyboard, then tapped her manicured fingernail against the desk as she searched for the name. "Dr. Hampton is on the second floor; suite 251."

"Thank you so much."

"You're welcome. Please enjoy your visit at the Hammond."

As she made her way toward the steps, the hairs on Breanna's arms rose. For the life of her, every person seemed to have stopped in their steps and watched her every move like they were waiting to point at her and cover their mouths as they gossiped about her.

Why didn't she just turn around and go the other way? All she had to do was take her black ass back down those steps and make a beeline for her car. Elijah didn't need to know she was here. Yet, she marched on, hoping this was the first and last time she had to do this crap.

Breanna stepped onto the dark almond wooden floor and listened to the heels of her flats slap the ground while she walked. She stopped. Suite 251 stared at her. She closed her eyes and took another deep breath. Nathaniel's warm embrace called was calling her name.

She knocked on the door and waited. If no one answered the door, she could make a break for the stairs and run out the joint. But the damned door just had to open.

"Breanna." Dr. Hampton stood in front of her and smiled. Her deep honey brown dreadlocks draped over her shoulders in what looked like waves over the black and white ruffled suit jacket she wore. Her skin smooth almond brown skin glimmered. Her cozy brown eyes were invitingly calm. "Please, come in. Mr. Bryson and I have been waiting for you."

Breanna walked inside. She saw Elijah sitting on the couch in his blue denim button-down shirt over a white t-shirt. The blue jeans he wore didn't have any holes in them for once. He smiled at her slightly and moved to the side, giving her room to sit down.

Dr. Hampton motioned for her to take a seat. "I'm glad you're here. I understand lunchtime traffic can be rather relentless."

Breanna nodded. "It's worse coming from Soul Bistro."

Dr. Hampton grabbed a coffee mug and notepad from her desk and sat in front of them in a black leather recliner. "So, you're the lady who bakes my favorite cinnamon pralines." She smiled. "You know how to make home with a twist."

"You're from Louisiana?"

"The very best of Baton Rouge, I must say." She eyed Elijah and Breanna, noticing how they sat apart, and nodded. "Do the both of you always sit so... far apart from each other?"

Elijah looked at Breanna and then turned his attention to Dr. Hampton. "We always don't. It's just when we're—"

"We're not able to see eye to eye sometimes," Breanna interrupted him.

Dr. Hampton nodded once more. She eyed them both and smiled. "Well, I would love to get to know the both of you a little better." She took a sip of her coffee. "So, I would like for you to look at those pictures I have on the wall above my desk and choose just one to describe the other person. I want your full honesty."

Elijah sat up from the couch and examined the pictures on the wall. His eyes darkened from his furrowed eyebrows.

"Do you see one that best describes your spouse?" Dr. Hampton stared at him and scribbled in her notepad.

Elijah shrugged. He rubbed his beard with his thumb and index finger, looking for the best choice.

Breanna scoffed. Each picture was of the same couple hidden by a silhouette but in unique events. She found it funny that every picture described Elijah in a way. "It's rather hard for me to only pick one."

"Really, Ms. Ellis?" Dr. Hampton scribbled in her notepad once more. "You're the first person who has ever said that."

Elijah glanced at Breanna, then back at Dr. Hampton. "It's the same for me too."

"This is interesting," Dr. Hampton stated. "Both of you see one another in every picture. Would both of you like to explain to me why?"

Elijah rubbed his temple. "Breanna is beautiful, talented, and kindhearted, but with me, all she shows me is her beauty. Her heart seems shut off from me now."

"Breanna," Dr. Hampton gestured for her to speak.

"I see someone who is alluring; someone who is nurturing. But that nurture becomes control."

"So, I can assume that your relationship started off good until something happened, correct?" Dr. Hampton placed her notepad on the floor and leaned closer to Breanna and Elijah.

"I got pregnant two years into our relationship."

"How was the news of the pregnancy received by yourselves? By your family members?"

"Well." Breanna cleared her throat. "I was twenty-three years old, and I was terrified. But I was with the person I loved more than anything."

Elijah took a deep breath. "I couldn't stop smiling when I found out Bree was pregnant. I thought my mom and dad would be disappointed with me, but they weren't. They were thrilled. But Mom and Dad told me it was going to be tough."

"So, you had support from your family, Elijah. That's good." Dr. Hampton stared at Breanna. "What about you, Ms. Ellis?"

"Well, Dr. Hampton—"

Dr. Hampton held her hand up and smiled. "Please call me Dr. Shelby. I don't want you to feel uncomfortable with me."

Breanna's shoulders dropped. She couldn't pinpoint what it was, but Dr. Hampton made her feel so peaceful. "Well, my mom wasn't too thrilled about the news. But my dad, his wife, and my older sister were excited for me. They couldn't wait to meet Isabella."

"Okay," Dr. Hampton nodded. "Why didn't your mom like the news?"

"She." Breanna hesitated.

"She doesn't like me," Elijah said, finishing Breanna's statement.

"Interesting. Why doesn't she like you, Mr. Bryson?"

"My mom thinks I made a mistake having a baby by a man who is of a different race than me." Breanna pulled a strand of her hair behind her ear. She looked into Elijah's eyes and took a deep breath.

"So, race is an issue for your mother, Breanna?"

She nodded. "My mom thinks white men are deceptive."

"And is he deceptive?"

Breanna shook her head. "He's just controlling."

"Breanna, I never tried to control you. I only wanted to protect you." As Elijah tried to touch her hand, Breanna snatched it away from him. He sighed. "You endured a high-risk pregnancy, Bree."

Dr. Hampton smiled at Breanna. "We've got something in common, Ms. Ellis. I had a high-risk pregnancy with my second child."

"What made your pregnancy high risk, if you don't mind me asking."

Dr. Hampton took a sip of her coffee. "I had preeclampsia—something I wouldn't wish on my worst enemy. My husband knew my job wasn't that stressful, but there were times I didn't follow the doctor's rules, and there were times I followed them."

"What happened?" Breanna asked.

"Oh! I had elevated blood pressure, my urine had way too much protein in it, and my child was in distress. Instead of having a vaginal birth like the way I wanted, I ended up having a cesarian delivery."

Breanna looked away from Dr. Hampton. "I was able to have a vaginal birth."

"That's a blessing," Dr. Hampton said. "But from your facial expression, there's seems to be some regret."

Elijah sighed. "Her mother never came to the hospital to see Isabella when she was born. My mom and dad did and so did her sister, Amber."

"It sounds like, Breanna, that your mother's opinion has a sturdy place in your heart."

97

"My mom has always been there for me. She'd never left my side until that day."

"Have you talked to her about this?"

Elijah stared at Breanna. He extended his hand toward hers and grabbed it.

She rubbed her shoulder and then wiped away a tear. "That's the one thing we never talk about. I think that's because of my father."

"Mr. Marvin is a good man, Dr. Shelby," Elijah said. "When I first met him, he accepted me immediately."

"But he can't accept my momma's apologies. That doesn't seem like a good man to me, Elijah."

"Have you talked to your mother and father about their divorce?" Dr. Hampton tilted her head to the side.

Breanna shook her head. "I don't have a relationship with him anymore."

"Breanna, you sound like you have deeper wounds than you believe you do," Dr. Hampton stated. "And these wounds are affecting your relationship with Elijah. How often are the two of you intimate or emotionally responsive to each other?"

"Not much," Elijah answered. "Sex was never an issue for us until a few months ago."

"Okay. What about positive emotional responses?"

"All we do is argue, Dr. Shelby," Breanna said. "Elijah... won't talk to me."

"Is this true?"

"I talk to her all the time, Dr. Shelby," he answered. Elijah raked his hands through his hair. "When she blames me for stopping her from living her life when she was pregnant, I feel horrible. But I would do it again if it meant that I wouldn't have to see her go through that."

"So, you've seen this before, Elijah."

Breanna stared at him with narrowed eyes. She folded her arms across her chest. "Are you trying to tell me you got another woman pregnant?"

"No!" Elijah answered. "I... I... seen it happen before to someone...."

"I'm assuming this was a relative. A close relative, yes?"

He nodded.

Breanna slumped back onto the couch. "You do this every time, Elijah."

"Ms. Ellis," Dr. Hampton said, holding her hand up. "It's good to know the problem is being addressed, but chastising Mr. Bryson won't solve it. He will eventually tell you whether it's in front of me or behind closed doors with you."

She watched Elijah wipe a streaming tear from his eye. His beige skin became pinkish red. Why wouldn't he say who the relative was? Why would he hold on to something like that?

"Eli," Breanna stared at him. "Did this relative pass away?"

"No, but she went into labor early and nearly died during childbirth," he replied.

"Will you ever tell me who it was?"

Elijah sighed as wiped away another tear. "When I'm ready to."

Breanna looked away from him. There was way much more to this story than he led on. Whoever the person was, she had a crucial part in his life.

Dr. Hampton got up from her chair, grabbed two wristbands from her desk, and handed them to Breanna and Elijah.

"What's with these?" Elijah surveyed the beaded band.

"I like to give these to every couple I work with," Dr. Hampton replied. "These bands have three meanings."

Breanna stared at Dr. Hampton with furrowed eyebrows. "What are they?"

"Communicate, comfort, and confidence," she replied. "I would like for you to try to bond within the next two weeks until our next session."

Breanna stared at Elijah for a moment. She couldn't believe it took a damn therapist to get him to talk. But it was more than he ever spoke of. Had she moved too fast with Nathaniel? If Elijah changed, would she have been willing to take another chance?

With Elijah, though, everything wasn't at face value. Breanna had to remind herself of that. One day, he would do or say one thing, and then the next, it would be a complete 360. How was she supposed to trust him when he wouldn't tell her who the relative was that nearly died during childbirth? She sighed. Communication was never Elijah's strong suit. It never would be.

She watched Elijah shake Dr. Hampton's hand and leave out of the room. She heard him clear his throat on the way out the door.

"Ms. Ellis," Dr. Hampton said. "You and Mr. Bryson have been through a lot, but you've endured more hardship with your family than with your boyfriend. I would love to talk with you alone if you like."

Breanna shook the woman's soft hand. "I'll think about it."

"Please do," she said. "You may find the peace you've been searching for."

Breanna looked at her. Her eyebrows were drawn together. There was something so calming, so trusting about Dr. Hampton. She must have been superhuman or something. She gave a half smile. "Do you have a business card?"

"Sure do," Dr. Hampton said, handing her the card. "I look forward to talking with you soon, Ms. Ellis."

Breanna smiled at her as she left out the room. She looked around the area. Elijah didn't waste any time getting back to work. With the way he acted, it seemed as if he didn't want to come back. Well, at least she still had a little time to herself before her second shift started. With only an eight-minute drive home, Breanna was going to have two whole hours to herself.

Breanna made her way down the steps and walked through the lobby. She stared at the other pictures hanging on the wall and smiled. This place was way better than the Hamilton Art Museum downtown. The receptionist smiled at Breanna as she waved one hand. The people at this building were too much for her. All the constant niceness was uncalled for.

Superficial attitudes on the outside, and money-hungry backstabbers on the inside.

Now, she sounded like Momma.

Still, Dr. Hampton's words lingered in her head as she stepped into the parking lot and strolled to her car. She unlocked the vehicle from a distance as she continued her trek. The sounds of Dwele's voice boomed from a man's car radio as he sat inside of it, bobbing his head. She smiled. She and Elijah used to do that too when they were in college.

Too bad it all came crashing to the ground. Breanna got inside of her car and looked where Elijah's truck was once parked. The man didn't waste any time leaving this place. He must have seen that fake shit too after trying to convince himself it was worth it. He should have just accepted the blame for what he did to her, and all of this would have been squashed. But he was too much like Daddy.

Had Daddy tried to make amends with Momma, they probably would have still been married. They probably would have still treated their children with love and care. That was all Daddy's fault.

Breanna drove off the parking lot, making a right turn to head toward Nathaniel's place. It would have been good to see him, but since she hadn't been staying at his place for the past few days, he probably didn't want to deal with her.

She came to a stoplight and sighed. The entire time they were in that counseling session and Elijah didn't so much as mention why he treated her the way he did. He always put on a good show, but he never followed through with his promises. No wonder why Daddy liked Elijah so much.

Breanna drove down Harvard Way. She should have gone to Nathaniel's place, but she didn't want to risk getting into an argument with him. The last thing she wanted was to lose the one man who honestly cared about her.

Turning left into their neighborhood, she waved at the neighbors standing outside. Maybe she could get a little peace without Elijah being around. Perhaps she could convince Nathaniel to come over for a while. Breanna pulled into the driveway and pressed the garage door opener. There was Elijah's truck, consuming every bit of space she had inside the garage. She scoffed. So much for the little peace she was going to get.

She parked her car and closed the garage door behind her. She stood at the door, not wanting to go inside. Elijah was just going to start some more shit she didn't feel like dealing with. She should have just shown up at Nathaniel's place unannounced and talked to him instead. But she entered the house anyway.

She tossed her keys on the dining room table and went upstairs. He must have been sleeping, Breanna thought. He had a hard time sleeping the night before.

"Eli," she said, entering their bedroom. She heard the shower water running. "Eli?"

She kicked off her shoes at the bathroom entryway and walked inside. The sound of Elijah's subtle breathing under running water made her raise an eyebrow. She opened the shower door and saw him standing underneath the showerhead. Water trickled down his hair and back. "Eli? What's wrong?"

"I had an asthma attack on my way out the building. The inhaler helped, but I still felt congested, so I got in the shower as soon as I got home."

"Are you okay?"

He glanced at her and nodded before looking away from her. "I'm good, Bree."

She looked at his wrist, noticing he was wearing the band. It was funny, she thought because she was wearing hers too.

"Breanna," Elijah coughed a bit. "I love you."

"I love you too."

"Is it real?"

"Yes."

"Then why does it feel like I've lost you?"

"Because you never wanted to talk to me until...."

"Now," Elijah replied. "Breanna, I always talk to you."

"You couldn't tell me who the person was that had a high-risk pregnancy."

"It's hard for me," he said, wiping the water from his eyes.

"Why is it so hard, Eli? Tell me!" Breanna frowned.

"Because someone else created more pressure than she needed. That someone was a person whom I loved dearly too."

Breanna stared at him and shook her head. "That reminded you of me?"

"It did."

"Elijah," Breanna got his towel down from the side of the shower door and held it out for him to dry off. "But I am not that person. You know that, right?"

"I know," he said. He cut off the water and got out. He stood before Breanna in the nude. Water dripped off the tip ends of his hair onto his chest and continued their roll past his abdomen. He grabbed the towel from her hand and then dropped it.

"Eli," Breanna breathed. "What's wrong?"

Elijah stepped closer to her and pulled Breanna into his wet embrace. He pressed his lips against hers, making her moan against his lips.

The warmth of his body felt so good against hers. He was so hard, yet so soft—she couldn't do this. Breanna couldn't do this to Nathaniel. She couldn't—she didn't want him to stop. One by one, she watched his fingers undo each button on her shirt. He stared into her eyes, biting his bottom lip.

God, he was so sexy when he bit his bottom lip.

Breanna grabbed his length and stroked it, feeling it grow bigger in her hand. Elijah moaned against her lips as she kissed her once more. He pulled the shirt off her back and lifted her from the floor. She wrapped her legs around his waist as he carried her to the vanity and sat her down on it. Her lips never left his as he unclasped her bra. Elijah caressed each nipple with his thumbs while trailing her neck and collarbone with his tongue and gentle nips.

As he made his way to her breast, he twirled his tongue around one of her nipples, making her suck in a breath and moan afterward. She felt the palm of his hand caress the small of her back. That was the one area she loved for his hand to travel to the most. It was more than just her pleasure spot; it was her gateway to orgasm heaven if he thrusted inside of her deep enough while caressing that spot.

He pulled her off the vanity and pulled her black slacks down her legs, trailing one of them with kisses as he made his way back up to her lips again. He turned her around to face the mirror.

Breanna moaned as his hands caressed the circumference of her ass. His hands were so soft, so inviting. She didn't want him to stop. She bit her bottom lip as she moaned, feeling his fingers slide her panties down her leg before his tongue found its way to her clit. Nathaniel couldn't find out about this. This would crush him if he knew.

Elijah stood to his feet and trailed his index finger down her spine, forcing her to suck in another breath. Breanna saw him bite his bottom lip again as he watched her twist her ass from side to side for him slowly.

"Elijah," she breathed. "I want to feel you inside me."

He turned her around to face him and kissed her once more. Elijah swept her off her feet and carried her into the bedroom. He placed her feet on the floor, turned her around to face the bed, and ran his hands over her breast and stomach.

"That's all I needed to hear." Elijah moaned in her ear. He guided her onto the bed until she was on all fours and positioned himself behind her. Elijah slid his fingers against the wetness between her thighs and replaced it with his tongue once more.

Breanna moaned, closing her eyes tight.

"Don't move," he commanded. "Let me give you what you're longing for."

She felt his length enter her core. She moaned aloud as she grabbed the bedsheets. Her vaginal walls clenched tight around his thick girth. It had been a while since she felt him inside her. "Elijah," she panted.

"Shh," Elijah whispered. "I'll go slow."

Her vaginal walls eased as he thrusted within her slowly. The feel of his hand on the small of her back teased her. His moans made her body tremble. The faint remnants of water on his skin slid onto hers. Elijah slid his hands up her spine and around to her breasts. He grabbed them, caressing her nipples with his fingertips as he guided her upward to meet him. Turning her head to the side, he kissed her lips, flicking his tongue into her mouth.

"I'm going to take all of my time with you right now, Breanna."

"This can't take too long. I've got to get back to work soon, Eli."

"You'll have time to recoup." He smiled. "But right now, it's my time."

She stared into his eyes, feeling his thrusts quicken in pace. Breanna wrapped her arms around his neck and grabbed his wet hair, running her fingers through his tresses. He tightened the grip on her hips as he quickened his pace a bit more.

"Eli," she breathed. "You're going to make me cum."

"That's the plan," he whispered in her ear and then nibbled on her earlobe. "But I'll let you savor this for a little while longer."

He slowed his pace, allowing her to catch her breath. Stopping, he pulled out of her and rubbed the tip of his length against the sensitive folds of her clit. She closed her eyes and parted her lips, moaning his name.

"You like that?" Elijah breathed against her ear in a whisper.

Breanna nodded, biting her bottom lip. His length filled her body once more as he slid back into her core slowly. Every inch of his thickness pressed against her G-Spot as he held her close to his body.

This was the best part about making love to Elijah. He always made her body feel like it was her first time with him. She honestly didn't care if she wasn't his first. The way he moaned her name when her body tantalized his gave her the confirmation he was beyond satisfied. The question she had to ask herself, though, was if she was still satisfied with him. Sure, she loved being around Nathaniel, but she never allowed him to touch her body. She only allowed Elijah that privilege. That had to change.

She had to decide who she wanted. Breanna moaned aloud, feeling his teeth gently bite the side of her neck. She had a big decision to make.

The soft touch of his hands on her curves of her body made her moan louder. As she felt his fingers trail a line down her torso, Elijah's fingers brushed against her clit. She moaned his name once more. He was too damn good in the bedroom.

Thrusting, he held her body tight against his. She listened to him moan against her ear. His deep breaths turned into a low growl. She closed her eyes as his length teased her G-Spot over and over. She clawed at his neck.

"Let it go, Bree," Elijah panted in her ear.

A euphoric vibration tingled in her pelvis and back as it surged its way through her body. Breanna screamed, hearing him moan aloud against her ear. She knew she would have to change the bedsheets before Isabella got home. She didn't need Shortcake, seeing remnants of white stains on the bed.

He kissed her lips, allowing his tongue inside her mouth. He stared into her eyes. "I love you, Bree."

"I love you too, Eli."

"I wanna make this work."

She stared into his eyes. Breanna hoped he was telling her the truth.

Chapter Eighteen

Two weeks and no phone calls. Ole dude must have been sexing her up good. Nathaniel watched Breanna get out of a red truck and walk toward the Hammond building alongside the man she supposedly left for him. No woman ever pulled this kind of shit on him. Yet Breanna wasn't just any woman. No. She was the woman that needed to be given a second chance with consequences. She needed to be taught a lesson.

Nathaniel got out of his white two-door BMW and leaned against it with his arms folded across his chest. Women like Breanna came a dime a dozen. They deserved to be placed on a pedestal, whenever they met his needs correctly, of course. But when they didn't fulfill his every request the way he wanted them to, he gave them something to remember him by. He smirked.

Had his parents decided not to uproot him from Tennessee because of some bitch alleging he knocked her up, he would have claimed Breanna as his. That ass was his, and nobody could touch it. And the white boy would have never been in the picture. Hell, he shouldn't have been in the first place. But that was okay. He knew how to handle him.

Nathaniel walked toward the building, getting a little closer to the vehicle they drove in. Ole dude was packing some heat. Some serious heat at that. A gun case that big meant two things. Either he was packing a ten millimeter or a forty-five. Nathaniel nodded, walking away from the truck. If there was one thing he knew about most white guys, it was their love for guns.

As he walked inside the building, he saw the receptionist and waved. He drew her eyes to him as he strode to her desk and leaned against it. His white button-down shirt flaunted the dark blue hue of the suit he wore. The silver Rolex he wore matched the silver ring he wore on his ring finger. Its single diamond lured women in his direction, making them disheveled and hot for him. Women didn't give a fuck if the men they wanted were married or not. As long as they could get their needs met, that pussy had a new home. His dick.

"You're looking good today, Melody." Nathaniel smiled at her. He eyed her, undressing her brown skin from the white blouse she wore. Her breasts pressed against the sweetheart neckline of the material, wanting him—no needing him to tap that ass right.

Her brown eyes perked up at his words. He knew what else perked up, too.

"Thank you," she answered. She smiled at him, biting her bottom lip a bit. "And you're looking mighty good today too, Mr. Morrison."

"Do I have any clients on my calendar today?"

The woman shook her head. Her smile never left her lips. "Not right now, but you have a three o'clock appointment."

"Who is it?"

"Tessa Chatman."

He smiled. His eyes and his ears. All he had to do was offer her some good, pleasing, and she was giving him everything he wanted. Older women were desperate; that's what made them easier targets. Had she not run ole boy away, she probably would have been married by now. Then again, older women were insecure. No man would want somebody's sloppy seconds. That's all she was, anyway.

"What are you doing for lunch, Ms. Melody?"

She smiled at him. "Wondering what you were going to be doing for lunch?"

"How about I meet you in my office in another thirty minutes?"

"Okay," Melody responded.

She wasn't Breanna, but Melody was going to get him over the hump until he had her in his bed again, begging and pleading his name. He smiled.

Chapter Nineteen

There it was in all its beautiful glory. Breanna's smile. Elijah hadn't seen her smile like that since Isabella was born. He couldn't remember the last time she sounded so giddy when she talked. The way she snorted when she giggled. The way she pushed her glasses up the bridge of her nose when she stared at him. This was the Breanna he wanted in his life.

Elijah pulled the visor down, trying to shield the sun's rays from blinding him while he drove. He glanced at her and smiled, not wanting this moment to end. "How did you feel about the second counseling session?"

Breanna shrugged. She tilted her chin toward the sun, letting the sunlight highlight her cheekbones. "It was a little more intense this time, but I didn't feel so overwhelmed like I did when we first went."

"That's good, right?" Elijah nodded.

She stared at him and smiled. "It is Eli."

Elijah heard her cell phone ring, causing the unwanted touch of an invisible finger to slide down his spine. He glanced at her as she answered. He prayed it wasn't her job. But the more her eyebrows furrowed and her lips tightened, the more he knew it was.

"Hey Howard," she answered. The sounds of shrieking white noise filled her ear and echoed throughout the truck. She pulled the phone away from it and scoffed. Breanna glanced at him and shook her head.

"Hello. Howard, I can't hear you."

His words broke through the sounds of white noise sporadically.

Listening to Breanna grunt out of frustration was cute, yet he knew Howard had other plans for her. "Is everything okay?"

"I don't know, Eli," she replied. Breanna put the phone on speaker. "Howard? Can you hear me now?"

"Oh! Thank God you answered. I needed you like yesterday," Howard said. "So, Leslie threw me her twos and left Tessa and two new hires here by themselves. I know it's your day off, but could you stop by for a bit and help one of the new hires with a recipe?"

Breanna closed her eyes and took a deep breath. "Sure, Howard. But I can't stay long. I have to pick up my daughter."

"Can't your boyfriend do that?"

Elijah glanced at her, frowning. "Is he serious?" he mouthed.

Breanna rolled her eyes, then shook her head again. "He can, but today is the day I go pick her up. We try to give each other a little leeway."

"Whatever. Get here as soon as you can, and I'll keep you only for thirty minutes."

"Twenty-five, and that's all you have, Howard."

"Fine. I'll see you here soon."

Breanna took another deep breath and exhaled through her nose as she massaged her shoulder. The brightness in her eyes dimmed. "Maybe it's time for you to leave that place."

Breanna frowned at him and then looked away. "I... I can't, Eli," she said. "I've got too much at stake there."

"Like what, Bree?"

"I helped him open Soul Bistro."

"You mean you opened the place on your own without so much as a thank you from Howard."

"He helped me buy my car, Eli."

"A car that you're still paying a high ass note for, babe. He's done nothing for you but be a pain in your side."

Elijah glanced at her, seeing the frown resting on her brow. Hearing her sigh, he shook his head. He didn't want to ruin this day.

"Howard's just," Breanna hesitated. "He's..."

"Going to owe you big time once he opens another restaurant in a different location," he said. Elijah pulled into Soul Bistro's parking lot and parked the truck. "That man wouldn't be anything without you."

She leaned over and pressed her lips against his. She gave a half smile. "I'll be right back."

He watched her get out of the truck and run toward the building until she disappeared inside. Howard was only using her for his needs, but Breanna wouldn't believe that, even if he was on fire. All she would do was fan the flames, then ask Howard how much water she needed to use to put him out.

Before Howard came running to Breanna to help him with the restaurant, she and Grandma Zora used to sell pastries from the house. Those were the best days of his life. He even put on ten pounds. But it was so worth it. They used to have the house smelling like apple cinnamon, strawberry shortcakes, and lemon zest. He closed his eyes and touched his rumbling stomach. If only he had some of Grandma Zora's fried catfish and spaghetti with the extra bottle of hot sauce, he'd be in heaven right now.

As he opened his eyes and looked out the window, Elijah jumped in his seat. Tessa stood by the driver's side window, beckoning him to roll it down. He sighed as he rolled the window down. If only Breanna knew what her best friend was up to, she'd be ready-to-use Ms. Betty along with her seven piercing friends.

He scoffed while shaking his head. He knew he would regret that, whether he appeased her or not. Somehow, it was going to find its way back to Breanna. "What do you want, Tessa?"

She leaned on the truck's door, getting closer to Elijah. "Is that how you're going to greet me, Eli?"

"It's Elijah."

"Oh, okay," Tessa said. She sucked her teeth. "I've been hoping to see you, and here you are."

"Again, Tessa. What do you want?"

"You." She licked her upper lip in a single stroke, flashing her tongue ring, then smiled. "If you would like to get to know me better."

Elijah placed both hands on the steering wheel and gripped it tight. "I think I know you enough, Tessa."

She giggled. "You see, a woman like me knows how to handle a man like you. Breanna can't handle you—"

"Tessa, I don't want to have anything to do with you. That's final."

"That's not what it looked like when I felt your ass the last time I saw you," Tessa grunted with a smile. "That thang was tight against the palm of my hand too."

Elijah frowned, then took a deep breath. If he could have given her a million-dollar wound, Tessa would have left him alone. "Get away from me, Tessa."

She frowned. "So, you gone talk to me like that, baby?"

"I'll do more than that if you keep fucking around with me."

Tessa backed away from the truck with her hands up. "I see somebody's in a mood. I'll just wait until it changes."

"You gotta long wait ahead of you, Tessa."

"I can't wait."

Elijah watched her walk back toward the restaurant. She stopped in front of the door and blew him a kiss. He closed his eyes and shook his head, then took another deep breath. Something about that didn't seem right. Whatever bullshit Tessa was trying to start, he didn't want to know the outcome.

Nathaniel hadn't been on her mind all day. The man she loved was finding his way back to himself, and she enjoyed every minute of it. Still, if it took Elijah all this long to get back to himself, how quickly was he going to revert? She couldn't just leave one man hanging and the other waiting on her beck and call. Breanna couldn't do that to either of them. This was too difficult of a decision.

She watched Kelvin flip the vanilla crepe like a pro. He was skilled for someone who had been scanning, labeling, and throwing boxes for the last five years of his life. She understood why Howard had him cleaning and bussing tables. He could carry more loads of dishes than she, Tessa, or Leslie ever could. But to train him to bake pastries too meant Howard was taking some severe shortcuts. This wasn't going to fair well.

Maybe that was the reason Leslie left. Perhaps she had gotten tired of being treated like crap. Yet, if she didn't start it, people wouldn't have beef with her. They probably would have still been friends had she not thrown her Ms. Perfect wisdom on everybody around her. Damn. That was nearly two months ago.

"Master chef?" Kelvin asked, staring into her eyes. "I don't think I have the technique down you showed me."

Breanna smiled. "Kelvin, you know you can call me Breanna."

"I know," he said, wiping away a fleeting drop of sweat from his forehead with the back of his hand. He sighed, flipping the last crepe onto the stack he created. "You're a pro at this. You've earned that title. Besides, Tessa was in here trying to flip a crepe, and she dropped the mixture on the floor."

Breanna covered her smile with her hand. If there was one thing Tessa tried to do that she epically failed at, it was cooking. She may have worked in a restaurant, but by no means should she have been around the stove. She could burn; it just wasn't in a good way. "She tried, Kelvin."

"A little too much," he replied.

"What else did she do?" Breanna laughed.

"She got a little too handsy."

"That sounds like she panicked."

Kelvin scoffed, raising his eyebrow. "If you call that panicking, then what does she look like under control?"

Breanna furrowed her brows and folded her arms across her chest. That was sort of the same thing Elijah told her some months ago, too.

Tessa walked into the kitchen with a grin. "Thanks for saving our butts, sis."

"You're welcome." Breanna smiled, watching her strut past her and Kelvin. She noticed she had a red bite mark on the side of her neck. "Somebody must have come through last night?"

Tessa covered her neck, then blushed. "I may be single, but this woman knows how to play the dating game." She laughed, pulling her long black natural tresses over her neck.

Breanna looked at the cellphone and glanced at the text notification scroll on her screen. Elijah must have gotten hungry.

"Hey, sis," Tessa said, walking toward Breanna. She took her by the arm and pulled her near the back door. "I got something I need to tell you."

Breanna sucked in a breath for a moment. "What's up, Tessa?"

"I didn't know how to tell you this, but Elijah sometimes meets with an older man that looks like you and Amber. Whenever they're together, he has Isabella with him."

Breanna frowned. "What?"

"Girl, yes," she said, surveying her surroundings. "I think Elijah must have thought I wasn't here, but I saw them because Leslie served them some of the desserts you prepared the night before."

She looked away from Tessa. Her frown grew darker. "He lied to me."

"I didn't know if you knew."

"Elijah told me he wouldn't take Isabella to see my father."

"I think now's the time to drop his ass like a hot potato and get back to your real man."

This was just too damn good to be true. Everything within her soul wanted Elijah to change, and he had been taking Izzy to see her father and his wife, Regina. She couldn't believe she trusted him to change. What was even the purpose of going to counseling if he was going to lie to her?

"I need to go," Breanna said. "I gotta go pick up Isabella."

"I'm sorry, sis."

"Don't be," Breanna said, pushing the back door open.

Walking inside, she saw Kelvin dressing the crepe cake. She smiled, watching him slide the long spatula alongside its edges. This guy was truly gifted. "Kelvin, this is gorgeous."

111

"Thanks, Master Chef," he replied. He noticed Tessa walking inside the kitchen and frowned.

"Listen, I have to go, okay."

Kelvin nodded. "I'll be here bright and early."

Breanna walked out the kitchen. Her footsteps quickened as she walked through the dining area. Why did Elijah do that to her? Why would he break the one request she pleaded with him never to do?

As Breanna made her way outside the building, she walked toward the truck. Elijah was going to regret ever lying to her about Izzy seeing her father.

"Hey, babe," Elijah said. He watched her climb inside the truck, then slam the door shut. He frowned. "What's wrong?"

"You. That's what's wrong."

He palmed his face, then rubbed his temple. "Breanna, I thought we were on a good path today."

"We were," she retorted. "Until Tessa told me you've been taking Izzy to see my father."

Elijah stiffened. He closed his eyes and sighed. "Breanna, Isabella needs to know who your father is. You shouldn't deny her that."

"That man has caused nothing but pain in my life."

Elijah clenched his teeth. "Breanna, your father isn't a bad person. He just found himself in an unpleasant situation."

"How the fuck do you know so much about the man, huh?" She yelled. "Answer me!"

"Because if you would sit down and ask your grandmother to tell you the truth, she would tell you. This isn't Mr. Marvin's fault at all."

Breanna folded her arms across her chest once more. "I don't want to hear any more of your lies, Elijah. Let's just go pick up Izzy."

Elijah grabbed the steering wheel, then hit it with his fist, causing the truck's horn to sound off. "I know I lied to you about not taking Izzy to see your father, but you're going to let Tessa fill your head with bullshit when she just tried to come onto me again."

"There you go lying again, Elijah."

"That bitch is going to screw you over in the worse way, Breanna. You best open your eyes before it's too late."

"Just drive."

Elijah reeved the truck's engine and sped off the restaurant's parking lot, leaving a plume of smoke settling in the spot the truck rested.

Tessa stepped outside the restaurant and pulled out her cellphone. "Ya' girl should be coming your way tonight, boo."

Nathaniel laughed seductively over the phone. "Good."

Chapter Twenty

Nathaniel sat up from his couch and stared at the door, listening to the soft tapping of knuckles against it. A wry smile pulled his lips as he stood to his feet. He peeped through his blinds. Breanna was back where she belonged. She stood outside the door, wiping tears from her eyes. Her sobs echoed faintly through the glass. He smiled. Ole dude had had his time with her. Now it was his turn. He just had to keep the white boy from looking like the hero.

Nathaniel opened the door and stared at a teary-eyed Breanna. She walked inside and wrapped her arms around his neck. She cried on his shoulder, muttering incoherently against him. Nathaniel held her tight, caressing the smoothness of her exposed arms with the tips of his fingers. He inhaled the sweetness of honey and mango butter in her hair. He smirked. Sorry, Mr. Bryson. What was once his now had his name branded on it.

"What's wrong, Beautiful?"

"Elijah lied to me," she whispered.

"Listen," he said, lifting her chin with his index finger. Nathaniel looked into her brown eyes and smiled. "I understand you're trying to make sure your little girl still has a family, but you gotta let him go."

"I just feel so hurt."

"You shouldn't be. You're with me now." Nathaniel took her by the hand and led her into his dimly lit living room. Jill Scott's voice harmonized throughout the sound system he recently installed. He beckoned for her to sit down on his black leather sofa, then kissed her forehead before whisking his way into the kitchen.

Nathaniel switched on the light, illuminating the kitchen's eggshell white and Dorian gray ceiling-high cabinets. A stainless-steel range hood hovered over a high-end stainless-steel gas range. He grabbed an empty tumbler from the cabinet, rinsed it out, and pressed it against the refrigerator's water dispenser, filling it halfway.

Nathaniel overheard Breanna's crying fade down the hall and into the bathroom. He walked into the living and picked her phone up from the sofa. Ole dude wanted to talk to her; he wanted her to come home. He smirked, copying Elijah's number to his phone. He noticed a picture of Elijah holding Isabella in his arms. The overly cheerful smile on his face made Nathaniel's stomach bubble a bit. There wasn't a wonder why Breanna wanted someone better. White boy looked as if he couldn't handle himself, let alone handle a black woman like her. Then, they bring this amalgam of a child into the world. Why would she even let him in, to begin with?

No doubt. That little girl was breath-taking. With eyes like her father's coupled with the smile and skin complexion of Breanna's, she was going to rip some fool's heart from his chest and steal his money all at once. He knew it wouldn't be easy to win her over, but Nathaniel knew he could, as long as he made all the right moves.

He rubbed his groomed beard with his index finger and thumb. He sent Isabella's photo to his phone. His smile widened. All he had was time now. Ole dude was going to do the rest for him.

He heard the bathroom door open and quickly returned Breanna's phone to the previous screen she had it on. Nathaniel laid it back down on the couch and bobbed his head to the music.

Damn, winning felt good.

He ran back into the kitchen and snatched a bag of his favorite sea salt and vinegar kettle chips off the bar, then returned to the sofa. Breanna's footsteps trailed down his hallway. She was right on time.

She stood before him, wiping a tear from her face. "Nathaniel."

"What's up, Beautiful?" He put the bag of chips on the sofa and walked toward her. Nathaniel took her into his embrace and stared into her eyes, losing himself in them. He kissed her, flicking his tongue in her mouth. Nathaniel felt her body relax against his. Breanna was on her way to letting him tap that ass.

"Thank you for this," she whispered against his lips.

Kissing her deeper, Nathaniel flicked his tongue inside her mouth again. The taste of her cherry flavored chap stick teased him more than he thought it would have. He couldn't wait to feel her lips and tongue licking on his big dick. Hell, he couldn't wait to hear her slurping and gagging on it. He lifted her from the floor, and she instinctively wrapped her legs around his waist.

Nathaniel carried her down the hallway and kicked the door to his bedroom open. Before she went on her two-week stint away from him, Breanna had spent many of her nights lying in his bed next to him. Nights where she could have been pleasing him instead of teasing him. Tonight was different, though. Tonight, Breanna was going to give him the one thing he'd been craving, and he could damn sure taste it.

He laid her on the bed, letting his hand crawl its way up her shirt. He grabbed her breast as he kissed her deeper. Breanna's body was a work of fucking art. Her curves. The angles in her legs and back when she arched them. Fuck! Breanna was going to make him bust one before he even got inside her.

He heard her phone ring in the background. Breanna turned her head away from him and sat up from the bed.

"Breanna," Nathaniel frowned as he stared into her eyes. "What's wrong?"

"That's probably my daughter calling me." She stood up from his bed. "I can't do this, Nathaniel."

Nathaniel sucked his teeth as he nodded. "You know he's pulling this shit to trap you. All he wants is to keep you down."

"Elijah's never done that," she said. Breanna closed her eyes. Another tear slipped from underneath her closed eyelids. "Isabella may have snuck off with his phone to call me."

"You deserve better than that, Beautiful."

"I can't do this to her, Nathaniel," she said, walking toward the door.

Before he said her name again, Nathaniel grabbed her by the wrist and snatched her back toward him, forcing her to stare directly into his eyes. He squeezed it harder, refusing her to walk out his bedroom. "If you keep falling for this shit, Breanna, you ain't going to ever be happy. Is that what you want?"

"Please, Nathaniel. You're hurting me," Breanna pleaded.

"I'm hurting you?" He snapped. "Ole dude has hurt you worse than I ever would."

"Please! Let me go, Nathaniel."

He pushed her away from him, causing her to stumble and fall. Her wrist clipped the pointed corner of his old wooden nightstand, a nightstand that had seen several gorgeous women's faces face plant it after they refused him. He didn't want Breanna to be one of them, but Nathaniel had no problem introducing the two if she forced his hand.

"Breanna," he said, getting on the floor next to her. "I'm so sorry, Beautiful."

She stared at him with wide eyes as she held her wrist. "I need to go."

"Breanna, baby girl. I'm really sorry."

"It's okay, Nathaniel. I just need to go." She sobbed.

"Please, Breanna," Nathaniel said. He grabbed her arm. "I didn't mean to hurt—"

"I really need to go." She pulled away from him once more and quickened her footsteps down the hall.

Nathaniel followed her down the hallway and watched her grab her phone off the sofa. She jetted out the front door as if she had never been there. He stood in the opened doorway, watched her jump into her car, and peel out of his driveway like she was driving in the Indy 500.

Slamming the door shut, Nathaniel cursed aloud, then punched it. A broken imprint with his knuckles now decorated his front door. He had to fix that. No. Breanna had to fix that. She had some balls for leading him on—for backing out, giving her body to him. She owed him. Big time.

Chapter Twenty-One

The moon followed Breanna through the gray clouds as she drove down a dark road. Tree branches covered many of the streetlights scattered about the pavement. She glanced at her wrist as she sped down the street. The remembrance of Nathaniel's fingers left a stinging imprint upon her flesh. The deep furrow in his eyebrows was something she'd never seen before. He wasn't that kind of man. Nathaniel just wasn't.

She turned on her radio. Musiq Soulchild's voice flowed throughout the cabin of her car. A smile tugged at her lips before returning to their tightened state. Elijah had every Musiq Soulchild CD to date. He even kept them in good shape. She chuckled slightly, smiling again. Bless his heart. The man still owned CDs. Moving him over to digital music was like scraping nails against a chalkboard.

And no matter what song of Musiq Soulchild's played, Elijah would hold up an index finger and shriek every lyric out of tune. She shook her head and chuckled once more. That was the love of her—Breanna cursed under her breath.

Elijah meant more to her than she realized, yet all he did was continuously stab her at her heart. She couldn't trust him like the way she used to—like the way she wanted to.

She sighed. Why couldn't things be the way they used to be between them? Why?

Elijah wouldn't change. It was like him to damage her emotions whenever he felt like it. But what happened at Nathaniel's place took her breath away. He would never hurt her. Breanna knew that. Besides,

Nathaniel wasn't that kind of man. Yet, the side of him she witnessed tonight said something different. It yelled in her ears, forcing her to leave as fast as she could.

But regardless of how angry Elijah got with her, he never raised his hand at her and clenched his fists. He would always walk away from her.

Nathaniel was just protecting her. She couldn't fault him for that. She wouldn't blame him for trying to love—was it really love he had for her? Or was it lust clothed in an angel's white robe?

Breanna sighed. It wasn't like he was trying to hurt her. Nathaniel was just—she took a deep breath and released it through her nose. He needed room to breathe right now. That's all. The man she had fallen for again wasn't the same guy she dated back in high school. Hell, she wasn't the same woman either. Breanna knew she brought a lot of baggage into their relationship, but she didn't think he would have reacted that way. He should have been more—what happened, happened. They both needed time to heal.

Breanna pulled into her and Elijah's driveway and parked her car. She noticed a black Lincoln Corsair parked near the mailbox. She rubbed her temples and sighed. Maybe she moved too fast with Nathaniel. Perhaps she should have left Elijah years ago. Breanna rested her forehead against her palm. If anybody knew how to handle situations like this, it was Momma.

She got out the car and made her way to the front door. As she was about to slip her key into the lock, Elijah opened the door. He stared at her. His eyes were streaked with red lines; his eyebrows furrowed.

"Elijah, I need to—"

"You need to talk to him before it's too late," he said, cutting her off.

She frowned, overhearing another man with a gruff voice talking in the background. "What? Who are you talking about?"

She stepped inside the house and stood by the dining room table. The crease in her eyebrows deepened as Daddy stood before her.

Elijah closed the door and walked toward her father.

"Breanna," Daddy spoke.

Breanna looked away from him. Her arms were folded across her chest. "What do you want?"

"Elijah invited me over." He stepped closer to her. "I haven't seen my little girl in so long."

"I'm not your little girl anymore." She stared at him with narrowed eyes. "That changed when you left, Momma. Remember?"

"I remember," he replied. "But there's something you need to know about that."

"I don't feel like hearing your lies, Daddy."

"Then, you need to stop listening to your mother's lies too."

"Momma's never lied to me."

Daddy smiled as he nodded. "Well, if she doesn't lie to you, then she should have told you about your Aunt Aubrey."

"Aunt Aubrey?" Breanna scoffed. "All you do is make up—"

"If you ever wonder who your sister resembles, it's your Aunt Aubrey. The same aunt your Aunt Pauline hated."

"Come on, Daddy. Aunt Pauline may be a little crazy, but she isn't a bad person."

"Sure, she isn't."

Breanna rolled her eyes. "Are you done?"

"Don't take that tone with me, Breanna."

"Or what? You're going to hit me like you hit Momma."

"I've never hit your mother, but the other man she cheated on me with did."

Breanna stiffened. "What are you talking about?"

"Breanna." Daddy took her by the hand. His fingers coursed over the forming bruise on her wrist as he stared at it and sighed. "I made the horrible mistake of cheating on your mother with your Aunt Pauline. I never forgave myself for what I did to her, but she did. Your mother took me back—"

"You're lying," Breanna said, interrupting him. Tears welled in her eyes as she pulled her hand from his.

"Breanna, when I thought your mother was okay, she wasn't. What I did to her hurt her more than I realized. Sure, I told her what I had done, but it didn't change the fact she hid her other relationship from me for six months."

Breanna stared at him with narrowed eyes. "I can't believe you would even stoop so low to lie about Momma and Aunt Pauline. I just can't believe—"

"—You don't have to believe me now, Breanna. You'll just have to find that out on your own." He looked back at Elijah and nodded. "I better get back home."

"You really should." Breanna stared at him. He had some nerves coming into the space she shared with Elijah and lie to her face. Daddy always made it his prerogative to make Momma look like she was the one in the wrong. She hated him for that. She hated him for always leaving those who needed him the most behind. She didn't need him. Hell, she would never need him ever again in her life.

"Don't make the same mistake your mother did Breanna," he said as he stood in the doorway.

"Just leave, Daddy. Now!"

119

Watching him leave their home, Breanna focused her attention back on Elijah and rolled her eyes as she scoffed. The crinkle in her eyebrows deepened as she pursed her lips outward and folded her arms across her chest.

"How dare you invite that man here?" Breanna grabbed her keys from the dining room table.

Elijah frowned. "How dare you not let your father talk some sense to you?"

"He left Amber and me for that bitch he cheated on Momma with, and for whatever reason, my stupid sister still loves him like he'd done nothing wrong."

"Didn't you hear what he said?" Elijah sat on the sofa and raked his fingers through his hair. "It doesn't matter what I try to do. You'll block my attempt to reason with you."

"Because you held me back from pursuing my dreams and my goals, Elijah," Breanna retorted.

He stared at her, then stood from the couch. Elijah reached his hand toward her wrist and frowned. Shit! The last thing she needed him to do was to find out Nathaniel had mistakenly hurt her. "What happened to you?"

"Nothing," Breanna said, hiding her hand behind her back.

"Breanna, those look like fingerprint marks. Who hurt you?"

"Nobody."

"You can lie to me about many things, but bruises, scrapes, and cuts ain't one of em'."

Breanna scoffed. "I must have hit my wrist on my way out of Momma's house."

He stared at her with a raised eyebrow. "Breanna, you can tell me what happened."

"That's what happened, Eli. Besides, you wouldn't give two shits about me anyway if you can't control me."

"Damnit, Bree," he hissed. "Every fucking time I try to talk to you, you pull this bullshit. You need to wake up."

"I need to wake up," she yelled. "How about you try telling me why you kept me as your slave, and maybe then I'll wake up from this nightmare."

"Really, Bree?"

"The shoe fits, doesn't it, Eli—"

"Stop it!" Isabella yelled. The child stood at the foot of the stair in her pink and white pajamas, then sat on the stair. She wiped away streaming tears as her body trembled from her sobs. "Please, Mommy! Please, Daddy! Stop!"

Daisy sat beside her and nuzzled her cheek with her nose before placing her head in her lap.

Elijah frowned at Breanna as he made his way toward Isabella. He scooped the child up from the step and held her tight in his embrace. "It's okay, Izzy. Sometimes, Mommy and Daddy have disagreements."

She rested her head on his shoulder. Her body continued to tremble as she sniffled and sobbed.

Breanna closed her eyes and sighed. What was becoming of her? Her daughter heard her yell and curse at the very man who no one could replace. Was it worth hurting her daughter this way? Was it worth having to see her parents throw grenades and call for airstrikes against each other to come to a moot point? It was time they tried to work things out. It was time—was it going to be the same process over again with Elijah? Was he going to treat her the same way as he'd always done?

Breanna stood beside Elijah. She moved some of Isabella's hair from the side of her face so she could see it. "Shortcake, I love you and your daddy very much."

Isabella looked up from Elijah's shoulder and stared into Breanna's eyes. "If you truly love us, why do you always leave us at night. Why can't you come home like normal mommies do?"

"Because I need to make sure you have everything you need to be happy."

"I have my mommy and daddy," Isabella replied through labored breaths. "That's all I need."

Breanna watched the child put her head back on Elijah's shoulder. She covered her mouth and coughed. "Mommy," she said, struggling to breathe. She shut her eyes tight.

"Izzy?" Breanna shook her arm. Her eyes were wide. "Izzy?"

Elijah sat her on the sofa. "Breathe slowly, Shortcake."

"It hurts, Daddy," Isabella wheezed.

"Go into the bedroom and find her inhaler. It should be on the dresser." Elijah rubbed her back in a slow, circular motion. "It's okay, Shortcake. Daddy's right here."

Breanna dashed up the stairs and down the hall into their bedroom. Knocking over bottles of perfume and deodorant, she grabbed the inhaler. Elijah's name was on it. She frowned. Why was Izzy using his inhalers?

She ran out the room and down the steps. She couldn't remember if she had taken every step or not. Breanna handed Elijah the inhaler and watched him administer the medicine to their daughter.

"Take a deep breath, Isabella," Breanna said, sitting next to her. She took the child's hand in hers and squeezed it.

Elijah kept his hand on her back as she continued to wheeze. He administered another pump of medicine and watched her continue to fight for air.

Breanna stared into his steel-blue eyes. "Why isn't the medicine working, Eli?"

Elijah picked Isabella up from the sofa and walked past her toward the backdoor. The two of them disappeared into the semi-lit darkness. Breanna ran to the back door. She pressed her hand against the glass, hearing Musiq Soulchild's voice blare from his phone's speaker. She watched him rub the back of her head as he danced with her in his arms.

Breanna let Daisy run out before her as she stepped outside and stood next to them. Isabella rested her head on her father's shoulder as she breathed normally.

Locking her eyes with Breanna's, Isabella stared at her. "Mommy, please don't leave me again. Please"

"I won't, Shortcake."

"You promise?" The child mustered a smile, never breaking her gaze.

Breanna smiled, then sniffled. "I promise."

She watched Elijah sway from side to side as he continued to rub his daughter's back. His eyes were closed as he hummed to the tunes of the song. The child closed her eyes. A faint smile tugged her lips as she breathed steadily.

Breanna turned from them and closed her eyes as she covered her mouth. A single tear streamed down her cheek. Isabella was suffering because of them... because of her. She wanted Elijah to be the man she needed him to be, but that wouldn't happen anytime soon. Nathaniel was the man she deserved. He may have gotten a little angry with her, but he knew how to talk to her. He knew how to treat her right. She knew what she had to do.

Chapter Twenty-Two

A thunderous clap woke Elijah from his sleep. He watched the tree branch's shadow dance about on the floor as the wind whipped them from side to side. He moved his hand to Breanna's side of the bed. She was gone. Again. This marked the fifth night in a row.

A week ago, she promised their daughter she wouldn't leave again. That was some straight-up bullshit. Elijah wanted to believe her; he wanted her to prove him wrong. Instead, she proved him right. Breanna didn't love him anymore, and she damn sure wasn't trying to be a mother to Isabella anymore.

She was like springtime. One moment, Breanna was a lustrous flower, soaking up the radiance of the sun's rays. And the next, she was like thunder, lightning, and hail pounding on the bedroom's windowpane, keeping him awake at night.

Honestly, Elijah couldn't say that he loved her the way he used to. She was the one woman that tamed him, that sculpted him into a better version of himself. Yet, she was the same woman that made him stress out more than he ever had in his entire life. Even Morgan didn't stress him out this bad.

Breanna was right about one thing, though. He needed to tell her about his mom's ordeal with her grandmother. She needed to know so she could understand why he was so protective of her when she carried Isabella for those precarious nine months. Breanna needed to know her own mother threatened to have him arrested and charged with rape. She needed to understand how her father saved his life. Breanna needed to know how her mother cursed him out when he tried to tell her about the birth of her granddaughter. Ms. Gwendolyn had nothing to do with Isabella until Mr. Marvin got involved.

Regardless of if Breanna believed him or not, she needed to know. He got out the bed and walked into the bathroom. Four o'clock blinked on the clock's screen. At least she was home long enough to tuck Isabella into bed.

He placed his hand on his chest. Asthma decided to give his lungs a bit of a squeeze, making breathing a difficult task. This was happening every night now. He shook his inhaler and pumped the medicine into his mouth. He closed his eyes and took a deep breath.

This was only a temporary fix.

Opening his eyes, Elijah looked in the mirror, then at the inhaler in his hand and sighed. The damn thing was nearly empty. He had to save what was left in case Izzy needed it more than he did. After having to choose between health insurance and bills, he knew he couldn't afford to waste his money on the benefits Morgan offered him. He had to make sure he and Isabella had enough medicine since they were using the same pump now.

Going into business with Morgan was the best decision he made, but Breanna's help with the insurance would have been even better since Morgan believed the most expensive benefit carriers were the best for her partners. Dr. Ackers tried his best to find a generic brand that would treat her asthma, but those only scratched at the surface of her attacks. It was always those damned 400-dollar inhalers that did the trick. The problem with that was he couldn't spend that kind of money every month along with the other many bills he had.

Perhaps if he tried talking with Breanna again—that was out the question. The countless times she said she would get Izzy's inhalers, she never turned up with them. That was nothing but Howard's doing. One minute, he wanted her to be a full-time pastry chef, and the next minute, she was the cashier.

All the man ever did was use her. The only reason he helped her buy that damn car was so he could keep her under his thumb. Breanna was just too stupid to see that.

Elijah took a deep breath. Relief washed over his core from loosening pressure asthma's hold had on his lungs. Feeling a tickle in his throat, he tried not to cough too loud so he wouldn't wake Isabella. She would have tiptoed inside his bedroom and asked him a million questions about why Mommy wasn't helping him through his asthma attacks anymore. He didn't want her to worry herself into an asthma attack. Elijah closed his eyes. His life had turned upside down in a matter of two months. Sure, they argued over the years they had been together, but it was nothing compared to this. When Nathaniel waltzed his way back into her life, Breanna changed. The way she spoke to him, the way she refused to keep eye contact with him, the way she snapped at him for even breathing the wrong way. That all screamed she wanted out. Maybe he needed to give her what she wanted.

As Elijah turned off the light in the bathroom, he noticed his bedroom door was ajar and glanced at his bed. Isabella curled up on her mother's side of it. Daisy was curled up next to her, resting her head on Izzy's legs. He climbed into the bed and kissed her forehead. He rubbed Daisy's head and smiled.

"Daddy," Isabella said tiredly. "Mommy doesn't love me anymore, doesn't she?"

"No, Shortcake." He pulled the cover over her shoulders. "Mommy loves you so much. She's... having a hard time...."

"With what?"

"The sudden changes happening in her life." Elijah smiled at her.

"But Daddy," she sobbed. "Mommy promised she wouldn't leave me again. She promised to stay with me."

He kissed her forehead again. "I know she did, Izzy. Something must have happened that required her attention. She'll be back home." Elijah lied to her with a straight face. "She'll make it up to you, Shortcake."

"I want my Mommy back." She covered her eyes and cried.

Elijah sat up in the bed and beckoned for her to come into his embrace. He rocked her from side to side. The cool wetness of her tears flooded his forearm as she continued to sob against his tank top. "She'll be back, Izzy."

He closed his eyes, then swallowed hard. Why couldn't he be honest with his daughter?

Breanna chose who she wanted in her life, and it damn sure didn't involve him or their daughter. What took them years to build, Nathaniel tore it apart in a matter of two months. His family lay scattered in pieces because of Nathaniel... because of Breanna's broken heart... because of his unwillingness to tell his girlfriend, his wife, the truth why he refused to watch her suffer like Mom had.

Elijah prayed Breanna would prove him wrong. He prayed she would come back home and rebuild the pieces of their broken family. But that was a lot to ask for. It was way more than she could promise. It wasn't foreseeable for Isabella's future—he wanted Breanna to prove him wrong. No. He needed her to prove him wrong. But knowing Breanna's state of mind now, Elijah's hopes and prayers would fall on death's ears.

Kissing the back of Isabella's head, Elijah hummed his favorite Musiq Soulchild song, hoping that would help Isabella fall asleep. He needed Breanna to prove him wrong. He pleaded for it.

125

Chapter Twenty-Three

The rhythmic tunes of sesame Street stirred Elijah from his sleep. He stared at the clock. 9:35 am flashed back at him. He stood from the soft mattress and looked around the room as he stretched. Isabella was gone. It was just him and Daisy, who laid sprawled on her back with a paw in the air. He shook his head as he smiled. She was the easiest-going dog he ever owned. Too bad JoJo Bean couldn't have been like Daisy. That dog went to doggy heaven mean.

The distant sounds of laughter coming from downstairs caught Elijah's attention. He stretched once more before switching out his pajama bottoms for some gray sweatpants and sliding them on. Usually, he'd walk around with his tank top on since company wouldn't come around so early in the morning, but if that were Mom downstairs with Izzy, he wouldn't hear the end of "Eli, I taught you better than that," lecture. The smell of bacon and eggs graced his nose as he walked down the stairs. He heard Isabella giggle at a Donald Duck sounding voice. He stepped into the kitchen quietly and stood behind his daughter and sister and listened to them sing along with the Duck Tales theme song. He smiled. At least this took his mind off Breanna for a moment.

Katrina turned around and stared at him with wide ocean blue eyes, then grinned. "Big brother!" She ran toward him and wrapped her arms around his neck.

He gasped for air as she tightened her grip. "You're choking me, Kat!"

"Sorry, big brother," she said, loosening her hold. "I haven't seen you in like forever."

"When did you get back?"

"I've been back for like a week and a half now," Katrina replied. "Mom and Dad, let me roost up in my old bedroom until my townhouse is finished."

He smiled. "So, how was Atlanta?"

She stared at him with a wry smile. "Well, I met this guy there."

Elijah planted a kiss on Isabella's forehead and walked toward the refrigerator. "So, who do I need to interrogate?"

"Oh my God, Eli." Katrina scoffed. "Do you always have to do that to every guy I meet?"

"You're my baby sister."

"And my auntie," Isabella said, struggling to peel the orange in her hands. She smiled, successfully peeling the biggest piece of the peel off the fruit.

"That's right, Izzy. Auntie Kat needs to be careful."

"You know, Eli, I am twenty-four years old, and I've got a good head on my shoulders."

"I know." He smiled. "But I'm thirty-one years old, have a little more experience than you do, and protective by nature."

Isabella giggled as she finally peeled the last piece of skin off the orange.

"Are you agreeing with your daddy, Busy Izzy?"

Elijah watched Isabella nod as she smiled. She needed that. She needed to smile when the one person who needed to be with her kept disappearing from her life.

"Anyway," Katrina said. She set three plates on the island. "His name is Miguel Matias, and he's so awesome. He's an optometrist, twenty-six years old, and lives here in Kentfield."

"Okay, so you met him while he was on vacation too." Elijah grabbed three tumblers from the cabinet and set them beside each plate.

"Yes. I did, Eli." She eyed him the way Mom did whenever she had something big to reveal to him. Kat was truly mom's replica.

He stopped in his tracks. "Did you invite him to dinner at Mom and Dad's house tomorrow?"

She hid her red cheeks and smile behind her hand. "Ye... yeah. I did."

"Kat," Elijah chuckled. "You know Mom's going to flip."

"Then please tell Breanna to come too. I've missed her so much. I know she'll back me up."

Elijah stared at her, then shook his head. Katrina's smile faded to crinkled eyebrows and slightly parted lips.

"I'll tell you about it later," he said. He sat next to Isabella, took the orange out of her hand, and tore it into several slices, popping a piece into his mouth.

Katrina stared at him as she served them their food. "Well, how about I take Busy Izzy with me today for a girls' day out and maybe spend the night at Gigi's house?"

Isabella stared at him with wide eyes and a big smile. "Can I, Daddy?"

He nodded. "You sure can, Shortcake."

He heard his phone ring from upstairs. He thought he'd brought the damn thing with him, but as always, he left it any and everywhere most times. If he could, he would have chucked it into the pond in their neighborhood and said he lost it if he knew how to turn off the GPS tracker Breanna programmed on it. Elijah took a bite of his bacon before excusing himself from the island and taking the long walk back to his bedroom. Once inside, he saw his cellphone and checked it. There were no missed calls or notifications. Elijah heard the phone chirp again, then stared at Breanna's nightstand.

That wasn't his phone. It was Breanna's.

He went to the piece of furniture and opened the top drawer. She left her phone at home. She was in a rush to get out.

A text notification woke the device from its dark slumber. Elijah picked it up and frowned, seeing Tessa's name and picture smile back at him, taunting him maliciously. Not wanting to look at the message, he placed her phone back inside the drawer until it chirped again.

He unlocked the device. Had Breanna known he had her passcode, she would have murdered Elijah where he stood. That was a little secret he would take to his grave. The screen lit up, displaying the baby picture of Isabella playing with her feet. He didn't need to go through it, but something wouldn't let him put it down.

Elijah held his breath for a moment as he skimmed through the text. Tessa was probably just on her usual rant about how she needed to leave him... about how he was no good—she was going to meet her and Nathaniel at the Foreman Club tonight, he read. Tessa suggested Breanna wear that little black dress that hugged her body in all the right places. That little number was going to make everything better with Nathaniel, she proclaimed.

Elijah gripped the phone in his hand, cracking the screen in the corner. A tear streamed down his cheek as he bit his bottom lip. Breanna lied to him. For two whole fucking months, she'd been laying up with the very man that she claimed was only a friend.

Chapter Twenty-Four

Breanna lied to him. That's all he could think about. He clutched the phone in the palm of his hand and took a deep breath. The man she claimed as a friend was more than that. Nathaniel Morrison was the man who was going to replace him in every aspect of her life. He was the main reason Isabella no longer had a loving mother.

Her phone chirped in his hand again. Nathaniel sent her a heart and smiling emoji. He couldn't wait to see her tonight, he said in the text. He couldn't wait for them to get back to his place so they could have a little one on one. Elijah let her phone slip from his fingertips as he sat on the foot of the bed. Tears flooded his eyes before rolling down his cheeks. Why didn't she tell him the truth? Why didn't Breanna tell him she didn't love him anymore?

The front door gave a whiny creak as it opened. Elijah closed his eyes and sighed. Mom did him a huge favor for letting Isabella stay with her and Dad for the weekend. And since Katrina was home, Izzy didn't have room to worry about her mommy and daddy not liking each other.

Thank God Kat came when she did. Isabella didn't need to see the rage waiting behind his smile at breakfast. Their daughter didn't need to see him pace the floor for hours after reading the message. She didn't need to hide her tears, wondering why her mommy chose another man over her. Isabella didn't deserve this.

"Elijah," Breanna called. "Have you seen my phone?"

He listened to the hesitance in her voice. He listened to how her heels clacked against the wooden stairs. Seven years. Seven years and the love of his life was now a figment. She was... another man's woman... another man's love... another man's pleasure. He grazed his teeth against his bottom lip. A tear slipped down his cheek. Seven years.

"Elijah," Breanna said, opening the door. She saw her phone sitting next to him. "Eli—"

"Don't. Just don't, Breanna," he snapped, cutting her off. He sighed, trying to keep from balling his knuckles into a fist. Elijah stared at her, noticing the little black dress she wore. It hugged her body in every right place, making him anticipate more to come. It illuminated her caramel brown skin just right—just like the way he loved to see her. Her raven tresses laid in beach waves between her shoulder blades. She was the woman who belonged to another man. "You lied to me."

She frowned. "About what, Eli?"

"Nathaniel!" Elijah yelled. "You lied to me about Nathaniel."

Breanna stiffened; her eyes widened at his words. "Elijah," she stammered. "I... I... wanted to tell you, but—"

"—But what, Breanna," Elijah said. "I'm trying as hard as I can with you, and nothing's getting through to you. I love you more than you would ever love me. Why can't you see that?"

"Because I'm afraid of you hurting me again," Breanna retorted. "I'm afraid you'll stop me again. I can't let you do that to me anymore."

"Then, what about the counseling?" He asked, standing to his feet and stepping toward her. "Hasn't that helped you at all?"

Breanna swallowed hard. "It's opened some wounds I thought were healed. Now they're just scabbing over again."

He frowned. "Why, Breanna?"

"Because all I can think about is how you and my father are alike. I think about how he left my mother because he couldn't deal with her anymore. You remind me of my fucking father."

Elijah ran his fingers through his hair and sighed. "Mr. Marvin isn't a bad person, Breanna. Mr. Marvin sided with the just when your mother didn't want to. You can ask Amber that."

"So, now you're going to keep making my mother look like the villain?" She looked away from him and scoffed as she shook her head. "That's the shit I'm talking about right there, Elijah. Both of you want to blame my mother for something she didn't do."

He shook his head. "You need to sit down and talk to your mother."

"I'll talk to her when I get ready to." Breanna snatched her phone off the bed and made her way out the door.

Elijah closed his eyes for a moment, then followed her. And like Ms. Gwendolyn, Breanna was pigheaded and hard to get through. Still, he was determined to push that to the side tonight. He had to. "Breanna, please don't walk away from me."

She turned toward him, stopping him in his footsteps toward her. "So, you can hold me back again. No, thank you."

His eyebrows creased. "I've never tried to hold you back, Breanna. You need to get that shit out of your head."

"So, when I was pregnant with our child, you never tried to stop me from getting my degree? You never tried to stop me from leaving the house? You never tried to stop me from working? Is that what I'm hearing, Eli?" Breanna asked, pressing her fingertip into his bare chest. "You're every bit of the piece of shit my father ever was and will be."

Before he could even think of his next step, Elijah grabbed Breanna by the waist and pulled her into his embrace. He held her tight against his body, resting the palm of his hand on the small of her back. He wouldn't let her back down from this. "You're not walking away from me, Breanna. Not until we've solved this."

"Let me go, Elijah," she said, struggling against his hold.

"Why are you letting this man tear our family apart?"

"Because you already tore it apart, Eli," she hissed. She stared into his eyes with her narrowed ones. "I've told you time and time again that you're the reason I hate coming home. You're the reason—"

"You hate looking into Isabella's eyes, right?" He asked, pressing her body tighter against his as she squirmed. "Don't you love her, Breanna?"

"Let me go, Elijah."

"Answer the question, Bree."

"I love Isabella. I love her endlessly—just like I love you." Breanna pulled away from him. Tears welled in her eyes. "You once told me you'd never hurt me, and you did. I couldn't see myself loving you anymore."

He ran his fingers through his hair once more. Elijah took a deep breath and released it slowly. "I thought I was going to lose the both of you."

"What?"

"That day when we were getting ready to leave my apartment for class, I watched my pregnant girlfriend walk out the front door and collapse," he said. Another tear slipped from his eye. "You were two months pregnant, and you were unconscious for about three hours. I was scared, Bree."

Breanna closed her eyes. Tears streamed from underneath her closed lids. "Why didn't you tell me that?"

"I had to be strong for you both," he sniffled. "Because I couldn't... handle the idea of losing the only woman who loved me for who I was.

I couldn't watch what happened to my mom happen to you all over again."

Breanna covered her mouth and closed her eyes once again as she shook her head. "Why didn't you tell me this, Eli?"

He pulled her back into his embrace. "It was hard for me to, Bree," he said. "It was hard for me to watch my grandmother attack my mom every chance she got. I sat back and watched my mother nearly die because my grandmother wanted to see her hurt for taking her baby boy from her."

"That put unnecessary pressure on her body than she needed," Breanna said.

"My grandmother hated Mom because she came from a wealthy family. She thought my mother was out to hurt my father."

Breanna stared at him. "You feel the same way about my mom, don't you?"

He looked away from her. "Your mother, Ms. Gwendolyn, accused me of raping you. If your dad hadn't come to my aid, I would have been in jail."

"Momma would never do that."

"But she did, Bree." Another tear streamed down his cheek. "That's why she didn't come to the hospital when Izzy was born."

Breanna frowned. "I can't be... believe this. All this time, Eli—you held this back from me."

He nodded. "I shouldn't have, but I did," he whispered. "I didn't tell you because I wanted to protect you and Isabella. But I was wrong. We were both wrong."

"You gave me no choice, Elijah."

"You assumed I gave you no choice, Bree," he said, frowning. "But you chose this on your own."

Breanna stared at him. Tears streamed down her cheeks. "I did," she sobbed. "I just wanted you to let me live. I just wanted you to talk to me. I just wanted you to—"

"Be understanding," he said. Elijah stared into her water-filled eyes. "It won't change overnight, but I want to try my hardest to make this work with you. Will you do the same for me?"

Elijah kissed her forehead, then tilted her chin upward with his index finger. He wiped away her tears with his thumbs, losing himself in her brown eyes. He pressed his lips against hers, taking in the suppleness of her medium-full lips, and the sweetness of her cherry chap stick.

"Elijah—I—I need to go," she whispered against his lips.

He gripped her tighter, unzipping the zipper to her dress and exposing her shoulders.

132

"Not tonight, you don't." Elijah kissed her deeper, invading her mouth with his tongue. He felt her fingernails dig into the skin on his lower back, then swept her off her feet and carried her into their bedroom. He yanked her cellphone from her hand and tossed it on the nightstand.

Elijah placed her feet on the floor and turned her around, pressing his bulge into her back. Her ass ground against his awakened length as he listened to her suck in a breath. Elijah slid the dress down her torso and over her hips, allowing the soft material to pool at her ankles. He pressed his hand against her stomach and trailed his fingers against the line leading from her navel into her red French lace panties. His fingers slid to her clit and caressed it. Breanna gasped as she rested the back of her head against his shoulder. Her breasts nearly spilled from her red lace bra as she breathed deeply.

"Elijah," she gasped. "Please—we shouldn't—you need to—don't stop."

"I won't, baby," he breathed against her ear.

Kissing the side of her neck, Elijah bit it, making her tilt it further into his teeth. She arched her back, grinding her ass harder against his rock-solid bulge. He turned her around to face him, then kissed her again. Her fingers unraveled the drawstring of his sweatpants as he guided her to the bedroom wall next to the window. Elijah pressed her back against it, slid his pants down over his hips, and stepped out of them. His full length stood to her attention.

The soft-touch of her palm and fingers wrapping around his length and caressing it made him throw his head back and suck in a breath. Breanna continued her slow caresses around his length, stroking him from the base to the tip. His breathing labored, and his heart raced from her touch.

Her body may have belonged to another man, but her heart was still his. No matter what Nathaniel tried to do to pull her away, he couldn't erase the seven years of laughter, the seven years of tears, the seven years of anger and pain, nor the seven years of raw intimacy they shared among each other.

"I want to taste you," she whispered next to his ear while still stroking him.

"Breanna," he said. He watched her kneel before him. "You don't have to do that if—"

Moans escaped his lips as she twirled her tongue around the tip of his length. She kissed the side of it before taking him into her mouth. He held the back of her head, guiding her slow ebbs and flows around him. Every kiss, every lick, and every slurp sent ticklish vibrations through his body.

"Breanna," Elijah groaned. "I'm going to explode if you keep this up."

She looked up at him with her round almond eyes and twirled her tongue around his tip. "That's what I'm hoping for."

Elijah moaned louder, feeling her hand take over where her mouth left off. He placed his hand against the wall, hoping he wouldn't climax so soon. But if he did, Elijah had another round in him left. He was at her mercy, and he adored every moment of it. He moaned; his body was nearing an early orgasm.

Elijah lifted her chin with his index finger and helped her from the floor. He pressed her back against the wall again and bit his bottom lip. "My turn."

He turned her body around again and slowly slid her panties down her legs. Elijah maneuvered them around the black peep-toe heels she wore, tossing them aside. Sliding his fingers down her spine, he trailed the circumference of her plump ass cheeks and found his way to her clit. Elijah caressed it, making her moan and move against his fingers. He pressed his body against hers, making her suck in another breath as she moaned his name.

"I love you, Bree," he said, kissing the back of her neck.

"I love you too, Blue Eyes."

He entered her, pushing his length deep until he met her G-Spot. Her moans and arched back caused him to nearly climax again. He kissed the back of her head, thrusting his length deeper rhythmically within her. Elijah grabbed both her hands and rose them above her head, intertwining his fingers with hers.

"Oh, God!" Breanna panted. "You feel so good."

He released one of her hands and grabbed her hip, guiding her body to meet his quicker thrusts. "You like that, baby," he said, grabbing her other hip.

She nodded. Her fingernails clawed at the paint on the walls. Her moans and panting made him close his eyes. A deep groan emitted from his throat as he slowed his pace, wanting this moment to last as long as it could.

Her leg curl around his as he deepened his thrusts. Breanna stared at him from the corner of her eye and bit her bottom lip. She moaned his name, then smiled at him before parting her lips to moan his name again. The muscles and arch in her back became like a work of art as she turned to the side to meet his lips. Her small breasts bounced from his thrusting.

Elijah pushed her hair away from her shoulder and kissed it. "You're so beautiful."

He quickened his thrusts again, causing Breanna to call his name as her hand pressed against the uncovered windowpane. If anyone were looking, they best had enjoyed the show with a bowl of popcorn and a cup full of Coca-Cola.

"I'm so close," Breanna breathed.

He stopped, pulled out of her, and turned her around to face him. Elijah stared into her eyes, then kissed her lips, savoring the sweet yet tangy flavor of his own essence mixed in with her cherry flavored chap stick she loved to wear so much.

He stared at her for a moment before sweeping her off her feet. He carried her to their bed and laid her body down on the plush comforter. One by one, Elijah pulled off her peep-toe heels and threw them to the floor. He crawled in between her thighs and rested his body on top of hers.

"Breanna," Elijah breathed, staring into her eyes. He knew this moment wouldn't keep her with him. That was clearly written in her eyes. But he had to let her learn from this if they were going to rebuild their relationship. Still, He just couldn't let her shatter Isabella's already wavering heart into pieces. She had to make a choice. "I will always love you. No matter what you do after tonight, I need you to be here for Isabella. Can you promise me that?"

She closed her eyes, turning her head to the side. Her body trembled beneath him.

Elijah caressed her cheek and then turned her face to meet his. He noticed a tear rolling down the side of it and wiped away the tear with his index finger. He kissed her forehead. "Promise me, Breanna."

"I promise," she whispered.

He entered her again, making her gasp. Intertwining his fingers with hers, he stared into her eyes as he deepened his thrusts. She arched her back as he licked her neck. Elijah quickened his pace and kissed her lips, savoring the remnants of her fading chap stick and his own essence. Her moans vibrated against his lips, making him hit her G-Spot with every thrust.

A deep yet muffled buzzing erupted from Breanna's cellphone as it moved about on the wooden nightstand. He slapped it off the piece of furniture, sending it sliding underneath the bed. The last thing he needed was to hear that damn phone chirp again.

Her vaginal walls clenched his length as her essence secreted around him. As Elijah sat on his knees, he grabbed her waist and guided her body to meet his thrusts. Breanna clinched the bedsheets and closed her eyes tight.

"Eli," she moaned. "God, I'm so close."

"Give it to me, baby," he panted. "Please, Bree."

Her screams filled the room as he continued to thrust within her. Gripping her waist tighter, he pushed his length into her deeper, hitting her G-Spot and making her climax again. He groaned, feeling pulsating waves of pleasure course through his pelvis, his spine, and his stomach.

Elijah kissed Breanna's forehead and smiled as he listened to her subtle breathing. He pulled out of her and laid next to her. Breanna was fast asleep. He moved a strand of her hair from her face and traced the contour of her jawline with his index finger. Nathaniel couldn't have her. But she had to be the one to make that call.

❦❦❦

Tessa stood beside Nathaniel. Every vein in his forehead and hands seemed to have swelled as he tapped his foot on the ground. He sucked on the toothpick in his mouth. His brows creased further into a scowl with every minute that passed by. Breanna best had answered her phone. The last time she pulled this stunt, Nathaniel put a hole in his front door.

"Ya girl said she was supposed to be here about twenty minutes ago." Nathaniel stared at her. He turned his attention to another young woman walking into the restaurant and smirked, eying the sway of his hips in her skin-tight leopard bodysuit.

Tessa shook her head, glaring at him with pursed lips. "Breanna told me she was going to get her phone. She'd left it at home."

"Let me guess. Ole dude is at home too, am I right?"

Tessa nodded, then sighed. "That doesn't mean she stood you up to be with him, Nathaniel. Elijah's just all in his feelings right now."

"Ole dude lost what he had; she's mine now. He better respect that." Nathaniel stood from the stool and adjusted his blue mosaic silk shirt, rolling the sleeves into cuffs to show off his gold and blue Rolex watch. The black slacks and Stacy Adams he wore made the shirt dazzle before her eyes.

If Breanna got into an argument with Elijah, Tessa knew that always led to one thing between those two. Sex.

"I'm gonna call her again," Nathaniel said. He stepped away from the bar and walked toward the entrance before she had the chance to respond.

God, she hoped Breanna didn't sleep with Elijah. It took her a good little minute to convince him Breanna just needed some time to see her daughter. But Nathaniel wasn't feeling that. He wasn't trying to hear any of that. He just wanted her ass where he could see her.

136

"So, your friend just went back home to get her phone, right?" Nathaniel stared at her. His furrowed eyebrows darkened his brown eyes.

"That's all she went to do."

He smirked, nodding his head at her reply. "Then, tell me why I heard her ass moaning and screaming ole dude's name when I called her."

Tessa frowned. "She wouldn't do that to you, Nathaniel. She wants to be with you."

"She wants to be with me, huh?"

"That's what she told me before she left my place to go to work."

"Breanna just so happened to have left her phone at home. I get it now." Nathaniel sat at the bar again and beckoned for the bartender to come his way.

"She was in a rush, Nathaniel. She and Elijah had gotten into an argument, and she didn't feel like listening to his sorry ass excuses anymore."

"But the bitch still finds her way back on white boy's dick." Nathaniel gulped the shot of whiskey, then beckoned for the bartender to pour him another. "Is she coming back to your place tonight?"

"She said she was picking up her clothes before making her way over to your place."

"Good," he said, taking down the last shot. "I can't wait to see her."

Chapter Twenty-Five

Breanna watched him sleep. Strands of Elijah's hair lingered over his eye. No matter how much they fought, it was these moments that made her love this man more and more. But she couldn't forget he was the same man that held her back from living her life. Elijah was the same man that promised her he would tell her everything. He was the same man Momma pegged to break her heart and hold her back. He was a wolf in sheep's clothing. She didn't deserve what he did to her. She didn't need his—was Momma wrong about Elijah?

As she got out of the bed, she grabbed her black dress and slid it back on. Breanna zipped it up slowly, then tiptoed toward the window and grabbed her pumps. A flashing light from underneath the bed caught her attention. That could have been Nathaniel calling her. He was probably ready to cut ties with her if she didn't make it up to him.

Breanna gingerly got on all fours and reached for her phone. She grabbed it, noticing the number of notifications she had on it. She heard Elijah moan, then shift in the bed. Breanna stared at him for a moment as she stood to her feet. He had seen a lot of bullshit from his grandmother. Never in her life did she ever hear him talk badly about her. Elijah only had but the sweetest stories to tell about the woman. So why didn't he mention the truth? Why didn't he ever tell her Momma tried to have him arrested and charged for rape?

She knew Momma didn't like Elijah, but that just seemed so farfetched. Then again, he painted his grandmother in the sweetest way, and she tried her damnedest to hurt Mrs. Lori. Maybe he and

Daddy were right. Perhaps it was time for her to sit down with Momma and ask her why she didn't come to Isabella's birth.

She tiptoed out of the bedroom and then down the steps. As Breanna reached the first floor, she heard him cough and clear his throat. She closed her eyes.

Why are you doing this, Breanna? This doesn't feel right.

For the life of her, she couldn't understand why she didn't want to leave the house. She couldn't understand why every footstep she took toward her car was a footstep in the wrong direction.

She opened the front door as quietly as she could and pulled it closed until it clicked shut. Breanna slid on her heels and ran to her car. She hopped inside of the vehicle, cranked it up, and sped out of the driveway. Dred lingered in the pit of her stomach as she made her way out the neighborhood.

"It's 12:30 in the morning." Breanna stared at the clock as she sped toward the intersection leading her toward the highway. "Shit! I hope Tessa's around. Google, call Tessa."

"Calling Tessa Chatman," the woman's voice replied through the car's speakers.

Breanna waited, hoping to hear Tessa's voice sing hello. But she never answered. That wasn't like her to miss her calls. Tessa was the one who would pick up on the second ring. She passed a slower-moving car on the expressway and made her way toward the I-40 ramp heading toward Nashville.

"Google," Breanna said. "Call Tessa."

"Calling Tessa Chatman," the woman said.

Breanna waited to hear Tessa's voice, yet she never answered. She frowned. The hairs on her arms stood as she took the exit toward Franklin Street. One by one, bell-shaped streetlights illuminated her path toward her best friend's place. Historic buildings sparkled with Christmas-styled lights like the establishments on Cooper-Young did in Memphis. Stopping at a red light, she saw a little girl skipping ahead of her parents. She stared at them for a moment. The little girl looked like Isabella. Her mother had beautiful long red hair that flowed over her ivory-toned skin, and her father had dreadlocks reaching the small of his back. His skin was like chocolate. That was her and Elijah. That was them happy together. That was—was she doing the right thing?

With the light's permission, Breanna pushed her foot on the pedal, leaving the happy family a figment in her rearview mirror. She made a right turn on Franklin Street and drove down the street. Every house on the road was either a Craftsman or Bungalow-styled home. This area, along with another neighborhood in Kentfield, were the only streets that restored their 1940s homes.

She glanced at a house close to the four-way stop. Its stonework and vibrant spring pastel colors stood out among the others. The landscaping made the place look so elegant, so vibrant. Breanna stared at a lit-up sign in the yard and noticed AJ's and Elijah's names on it. They were the ones who rehabbed that house. Elijah.

She pulled into Tessa's driveway and noticed a white BMW X5 sitting in the driveway. Breanna frowned. Tessa mentioned nothing about one of her men coming through. That was probably why she never answered the phone. Breanna chucked. Tessa was too busy getting busy.

She dug inside her purse and pulled out Tessa's spare key. It was a good thing she swiped it off the bar. She would have never gotten inside the place. As she got out of the car, she heard a dog howl in the distance. She looked around the neighborhood. Why did it feel like something was trying to keep her from going inside the house?

Breanna made her way to the door and put her key inside the lock. The door was already open. She frowned as she walked inside.

"Tessa," Breanna called. She stood in the foyer and placed her car keys and Tessa's spare key on a table near the entryway. "The door was still open."

"I know," Tessa replied. She stood behind Breanna in the arched hallway.

Breanna jumped. "Tessa. Girl, you scared me."

"Um... Bree." She hesitated. "You should talk to Nathaniel."

"I know. I was just stopping by to pick up some clothes so I could make my way over to his place," she replied. "I kind of figured you had somebody over for the night."

Tessa rubbed her neck, then looked away from her.

Breanna frowned. "Tessa? What's wrong?"

"She can't vouch for you anymore, Breanna." Nathaniel walked out from the first bedroom behind her and stood in front of Tessa. He smirked at her, moving his neck from side to side, cracking the bones.

She jumped as she glared into his eyes. His smirk transitioned into a grin. A grin Breanna wasn't used to. "Nathaniel. I'm so sorry. Elijah held me up—"

"He did more than hold you up."

"What are you talking about?" She watched him walk closer to her, cracking his knuckles. She stepped away from him with wide eyes. Her heart pounded near the top of her throat. Breanna bumped against the wall. His eyes darkened as he stood in front of her.

"I'm talking about you fucking white boy," Nathaniel retorted. He stroked the side of her cheek with his index finger.

"I... I didn't—"

140

"You didn't, huh?" He looked at Tessa and smiled at her, then returned a motionless look back at her.

"No. I didn't—"

"Bitch, I wish yo' ass would keep lying to me. I heard you screaming his name over the phone when you answered." He grabbed her arm and jerked her toward him. "Yo' ass keep going back to ole dude, but you won't offer me the cookie."

"Nathaniel," Breanna hesitated, watching his fingers clench around her forearm like a vice grip. She winced. "It was a mistake. One thing led to another and—"

The searing sting of his hand across her cheek caught her off guard. She stared at him with wide eyes, then held it. She stepped away from the wall into the center of the living room.

"Where are you going, Bree?" Nathaniel smiled as he stalked her. He grabbed her by her throat and threw her against the wall. "You think you gone leave me hanging?"

He slapped her hard in the face again, causing her to fall to the floor. Breanna touched her bottom lip. She winced again as she touched the stinging split. A splat of blood rested on her fingertips.

"Please stop," Breanna pleaded.

"You want me to stop?" he yelled at her. "I'll stop."

Nathaniel held his hand out to help her off the ground, then smiled at her. Breanna hesitated. The look in his eyes said he wasn't done with her yet. Still, she took his hand, hoping he wouldn't hurt her anymore. This wasn't the Nathaniel she knew back in high school. Hell, this wasn't the man she had been dating for the past two months. This was a man she didn't know. And she made the biggest mistake of still trusting him.

His fingers slinked their way around her throat again and squeezed. She closed her eyes as she struggled to breathe. "Please... stop."

"I'll stop when I'm ready to." He lifted her from the ground and shoved her against the yellow and green wallpapered accent wall in the living room. Breanna's shoulder hit the edge of the bookcase. Its sharp point punctured her shoulder blade. She screamed. "I think I'm just getting started."

Breanna fought her way from his grasp and ran into the kitchen. She tripped over her own two feet and fell to the floor. She clawed at the shoes on her feet and threw them off one by one. The sound of his growl, like panting, lingered behind her as she scurried to her feet. Her eyes widened, feeling his hand grab a handful of her hair. She screamed. His fist connected with the back of her head like two bucks fighting over a doe. Nathaniel drug her across the wooden floor extending from the kitchen into the living room. Breanna stared at

Tessa sitting on the couch. She just sat there and did nothing. Her raised eyebrows and wide eyes said one thing. But when she looked away from her, that told Breanna everything she needed to know about her best friend. She pulled out her cellphone and stared at it.

"Tessa! Help me!" Breanna pleaded, holding her hand out to her.

Tessa looked at her for a moment, sighed, and returned her attention back to her mobile device as if nothing happened in front of her. Her own best friend wouldn't extend a hand; she wouldn't even call the police. Breanna screamed from the hard stinging connection of Nathaniel's shoe with her ribs. The pain surging through her body danced between the urge to vomit and boiling water doused upon her skin. She could no longer tell which was worse. Everything pulsated. This was far worse than natural childbirth.

"Let this be a lesson learned," Nathaniel huffed. He kneeled beside her, smiling at her trembling. "Don't you ever fuck off on me again, Bree."

Tears streamed from her eyes. She laid in a small puddle of her own blood and tears. Nathaniel lifted her face from the floor with his index finger and thumb. His cognac brown eyes gleamed in her pain as he stared at her.

"Do you understand me?"

Breanna nodded, still trembling.

He slapped her hard in the face again. "Say something, bitch."

"I... I under... I understand," she whimpered.

He smiled. It was the same smile Breanna remembered the first night she reconnected with him at Soul Bistro. She watched him leave out the house and slam the door behind him. She heard Tessa's footsteps walk down the hallway. Another door slammed shut in the distance. She curled up into a fetal position and sobbed.

She needed Elijah to hold her. She needed to be back in his arms again. Breanna needed to forgive him before it was too late... before Nathaniel took her life.

Chapter Twenty-Six

A clock stared at Breanna as she stirred. It's stale red 3:37 am reminded her how long she had been out. She gripped the bedsheet and held onto it, feeling its softness caress her fingertips. She looked around the moonlit room. It spun a bit as she moved her head. Plush wetness greeted her tips as she slid her fingers past her face. How the hell did she get in the bed?

She groaned as she rose from it. Her side twinged with pain as she from the little motion she took to stand to her feet. She ambled across the wooden floor holding her side.

Thank God, Nathaniel didn't get too happy and send her to visit Grandma Isabella.

She noticed a trail of her own blood grace the floor. It was still fresh. Tessa must have pitied her and drug her into the room she once slept in for the past couple of nights.

She stepped toward the bedroom's entrance and stared at Tessa's closed bedroom door. Breanna covered her face with her hands and sobbed. How the fuck did she let things escalate like this?

Tessa was supposed to be her best friend. She was supposed to have been the one she went to for advice. She was supposed to—Tessa was everything Elijah said that she was. Elijah even warned her she would hurt her if she gave her a chance, and like a fool, she didn't listen. Breanna was just like... Momma.

Breanna hobbled back toward the bed and ripped the clean pillowcase off the pillow she lay on. She stumbled as she walked toward the dresser. Her entire head pounded. She opened the top drawer, pulled the little clothes she had out of it, and stuffed them in the case. Breanna spotted a black pair of leggings and one of Elijah's old t-shirts she must have grabbed by mistake. She sobbed, then winced from the pain of sucking in too deep of a breath. One by one, she slid each leg into the thin leggings and then slid on Elijah's shirt without crying aloud from the surging pain playing in her side.

As she hobbled to the closet and opened it, she saw a pair of Tessa's old scuffed up, dirt ladened tennis shoes and reached for them. Pain radiated from her shoulder blade to her shoulder, then lingered at her side again, making sure she knew its presence was still with her. Something may have been broken. She stood up straight and tried to breathe through the pain. It wasn't working as well as she hoped.

Breanna hobbled inside the ensuite bathroom and stared into the mirror. The print of Nathaniel's hand turned portions of her caramel skin puffy and red. Her bottom lip was still busted and swollen more than ever. The good thing was it no longer oozed. That's if that was a good thing. She winced as she touched her face. A tear slid down her cheek. Elijah would have never done this to her. He would have never—all of this was her fault.

She ripped her happiness to shreds because of issues that could have been dealt with. But Breanna refused to talk to him; she refused to listen to him. She had gotten what she deserved. Breanna... needed help. She needed... comfort. She needed to talk to Momma.

The clicking sound of Tessa's door unlocking made Breanna stiffen. She stared at the corner of the mirror, noticing a small picture of her and Tessa posing together as they slurped a strawberry smoothie from a massive cup with two red straws. Tessa wasn't her best friend; she was her best enemy.

She grabbed the pillowcase from the bed and hobbled out the room. Pain surged through her side and the back of her head as she walked.

"Keep pushing, Bree," she muttered to herself.

She saw her car keys on the table inside the foyer, sitting next to Tessa's spare house key. The bitch would never have to worry about her borrowing the damn thing ever again. Breanna snatched her car keys off the table along with Tessa's spare key and walked out the front door. She threw the spare key into the neighbor's bushes, then winced in pain. She grabbed her side, feeling the stinging rip of pain surge through it again. That was worth the discomfort. She left the door wide open as she limped to her car. If Tessa couldn't lift a hand to help her, Breanna couldn't close the door behind her. Perhaps someone or something would find her house cozy enough to take shelter inside.

Breanna opened her car door and got inside. She cried out in pain as she sat down. Driving was the last thing she needed to attempt, but

144

it was either suffer in pain or deal with the shame of getting help from Regina.

Maybe Regina would shame her. Perhaps she would—with the way she talked to her stepmother, Breanna wouldn't have blamed Regina for not treating her injuries. She struggled to close the door, then cranked her car. She backed out the driveway and drove down the street.

She held her side as she tried to keep her sights on the dark road. Between the pain wracking her body and the streetlights burning her eyes, Breanna couldn't tell which was worse anymore. She knew she couldn't stop. She had to keep moving. Breanna had to get back to Elijah and Isabella. But she had to straighten shit out with herself first before she ran back to them again.

She parked at a gas station close to the expressway and surveyed the area, hoping Nathaniel didn't follow her around the block so he could beat her senseless again. She dialed Regina's number and listened to the phone ring. At this time of morning, her stepmother wouldn't answer her phone. She had other patients she had to deal with.

"Hello?" Regina asked cautiously.

"Regina." Breanna winced in pain.

"Breanna? Sweetheart, is that you?"

"Yes, ma'am." She sobbed.

"What's wrong?"

Breanna winced in pain again. "I need your help."

"Breanna, did you get into a car accident?"

"No," she said, sobbing aloud.

"What happened, Breanna? You can tell me."

"Someone hurt me."

"Oh my God! Are you bleeding? Is there anything broken?"

"Everything hurts, Mom." Breanna cried.

"Are you able to get to Highland Memorial Hospital?"

"I think so."

"Listen, sweetheart. I want you to stay on the phone with me until you get here. I'll be waiting outside the emergency entrance, okay."

"Mom," Breanna said, whimpering. "I'm so sorry for how I treated you."

"Sweetheart, we'll talk about that later," Regina said. "Right now, I just need you to use your Bluetooth headset and drive."

"Yes ma'am."

Breanna pulled off the parking lot and drove toward the expressway. Thank God, Highland Memorial was only twenty minutes from where she was. She still had to get there in one piece, though. If something would have happened to her, Elijah would have been able

145

to move on and be happier. He would have found new love; he would have been—she couldn't think like that. Not now. She had to keep moving.

As she passed the exit sign for Nashville, a car in front of her suddenly cloned itself. Its blurry twin forced her to rub her eyes. Her heart raced as she squinted. Nathaniel hit her harder than she thought he had.

"Mom," Breanna spoke.

"Are you okay?"

"I'm seeing doubles."

"Shit!" Regina took a deep breath. "Breanna, I'm going to need you to keep your eyes focused on every sign you pass. I think you may have a head injury."

"I don't feel so well either. I feel a lot of pressure on my side." She stared at each sign, hoping she wouldn't have a car accident.

"Do you see the exit for Highland Memorial yet, sweetheart?"

Keeping her distance, Breanna followed the car in front of her. It was the only thing she could somewhat see straight. "No."

"Tell me what you can see. Maybe I can get you here on a different route."

Breanna squinted at a sign for Toots Blvd and sighed, thankful she wasn't completely out of it yet. "I can take the exit for Toots. It's coming up in another half mile, I think."

"Okay. Take the exit and stay focused on the road. There aren't too many streetlights going down that way, so that'll be the best route," Regina replied.

Breanna took the exit for Toots Blvd. and drove toward another four-way stop. A white SUV pulled up close behind her. Her heart raced again. Darkness kept her from seeing the person's face who drove the vehicle.

She drove through the stop sign, hoping the vehicle wouldn't follow behind her. But without fail, it followed her. "Mom."

"Breanna, are you okay? Are you still seeing doubles?"

"A little, but I think someone may be following me."

"Okay, Breanna. Go through the next stop sign and see if the person goes through the stop sign with you."

"Yes, ma'am."

Breanna held her breath as she drove through the second stop sign. Maybe the first time was by incident, but when she noticed the SUV followed her without stopping, Breanna knew it wasn't by accident. She pressed her foot on the gas pedal, sending the black sedan bolting through the other stop sign. The SUV zoomed behind her. Nathaniel. He was out to finish the job, regardless of if he had onlookers or not.

146

Breanna made an abrupt right turn onto Pelter Street. Her tires screeched as she pressed the pedal to the floor. After that stint, she would need some more tires, but she had to live to see another moment before worrying about something as minuscule as that.

"Breanna, are you okay? I heard your tires. What's happening?"

"I'm okay, Mom. I'm getting closer to the hospital."

"Where are you?"

"On Pelter Street."

"You're only three minutes out, sweetheart," Regina said. "Just keep driving."

She drove through a quiet neighborhood, hoping she wouldn't see the SUV following her again. A bright green iridescent sign for Highland Memorial caught her fading sight. She sped down the street, hoping no one was walking on the street at this time of morning. She'd already suffered a beatdown. She didn't need to add jail time to that too.

She sped toward the emergency exit and entered the parking lot with smoke behind her. Breanna stopped the car and opened the door. Regina ran toward her car in her green floral scrubs and white clogs. Her wide eyes and labored breathing said more to Breanna than her own mother ever showed her in her lifetime. She placed one foot on the ground and collapsed to the pavement. Struggling, she braced herself to stand to her feet only to slump back to the rough surface. The coolness of the pavement eased some of her pain away as she lay on the ground.

"Breanna!" Regina kneeled next to her and touched the back of her head. Wetness graced her fingertips. "I've got to get you into a room quick."

Breanna held her head as her vision blurred. She squinted, noticing the white BMW X5 drive into the lot and sit there for a moment before driving off. Nathaniel was waiting for her to move; he dared her to move. Breanna sobbed. She caused this to have her better slice of life. Was it worth it?

Chapter Twenty-Seven

Rays of bright light stung her eyes as she opened them. The sound of trumpets and horns playing harmoniously together prompted Breanna to sit up in the bed she laid in. Pain danced through her side, taunting her for making the wrong move. A tear slid down her cheek as she winced. How could she have allowed this mess to happen?

Nathaniel was supposed to be the man who understood all her frustrations; he was supposed to be the man who she could talk to no matter the issue. Instead, he was the wolf lurking about with a sheep's wool around his body, waiting to maul her when she got close enough. She closed her eyes as she touched the tender puffiness on her cheek. A man wasn't supposed to put his hands on a woman. Daddy always stressed that. But Momma... she never said a word about abuse. Never.

"Knock, knock," Mom sang, walking inside the room. "How are you feeling, sweetheart?"

Breanna smiled and nodded, trying to hide the lingering pain. "I'm better than I was last night."

"Breanna," Mom said. She sat on the side of the hospital bed next to her. "Can you be honest with me?"

Breanna nodded once more. She stared into her stepmother's eyes. There was always love for her in them. Hate didn't exist in them. It should have, though. With every slick word, mocking glare, and eye-roll Breanna ever gave to this woman, Mom never tried to get back at her. She was patient with her. That was something she needed to learn... something she needed to understand.

"Who did this to you?"

"He was—" Another tear slipped down her cheek. "Someone I was dating."

"Breanna." Regina swallowed hard. "Does Elijah know about this?"

Breanna nodded. More tears streamed down her cheeks as she covered her mouth and sobbed. "I made a horrible mistake, Mom. I ruined Elijah and Isabella's lives. I ruined what we had together."

Mom took Breanna's hand into hers and squeezed it tight. "Breanna, mistakes are a part of life. That's how we become better individuals. But if you choose not to fix it, then it becomes a problem. You've got to fix this."

"How?"

"Start by asking God for forgiveness."

Breanna sobbed. "Why would he forgive someone like me?"

"Because every saint was a sinner, and a sinner can become a saint."

"Do you think Elijah will ever forgive me for what I've done?"

Mom sighed and squeezed her hand tighter. "If you're willing to be patient with him, listen to him, and talk to him, Elijah will forgive you. But don't forget to forgive yourself in the process too."

Breanna wiped the streaming tears from her eyes and nodded. Mom was right. Forgiveness was her starting point, but like hell, would it be easy, especially since she had to forgive herself. She took a deep breath. A surge of pain jolted through her side. This road would be difficult to travel, but she knew where she had to begin. "Mom... can you forgive me?"

Mom smiled. A tear fell from her eye. "I forgive you, Breanna."

She took Breanna into her embrace and kissed the side of her cheek. Breanna rested her head on Mom's shoulder and sniffled, trying to hold back her tears. The tears won that battle. The sharp stab-like pains flowing through her side subsided as she cried on her shoulder. Mom's embrace was so warm, so comforting.

Momma used to hold her in her arms like this until she and Daddy divorced. The warmth of her arms never embraced her anymore. But they never embraced Amber at all, from what she remembered. Momma would just leave Amber standing in the middle of the floor, crying.

No wonder why Amber hated her and Momma. She didn't grow up with a loving sister or mother who cared about her. She grew up by herself until Daddy came and got her. What kind of mother would do that to her own child? What kind of—she wasn't too far from being like Momma. Daddy and Elijah were right. She needed to talk to her.

She needed to know who Aunt Aubrey was and why she never talked about her youngest sister. Breanna needed to know why Momma only talked about Daddy's affair and never about her own. She needed to know why Aunt Pauline always wrinkled her nose up at Amber every time she saw her. There was just too much mess her family left uncleaned.

There was too much baggage Momma held onto. Sure, she may have had the nice car, the big house, and even the bank account to flaunt her status as a divorced woman, but the way she raised her and Amber was like one choosing the finest boy at school to take to the junior prom who was a complete asshole versus the nice guy who wore braces and suspenders.

Dr. Shelby was right. Momma had a stronghold in her life, and it was costing her everything she loved and cherished.

"Mom," Breanna said. She rose from her shoulder and gazed into her deep brown eyes. "Have you ever tried talking to my mother?"

"On several occasions." Mom nodded. "She just didn't want to talk to me."

Breanna frowned. "Why?"

"Well, your mother said she didn't want to deal with her ex's mess." She sighed. "So talking to me was out the question."

"So Momma gave an excuse, right?"

"She did, but that didn't stop me from trying. It wasn't until your father and I made our relationship official that she began referring to me as the other woman."

"That makes no sense, Mom. My mother said you were the one Daddy had an affair with."

"No, sweetheart. I wasn't the one," she replied, shaking her head. "It was her sister, Pauline, he had a one-night stand with."

Breanna looked away from her and wiped a falling tear from her eye. Had Momma lied to her about Daddy's affair? "Daddy told me the same thing."

"Whatever your mother told you about us isn't true. Your father and I met a year after their divorce. He came limping into this very hospital because he stepped on a nail, and I was the one who gave him a tetanus shot."

"Why would Momma lie to me?" Another tear slipped down Breanna's cheek. "Why?"

"Ms. Zora told me her husband had an older sister named Vivian."

"Grandma Zora didn't like it when she came around me and Amber."

"She had good reason to. You see, Vivian grew up in a time where brighter skin meant better treatment."

Breanna examined the hue of her caramel brown skin. Great Aunt Vivian always brought her toys when she was a little girl, but she never gave Amber anything. "That's why Amber used to cry whenever she came around."

"Mmm-hmm." Mom nodded. "Ms. Zora told me she didn't like Aubrey or Amber because of their darker skin tone. But she loved you, your mother, and Pauline."

"Because we're bright-skinned."

Mom nodded once more. "Yeah."

"I don't blame Amber for hating me."

"Amber loves you, Breanna. Please don't think otherwise."

"I don't see how. I always got affection from Momma, and she never received so much as a hug and kiss from the woman."

She smiled at Breanna, then moved a strand of her hair behind her ear. "Do you remember when you two spent the week with your father and me when you were twelve years old?"

Breanna smiled as she nodded. "That was the summer when you and Daddy snuck us inside the movie theater to see Miami Vice."

Mom smiled, flashing her perfect white teeth. "The both of you wanted to see that movie so bad because you had a crush on Jamie Foxx—"

"And Amber wanted to see the lady who played Tia Dalma from Pirates of the Caribbean."

"I had never seen you two so happy together," she said. Her smile faded. "That was the same night Amber begged me not to let you go back home because she didn't want you to change."

One by one, tears slid down Breanna's cheeks. She wanted her sister to love her again. She wanted Elijah and Isabella to know she could change for the better. Breanna wanted—no, she needed them to know that. She needed to change for them and herself.

She hugged Mom again, resting her head on her shoulder as she sobbed. Leslie was right, too. She just hoped the mess she caused wasn't too much to clean up.

Chapter Twenty-Eight

Elijah closed the tailgate to his truck and wiped the sweat from his forehead. A droplet of rain splashed onto his forearm. He stared into the sky and watched the gray clouds consume the sun like Pacman. A cool spring breeze played with his hair. Streaks of lightning danced about in the near distance. Kentfield and springtime. The two never liked each other.

He watched as the rest of his crew pack up their gear and rolled off the pavement before the storm came rolling through. These were the days he loved the most. He could go home and lay beside Breanna if she were home for her break. Thoughts of her smiles and giggles rummaged through his head as he took a deep breath. He could still smell the sweetness of honey and the savory hickory-smoked bacon in her hair when he nuzzled her. He longed for that right now. But that wouldn't happen anytime soon. She was too busy laying up in Nathaniel's bed to even think about him or Isabella.

AJ walked toward him, pulling on his baseball cap. "Yo' man. You alright?"

"I'm good, bro," Elijah replied. "Just can't believe how much we've accomplished in the past two months."

He nodded, viewing the houses erected around him. With the help of Morgan's team, they would be finished by the midpoint of summer. They already had four houses fleshed out. All he and AJ needed now was the design team to come in and work their magic.

Elijah sighed. He stared at AJ for a moment and looked away. Thunder clapped, sending a rumbling resound about them.

"Man, are you sure you're okay?" AJ placed his hand on his shoulder.

He shook his head. "I'm not."

"Breanna again?"

Elijah nodded. "She's been cheating on me."

AJ's mouth fell open. "You serious, E?"

"I wished I wasn't."

"Damn, bro. I hate that's happened to you. I thought the counseling was working."

"Breanna and I went for two weeks. Shit got real when Tessa told her I had been taking Izzy to see Mr. Marvin."

"That bitch gets on my fucking nerves, yo'. I was so glad when Leslie quit that place. All Tessa does is start shit cause' she wants attention."

"Trust me. I know." Elijah's cellphone buzzed in his back pants pocket. He reached into it, pulled out the device, and stared at it. Isabella's teacher wanted to speak to him again. This shit was getting worse. "I told Breanna time and time again Tessa had been pushing up on me. She didn't believe me."

"Tessa's going to fuck around and get hurt." AJ waved at the last few people leaving the lots.

"Then give me front row tickets so I can see that shit in action."

They laughed. Elijah needed that. Though not at the expense of someone getting hurt, he didn't mind seeing Tessa get what she had coming for her ass.

"Hey, man," AJ said. "Don't stay out here too long. The news is forecasting some bad weather for the next two days."

"You know what that means, AJ."

"Sleep. Much needed sleep." AJ rubbed his shoulder as he rotated it. "I'm going to need it. Leslie and I are babysitting the twins for the weekend again."

Elijah smiled. "Big bro's back in town?"

"Yep," AJ replied. "And taking all the good food too."

"Did your mom, by chance, make her famous pound cake?"

"Along with the fried chicken, the green beans and potatoes with bacon, and her cornbread." AJ pursed his lips as he folded his arms across his chest. "And knowing Robert, he probably took all the fried chicken necks and backs."

Elijah shook his head. "I hope she has enough for an extra plate."

"Then, you better drop by before Robert saps everything up."

Morgan walked toward them. She glanced at the gray clouds rolling in the sky and waved at them both as she smiled. Her eyes never left Elijah's.

153

AJ stared at her, then at him. His eyebrows furrowed. "She seems infatuated with you again, E."

"You think so."

"I know so." AJ pulled his cellphone out his pocket. "She's cool people and all, but I'd be careful if I were you."

"I'll be careful, bro. She's just... being friendly."

"Like she was back when we were in college," AJ said, sighing. He eyeballed Morgan, then returned his attention to Elijah again. "I know you're hurting, but I don't think Morgan should be the one you turn to."

Elijah frowned at AJ. He knew his best friend was right. Morgan wasn't the best person. Yet, she was the only person who made him feel at peace when Breanna left. She was the friend he could lean on when he needed to vent. He sighed. "I'll be careful, bro."

"Be careful about what?" Morgan stared at them both. A smile pulled her full lips, exposing her straight white teeth.

"Be careful in this storm," Elijah replied. He stared at AJ, then nodded once. "It looks like it's going to be pretty bad."

"That it does," AJ said. "I better get going, so I can pick up Kourtney and Khloe."

"See ya', AJ." Morgan waved at him.

"I'll stop by your mom and dad's house to get a plate soon."

"Alright, E. I'll see ya' soon." AJ dialed a set of numbers on his phone. Its rhythmic dial tone sounded like a jingle for a commercial as he walked to his car. Another streak of lightning flashed in the distance. Rain poured to the ground just as he got inside his vehicle. AJ cranked the car and honked his horn, waving at them both as he drove off the lot.

Morgan turned her attention to Elijah. That smile never left her lips. "How are you doing, sunshine?"

"I'm good, Morgan."

Her eyebrows crinkled, her lips pursed. "Are you sure? You seem like you're hurt."

He smiled, faking his contentment. Morgan's intuition hadn't left her at all. They were probably more hyper-vigilant than they were back in college. "I'm good, Morgan."

"Well, if you like, a friend of mine and I are heading to Cee Cee's Bar and Grill tonight," she said. "That's if the storm isn't still so bad and all."

Elijah rubbed his temple. He wanted Breanna. He even tried to talk to her and smooth things over. Elijah wanted to... he needed to be happy. If Breanna searched for someone better to make her happy, he needed to do the same. She wouldn't come back home tonight, anyway. "I'm game."

Morgan's smile widened as she nodded. "That's the spirit, Sunshine."

"Morgan," he said, touching her shoulder. Her skin was so soft underneath his fingertips. He sucked in a breath from its delicate response to him. It was like what it used to be back in college. "Thanks."

"For what?"

"For being there when I need it."

"Sure," she replied. She narrowed her eyes. "Are you sure you're okay?"

He stared into her brown eyes. "No. I'm not."

Morgan stepped closer to him and pulled him into a hug. "That's what friends are for, right?"

Elijah stared into her eyes once more, losing himself in them. "They are."

He sucked in another breath as he drew closer to her. Morgan's body pressed against his, making junior stiffen. The heat of her breath graced his lips. His hand floated to the small of her back. Elijah closed his eyes, then bit his bottom lip as he looked away from her. This wasn't right.

"Elijah," Morgan breathed. "What's wrong?"

He stepped away from her. "I'm sorry, Morgan. I'll see you tonight."

She watched him walk away. That same smile pulled her lips again as she bit her bottom lip and waved at him. Elijah walked through the rain to his truck. He had to be better than Breanna. He just had to.

Damn. Morgan was what he needed right now. She was who he longed to have underneath him in his bed. She made him feel like himself again. She gave him what he'd been craving from Breanna. Love.

He got inside his truck, cranked it, and gripped both sides of the steering wheel. Maybe it was time for him to end things with Breanna. Perhaps it was time—maybe he needed to give Breanna one more chance.

He drove off the lot, leaving Morgan standing inside the opened skeleton of one of their new builds. At least it had drywall and roofing protecting her from the rain.

"I shouldn't have left her," he muttered to himself. He sighed. He should have taken Morgan home.

Chapter Twenty-Nine

M om said that the first step to correcting a mistake was forgiveness. Breanna stood from the hospital bed and pulled on a pair of jeans her stepmother bought her. She tied a knot at the bottom of Elijah's shirt and sat back down. This was going to be the most difficult thing she did. But it had to be done. She ruined too many lives—innocent lives that didn't deserve the likes of her trampling all over them.

Breanna pulled Dr. Shelby's card from her purse and held the piece of thick glossy paper in between her index finger and thumb. She stared at it, grazing her teeth against her bottom lip.

For the past three days, she had been fighting herself to call Elijah and tell him she wanted to start the counseling sessions with him again. Yet Breanna knew she had to do this on her own. She had to solve her own problems.

She sat on the bed, grabbed her phone from the tray, and pressed each number slowly. She took a deep breath as she pressed the last button.

You've got to do this, Bree.

She listened to the phone ring and sighed. A small part of her begged for Dr. Shelby not to answer—that part of her wanted to believe all she had done to Elijah and Isabella wasn't her fault. She closed her eyes, hoping she'd answer. She had to push past the idea their pain wasn't her fault bullshit when she very well knew it was.

"This is Dr. Shelby Hampton speaking."

"Dr. Shelby." Breanna's voice cracked, forcing her to clear her throat. "This is Breanna Ellis."

"Yes," Dr. Hampton said melodically. "How are you?"

"I'm... I'm..." Breanna stammered. "I'm not good, Dr. Shelby. I need your help."

"What's wrong, Ms. Ellis?"

"I..." Breanna covered her mouth and sobbed. Tears slipped down her cheeks. She took another deep breath and wiped the tears from her face. "I entered into an abusive relationship."

"With Mr. Bryson?"

Breanna closed her eyes. "With someone else."

"Ms. Ellis, are you and Mr. Bryson currently together?"

"Yes."

"Okay," Dr. Hampton said. "Ms. Ellis, I would love to talk to you more about this tomorrow afternoon if you are available."

"I can be," Breanna replied.

"I'm glad you called me. When Mr. Bryson called and informed me you two would no longer be seeking my services, I wondered if you two separated."

"We hadn't." She hesitated to speak. "I hurt Elijah and Isabella more than I ever imagined, Dr. Shelby."

"Ms. Ellis," she spoke. "First and foremost, I am proud of you for admitting what you've done, but you mustn't beat yourself up. You must take the first step in getting back on track."

"I understand."

"This is your road to recovery. I want to help you as much as possible."

"Thanks, Dr. Shelby."

"I'll see you tomorrow," she said. "Have a good day."

"You do the same," Breanna said, ending the call. She held the cellphone to her chest and sighed once more. She looked around the room, examining the four white walls surrounding her. Hearing footsteps behind her, she turned around and smiled. Mom stood in the doorway.

"Looks like you're free to go, sweetheart," Mom said. She walked inside the room and stood before Breanna. Her pink scrubs complimented her brown skin. "Are you going to tell Elijah what happened to you?"

Breanna inhaled, then exhaled through her nose slowly as she rubbed her temple. "I don't know if I should."

"I think you should, Bree." Mom sat next to her. "He needs to know the truth."

She looked at Mom and gave a half-smile. "You're right, Mom. I just don't know how or where to start."

"Start by telling him you want to talk to him," Regina replied.

157

Breanna nodded. If she didn't tell him the truth, he would be furious if he'd found out on his own. She had to let him know. She had to get a restraining—she had to steer clear of Nathaniel. All that piece of paper was going to do was piss him off further. Yet, he was still out there, anticipating her every move. How would she tell him without putting Isabella and Elijah in harm's way?

"Do you need a ride home?"

"No, ma'am." Breanna leaned over and hugged her stepmother. "I called Grandma Zora earlier. She should be here in about another five minutes."

"Okay, sweetheart." Mom rubbed her back. "If you need anything, Breanna, don't you dare hesitate to call me or your father."

"I won't, Mom."

Her cellphone vibrated in her hand, luring Breanna to stare at it. Grandma Zora's smile graced her screen. She didn't want Momma freaking out about why she had bruises and scrapes all over her body, so she called the one person who would chew her out and love on her at the same time. Grandma Zora.

"Hey, Grandma," Breanna said. She took her discharge papers from Mom's hands and kissed her cheek.

"Breanna, I'm outside waiting for you, baby. Are you feeling better?"

"Yes, ma'am. I am."

"Good. I made us some chicken pot pie if you're hungry."

Breanna patted her stomach as it growled. Just thinking about Grandma Zora's food made the lingering pain dissipate. "I am, Grandma. I'm on my way downstairs."

She walked out the hospital room and made her way down the hall. This was her step to recovery. This was her way back to Elijah and Isabella.

Chapter Thirty

A loud telephone ring and vibration against wood jolted Elijah from his sleep. He sat up and glimpsed around the dark room. The light from the master bathroom spread across a small portion of the floor. Droplets of sweat were speckled across his forehead. He wiped them off with the back of his hand, then rested it against the pillow. The room finally stopped spinning. He closed his eyes tight and sighed. That was the last time he was drinking whiskey.

He heard Isabella coughing from a distance and got out of bed. Elijah grabbed his phone and stared at it. 5 am gawked at him with its bold white number and lettering. He swiped down on the device, revealing the notifications. Breanna called. She hadn't been home for the past two weeks, and now she wanted to call. She wanted to talk to him like nothing ever happened. She wanted—he didn't have time to play games.

He stepped out his bedroom and entered the hall. He cracked Isabella's door open and peeped inside. She hugged her Princess Tiana doll tight as she slept. Daisy was curled up next to her. He smiled, then closed his eyes. Breanna would have been standing behind him. Her nose would have been pressed against his shoulder blade, trying to peep over it to watch Izzy sleep. He longed for that again; Elijah needed that again.

He staggered into the bedroom and took a deep breath. It was going to be a minute before the whiskey released its hold on him. He closed the door behind him and grabbed his phone off the nightstand. Elijah's brows furrowed deeper the longer he stared at it. He never thought

Breanna was this unhappy with him. He never thought she would start seeing someone else because of him. But he did nothing wrong. Elijah wanted to see his future wife and daughter healthy. He wanted to prove Gwendolyn wrong. He wanted—Elijah sighed.

He hesitated, hovering his thumb over the phone. Exhaling, he dialed her number. Each press of his digit against the touch screen played a melodic tone. He held the phone to his ear and listened to it ring.

"Eli," Breanna answered.

"Bree." He raked his fingers through his hair. "Where are you?"

"I'm—" she inhaled, then exhaled loudly. "I'm with my grandma."

"Are you okay?"

She sobbed. "I'm... not okay, Blue Eyes."

A tear rolled down his cheek. Breanna gave him that nickname when she couldn't remember his name after meeting him for the first time. But she used it so much that it became his official pet name for him. Mom and Dad would tease him about it. But he loved every moment of it until now. "What's wrong?"

"You were right about Tessa," she said. "I should have listened to you."

"What happened?"

"She hurt me."

"I'm sorry that happened, Bree," he replied, not too shocked by her statement.

"Eli, I was—" Breanna took another deep breath. "I want to talk to you."

"Bree." Elijah frowned. "You don't have to be afraid to tell me what's wrong."

She sniffled. "Where do I start?"

"By telling me the truth, Bree."

"Nathaniel... he... hit me."

Elijah gripped the phone tight as he clenched his jaws. "What? When?"

"About a week ago. Tessa watched it happen."

"She didn't call the police. She didn't help fight him off you." Elijah tightened his lips, gritting his teeth. "Was he worth that, Breanna?"

She sobbed. "He wasn't, Eli—I fucked up. I fucked up bad."

"Then let's talk about this. Can you come home now?"

"Not now."

"Why not?"

"I've got to go to work in a few more hours."

He nodded once. The frown never left his brow. "Are you playing with me, Bree?"

160

"I'm not," she spoke. "I want to set everything straight."

"Come home tonight. We can talk then."

"Elijah?"

"What, Bree?"

"Do you hate me?"

He sighed. Every fiber in his being burned to say no, but a small inkling longed to yell out yes. That was the part of him that grew tired of her and wanted to kick her ass to the curve. "No. I don't hate you. I just want to know why you did this."

"I understand," she replied. "Will Isabella be at home tonight?"

"She's going to my mom and dad's house tonight."

"Okay. I'll see you then."

"Breanna?"

"Yes, Eli."

"I love you."

"I love you too."

Another plate crashed onto the ground. Its shattered pieces scattered about the kitchen floor. Breanna glared at Tessa as she and Howard cackled in the near distance. She noticed Kelvin glaring at her former best friend, then glimpsed to Latasha, scrambling to catch the other plate sliding from the stack toppling in her arms. She was the other new hire Howard purposely looked over for training. Or a cover-up for the last three people who walked out last week during the restaurant's rush lunch hour. Breanna took a deep breath as she kneeled to collect the pieces of broken porcelain from the floor. Only one more hour, and she could fly out this joint.

"Ms. Breanna," Latasha said. She kneeled next to her with a small broom and dustpan and swept up the small, shattered pieces. "I'm so sorry about this."

Breanna looked at Latasha and smiled. "You're fine, Latasha. You needed help."

"But my help just walked out the kitchen with the boss."

She sighed. "I know."

"Ms. Breanna," Latasha said, sweeping up the last piece of the broken plate. "I really appreciate you helping me last week."

"No worries, Latasha." Breanna stood to her feet and grabbed the garbage can, dumping the shattered pieces inside. "It's the least I can do since you closed the restaurant with me last week."

Latasha pursed her lips, then looked away from her. She emptied the remaining contents of the dustpan into the garbage. "Ms. Breanna?"

Breanna stared at her with wrinkled eyebrows. "What's wrong, Latasha?"

"When you were out earlier this week, Kelvin and I overheard Tessa talking about you and your boyfriend."

Breanna leaned in closer to her. "What did she say?"

"She said that you didn't know how to please a man like him. That's why she was going to clean up what you messed up."

Breanna gripped the edge of the garbage can. "She did, huh?"

Latasha nodded. "She's even made Kelvin feel uncomfortable too. She groped his ass yesterday. I had to walk him outside to keep him from ripping her ass a new one."

Breanna gazed at Latasha, watching her lips move. The sound of her pounding heartbeat drowned out her co-worker's voice. Tessa wasn't the guru Breanna thought she was. She was the bitch tearing shit apart because she wanted what she couldn't have. How stupid could she have been?

"Excuse me, Latasha," Breanna said calmly. "I need to go handle something."

"Ms. Breanna," Latasha said, blocking her path. "What are you about to do?"

"What I've should have been listening to in the first damn place." Breanna moved past Latasha and stepped through the kitchen's double doors into the hallway leading toward the break room. She overheard Tessa's cackling from down the hall.

Bitch had some fucking nerve to laugh.

Nearing the door, Breanna frowned as she grabbed the knob. This was the same woman who watched Nathaniel beat her; this was the same woman who claimed she would always have her back. Breanna twisted the doorknob and pushed the door open.

Tessa sat on the couch with her phone pressed against her ear. She gawked at her with wide eyes. She rubbed her neck as she kept her eyes on Breanna.

"Imma call you back," Tessa said, ending the call.

"So, you've been trying to break me and Elijah up this entire time, right?"

Tessa shook her head as she stood from the couch. "Bree, that wasn't my intention. I know you didn't love him anymore, so I was just trying to help a sista out."

Breanna frowned. "Help me out. You lied to me."

"I didn't lie," she snickered. "I just told you what you wanted to hear. I was looking out for you, Bree—"

162

"Don't you even say some bullshit like that, Tessa." Breanna stood in front of her. Her frown deepened the creases in her nose and forehead. "You were the very person who I trusted, and like a fool, I let you play me."

"Didn't you have a good time with Nathaniel? Didn't he make you feel good?"

"He made me realize I had a good man at home the entire time while I was with him."

"That wasn't what you told me when you were laying in his bed before you ran back to Elijah."

The burning sting of Breanna's hand across Tessa's cheek sent her falling back onto the couch. Tessa glared at her as she held her cheek.

"Bitch, did you just slap me?"

"I got more where that came from."

Tessa sprang toward her, grabbing a handful of Breanna's hair. Panting hard, Tessa jerked her across the floor toward the table. Breanna covered her face with her forearm as she slammed the wooden piece of furniture face first. Pain and numbness radiated through her limb for a moment. Like hell, she would fall victim to this shit again.

Tessa's grimy hand latched onto her hair once more and rose her from the table. She elbowed Tessa in the stomach, then kicked her in the shin with the back of her heel. Tessa stumbled away from her, holding her stomach and grunting in pain. That was the same pain her so-called best friend watched Nathaniel inflict on her—the same anguish Tessa ignored.

Breanna turned toward Tessa and glowered at her with narrowed eyes. She inhaled and exhaled deeply. She needed to feel the never-ending pulsating ache like the way she had when Nathaniel hit her in the back of her head. Tessa needed to experience her muscles tear all at once, like the way Breanna had when Nathaniel drove his foot into her back.

She lunged toward Tessa and tackled her to the dirt-ridden black-and-white checkered board marbled floor. She gripped a handful of Tessa's hair, clenched her fist, and slammed her knuckles into her face. Breanna watched Tessa's skin redden from the pressure of her fist, hitting it repeatedly. Blood seeped from Tessa's nose. Her shriek like screams numbed Breanna's ears as she screamed out for help.

That's why Nathaniel kept hitting her. It wasn't hearing the agony; it was seeing it. He took pleasure in her pain. He bathed in it just like Tessa had.

Readying herself to punch Tessa again, a pair of arms wrapped around her waist, yanking her away from Tessa. She wrestled to get out

163

of the hold as she watched her other co-worker drag a kicking and screaming Tessa away from her and shove her into the corner of the room like she was a child.

"Master chef," Kelvin said. He pulled her out the room and held her against the wall. "You gotta calm down."

Howard and another busboy ran into the break room to get Tessa. Her feet drugged the ground as they guided Tessa out the room. Her kicks and screams were like a rabid animal trying to attack its prey. Too bad she wouldn't get a second chance at their scuffle. If Tessa did, it would have been a definite K.O. for her, for sure. Her incoherent grunts and curses resounded into the hallway from the other room.

Latasha covered her mouth. Her widened eyes spoke volumes. She glanced inside the room, then back at her. "I knew I should have gone with you, Ms. Breanna."

"I didn't want you getting involved," Breanna said. She glanced at Kelvin, then at Latasha again and sighed. "I need you to keep your job for your baby and little brother."

Latasha smiled. "Thanks for caring about me, Ms. Breanna, but you know I got your back."

"I know you do," she replied. "But I can't let you do that. Not for me anyway."

"I should fire her for letting you do something so stupid, Breanna." Howard swayed toward the three of them. The mascara he wore made his frown more dramatic. "I can't believe you would do something like this."

Breanna stepped away from Kelvin and stood in front of Howard. "Don't fire her for something I did. Just fire me instead."

He scoffed. "You're right, Breanna. I should fire you... and Latasha."

"Please, Howard," Breanna said, stepping closer to him. "I'm the one who hit Tessa. Not Latasha."

He tightened his lips as he stared at her and Latasha. He nodded. "You're right about that, too. Both of you will get extended schedules."

Latasha frowned. "But Mr. Howard, it's hard enough as it is to find a babysitter to take care of my babies."

"You shouldn't have opened ya' legs up to every bastard with a swinging piece then, honey," he replied, rolling his neck to every word he spoke.

Latasha's knuckles cracked as she clenched them in a fist. She stepped toward him, staring him down with squinted eyes. "The fuck you just say to me—"

Breanna held her arm out, keeping her away from Howard. She stared at her, then shook her head. She directed her attention back to Howard and frowned. "That was low, Howard."

164

"It's not low if it's true."

Kelvin shook his head. "Naw, boss man. That shit's low as hell. You need to apologize to Latasha for that."

Howard huffed. "Then if all of you want to be in the same boat together, that's fine by me. Now you all have extended schedules. Breanna, I'll see you at noon. Latasha and Kelvin, I'll see you here at 2 pm. Your end times will be determined tomorrow as I see fit. Comprende?"

Breanna nodded as she kept her eyes trained on him. "We do, Howard."

"Good. Now get the hell out of my restaurant."

Breanna watched Kelvin and Latasha walk inside the break room and gather their things from their respective lockers. She eyed Howard and frowned. Whenever he called her, she was there, front and center. Whenever an employee fucked up a customer's order, she was there to soothe things over. Whenever Howard called in because he wanted a little playtime with the guy he was messing off with, Breanna was there to cover for him. Now, this?

"Why are you just standing there, Breanna?" Howard stared at her as he folded his arms across his chest.

Breanna gave a half-smile. "Nothing."

"Are you sure?"

"I'm positive," Breanna said. She walked back into the break room, opened her locker, and grabbed her purse. Elijah was right. It was time for her to leave this place. Hell, she should have thrown her twos like Leslie did weeks ago, but she needed to line some things up before she left. Breanna sighed. Why didn't she listen to Elijah sooner?

She stepped out the room and felt Howard's glare burn her skin as she strode past him. Had this been two months ago, she would have been running to him and Tessa to complain about what Elijah had done to her; what she was going to do if Elijah kept acting like a bitch. Well, who was the bitch now?

She trekked past the dining customers. Their eyes reverted to her as she kept her attention focused on the double doors ahead of her. A rather tall man sat at a table in the center of the restaurant by himself. He was the only one who kept his eyes on her as she walked. Looking toward his way, she noticed him nod. He smiled as he softly clapped his hands. She smiled at him, returning his nod. He wasn't just some ordinary customer. That man was somebody of great importance.

The way he would sit upright in his seat with one leg crossed over the other. The way he would place his salad and dinner fork adjacent to each other when she served him. The way he would tap either side of his mouth with his napkin after consuming a slice of cake or beignet.

He was more than just a foodie. He was a man who could make or break Howard's restaurant. He was, she hoped, the man that was going to teach Howard a valuable lesson.

Breanna walked out the door. The night's calm spring winds brushed against her cheek. The melodies of a nightingale made her smile while he strode to her car. A pair of headlights blinded her for a moment, then turned off. She frowned, scoping out the area. The sound of a cranking engine caught her attention. The lights flashed on and off again. Its familiar hum made her eyes widen. That couldn't have been him.

Her phone rang. Nathaniel's name panned across the screen. Breanna unlocked her car as she ran toward it. A white SUV drove behind her, forcing her to run faster.

Why the hell did you have to park so far away?

Breanna panted. How did Nathaniel know she was working tonight? She hadn't spoken to him since the—Tessa. That's who she was on the phone with. That bitch had planned this mess from the jump. The piercing sounds of screeching tires, clanking steel, and the smell of hot smoking rubber made her look back. She placed her hand over her heart, then jumped into her car. Thank God for people who didn't know how to drive while inebriated.

She watched Nathaniel glare at her as she cranked her car and sped off the parking lot. He wasn't done with her. She knew he wasn't. God, what had she gotten herself into?

Chapter Thirty-One

What the fuck had she gotten herself into? Breanna wiped a streaming tear away from her cheek. Those cognac brown eyes of Nathaniel's hid the seething, fire-breathing monster waiting behind them. Never in her life had she been kicked and shoved by a man until now. Elijah never drew his fist at her. Elijah.

Thunder clapped in the distance. She pushed her foot on the gas pedal, hoping to keep as much distance between her and Nathaniel. That fender-bender saved her ass. Yet that didn't mean he wasn't still out looking for her. Maybe it didn't hold him back as much as she'd hoped, or fear had taken over her brain completely.

She guessed the rain helped disguise her black car. But even that, too, would have been a failed attempt if he pulled up behind her. Noticing a car pull up beside her, Breanna held her breath, praying to God it wasn't Nathaniel. Raindrops the size of quarters splashed onto her windshield as she kept her eyes trained on the vehicle driving past her. She gripped the wheel tighter and exhaled. She had to get herself out of this mess.

Elijah had nothing to do with her now, especially since Morgan made it her every waking moment to be in their business. The bitch had some nerves. But deep down inside, Breanna didn't blame her. She allowed the one man who had given himself to her relentlessly to finally say he was ready to kick her ass to the curve.

Raheem DeVaughn's voice blared through the car's cabin. Tessa was the last person she wanted to speak to. After she sat and watched Nathaniel beat her and then professed how she would snatch Elijah up,

Breanna saw Tessa for who she was—a thirsty whore waiting for someone else's sloppy seconds. She was the one woman who was supposed to have her back when she was the one woman trying to stab it.

Breanna sniffled. Leslie felt stabbed in the back by her own best friend, too. Karma snuck its way into her life and pile drove it. Hell, she deserved it.

"Okay, Google," Breanna said, wiping away her tears. "Call Elijah."

"Calling Elijah Bryson," the woman's voice responded.

She listened to the phone ring until it went to voicemail. That was the same from Amber and Leslie when she called them. No word from her best friend. No word from her sister. And now, Elijah. No one wanted to speak to her. No one wanted to hear her bullshit ass lies. Had she listened to him when he tried to apologize to her at the counseling session, Breanna would have been in a better spot than this. She came to a stop at a red light and covered her mouth, sobbing aloud.

"I'm so stupid," she muttered to herself.

Her cellphone rang. An unknown number flashed on the screen. That could have been anyone, or it could have been Nathaniel toying with her again. She drove toward the park's entrance and pulled into the dark parking lot. Breanna surveyed her surroundings, making sure no other cars followed her. She turned off her headlights and exhaled. The phone rang again. Whoever this person was, they weren't giving up.

"Hello," Breanna answered, hoping it wasn't Nathaniel on the other end.

"Bree," Elijah breathed.

Breanna's heart raced. "Elijah?"

"Yeah, it's me," he replied. "My battery died, so I had to use my business phone."

Breanna sighed. "Are you still at home?"

"I am, Bree. I was hoping..." he paused. "You were still coming home so... we could talk."

"Breanna grazed her teeth against her bottom lip. "I can come home."

"I'll see you when you get here."

"Eli—" The phone call ended. Seven years and Elijah was never short with her; he never yelled or raised his hand at her. He chose the road less traveled when dealing with her. But never did he explode in rage. She changed all that.

She turned on her headlights and drove off the lot. She made a right turn onto the dark street and drove. She sat in silence while driving through another green light. Maybe he finally wanted to get full custody

168

of Isabella. Or perhaps he wanted to rekindle his relationship with Morgan. It would hurt like hell, but it was better knowing now than not at all.

Breanna made a left turn into their neighborhood and sped down the street. Her heart drummed against her chest. What would she say to him after not coming home for weeks? Hell, how would she respond to her? She pulled into the driveway and pressed the garage key opener, waiting for the giant door to lift. Breanna saw Elijah's big red Chevy pickup and parked next to it. She took a deep inhale, then exhaled slowly. She couldn't face him. Not now. She had pulled this man through troughs of mud and muck. The last thing she wanted to do to him was break him.

Breanna pressed the button to lower the garage door, got out the car, and walked inside the house. The light in the mudroom guided her through the dark hallway. She trekked carefully in the dark, hoping she wouldn't step on Daisy's tail. The lamp in the family room gave her enough light to walk with ease as she neared its entrance.

Breanna noticed Elijah's silhouette sitting on the couch as she walked inside. No telling how long he had been sitting there. It was a good thing Izzy went to Mrs. Lori and Mr. Jonah's house; she would have freaked out seeing her daddy sitting in the dark.

"Elijah," Breanna said, switching on the main light. She sat next to him on the chocolate-colored sofa. She noticed another tattoo on his inner left arm.

He stared at her for a moment, then looked at the black television screen. "Breanna."

"When did you get that?" She pointed at the tattoo.

"When did you start caring about me?"

"I've always cared about you, Eli," Breanna retorted.

He scoffed. "Bullshit, Bree."

She eyeballed the shot glass sitting on the ottoman. Elijah wasn't much of a drinker, especially of the heavier liquors. He hated the heated, prickly sensations that trailed his spine whenever he did. She guessed tonight he needed it.

"Are you drunk, Eli?"

He stared at her and smirked. "Well, thanks for caring about me, Bree, but I only had one shot."

Breanna looked at the black television screen and stood to her feet. "I should probably leave."

He grabbed her by the bruise resting on her arm and stood to his feet, noticing her wince. He frowned. "Did I hurt you?"

"It wasn't you." She rubbed her arm.

169

"Did he hurt you again?" Elijah cupped her chin with his thumb and index finger. His touch made her close her eyes. A tear fell upon his hand.

"His response was my fault. I made him do this—"

"He should have never put his hands on you, Bree. Don't you dare take up for him." Elijah interrupted. He walked away from her, raking his fingers through his hair. "Of all the crap we've been putting each other through for the past two months, was it worth you getting hurt by some man you cheated on me with, Bree? Was it?"

Breanna narrowed her eyes. A nagging pain lingered above her eye. "I never slept with Nathaniel," she snapped. Tears streamed down her cheeks. "I couldn't."

Elijah stiffened. The crease in his brows lessened. "Why?"

"Because it wasn't you, Elijah," she sobbed, wiping her eyes. "Every time I kissed him, I saw you. Every time I lied next to him in his bed, I thought of you—I was wrong for what I did to you." She turned from him, burying her face in her hands.

Elijah stood behind her, hesitating to touch her shoulders. He let his arms fall to his sides, then looked away. "You did this because of me."

Breanna's tears ceased. She saw a single tear stream down his cheek as she turned to meet Elijah's face.

He stared into her eyes. "You're a strong, beautiful black woman that didn't need the likes of a white man putting you in a position of powerlessness, Breanna. I'm sorry."

She slumped to the sofa in tears. She covered her face with both hands again and cried. "You don't need to apologize to me," she mustered. "I was too pigheaded to see what you were trying to do for me and Isabella. We are alive and well because of you."

"That doesn't change the fact I kept you down," Elijah said, sitting behind her. He wrapped his arms around her waist and rested his head on her shoulder. "I fell in love with your strength and beauty. I'm ashamed I kept you from being strong, from being who God made you to be."

"Elijah," Breanna whispered. "That doesn't excuse what I did to you. I'm worthless—"

"Don't say that," he said, holding her tighter in his arms. Feeling her arm, he glided his fingertips across her skin, barely touching the bruise. "Can I see your arm?"

Breanna nodded. She watched him roll up the sleeve of her white blouse and survey the blueish black mark Nathaniel imprinted upon her. His fingers slid across the tender redness surrounding the mark again, demanding his attention.

"I've got a medical kit in the bathroom upstairs," he said. "You made me buy it a year ago, remember."

"I remember," Breanna replied. A smile tugged at her lips.

He stood from the sofa and gestured for her to take his hand. Elijah stared at her knuckles as she placed her hand into his. A frown darkened his steel-blue eyes. "What happened to your hands, Bree?"

"I guess I forgot to mention I got into a fight with Tessa tonight too."

He chuckled. "Are you serious?"

"She had that shit coming."

"But from you, Bree?"

"Like I said, Eli, she had that coming to her."

He smiled, pulling her from the couch. He guided her toward the stairs, still holding onto her hand. Every step, every anticipated breath, reminded her of the first time they made love in this house. The kitchen, the stairwell, the wall in the hallway upstairs. Every area of this house became their bedroom. But that was no longer a fact. What she did to him shifted the house into a battleground.

Breanna followed Elijah into the bedroom and watched him switch on the bedroom light, leading her into an already lit master bathroom. She stood against the wall, waiting for his next move. He looked through the bottom cabinets and pulled out the medical kit. Elijah opened a bottle, a roll of brown wrap, and some IcyHot. "Come here." He beckoned for her to come closer to him.

Breanna stood in front of him, staring into his steel-blue eyes. His beard had grown since the last time she saw him.

"Take off your shirt," he said.

She nodded, unbuttoning the blouse and letting the garment fall to the floor. She stood in her black bra, work slacks, and flats, trying to maintain her composure and not jump his bones.

The stroke of his fingers against her skin made her suck in a breath. The coolness of the cream and warmth of his fingers waged a minor war upon her skin, sending goose pimples down her forearms.

"I'm almost done," Elijah said, wrapping the thin material around her arm. He turned on the water and washed his hands of the pungent ointment. He stared into her eyes, pulling her closer to him. The bulge in his sweatpants pressed against her abdomen. His fingers slid between her shoulder blades like a trickle of water against glass.

Breanna reached for his loose tank top, pulled it over his head, and let it fall to the ground in a heap. His lips pressed against hers, making her moan against them. "I love you," she whispered.

Elijah gazed into her eyes and smiled. "I love you too."

He kissed her deeper as his hand slid down her torso and into her pants. The warmth of his fingers moved past her panties and pressed against her clit, massaging it slowly. She sucked in a breath as she closed her eyes.

"I want these off," he whispered against her ear.

As Elijah unbuttoned and unzipped her pants, Breanna kissed the center of his chest. She ran her fingers over one of his nipples, then replaced it with her tongue. Breanna heard him suck in a breath. His fingers tilt her chin to meet his lips once more. He kissed her and allowed his tongue to play with hers.

"I want you," he breathed against her lips. He pulled her pants down her hips and hoisted her onto the vanity, spreading her legs to accommodate his shaft. He unclasped her bra and tossed it to the ground. Elijah caressed her nipple. It rose under his caress.

He ran his hands through her hair as he kissed her and sucked on her neck. The wetness of his tongue gliding against her neck nearly made her orgasm. "Do you want me out of these?"

Breanna nodded, already unraveling the strings to his pants. She slid them down his hips and watched them pool around his ankles. He stepped out of the sweat pants. His black boxer briefs seemed too small to house the bulge that nearly spilled out of them.

He stared at her black French lace underwear. A wry smile tugged at the corner of his lips. "Are you attached to these?" Elijah asked, tugging at them.

"I am," she breathed. "Please don't—"

"—Too bad." He ripped the thin material in half with one try. His muscles remained tensed.

There were times Elijah reminded her he didn't need to show off his strength; his strength spoke for itself. Whenever he threw old tubs out of windows, hauled run down cabinets out of kitchens, and carried stacks of wood plies on his shoulders into the houses he and AJ rebuilt, he did it with modesty. Then, there were times where raw strength showed itself—that was the strength she delighted herself in seeing because she knew it would never end with just one round.

Elijah pulled her closer to feel all of him as he rubbed his fingers against her clit again, making her wetter. God, this man knew how to work her clit.

Breanna moaned as she bit her bottom lip. She watched as he sunk between her thighs. The inviting pressing of his tongue made her gasp. Its thick wetness tickled her throbbing clit. Her body jerked from his long cat like strokes. She had to compose herself, hoping she wouldn't orgasm too soon. She grabbed his hair as her breathing labored. "Oh, God! Elijah."

He kissed and sucked on her outer lips, making her climax. "Sounded like you enjoyed that?" He asked, standing in between her thighs again.

She nodded, trying to compose herself. It wasn't working. Breanna watched as he stood back from her, slid his underwear down his hips, and let his length tantalize her mind and body. He smiled, placing himself back between her thighs.

"Tell me now if you want to stop," he said. He stared into her eyes, intertwining his fingers with hers.

Breanna kept her eyes locked on his and nodded.

Elijah stroked his length with her wetness, lubricating it as he kissed her. He entered her, keeping his lips on hers. Breanna wrapped her arms around his shoulders and buried her face in his neck as he thrusted. She moaned, wrapping her legs around his waist. She gazed into his eyes and kissed him once more. With every thrust, his length reached her G-spot, teasing it. She groaned his name louder, making him rotate his hips as he pushed his length within her faster.

Elijah slowed his pace, making her dig her nails into his shoulder blades. He pulled her closer to the edge of the vanity, deepening his thrusts. He moaned against her lips as he kissed her. Sweat rolled from his forehead onto her collarbone. He threw his head back and groaned as he quickened his pace.

She moaned aloud. His body invaded her senses, causing her to clench her vaginal walls too soon. For once, she wanted to match his stamina instead of waiting for the next round to ensue. She felt his hand press against the small of her back—the one spot he knew he could get her to climax a waterfall.

"I'm so close," Breanna breathed. "I'm about to—" she moaned, feeling her essence roll down her inner ass cheek.

He lifted her from the vanity while still inside her and walked her into the bedroom. He laid her on the bed and started his endeavor all over again. "You know I've got more where that came from," he smiled.

Breanna gripped the bedsheets and closed her eyes. She knew he didn't care how many times he made her climax. As long as he made her moan his name first, that was all that mattered to him. Elijah slowed his hips and rotated them once more, making his length vibrate against her G-spot.

Breanna bit her bottom lip, savoring every moment of pleasurable torture. She watched Elijah shift to his knees as he placed one of her legs on his shoulder. Breanna sucked in a breath, then moaned louder, feeling his length in her stomach. He quickened his pace, forcing her to arch her back. She watched Elijah close his eyes and threw his head back once more, moaning her name. Breanna loved to hear him call her name as he neared his peak. The way he would groan, then breathe deeply before sucking in a breath would make her orgasm twice before he climaxed. He knew how to keep her anticipating for more. He lowered himself to meet her lips and kissed them.

Breanna wrapped her legs around his waist again as he intertwined his fingers with hers. He buried his face in her neck and kissed it. His labored breathing made her vaginal walls clench around his length once more. Elijah moaned. She knew he couldn't hold on any longer.

He kissed her, then gazed into her eyes. "Cum for me, baby," he moaned.

"Elijah," she panted. "I'm all yours." Wave after wave of vibrations coursed through her body as she screamed through her climax.

He held her hands tight as he groaned and trembled after climaxing inside of her. His breathing labored against her neck. "I love you, Bree."

"I love you too, Blue Eyes."

He smiled. "I love it when you call me that," he said. Elijah slid out of her and laid next to her, pulling the cover over them both.

"I've missed you, Eli," she hesitated. "I've—"

"—Let's not ruin the moment, Bree," he said. He kissed her forehead.

She looked away from him. "We can't always avoid the subject, Eli."

"You're right. We can't always avoid it, but we can start working on getting us right."

Tears welled in her eyes. Why couldn't she have tried working with him the first time instead of running back to Nathaniel? Why couldn't she have listened to Elijah when he tried to apologize? She sniffled. All of this happened because of her. Whether she wanted to take the blame or not, Breanna was the reason they were at this moment. "How do we fix us?"

He kissed her forehead once more. "One day at a time, pray a lot more, continue our couples' counseling," he replied. "All I know is that I can't see myself with anyone else but you."

"Eli—"

"Marry me, Breanna."

"But Elijah, what happens when we can't work shit out?"

"Tell me what marriage is perfect, and I'll get us set up to visit them in the morning ASAP."

She sighed. "I'm not the woman you fell in love with seven years ago."

"You've changed," Elijah said. "So, have I. That still doesn't change the fact I want you to be my wife."

"And if I hurt you again?"

"We'll work through it, Bree." He stared into her eyes. Reaching over her head, he grabbed a small black box off the nightstand. He opened it, pulling out a small gold ring with a small butterfly in place where a diamond should have been. He slid it on her finger and held her hand against his cheek. "You don't have to answer me now. I would rather you think about this."

Breanna lost herself in his steel-blue eyes. As much as she wanted to scream yes and jump on top of him like those women did in those romance movies she watched too much of, she couldn't. Breanna couldn't force herself to say yes, knowing the other man she started a relationship with wouldn't allow her to say yes.

Elijah was right. They needed to fix them, but she needed to fix herself more than she ever thought she needed to.

Chapter Thirty-Two

His warmth was still present where Elijah once laid. The subtle drizzle of falling water hitting tile soothed her ears. She smiled as she inhaled the tangy yet subtly sweet smell of lemon and mint. Breanna pulled the comforter and bedspread over her exposed breasts and snuggled her nose against the softness of her half plump half flat pillow. It had been a long time since she felt comfortable being in Elijah's embrace again. Maybe things were getting back on track.

"Bree," Elijah called from the master bathroom. "What time do you have to be in at work today?"

Breanna rose from the bed and grabbed her cellphone from the nightstand. She stared at the clock, watching 10:35 flash to 10:36 am. She sighed. Twelve o'clock was coming way too fast.

"I've got to go in at noon."

"Really?" Elijah said from afar. "When did Howard change your start time?"

"When I beat up his bestie." Breanna stood from the bed in the nude and sashayed across the room. Her small breasts and plump ass jiggled as he walked toward the dresser. Opening it, she heard a deep, muffled rattle on wood. She glanced at Elijah's cellphone, noticing he'd never charged it. He has a sheer hatred for that phone.

She heard the rattle again as she pulled on a white tank top and a pair of black boyshorts. She frowned. He said his battery died on his phone. How in the hell was it still working after not being charged through the night?

Breanna closed her eyes and sighed. Maybe that was his work phone. She heard the muffled rattle again, then walked toward his nightstand and glared at it. Morgan's name scrolled across the screen. She'd texted him three times.

They were business partners. Morgan had all the right to call, scream, rant, and curse about how the business was and wasn't going. She couldn't stop her from calling or texting. Breanna understood that, but something didn't sit right with her. Something felt off.

Elijah's phone illuminated before her eyes, displaying Morgan's latest text on the screen. Breanna touched the device and woke it, sending it directly to its messages.

Morgan: Morning, Sunshine. You never texted me back last night about our date. Are you good for tonight?

Breanna closed her eyes and took a deep breath. So, now he was doing the same thing she had done to him. She deserved this. After the hell she put him through, Breanna knew it was a possibility he could have been seeing someone, too. But Morgan, of all people? Better yet, date last night?

Elijah strode into the bedroom with a towel wrapped around his waist and a bright smile on his face. Water dripped from the tip ends of his hair onto his back and chest. But when he noticed Breanna glaring at him, his smile faded to solemness.

"Bree, what's wrong?"

She folded her arms across her chest. "So, you were supposed to go on a date with Morgan last night, right?"

He scoffed. "Date?"

"Yes, Eli. A date with Morgan. Your ex-girlfriend, current business partner. You do the math."

Elijah took a deep breath as he rubbed his temple. "I was going to meet her and a couple of her friends at the bar for a drink, but I didn't want to go."

"Are you being serious with me right now, Elijah?"

"Bree," Elijah said, coughing. He rubbed his chest, then took a deep breath. "It wasn't that kind of date. Why can't you get that through your head?"

"Because you're no better than I am."

Elijah looked away from her, tightened his lips, and nodded. "I'm no better than you, huh?"

"I can't believe you would pull some shit like this."

"Oh my God!" he huffed. "Woman, I don't know where the fuck you get your logic from, but going to the bar with a friend is nothing compared to laying up in another person's bed."

177

Breanna laughed sarcastically. "I can't believe you would judge me, Eli."

"You cheated on me, Breanna. How the fuck do you justify that?"

"I won't stand here and try to justify that. I know I'm wrong, but you can't have it both ways either, and you know that."

"I'm not trying to have it both ways, Bree." Elijah glared into her brown eyes. "I'm trying to work things out with you."

Breanna walked to her side of the dresser and opened it. She pulled out her black slacks and white blouse, then turned toward Elijah and frowned at him. "Then why in the hell is Morgan begging to go out with you, then?"

"I told you, Bree. We only had drinks before. That was it."

"But a date, Elijah?"

"You know what," Elijah spoke. "I don't know why I even try with you, anyway. You think everything is my fault in the first fucking place, so you might as well go back to Nathaniel and get your ass beat again."

"Fuck you!" Breanna yelled.

He nodded as he smiled wryly. "Give me my ring back."

Breanna slid the ring off her finger and tossed it at his feet. She slid on her black slacks and pulled on her white blouse over her tank top. "I don't know what I was thinking to even accept it."

"Take your ass somewhere else, Bree." Elijah sat on the bed, rubbing his chest. "I'm sick of you, anyway."

"You're sick of me, Eli," Breanna said, pointing at herself. "You've got some nerves—"

"Get the fuck out of my house, woman!"

Breanna stared at him with narrowed eyes. A scowl she'd never seen before darkened his steel-blue eyes. She slid on her black flats, grabbed her cellphone off the nightstand, and marched out of the bedroom. She ran down the steps, then made her way down the hall toward the garage. Why did she even think she could go back to normalcy with Elijah again? Why?

Breanna slammed the door behind her and opened her car door, hopping inside it. She gripped the steering wheel, then rested her head on it.

"What the fuck did I just do?" she muttered to herself.

Reaching for her keys inside her purse, she cranked her car, then opened the garage door. She backed out the driveway and sped down the street. A tear slid down her cheek. She'd never in her life heard Elijah talk to her the way he did just now. Hell, even the way he stared at her made him seem like he was a completely different person. Breanna exhaled raggedly, trying to restrain her tears. This was still her fault.

As she brought her car to a halt at a red light, she reached for her phone. Highlighting a list of names, she found Dr. Shelby's number and dialed it. She listened to the phone ring as she waited for the light to turn green.

"This is Dr. Hampton speaking," she answered.

"Dr. Shelby." Breanna cleared her throat as she drove through the green light. "This is Breanna Ellis."

"Ms. Ellis. It's good to hear from you."

"Can I have a session with you tomorrow?" She squinted through the tears as she turned right onto another street.

"Sure," Dr. Hampton said. "It's ahead of schedule, but I can fit you in. One of my other clients had to cancel because he's going to his ex-wife's wedding, so you know how that goes and all."

"I fucked up."

"Ms. Ellis, what's wrong?"

"Elijah proposed to me last night, but we got into an argument this morning. I think I just ruined what we had."

"Ms. Ellis," Dr. Hampton said. "First, you need to take a deep breath and then clear your mind."

Breanna took a deep breath. She turned left into Soul Bistro's parking lot and parked her car. She noticed Tessa's car from a distance.

"Now, take your time and tell me what you said to him."

Another tear slid down her cheek. "I noticed a text on his phone. It was Morgan. She wanted to go out with him, and I think I may have taken things out of context."

"Okay," Dr. Hampton sighed. "I think we need to talk about thinking things through before jumping to conclusions, Ms. Ellis."

"You're probably sick of me by now."

"Why would you think that, Ms. Ellis?"

"Because everyone I've hurt is sick of me. Elijah. Amber. Leslie. Isabella. My stepmother. My dad. They hate me, Dr. Shelby."

"They don't hate you, Breanna," she stated. "They just want the best for you. And I'm not sick of you. I only want to help you. That's why I insisted."

She covered her mouth with her hand and sobbed. "I'm a mess."

"No, you're not a mess, Ms. Ellis. You're a work in progress."

Chapter Thirty-Three

Why couldn't Breanna just listen for once and not be so damn stubborn to reason with? Why couldn't she think things through before opening her mouth? Elijah took another painful, deep breath as he rubbed his chest. Just one more day until payday, and he was on his way to buying another inhaler for both him and Isabella. Had Breanna been thinking more about her family than herself, he wouldn't have been so bent and twisted out of shape. So much for depending on a woman who cheated on him.

He took a single pump of forced air into his lungs, hoping that would stave off the festering asthma, kicking and shoving away at his inner workings. He closed his eyes and took another deep breath. It wasn't so painful this time.

He stared at the ring in the palm of his hand and clenched his fingers around it. The one woman he believed was his one ripped his heart into shreds. He just couldn't understand why he put up with her shit this long. He sighed. That was his granddad through and through. That man believed in fighting hard for what he loved. Even if it weren't meant for him, Granddad Cameron strove after it anyway for a different result. He guessed Dad was right, too. If her love was worth fighting for, he couldn't give up on her. He and Granddad were cut from the same thread of cloth.

Still, Elijah knew he had to let Breanna go at some point. Or did he just need to work a little harder at making her understand? He raked his fingers through his wet hair and stood from the bed. He walked toward his phone, grabbed it off the nightstand, and stared at it.

Breanna's beautiful smile stared back at him, pleading for him not to stop fighting for her.

Elijah dialed her number and placed the phone against his ear, listening to it ring. He sighed as he heard her voice mailbox answer for her for the third time. "Bree, I think we need to sit down and talk like adults. Call me back when you can, okay. I love you."

Elijah placed the phone on the nightstand again and made his way to the dresser. He wheezed, then put his hand on his chest, trying to catch his breath. He took another pump of forced air into his lungs and cleared his throat. It was a relief for the moment, but Elijah knew he needed more to combat this looming attack.

As he heard his phone ring, Elijah yanked it off the piece of wooden furniture. "Hello."

"Hey, Daddy," Isabella sang. "Gigi and I made breakfast for you if you want some."

He mustered a smile. "Thanks, Shortcake, but Daddy's not hungry right now."

"Daddy," Isabella spoke. "You don't sound like you feel so well."

"I'm okay, Shortcake."

"Are you sure?"

Elijah coughed, then wheezed a bit. He cleared his throat again. "I'm sure."

"Okay, Daddy," she said hesitantly. "Gigi wants to speak to you."

He dragged his hand over his face as he heard Isabella hand the phone over to Mom.

"Eli," Mom said. "Are you okay? Do you want me to drop off Izzy and your breakfast?"

"I'm good, Mom."

"Do you have any more inhalers?"

He paused, knowing Mom was going to be able to tell he was about to lie. "I'm good, Mom."

"Don't lie to me, Eli."

"I only have one left," Elijah sighed. "I get paid on Friday, so I should be fine."

"Do you want me to buy your inhaler? I can if you need me to."

"Mom, you don't have to." He put the phone on speaker and then placed it back on the nightstand. Elijah pulled on some blue boxer shorts and grabbed a pair of jeans from the top dresser drawer. He pulled them on, then stumbled backward. It was getting worse with every step he took. He rubbed his chest. That old familiar tightness clenched it again. God! He didn't need this right now. "It's just taking a little longer than normal for my asthma to subside."

"Where's Breanna?"

181

"She's at work, Mom."

"Damn it," she huffed under her breath. "You may need to go to the hospital. You sound out of breath."

"I'm okay, Mom."

"Okay," Mom said. "But that doesn't mean that I won't buy you an inhaler, understand."

"I understand, Mom."

"Good," Lori replied. "I'm going to drop Izzy off at the house on my way to the pharmacy, okay."

"Okay, Mom."

"I love you, my son."

"I love you too, Mom."

Elijah ended the call. He noticed another text from Morgan and mustered a smile. She wanted to know if he was okay, it read. She wanted to see if she could stop by and check on him if he didn't answer soon. Elijah sighed. He wanted to call Breanna again. He wanted to work things out with her, but the continuous calls and voice messages wouldn't change a thing if she didn't answer them. Elijah picked up the phone and responded.

Elijah: Hey, Morgan. You can stop by tonight.

Morgan: It's good to hear from you, Sunshine. What time do you want me to swing by?

Elijah: You can come by around five or six.

Morgan: Great! I'll be there to harass you at 5:30. See ya' then, Sunshine.

Still staring at the phone, he redialed Breanna's number. He listened to it go to voicemail, then rubbed his chest once more. "Breanna, I want us to work through this. Call me back. Please."

Elijah coughed harder, feeling his lungs constrict as he breathed deeply. He grabbed hold of his chest. Tightness seized it for a moment, then released after taking another pump of forced air into his lungs. This was going to be a long day. A very long one.

Chapter Thirty-Four

E very time daddy coughed, he struggled to breathe. And with every breath he took, he wheezed louder and louder. Isabella noticed him as he placed his hand against the island to catch his breath again. That was the third time she witnessed him do that. She'd never seen him so bad off. Didn't Mommy know about Daddy's asthma today? Didn't she even care anymore?

She sat on the couch beside Daisy and rubbed her head. She heard Daddy cough again. This time, it sounded like he coughed up an old hairball that had been stuck in his throat for ages. She closed her eyes and took a deep breath. This was her fault. If her stupid asthma hadn't flared up a week ago, there would have been enough medicine to go around for them both.

Why did Daddy have to share his inhalers with her now, anyway? Didn't that pretty lady care enough to help him buy the inhalers he worked for? She tightened her lips at the thought. Maybe she and Mommy had something in common. Maybe they only liked Daddy, but they didn't love him enough to care about his needs.

She couldn't understand why some women like those two only cared about their own needs. That wasn't the kind of person she wanted to grow up to be.

"Daddy," Isabella called. She stood from the couch and walked into the kitchen. She watched him as he sat at the island and rubbed his chest. "Are you okay?"

Elijah turned toward her and mustered a smile. His skin had become red as he took a deep breath. "I'm not feeling so hot right now, but Daddy will be okay. I promise."

"Are you sure?"

He nodded. "I'm sure, Shortcake."

"Do you feel like watching Duck Tales with me?"

"Are these the old ones or new ones?" He mustered to smile again.

Isabella placed her hand on her hip and grinned. "The old ones, Daddy. Only Mommy and I watch the newer ones."

She watched the smile fade from his lips as he stood to his feet. "Daddy, where's Mommy at now?"

"She's at work, Shortcake," he breathed. Daddy stumbled into the living room, then placed his hand on the back of the couch as he held his chest, panting through loud wheezes. "Izzy... call for...."

Elijah hit the floor with a thud. He grabbed at his throat as he fought to breathe. Isabella kneeled beside him and stared into his wide eyes. He stared into her eyes as he tried to speak. A tear rolled down the side of his face.

"Call... Mommy," he breathed raggedly.

She watched him fight to breathe as he rolled to his side. As Daddy tried to stand to his feet, he slumped to the floor. He held his throat as his eyes fluttered shut.

"Daddy!" Isabella screamed. Tears streamed down her cheeks. She shook his shoulder, hoping to make him stir. "Daddy! Please stay awake."

He stared into her eyes tiredly. "I... love... you... Izzy."

"Daddy?" Isabella shook his shoulder again. He never moved. "Daddy, please!"

She peered around the open area. Tear stains lined her cheeks as she stared at the only parent she had left in her life. "Help!"

She whimpered aloud. "Somebody, help!"

She heard Daddy's phone sound off upstairs, then sprang up from her father's side. Isabella dashed up the stairs. Daddy's phone lit up with a notification, then went black as it sat on the nightstand. She snatched it off the wooden piece of furniture, woke it up, and dialed Mommy's number as quickly as she could.

"Please, Mommy," she cried, listening to the phone ring. "You've got to pick up."

"I'm not currently available at the moment, but if you leave your name and your number, I'll get back to you as soon as I can. Bye."

"Mommy, you've got to come home. Daddy's having a really bad asthma attack. He can't breathe. Please, Mommy!"

She noticed the inhaler on the dresser and grabbed it. She ran downstairs. Daddy was still unresponsive. She noticed Daisy licking the side of his face and kneeled next to him. Isabella shook his shoulder again, waiting for him to move. But he never did. She pushed him onto his back, then heard a strained wheeze emit through his parted lips. He was still fighting to breathe. Maybe she could wake him up.

Isabella shook his shoulder. "Daddy! Wake up! Daddy! Please! Wake up!"

She redialed Mommy's number, waiting for her to answer. All she got was another prompt to leave a voicemail. "Mommy! Please pick up! Daddy's not moving anymore. He needs you, Mommy. Please help."

She frowned. Mommy wouldn't save Daddy. She had to realize that. Whatever was going on with her, she chose it over them. Isabella hoped Mommy was happy with her decision.

She dialed Auntie Amber's number and put the phone on speaker as she tried to shake Daddy awake again.

"Hello, my little munchkin—," Amber sang.

"Auntie Amber," Isabella said, hurriedly.

"Izzy? What's wrong?"

"It's Daddy," she cried. "He won't wake up, Auntie Amber."

"Fuck! Does he have anything in his inhaler?" Amber asked.

Isabella shook the inhaler, hearing nothing in response to her action. She pouted aloud. This was all her fault for sure. Daddy must have given his last drop to her when he needed it more than she did. "No. It's empty, Auntie."

"Oh my God! Listen, I'm about twenty minutes out, Izzy. Have you called your momma yet?"

"I have, Auntie. She won't answer the phone. Daddy said she was at work."

"Gawd damn it, Breanna!" Amber hissed. "Okay, I'm going to get there as quick as I can. Right now, I need you to be a big girl and call 9-1-1."

"Okay, Auntie Amber."

"Alright, sweetie, call them now."

As she ended the call with Auntie Amber, she heard several hard knocks at the front door. She stared at the large wooden slab as she wiped her eyes, then back at her daddy; Isabella didn't want to leave him lying on the floor by himself, but this was her only attempt at getting help. She stood to her feet and ran toward the door and opened it. This would have been a no-no for her to do if Mommy and Daddy saw her doing this, but Mommy wasn't around, and Daddy didn't have much time left.

She stared into the pretty lady's eyes. Tears continued to stream down both her cheeks. She must have heard him fall, Isabella wondered.

"Hey, pretty girl. What's wrong?" Morgan asked, cocking her head to the side like a playful puppy.

"My Daddy..." Isabella stammered. She pointed to him. "He won't wake up."

Morgan saw Elijah's limp body lying on the ground and covered her mouth. "Oh my God! What happened?"

"Daddy had an asthma attack. Please help him." Isabella said through hiccupping tears and whimpers. Tears streamed down her cheeks one by one. She watched the pretty lady run over to him, kneel beside him, and place her ear on his chest.

"Your daddy still has a pulse, but we've got to move quick. Call 9-1-1 now."

Isabella nodded as she wiped the tears from her eyes. Her fingers trembled as she dialed the three most important numbers she never thought she would ever dial. She couldn't lose Daddy; he was the only actual parent she had left in her life now that Mommy had left them. Whatever Mommy left them for, she hoped Mommy loved it more than she did them because Isabella no longer loved her. She just couldn't anymore.

8:45 pm stared at Breanna from a distance. Time couldn't have gone much slower than it was at the moment. She rubbed the back of her neck and wiggled her feet, trying to stop her limbs from creaking and aching. Between Howard's constant checking to see if they had their cell phones out after he threatened to fire them if he saw them out and Tessa's constant snooping around them so she could run and tell Howard if she saw them using them, she couldn't get a break. But that was a matter to be expected from those two now. Even more so, it was a matter of how long she was going to stand for their never-ending pile of smoking crap.

Breanna walked inside the kitchen and looked at Latasha and Kelvin as they slaved away over the stack of dishes Tessa kept bringing in for them to wash. Since Howard gave Mr. Sinclair and Ms. Olive the night off, she guessed he could place all the work on two people, knowing full well it was a Thursday night. Three people couldn't do all the work by themselves to feed over sixty people. Nope. Howard did it because he knew he would eventually make them get on their knees and grovel for him to make the torture stop. That was going to be the other way around.

"Hey, Ms. Breanna," Latasha said, looking in her direction. "I kept an eye on your phone for a while, but I had to leave it for some time."

Breanna gave a half-smile. "That's okay, Latasha. I really appreciate you looking out for me."

"No problem, Ms. Breanna," she replied.

Kelvin stared at them both and frowned. "You better make sure Tessa didn't fuck off with your phone. Howard had us taking out the trash and serving people for a little minute while you were working the front of the house."

"Thanks for the heads up, Kelvin," Breanna said. She glanced around the kitchen, then disappeared down the hall toward the break room.

She closed her eyes and took a deep breath once she got inside and closed the door behind her. She wanted to call Elijah the moment she stepped inside the joint, but Tessa gawked at her like she dared her to even try. It was funny how Tessa went from being her best friend to her best enemy. She should have listened to Elijah. This was a lesson well learned.

Breanna woke her phone and stared at it. She frowned. She had not one phone call, one notification, or even one text message. That was odd. Neither Tessa nor Howard didn't see her sneak it inside the kitchen. And she knew Kelvin and Latasha wouldn't say anything about her having it out, but for the life of her, Breanna couldn't figure out why. Maybe Elijah had honestly gotten over her, or Kelvin's paranoia of Big Brother spying on them unknowingly was being justified.

She swiped through every setting through her phone and noticed the small airplane icon lit up. She could count how many times she touched that damn thing, and her finger never went to the setting. That bitch fucked with her phone. But how? She didn't even know she had it out unless she was eavesdropping on her conversation with Latasha and Kelvin before she went out front.

A rapping at the door startled Breanna from her train of thought. She went to it and peeked through the window. Latasha stared back at her with drawn together eyebrows. She bit her bottom lip. Breanna didn't like where this was heading.

"Hey. What's up?" Breanna opened the door, letting her step inside the small room.

"Ms. Breanna," Latasha sat on the couch before her. She twiddled her thumbs around. "Mya spoke with me, and she said Tessa took your phone when Howard sent me and Kelvin out on trash duty."

187

"How in the hell did she get my phone? She didn't see me bring it inside the kitchen." Breanna sat next to Latasha with her phone in hand. "Only you and Kelvin saw it."

"I know," she replied. "But Mya said she saw Tessa with your phone when she was flirting with a customer who was checking out. She said knew it was yours because of the pocket-sized photograph you keep inside that clear case."

Breanna frowned, then stared at her mobile device. Mya described it perfectly. "She must have known I had it with me."

"What are you going to do?"

"Return the favor," Breanna said, gripping her phone tighter. "But first, I need to make sure my boyfriend is okay."

Breanna watched a rush of text messages, voicemails, and missed called flood her device as she disabled the setting. She shook her head. Elijah had called about five times. He still wanted to talk to her; he wanted to work things out between the two of them.

She swiped over to her voicemail app and stared at the list of voicemails she had. She pressed on the latest notification and held it to her ear.

"Mommy! Please pick up! Daddy's not moving anymore. He needs you, Mommy. Please help."

"Oh my God!" Breanna covered her mouth. Tears welled in her eyes. "Elijah!"

"What's wrong, Ms. Breanna?"

"My husband had an asthma attack. He's not breathing anymore."

Latasha stared at her with wide eyes. "Oh, my God! Ms. Breanna, do you want me to come with you?"

"No. I just need to get to him," she said. She grabbed Latasha's hand as she panned the room. Elijah wouldn't have been in this situation if she hadn't argued with him. Better yet, he wouldn't have been in this situation if she had just bought the damn inhalers. The man had to plead with her repeatedly, and now this. "Please let Howard know I had an emergency."

"I will, Ms. Breanna."

She sprung from the couch and dashed to her locker. She yanked her purse out the hand trapping contraption and slammed it shut. She ran down the hall toward the exit door. Its alarm blared throughout the hall and outside the building as she ran past the old-dented garbage cans sitting in the dim light. They sat next to a tall, cherry oak tree Howard couldn't keep vagrants and college students from sitting under. That's what he deserved for kicking and spitting at them rather than being nice to them.

Breanna stared at her phone and redialed Elijah's number. "Please pick up, Eli. Please, Blue Eyes."

She held her keys out toward her car and unlocked it. She stared at her phone again as she hopped over a small puddle of water. Not even a callback. This was far worse than she thought.

Not looking up, Breanna bumped into a firm body. The sounds of deep, husky laughter made her heart pump faster. Her eyes widened. It couldn't have been him. Breanna swallowed hard as she stared into his cognac brown eyes; the smile on his face didn't match his laughter.

"Nathaniel!"

He gripped her throat tight, digging his nails into her skin as he squeezed it. "I know you ain't been ducking and dodging from me, Beautiful. I've been trying to get in touch with you, and all you do is avoid me."

"You're hurting me," Breanna gasped. She stared into his eyes. "Please. Let me go."

"Where's the fun in that, Bree?" Nathaniel tightened his grip around her throat, causing her to cough and struggle against his hold. "Remember the fun we were supposed to have."

"Hey!" A man's voice yelled from afar. "Leave that woman alone."

As she felt his grip loosen from around her neck, Breanna jerked away from his grasp and kneed him in the balls. He stumbled away from her, grunting and holding his groin. She couldn't miss the opportunity to get away from him. Running from him, Nathaniel's growl-like grunts grew closer until his fingers latched onto her hair. Pain seared through her scalp as he snatched her back toward him.

Laughter emitted from the depths of his throat as he enclosed her in his embrace. Even in front of this stranger, Nathaniel was willing to teach her a lesson for not giving him what he wanted, regardless of if he wanted to watch or not.

"Don't you ever do that shit again, Breanna," Nathaniel hissed in her ear.

"Hey, man!" The man's voice grew closer. "I said leave that woman alone."

Nathaniel shoved Breanna to the ground and pointed his finger at her. "I ain't done with you yet, bitch."

Breanna trembled as Nathaniel loomed over her. The other man's shouting echoed in the background, dragging his attention away from her. She kept her sights on him until he marched toward the man. She glanced at her car, then back at the man who saved her life. Nathaniel stomped at him, taunting the man to throw the first punch.

"Yo' man," the man stood in front of Nathaniel. He was several inches taller than he was. "The fuck is your problem."

189

"This ain't got nothing to do with you, man," Nathaniel hissed mockingly. "Unless you want it to be."

Breanna gawked at the two men size each other up as if they were in a squared ring. She had to move. She couldn't let fear keep her on her ass and miss this opportunity for escape. She stood to her feet and eased away from them. Their cursing and taunts resounded throughout the parking lot. She ran toward her car, jumped inside, and locked the door behind her. Breanna cranked the vehicle and mashed her foot on the gas pedal, speeding past them. Breanna witnessed them shove each other until Nathaniel threw the first punch in her rearview mirror. A woman stood near an old black pickup truck someone left on the lot they tried to sell with her phone out, recording their scuffle.

Just a few minutes more, and she would have been at Nathaniel's mercy, begging for him to let her go. But listening to her and restraining himself weren't things he was trying to do. No. Nathaniel's priority was to make her pay an expensive price for what she hadn't given him. Sex.

She sped down the street. Pain surged around her neck from his hold. Breanna touched it and winced. The remnants of Nathaniel's fingers pressed against her fingertips. He would have done more to her in that parking lot if that man hadn't interfered. Sex may not have been his stopping point; it probably wasn't his stopping point anymore.

She sobbed as she drove. She caused every ripple effect happening around her. Elijah and Isabella didn't deserve what she had done to them. Breanna sniffled, trying to contain her tears. God! There was no telling how long Elijah had been without oxygen. Isabella must have been so scared, witnessing her daddy fight to breathe.

Had she taken the time to listen to Elijah instead of jumping to conclusions, they probably would have been married by now, maybe even had another baby. That's if her body would allow it. They would have been happier had she not gone sniffing out something grander.

I didn't have to put them through this, but like a fool, I did. God, how could I have been so stupid?

The loud blaring of a car driving behind her jolted her from her train of thought. She peeped at an elderly couple in the far-right lane. The man shouted and waved his fist in the air as the woman gawked at her as she clutched her chest.

She had to get to Elijah. He needed her, and she wasn't there for him. She wiped another fleeting tear from her eye. She let the one man who loved her for who she was fall victim to something that could have been prevented.

Breanna placed her hand over her heart. It thumped hard against her palm. Another car horn honked in her ear. The depths of its sound made her ears ring. She glanced at the driver, seeing him yell at her from a distance. She didn't have time for people slowing her down. She had to get to Elijah.

She made a right turn near the supermarket, sending the black Honda Accord zooming down the street.

Just hold on, Blue Eyes. I'm on my way.

She slammed her foot on the brakes as she neared a two-door sedan pulling out in front of her.

"I don't have time for this!" Breanna yelled. She zoomed past the driver in front of her, leaving a plume of smoke from her screeching tires in front of them. Another horn blared in her ear. This time, the driver flipped her off when she zipped past her. She had grown accustomed to the all too familiar sounds of car horns. Maybe, just maybe, they were trying to tell her something.

Her phone rang in her purse. She swerved into another lane, reaching for the mobile device. Another car horn blared at her yet again. The driver pulled up beside her and shouted at Breanna. She took a deep breath. She had to keep her cool. Breanna didn't need to add vehicular assault to her long list of crimes she had already committed against the ones she loved.

Grabbing her phone and peeping at it, Breanna glanced at Katrina's number scroll across the screen. She dialed her number and listened to it ring throughout the cabin of her car.

"Breanna!" Katrina answered. "Where have you been? I've tried to call you earlier, but your phone kept sending me to voicemail."

"Kat, I'm so sorry. Somebody stole my phone while I was at work."

"How—" Katrina paused, then said. "Never mind that. Listen. Elijah's at Highland Memorial East in room 450. He's doing better than when he got here three hours ago."

"Three hours ago? Oh my God!" Breanna sped toward the expressway and merged onto the nearly empty street. "Who found him?"

"Morgan, of all people," Katrina answered. "Thank God she was there, though. My brother would have been dead if she hadn't come over."

Breanna gripped the wheel tighter as she drove. "Is he awake? Can he talk?"

"He woke up about an hour ago," she replied. "You need to be here, Breanna. Isabella was so torn up when they took him back."

"Did the doctors let her see him when he woke up?"

"They did. That calmed her down, but she didn't seem like herself when I asked her about you."

Breanna sighed. "I've got to talk to her."

"It's not too late, Breanna. My brother and niece need you. Don't let Morgan sink her teeth into neither one of them."

"I'll do my best, Kat."

"That's all I'm asking for, Bree. I'll see you soon."

"Alright. I'll be there shortly," Breanna said, ending the call.

Morgan saved his life. The very woman they argued over saved his life. She couldn't be angry with her for that. She was grateful. But knowing Morgan, there would be something more in store for her when she got there. That was just her nature.

As Breanna got off the expressway, she drove down Toots Boulevard. Only a week and a half ago, Nathaniel put her in the same hospital she drove to. Her heart raced against her chest as she viewed the bright sign for Highland Memorial Hospital from a distance.

Driving toward Tessa's neighborhood, Breanna drove past several couples holding hands and smiling as they strode down the sidewalk. She had to prove to Elijah she still needed him. She had to prove that to him and Isabella. If she didn't have them anymore, she wouldn't know what she'd do without them.

She turned into the visitor's parking lot and searched for a parking spot close to the building. Everyone must have fought for the nearest parking spaces. She glimpsed at a red Dodge Challenger and parked next to it. It wasn't close to the building, but it wasn't too far away either.

Breanna stared at the black and white furry dice hanging on the rearview mirror inside the car and shook her head. There was no way Amber was here, too. She didn't need the extra added breathing down her neck. Yet, it wasn't like she didn't deserve it, though. Amber was a victim of her butterfly effect, too. Still, Morgan was going to do plenty of that on her own. She didn't need Amber's two cents, too.

A cool spring breeze graced her as she stepped out of the car. She closed the door behind her and pulled her collars up, hoping no one would notice the markings on her neck. She touched them. The imprints were swelling.

Breanna sauntered through the sliding double doors. Her eyes landed on an older woman sitting at the receptionist's desk. She pecked away at her keyboard, not paying attention to the people passing by the desk. Her glasses sat on the edge of her nose as she held her head high in the air, straining to see. She was the true embodiment of Ms. David, her seventh-grade algebra teacher, who reeked of gasoline and stale coffee beans whenever she stood around her to check her work. "Can I help you, miss?"

For the love of God, why did she have to look up now?

Breanna cursed under her breath. She didn't question the other people walking in? Why her? What had she done to get this woman's attention?

She stared at the older woman. "I've been here before, ma'am. I know where I'm going."

The woman stood from her chair and squinted, getting closer to Breanna. She reached her hand out to her. "Miss, did someone physically harm you?"

Breanna stiffened, pulling the collar of her blouse further up around her neck. "I'm okay. Really, I am."

That's what she had done to get her attention.

"Miss," the woman said. "Are you in any imminent danger? Do you need help?"

Breanna stared at the vestibule, then back at the receptionist. Her heart raced. She needed Mom to protect her the way she did when she was last here. She needed to get away from prying eyes, judging her for what she'd done to her family.

"Ma'am," Breanna said. "I'm fine."

"You don't seem fine to me," the older woman stated. "It looks as if someone strangled you."

"Please, ma'am," Breanna stammered. "I'm fine."

"I'm going to call the police to get you some help, okay."

As soon as the woman turned around, Breanna ran toward the elevator and pressed her back against the wall, hoping the woman wouldn't come looking for her.

"Miss," the woman called from afar. "Did any of you see a young black woman with strangulation marks on her neck?"

Breanna held her breath for a moment, hoping the woman wouldn't come around the corner. Hearing her voice trail off, she exhaled. The last thing she needed was people to bring attention to something she brought on herself.

A stale white light beamed on her head as she moved toward the dual elevators. It was the same light the doctors used to examine the injuries Nathaniel placed upon her flesh the first time. She looked around the vestibule and rubbed one of her shoulders. She noticed a couple walk toward her from the corner of her eye and darted her attention to the floor. She didn't need more people becoming detectives and examining her without her permission.

Once one of the elevator doors slid open, Breanna hurried inside and pressed the button for the fourth floor. She leaned against the wall. There was no telling what Mrs. Lori and Mr. Jonah would say when she got there. There was no telling how Isabella would react when she saw her.

193

Breanna ran her fingers through her long hair as a tear slipped down her cheek. She had to make this up to Elijah and Izzy. She didn't know where she would begin, but she knew she had to start somewhere. Breanna had to give herself that swift kick to the ass if she wanted to change for the better. She needed to listen more... she needed to learn from her mistakes more... she needed to do what everyone had been telling her to do. Talk to Momma.

Dr. Shelby would be proud of her if she heard her thoughts right now. Yet, that was easier said than done. That woman was freakin' Fort Knox when it came to family ordeals. But when someone did her wrong, Momma wouldn't hesitate to warn her. Hell, Momma scared her away from any risks she thought were the worst thing for her to do, especially dating Elijah. Maybe Breanna finally heeded her warning. Maybe Momma had more of a negative influence than she thought she had.

"They were right," she muttered to herself.

Breanna watched the elevator door slide open and stepped onto the fourth floor. Silence slapped her in the face as she walked down the hall. A steady hum from the drink machines gave her a little comfort as she walked toward the nurses' station. She passed the empty area, hearing voices in the distance. She stared at the room numbers, looking for room 450. It must have been a busy night, or trouble was brewing in the east.

She noticed a woman's long blondish red tresses sway from side to side as she paced the floor. Turning in Breanna's direction, Katrina smiled and ran toward Breanna, wrapping her arms around her shoulders.

"I've missed you, Bree," Katrina said in her ear.

Breanna rubbed her back. "I've missed you too, Kat."

"He needs you, Bree," Katrina stepped away from her. "I overhead Morgan talking shit about you when I was talking to my mom and dad."

Breanna sighed. Knowing that Morgan saved his life, she knew she wouldn't stop there. Nope. The woman had a conquest to take him back. But with the way things were going between them, Morgan may have been triumphant in her efforts. "I see you're still eavesdropping on your big brother."

"Only for his protection, Bree," Katrina replied. "Besides, I've never liked her."

"Morgan saved his life, Kat," Breanna caught a glimpse of Isabella holding onto Amber's waist. She rested her head on her sister's stomach. Her little body trembled. A frown deepened Amber's deep brown eyes as she looked in her direction. She pursed her lips, then rolled her eyes as she looked away from Breanna.

"I know she did, Bree," Katrina said. "But I don't like her. She's too damn arrogant."

"Trust me, I know," Breanna said. "We've had our run-ins. I just need to talk to him."

"Please do," she said. "I don't want Morgan slinky her lanky ass back into my brother's life."

Morgan already had. She just allowed it to happen. Had she not been trying to replace the one man that loved her for her every physical and emotional imperfection, she wouldn't have been in this situation right now. But she was. Breanna had to make that change for them, if that was all she could do.

"I will, Kat." Breanna watched her walk toward Mrs. Lori and Mr. Jonah and place her head on her dad's shoulder as she draped her arm around it.

I've got to solve this.

As Breanna caught another glimpse of Isabella, she smiled. She looked much calmer sitting in that chair by herself. Amber appeared from behind her with a bottle of water in her hand.

Shit! Amber was going to take her every frustration and then some out on her. And Breanna deserved it. She knew she did. For the way she and Momma treated her, she wouldn't blame for her reaction. Breanna took a deep breath and ambled toward the two of them.

"Hey, Shortcake, are you okay?" Breanna said, sitting next to her daughter. The frown on Izzy's face screamed at her. She glared at Breanna for a moment, then looked away from her. "Listen, Izzy. Mommy's very sorry for not answering the phone when I should have."

Amber stared at Breanna with narrowed eyes. "Seriously, Bree?"

She frowned. "Yes. I'm serious, Amber. I need to talk to my daughter."

Amber nodded, then chuckled. "Like the way you've been doing before. I don't think so."

"Amber, please," Breanna pleaded. "Just give me a few minutes to speak with her—"

"I don't want to talk to you," Isabella huffed, cutting her off. She folded her little arms across her chest and poked her bottom lip out. That frown never left her little face.

Breanna placed her hand on Isabella's shoulder. "Shortcake, I would love to talk to you. I want to apologize to you and Daddy."

"Why bother?"

"Izzy?"

"She's right, Bree," Amber stood next to Isabella. She beckoned for the child to come into her embrace. "Why are you even wasting your breath?"

"Because I love her, and I want her to know that I messed up."

Amber glared at her as she shook her head. A tear slid down Breanna's cheek as she watched Isabella hold on to Amber's waist and look away from her. She didn't want to fight with Amber. Hell, she didn't want to fight with her daughter, but she knew she had to take the punches if she was going to take steps to change.

"I think you may be all out of chances, little sis," she said, shrugging her shoulders. "But be my guest. Just know it's your fault."

Breanna stood from her chair and kneeled beside Isabella. The child refused to look her in the eyes. "Shortcake, Mommy wants to apologize to you. Will you accept my apology?"

"No," said Isabella. She hid behind Amber's leg.

"Please, Izzy. Mommy loves you so much."

"You don't love me." She looked away from her again as she held onto Amber's leg tighter.

Reaching for Isabella's hand, Breanna witnessed her snatch it away from her. Another tear slipped down her cheek as she neared her daughter. "But I do love you, Izzy."

"No. You don't. You don't even love Daddy."

"Please, Izzy. I love both you and Daddy."

"No. You don't," Isabella yelled. "Get away from me. I hate you."

Breanna stared at her with wide eyes. The weight of her words sat on her soul like a sunken boat at the bottom of the ocean. She couldn't tell what was worse. Being kicked in the back by a full-grown man or hearing her flesh and blood scream to the heavens that she hated her. "Isabella... you don't mean that."

"She does, Breanna," Amber said. The frown in her eyes dug in deeper than Isabella's words had. "You should leave. Now."

Breanna stared Amber down. Every fiber of her being burned with frustration. There wasn't any point in trying to get through to her sister, but she didn't blame her. She couldn't.

"Amber, I'm not trying to fight with you. I just want to talk—"

"That's a first, little sis," Amber chuckled. She stepped closer to Breanna with her arms folded across her chest. "What's wrong? You can't roll with the punches tonight?"

Breanna looked away from her as she rubbed her neck and frowned. That ole stinging sensation reared its head again. Amber was right about one thing, though. She was tired of fighting for all the wrong reasons.

"Stop it, you two," Mrs. Lori said, walking behind Breanna. She stood between the two sisters and glanced at them. "What would your father say about the way you two are acting right now?"

196

"He wouldn't be happy, but honestly, he probably wouldn't give a damn about me anyway," Breanna said. She stepped away from them. With the way she treated Daddy, she wouldn't have blamed him if he didn't care about her.

"Breanna," Lori said. She followed her. "Sweetheart, please stop."

Breanna stopped in her steps. The softness of Mrs. Lori's hand graced her shoulder as she wrapped her arm around one of her shoulders.

"What's wrong, Breanna?"

Breanna covered her face with both hands and sobbed. "Your son proposed to me earlier today," she replied, looking up from them.

Mrs. Lori covered her mouth with her hand. "He did?"

She nodded as she continued to sob. "But I fucked it up."

"How?" Lori pulled her closer to her.

"I cheated on him. I blamed him for ruining my life. I caused this asthma attack," Breanna said through tears. "I've hurt him and Izzy."

"You two need to work through this."

"I doubt if he'll listen to me, Mrs. Lori,"

She rubbed her shoulder. "Just try."

Breanna nodded. As simple as those words flowed from her lips, they were the most difficult things she ever had to do in her life. If Isabella's reaction toward her was extreme, there was no telling how Elijah would react.

"You've got to try, Bree. Even if you think it's fruitless, you at least tried."

Breanna turned around and embraced Mrs. Lori. That woman was one of the sweetest people she'd ever met. She was like her stepmother. Stern, but forgiving.

As Breanna looked up, she spotted Morgan gawking at her. A smirk rested on her lips.

And then there she was. The woman who saved her husband's life, and the same woman who came to snatch him out of her grasp. She watched Morgan shake her head as she stood in the doorway of Elijah's hospital room like a barricade. She hugged Mrs. Lori once more before training her eyes back on Morgan.

"I'm going to talk to Elijah now," Breanna said, stepping away from his mother. They both stared at Morgan. "I love you, Mrs. Lori."

"I love you too, sweetheart."

She walked towards Elijah's room and stood in front of Morgan. "Morgan."

Morgan snickered. "Breanna."

She swallowed hard. "I wanted to tell you thank you for saving his life."

"Y'all hear that." Morgan smiled. "The infamous Breanna Ellis wants to thank me for something she should have done."

"Please, Morgan. I didn't come here to fight with you."

"Sure, you didn't."

"I didn't. I just want to talk to Elijah."

She snickered louder this time. "Good luck with that."

Breanna stared at Morgan as she walked past her. That bitch had some nerves, yet she was still in her gratitude for saving her boyfriend's life. The outcome would have been grimmer had she not shown up. Still, Morgan's intentions were prominent as fuck. Breanna knew she was on an island all by herself. But she had a lifeboat; she hoped that lifeboat didn't have too many holes in it.

She locked eyes with Elijah as she entered the room. His eyes looked as if he hadn't slept in two days. He frowned at her as he watched her twiddle her thumbs before taking a seat next to him.

"Elijah... I'm sorry—"

"—Save it for someone else, Breanna."

"Eli, please give me a chance to talk to you."

"I've given you more chances than you needed, and you still hurt me. I'm done giving you chances."

"Elijah," she sobbed. "I didn't mean for any of this to happen."

"Are you sure about that, Breanna?" His frown deepened. "I maintained patience with you. I kept my cool with you. I even forgave you. And despite that, you cheated on me and then left me for dead."

"Elijah, I swear. I didn't mean to do any of this—"

"—I could've been like any other man out there and left your ass where you stood. Some of these men have even called me pathetic for still loving you," he retorted. "But I loved you enough to stand by you at your best and worst. That's what real men do, Breanna."

"Eli, please. I can explain."

He shook his head as he chuckled. His frown turned into a subtle smile. "Explain what, Bree. That you fell out of love with me five years ago. That you've been tired of me and Isabella and wanted your life back."

"No." Breanna sobbed, wiping a tear from her cheek. "That I fucked up. I ruined our lives searching for something I already had... with you and Izzy."

He laughed, then coughed. "Well, Bree. That's what happens when you fuck around with people. They get tired of the shit and leave."

"Elijah, I want us to talk this through."

"We're talking, Breanna."

"No, Eli," she said. She reached for his hand, hoping he would listen to her. But as she witnessed him snatch it away, she knew her chances

198

were gone. She covered her mouth as she sobbed again. "I know we can make this work."

"Are you serious with this shit right now, Breanna?"

She nodded. "I am, Eli."

"Well," he chuckled. "I'm serious too. Get your shit out of my house and leave. I'm done with you."

"Elijah, you don't mean that."

"I mean every word, Bree," he said. "Now, leave."

"Elijah, please."

"Leave, Breanna."

"Elijah," she sobbed.

"Get the fuck out of here," he hissed.

"Elijah—"

"What don't you get when someone tells you to leave?"

"That I'm not willing to give up yet."

He stared at her, shaking his head in disgust. "Sounds like stupidity to me."

"Eli—"

"Ya' best leave before I call for security."

She stood from the seat. Her head swam from his words piling up in her ears. She couldn't stop the tears from streaming. Then her neck pulsated once more like she needed more pain added to the pain she already felt. Nathaniel's faded grip swelled into painful memories. She rubbed it, feeling numbness in place of the pain.

"Breanna," Elijah said, glaring at her.

She found herself caught by his icy stare. Goose pimples formed on her arms from the frown sitting upon his eyebrows. Breanna rubbed her neck and took a deep breath, waiting for what he was about to say next.

"I want full custody of Isabella. The papers are on the dining room table."

She covered her mouth again as she shook her head. Her back hit the wall as she stepped away from his bedside. Pain danced its way across the base of her neck. Everyone she ever loved hated her; everything she ever had with them vanished because of stupid wants she thought she needed in her life.

"Eli..." Breanna stammered. Giving up her daughter was the last thing she wanted to do, but it was going to be for the best. Isabella no longer loved her, anyway. "I'll sign them."

Breanna turned her back toward him and placed her head against the door as she cried to herself. Her body hurt worse than the last time she was laid up here.

"Good. Now get the—"

"I'll get out," she sobbed. "I'm sorry."

Breanna stepped out the hospital room and passed Amber and Katrina by. Everyone's voices blurred into one as she trekked down the long hallway. All she could hear was her own heartbeat. It thumped hard against her chest with every beat. Her neck ached like a migraine now. The numbness traded its post with the stinging pain and left.

Mrs. Lori caught a glimpse of her neck as she passed her by and frowned. "Breanna, wait. What happened to you?"

She walked past the crowd of people huddled near rooms not too far from Elijah's room and kept her eyes on the floor. The sound of Mrs. Lori's voice faded into the background.

"There she is," the receptionist said, jolting her out of her train of thought. She ran in her direction alongside a nurse and a police officer. "Ma'am. Ma'am. We only want to help you."

Mrs. Lori walked toward the receptionist and stood in front of her. "What's going on with Breanna? Is she in any trouble?"

"She may be. She's got bruising on her neck that resembles strangulation," she replied, shaking her head. "And just a while ago, this officer got a report that a couple witnessed that very woman being assaulted in Soul Bistro's parking lot."

Mrs. Lori's eyes widened as she took a step back from the woman. She watched Breanna as she disappeared down the hall. She turned and stared at Morgan as she waltzed her way back into her son's room.

"When did this happen?" Mrs. Lori asked.

"Sometime between 8:45 and 9 pm tonight." The officer said, stepping closer to her. "Do you know her?"

"She's my daughter-in-law." Mrs. Lori glanced down the hall again. She was gone.

Breanna stood in the center of the moving room. Tears slipped down her cheeks until they rolled off the edges of her jawlines. She had got what she wanted. She got every bit of it. And because of it, she lost the people who loved her beyond her faults. Elijah and Isabella hated her. Hell, she hated herself.

Life was going to be different now. She had nothing else to live for. She didn't want to live for anything else. Breanna watched the elevator door slide open and entered the vestibule. She walked toward the hospital entrance; eyeing every assumingly happy couple as she strode. She covered her mouth and sobbed, hoping no one would see her. But from the looks of several people eying her walk by, she could tell they saw her for who she truly was. A stupid bitch who bit way more than she could chew.

Onlookers gawked at her as she walked past them. They must have been whispering about how she screwed her family over to be with another man. They must have been laughing at how she gave up her happiness to get her ass beat. They were probably calling and telling everyone they knew about what she'd done to Elijah and Isabella. To Daddy. To her stepmother. To Amber. They must have—Breanna panted as she panned the room with wide eyes. Several people craned their necks to look at her.

Confusion and concern were displayed on their faces as she stared at them. Coughing, she ran out the building and hid near the hedges. A dim streetlamp shined its weak light over her, barely casting her shadow on the ground. She wailed, then gasped for air. Tears flooded her eyes.

"Oh! My God! What have I done? What have I done to my family?"

Chapter Thirty-Five

Silence greeted her as she stood in the doorway. Its deafening hum and unnerving rattles festered in Breanna's ears as she stepped inside the house. This was no longer her home; she was now an intruder in this space she once called home. Breanna closed the door behind her, then rested the back of her head on the wooden structure. She peered around the foyer and family room. Pictures of her, Elijah, and Isabella hung about the walls. Their smiles were now distant memories. Memories she turned into nightmares. She was no longer welcomed here.

She stared at a picture of Izzy playing in a kiddy pool. Eli looked so frustrated, having fallen inside of it with their daughter. The grin on Izzy's face numbed the pain for a moment. Yet the thought of having to leave made it just that worse.

Breanna smiled as she brushed her fingers against the picture their daughter drew in her pre-k class. Elijah was so proud of it he called everyone to come see it. But she didn't. She sobbed, looking away from the pictures. Isabella was no longer her daughter. And Elijah... was no longer the man who loved her. She chuckled at herself. She ruined Elijah's heart for a man who wanted to beat her ass for not giving him what he wanted. How stupid could she have been?

Her phone vibrated against her backside for the fifth time tonight. Mrs. Lori wouldn't give up that easily on her, but Breanna already had. Five years ago. She pulled the device from her pocket and stared at it. Mrs. Lori's number scrolled across the screen again. She couldn't take that call. It didn't matter if Mrs. Lori loved her like she was her daughter. It was more of a matter if her son still loved her, which was a definite hell no. Elijah would have rather seen her burn at the stake than talk to her, and Breanna didn't blame him. She deserved that burning.

The air in the house became cool suddenly. Its warmth left her like she left Elijah and Isabella. Perhaps the house itself was trying to kick her ass out, too.

She stared at the inhaler lying on the family room floor and walked over to the small piece of white plastic. Breanna picked it up from the floor and shook it. It was empty. She covered her mouth and cried once more.

"How could I have been so fucking stupid?" she fussed at herself. "How could I have done this to them?"

Her phone vibrated in her hand again. She knew Mrs. Lori meant well, but she couldn't associate herself with her anymore. Not if Morgan would be around from now on. At least Elijah had Plan B ready to go.

As she took a deep breath and wiped her eyes, Breanna stood to her feet and made her way toward the stairs. One by one, she gingerly planted each foot on the stairs until she arrived at the second floor. Daisy ran up behind her, wagging her tail. At least she still loved her. But that would have changed too if she saw what Breanna had done to Isabella and Elijah. The dog would have finished the job Nathaniel started.

She rubbed the Labrador's head, then stopped to look at Izzy's door. It was ajar. Breanna walked inside, noticing Isabella's favorite Princess Tiana doll lying on the floor. She picked it up, placed it on the pillow Izzy loved to lie on, and laid it on their daughter's bed. This was the last time she was going to see her baby's smile, hear her baby's beautiful singing voice, and smell her baby's fruity pomade Breanna used in her hair. This was the very last time.

She nuzzled her nose against the pillow and cried. "I'm so sorry for what I've done to you, Shortcake."

Daisy hopped on the bed next to her and pushed her with her nose. The smile that sat on the dog's face made her flowing tears stop for a moment.

"I love you so much, Daisy," Breanna said, rubbing the dog's head. "But I can't stay here anymore. You gotta take care of Shortcake for me, okay."

Daisy barked at her as she wagged her tail. For some strange reason, Breanna thought the dog understood every word she spoke. She rubbed her head again, then rose from the bed.

She walked out of Isabella's bedroom, leaving Daisy inside, and strode toward the room she once shared with Elijah. The very room where every fight they had occurred. The same room where their nightly escapades would end. The same room where she decided to cheat on him with Nathaniel. Elijah was right for putting her out.

As she stepped inside, Breanna sat on the bed for a moment. This was the last time she would share space with the man she should have made her husband. This was the last time she was going to get to see his smile, hear his moans, and smell that soap he loved to bathe with so much. She wiped away another fleeting tear. This was all her fault. She couldn't blame this on anyone else except herself.

"Okay, Bree," she said to herself. She peered around the room, then lost herself staring at Elijah and Isabella's picture sitting on his nightstand. "You can't stay here anymore."

She rose from the bed and walked toward her side of the bed. Elijah had already set her duffle bag on the floor. He didn't waste any time. Breanna walked toward her side of the dresser, opened it, and pulled out her clothes. She tossed them onto the bed, then opened another drawer, starting the process all over again. She heard her phone buzz against the bed's comforter. Mrs. Lori couldn't change what she had done, but she knew that woman would have tried if she could. Breanna stepped to the bed and stared at it. Howard's name scrolled across the screen. She sighed. Not this idiot.

"Hello."

"You know something, Breanna. I'm sick of you and your drama."

"Then just fire me, Howard."

"I won't do that, considering what happened to your boyfriend and all."

"He's not my boyfriend anymore."

"Oh! Is he okay?"

"He's better off now."

"Okay," Howard responded hesitantly. "Listen, take two days off and recoup. You sound like you need it."

She pursed her lips. There was a stipulation coming with this. She could feel it in her bones. "I've started catering just this week, and I have a gig coming up on Sunday. It would be great if I could get you to bake your best pastries for the event. It's for a family reunion."

Breanna dragged her hand over her face and sighed. As much as she didn't want to do it, she knew Howard wouldn't let her down for not cooperating. "Okay. Just let me know how many people will be there, and I'll prepare enough for that many."

"Great! And seriously, Breanna, leave your shit at home."

The call ended. Breanna kept the phone to her ear as another tear slid down her cheek. Humming silence graced her ears again. She got up from the bed once more and walked inside the closet. There wasn't any need to take anything from here. She didn't have enough room in her bag to carry everything. Hell, Elijah could burn it all if he wanted. Breanna didn't care anymore.

She slid her fingertips across the smooth yet comfiness of Elijah's dress shirts hanging in the closet and closed her eyes. Remnants of his cologne, her perfume, and their essence combined lingered on the blue shirt she loved to see him wear. She grabbed the sleeve of it and pressed it against her nose. A picture fell onto the floor. As Breanna picked it up, she stared at it. She, Elijah, AJ, and Leslie all sat together at their favorite diner that night after final exams.

Their smiles were wide in celebration of passing Mr. Oliver's torturous statistics class. They knew they were all doomed to fail that course, but after the teacher's pet brought him a bottle of tequila, he passed everyone. Breanna caressed the picture with her fingertips and put it close to her heart. She was three weeks pregnant with Isabella then.

But that was then. That was the life she gave up for punches to her faces, kicks to her spine, and tight grips around her throat. She gave up her family for abuse. Breanna shook her head and slid the picture into her pocket. That would be the only lasting memories she had to remember the love she had with them.

She took a deep breath and held it for a moment before exhaling slowly. Tears cascaded down her cheeks like drops of rain sliding against glass. Back in high school, the Nathaniel she knew was the guy every girl fought and drooled over. He and Elijah were damn near the same height, except he had these smoldering cognac brown eyes that would make the girls blush in more areas than one. His chocolate brown skin reminded her of the first time she tasted chocolate ice cream with chocolate chips inside it. It was so creamy and smooth... so alluring. She closed her eyes. Nathaniel was charming, alright. He was charmingly deceptive.

She always wondered why his family rushed to move to North Carolina during the midpoint of their senior year. Sure, his father got that new job Nathaniel had been telling her about, but from what he used to say to her, they didn't plan on moving until after he graduated from high school. Something deeper, something much more serious, happened that made them move within a one-week time frame.

Breanna walked out the closet and back into the bedroom. She closed the drawers to the dresser, pulled her duffle bag onto the bed, and began folding her clothes. She stared at her phone again. Maybe

Leslie would answer her call. Perhaps she would—that was a fat chance of that happening. Breanna was the last person Leslie wanted to speak to, let alone give a shoulder for her to cry on. But she would never know if she didn't try.

Breanna dialed Leslie's number, held the phone to her ear, and listened to the call go straight to voicemail. She closed her eyes, waiting for the woman's instructions to end. "Hey, Leslie. It's Breanna. I was wondering if you would like to meet up at Carol's Diner in midtown sometime next week. If not, it's cool. You probably don't want to talk to me, anyway. Sorry I called." She ended the call and placed the phone on the bed once more.

She stood back from the soft mattress and ran her fingers through her hair. She didn't have anywhere to go. After paying that expensive ass car note Howard claimed he would help her with it, she only had $150 to her name. Getting a hotel home for the night was out of the question.

Maybe Grandma Zora would take her in again. But it was rather late. Breanna didn't want to wake Grandma from her slumber. She needed all the rest she could get after the last time she crashed there. Grandma stayed around her like clockwork, helping her heal from her injuries. Injuries Nathaniel gladly placed on her body. Momma would understand. She was happy to see her the last time she spent the night there. But that was because she and Elijah were fighting, and Momma begged her not to go back home to him. Instead, Momma insisted on her staying with Nathaniel. She sighed. Momma had a hand in breaking them up—No. She wouldn't blame Momma for something she had done. This was her own doing.

She dialed Momma's number and listened to the phone ring. Momma was never good at answering the first call.

"Breanna," Momma answered. "Why are you calling so late?"

Breanna took a deep breath. "I was wondering if I could stay with you tonight."

"Why can't you stay with Nathaniel? He's been good to you."

Breanna frowned. "He hasn't, Momma. I would prefer to stay with you."

"Oh, sweetheart. Did you two get into an argument?"

"It's a little deeper than that."

"Are you pregnant again?"

"No, Momma. I'm not," Breanna huffed. "There was a lot of shit that happened tonight, and I just wanted to stay with you, if you're okay with it."

"Alright, my baby," Momma said melodically. "I'll be up waiting for you, okay."

"Okay, Momma. I'll see you in a little while."

She ended the call and slid her phone back into her pocket. Breanna looked around the house, noticing how clean Elijah kept it. He was never one for things lying around. Just the smell of stale Cheetos and dirt made goose pimples crawl up and down his skin. That's what she loved about him. Yet he hated everything about her now. Hell, Elijah even hated the air she breathed. Tears streamed down her cheeks one by one again. There was no coming back from this. All she could do now was start over. But how?

She stuffed the remaining clothes into her duffle bag and cursed under her breath. She completely forgot about her shoes. So much for letting him burn everything she had.

She noticed her favorite lotion, perfume, and deodorant sitting on the dresser and grabbed them. She stuffed them into the too-tight bag and zipped it until it stopped just an inch from its closure. Even her duffle bag didn't want to deal with her. Breanna would have to resort to garbage bags if she wanted to take anything else with her. It was ghetto, but it was the only option she had.

Breanna left the bedroom and ran down the steps. She marched herself into the kitchen and looked around. There was a pile of dishes sitting in the sink. Usually, Elijah would have washed them, but he wouldn't be doing anything for a while after suffering from that horrible asthma attack.

She turned on the water and let it run until she saw steam. Breanna opened one of the cabinet doors beneath the sink and pulled out two garbage bags, dishwashing liquid, and a clean dish rag. She tossed the garbage bags onto the island, then turned her attention to the dishes that needed cleaning.

Breanna grabbed Isabella's favorite cup and took another deep breath as she held it in her hand. She squeezed some washing liquid onto the dishrag and scrubbed the cup until she was satisfied, or at least smelled like crisp green apples. The sound of rushing water allowed her to let her shoulders slump for the moment. Breanna didn't know how she would move on from this breakup, but she had no other choice. She got out what she put into their relationship. It was just going to be hard trying to move on without the loves of her life.

"It's too quiet," Breanna said to herself. She dried her hands off on a towel, reached into her pocket, and pulled out her phone. She woke the device, then quickly swiped left until she found her Spotify. Tapping on the R&B radio, Musiq Soulchild's smooth harmonies boomed through the speakers. She closed her eyes, listening to him sing about going half crazy. That's what Elijah felt with her; that's what she did to him. She closed her eyes, allowing tears to emerge from underneath her lashes and roll down her cheeks. She would never get over losing the two of them. This was a welted lash she had to endure for the rest of her life.

Breanna gazed at a steak knife lying inside the sink and picked it up. She examined it, running her fingertip over the smooth sharp edges of the utensil. Its sharpness pressed further against her fingertip. The music played incoherently as she brought it to her wrist. It could slice into her skin and cut into an artery and make her bleed out slowly. Her vision blurred as she pressed the utensil harder against her wrist. It would have been quick if she just only...

All you have to do is end it. They won't miss you.

The knife fell from her grasp as she stepped back from the sink, trembling. Her eyes were wide, and her chest heaved up and down. The last time she contemplated suicide, she overheard Amber and Momma screaming at each other about her. She recalled the gruffness in Amber's teenage voice. There was so much hurt and anger behind it when there should have been contentment there. That was all her fault then, too. That was the last time she and Amber lived together. That was the moment she thought Amber would have been better off without her in her life.

"If you're listening to me, God, please help me. I need you," Breanna whispered to herself. She took another deep breath and walked back to the sink. The sound of Lalah Hathaway's voice harmonized over the phone's speaker as she began washing the dishes again. Breanna at least had to finish what she started. It was the least she could do to make her exit a clean one.

"I'll clean up what I can and get the rest of my things."

Placing the last dish into the dish rack, Breanna shut off the water. She squeezed the remaining water from the dishrag and wiped the island down. She found comfort in wiping the piece of furniture down. There were so many beautiful memories made in this space. They were the last beautiful memories she would have to leave behind.

Breanna placed the dishrag back into the sink and grabbed her two trash bags off the island before making her way out the kitchen. She stood at the bottom of the steps and stared at the pictures hanging on the wall again. She didn't realize they had so many images until now. Breanna took the first step, then stopped, staring at a photo of her and Elijah holding hands and smiling at each other. She cried as she held the stairwell and ambled up the steps.

This was the hardest thing she ever had to do in her life. Even giving birth wasn't this hard. But this... this was like having her soul ripped out of her while watching it happen before her eyes.

She opened one bag upon entering the room and sat it next to her duffle bag. She walked back into the closet and gathered the shoes she wanted to take. Elijah could do whatever he wanted with the rest. There wasn't any need to keep any remnants of herself in the house. Though, Breanna had to admit she was shoe fanatic to her soul. There were shoes she collected she'd never worn. She was just like Momma. But for the life of her, she couldn't tell if that was a good or bad thing anymore.

She walked out of the closet with arms full of shoes and let them drop to the floor. She grabbed the garbage bag from the bed and tossed her shoes inside it. Breanna wiped a tear from her eye as she threw the last shoe into the bag. There was one last thing she had to do before she left the house. The one thing she dreaded the most. Snatching a pen off Elijah's nightstand, she ran back downstairs and stood at the dining room entry. She peeked at the thick white envelope lying on the table and walked toward it. There was no other way around this. There just wasn't. Even if she tried to fight for his love, to fight for Isabella's love, it wouldn't be enough. There was too much damage to remove by hand.

She sighed as she opened the envelope. The thick mass of papers sprung open in her face like the foldable fan Grandma Isabella used to fan herself with in church when the air conditioner broke down during a full service. She flipped to the last page of the document, not bothering to read through the material. It was already hard enough to soak in the reality that Isabella told her she hated her. Breanna didn't need to read it in writing repeatedly.

She saw the dotted line where she needed to sign and signed her name. Breanna laid the pen on top of them and took another deep breath. Her head swam for a moment. She wanted to make sure Elijah saw she signed them. The last thing she needed was for them to fight over Isabella.

She stared at another picture sitting on the dining room table and picked it up. It was a picture of her, Elijah, and Isabella playing in a field of leaves. Breanna grabbed it, then ran her thumb over their faces. This was the last time she was going to see her family. This was the last time she was going to step inside this house. This was the last time she was going to be happy. Another tear fell.

"I miss you both so much," she cried. "I don't know what I'm going to do without you two. I have nothing left to live for anymore. I have nothing."

Chapter Thirty-Six

Thunder clapped, reverberating through Breanna's Honda Accord as she pulled into Momma's circular driveway. A flash of lightning streaked across the clouded dark sky. Wind brushed against the trees, forcing them to sway from side to side. A cluster of green and yellow veined leaves fell to the ground in a scattered heap.

She and Elijah used to lie in bed together and watch the lightning grace the night sky when Isabella refused to sleep at night when she was just an infant. She wiped a cascading tear away from her cheek and shut off her car. The last thing she needed was for Momma to see her crying, especially over Elijah.

Breanna dialed Momma's number and waited for her to answer. Even while parked in her front yard, Momma still dillydallied around like no one wasn't waiting for her. She should have been used to that by now.

"I just unlocked the door for you, sweetheart," Momma responded.

"Thanks, Momma," Breanna said, watching Momma lean halfway out the door and gawk both ways before leaning back inside. "I'll see you in a sec." She emerged from the car and surveyed her surroundings. Sounds of rustling leaves and croaking frogs made her heart race. The last thing she needed was for Nathaniel to have followed her to Momma's house.

She observed the stately manors, more like miniature castles, sitting alongside Momma's mini mansion and shook her head. All that house and the owner couldn't turn on the freakin' light. Some folks didn't care if they lured people to come take their stuff. That always bothered her.

She couldn't explain why; it just did. She shook her head once more. That was something Daddy complained about too. She guessed she was more like Daddy than she thought she was.

Stained-glass solar lights surrounded her white and blueish-purple Perennials Amber gave her two months ago. They were lined in the shape of an "I" while some lined the sidewalk to the front door. Breanna was surprised she even accepted the flowers from Amber, considering how much love she showed her through the years. Momma probably loved those perennials more than the both of them from the way she talked to them and named them once she found a spot in the ground for them.

That was sad. Amber was by far prettier than a flower and deserved more attention than the greenery Momma cared for. But she couldn't say the same thing for herself, though. That woman would go on and on about Nathaniel. She'd already named him her future son-in-law, with no regard to Elijah. That was her fault. She painted this picture of this man who was sweet, understanding, and loving before he slapped her ass around. If only Momma knew... Momma wouldn't understand. She would only take up for Nathaniel.

Besides, he could do no wrong in her eyes. He was deemed to be the perfect gentleman. But had she known that he'd put her in the hospital and threatened to harm her if she didn't have sex with him, Momma would have been at the forefront of protecting her. That's if she didn't ask her a million questions about what she had done to make him upset and what she was going to do to make things up to him.

Breanna opened the back passenger door, then reached inside, pulling her duffle bag toward her.

"I ain't going to keep this door unlocked for you all night long, Bree," Momma yelled from the other side of the door.

Breanna shook her head again and sighed. Momma's voice could wake up a few sleeping cats and the neighbors across the street if she wanted to go an octave higher.

"I'm sorry, Momma, I was trying to get my bags."

"Get em' in the morning, Bree," Momma said. "I still got some clothes of yours in your old room."

After closing the door behind her, Breanna trekked toward Momma and pressed the button on her key chain, making the car's horn honk twice. Rustling bushes and hooting owls made her walk faster to Momma's front door. With Nathaniel lurking after her every move, she didn't want to risk giving him an easier target to attack.

Breanna stepped inside the house and pulled the door closed behind her. She locked it before Momma could turn on her heel and glare at her as if her head sat among a platter of fruits, cheeses, and vegetables.

She walked through the gallery and stared at the pictures hanging on the khaki-colored walls. There were so many photos of her and Momma posing together, yet there weren't any pictures of Amber to be found. A walnut-toned wooden and glass china cabinet sat against the main wall of the foyer. Every piece of porcelain Momma ever owned rested within that cathedral-like structure. From her figurines and fine china Daddy gave her for Christmas and birthday gifts to every ornament she ever collected while on her various vacations, Momma had it all stuffed inside that cabinet. There were even small, recessed lights inside the thing like it was a house or something.

"You like it?" Momma strode behind Breanna. "I just got those lights installed a couple of days ago."

Breanna smiled, losing herself looking into Momma's beautiful brown eyes. "I do."

Momma looked at her with narrowed eyes and pursed lips, held her head to the side, and frowned. "What's wrong with you, sweetheart? You seem distant."

"I'm fine, Momma," Breanna replied.

Momma pushed a strand of her long hair behind her ear, then cupped her chin, lifting it slightly. "Even when you were on the phone with me earlier, you sounded like you lost something."

"I'm okay, Momma," Breanna said. "I'm just—"

"Girl! What the hell happened to your neck?" Momma moved her chin upward and to the side, examining the welted bruises resting on it. "Did Elijah do this to you?"

"No, Momma. He would never hurt me."

"You best not be lying to me, little girl!"

"I'm not lying to you, Momma. Elijah's not abusive," Breanna answered. A frown rested on her brow.

"Maybe not physically, but damn sure emotionally."

Breanna stepped away from Momma's grasp and covered her mouth, trying to mask the sound of her sobs. She couldn't keep up the facade she was carrying on with anymore. "He's in the hospital, Momma."

For a moment, Momma's eyes widened before they settled into their "why do I give a damn gaze" She scoffed as she rolled her eyes, returning her attention to Breanna. "So, what happened to him?"

"He had an asthma attack and stopped breathing."

"Sounds like he got what he deserved," Momma scoffed again.

Breanna frowned at her. "Why would you even say something like that, Momma?"

"Because that man has done nothing but cause you pain and suffering, and on top of that, the asshole tried to bend you to his will."

212

She shook her head. Daddy and Elijah were right about Momma. She wouldn't listen. Hell, she wouldn't even show sympathy, let alone empathy, when she needed it the most. "He saved my life when I didn't realize it."

"That cracker kept you on your back nearly the entire time," Momma huffed. "I can't believe you would let someone like that in between your legs. I didn't raise you like that."

"But you raised me to take a beating, right Momma?"

A frown sat on Momma's brows. She folded her arms across her chest and stepped away from Breanna. "What the hell did you just say to me, girl?"

"You heard me, Momma. Did you raise me to take a beating?"

"I didn't. Why would you ask me something like that?"

"Because Nathaniel hit me, Momma." Breanna wiped away her flowing tears. "He's the one that put these bruises on my neck."

"What did you do to him to make him so mad, then?"

"What did I do?" Breanna frowned, pointing to herself. Hearing those very words come out of Momma's mouth made her feel like she was a little pouting girl who had just gotten spanked for tasting a cookie before dinner. "Did you hear what I just said, Momma?"

"I did." She frowned, placing her hand on her hip. "What did you do to make him so mad at you?"

"I can't believe you right now."

"Nathaniel is a good man, Breanna," Momma retorted. "You best treat him right."

"Just like the man who hit you when you cheated on Daddy?"

"What?" Momma stiffened where she stood. Her arms dropped to her sides. Her black silk robe slowly came undone. "Who told you that?"

"Daddy told me, Momma."

Momma darted her eyes away from her and raked her fingers through her grayish, reddish-brown, curly hair.

"Why did you cheat on Daddy?"

"Did he tell you that he cheated on me first?"

"Daddy told me. So did Mom."

Momma stepped closer to her and glared at her. "You dare call that bitch Mom in front of my face."

"Regina isn't the person who Daddy cheated on you with. It was Aunt Pauline. She was the one who betrayed you, Momma."

"You stop it. You stop this mess right now, Breanna."

"Is it true, Momma?"

She watched Momma storm away from her and into the kitchen. She swung the wine cooler cabinet door open on the side of the large

213

island she recently had redone some months ago and pulled out a bottle of blueberry Merlot. She pulled a wineglass from the cupboard and sat it next to it. "I can't believe you would come to my house and tell me this shit."

"Momma, why didn't you ever tell me that?" Breanna stood across the room from her. "Why didn't you tell me you cheated on Daddy too?"

"You know something." Momma pulled the cork from the bottle and poured it into the wineglass. Its reddish purplish color splashed about in the glass as it swirled around its circumference. "You ask too many stupid questions like your damn Daddy, Breanna."

"You never answered the question, Momma. Why didn't you tell me you cheated on Daddy too?"

"Because the bastard stopped fighting for our marriage a long time ago. I never signed up for that mess, Breanna, and you shouldn't have either."

"But I love Elijah, Momma."

"You think that's love," she said, taking a sip of the wine. "I call that situational slavery at its best."

"Situational slavery? There was nothing about that situational slavery. I love Elijah more than you ever realized."

"That's not love, Breanna. That's stupidity."

"That was love, Momma. Elijah took care of me when my pregnancy became too much for me to endure. He was always there for me. Where were you?"

"I was always there for you." Momma slammed the glass onto the island. "But you let that cracker impregnate you. That was your fault, Breanna."

"Yes, Momma," Breanna retorted, throwing her hands in the air. "Elijah got me pregnant. It wasn't planned, nor did we talk about having children. But it happened—"

"You let that man impregnate you, Breanna. You're just too stupid to understand that."

"I'm too stupid," she yelled. "How in the hell do you get off calling me stupid when you won't even acknowledge that your sister slept with your husband."

The sudden slap across her face caught Breanna off guard. She watched Momma pant as she rubbed the same cheek Nathaniel punched her in. In all her life, she never thought Momma would ever raise her hand at her, until now.

She stared into the eyes of her near doppelganger and frowned. Momma's long brown hair rested on her caramel toned shoulders in large loose curls. Her tight lips and frown bearing eyebrows imprinted

214

its image in her mind. The strap around her black robe loosened itself, exposing her sexy yet comfortable pink nightgown. The look in her eyes was something she'd never seen before. But Amber had seen it many times.

"I acknowledged it, Breanna," Momma screamed at her. "I acknowledged the fact that my sister fucked my husband, your father. But that meant little to me because I was seeing someone else at the time it happened. As far as I cared, Pauline could have kept him."

Tears welled in Breanna's eyes as she frowned. "So, it is true. You cheated on Daddy."

"As I said, Breanna. He didn't want to fight for me anymore—"

"Daddy fought for you, Momma. He honestly did, but you didn't love him anymore."

"I loved Marvin. I loved him very much, but," she said, looking away from Breanna. "He was controlling."

"How so, Momma?"

"Your father never wanted to see me excel in my career, so he stifled me."

Breanna's frown deepened. It all made sense to her now. When Momma got her feet off the ground and was engrossed in her career, she got pregnant with Amber within months of becoming CFO at the ad agency she used to work for years ago. She blamed Daddy and Amber for ruining the life she had. "Do you even love Amber, Momma? Do you even love me?"

Momma wiped a tear from her eye. "I love you, Breanna. Not even your stupidity will change that."

"But what about Amber? Don't you love her?"

Momma hesitated for a moment, then spoke. "I do."

"Do you really?"

Momma chuckled as she sat at the island. She took another sip of wine from her glass. "When Amber was a baby, she used to cry all the time. The only people who could settle her down were your father and your Aunt Aubrey."

Breanna stiffened. She remembered Daddy and Mom telling her about Aunt Aubrey. She had always wanted to know who she was and what she was like. But she never got a chance to know her more before the incident happened.

"Momma," Breanna said, folding her arms across her chest. "Why haven't you ever told me about Aunt Aubrey?"

"You were too young to know her, Breanna."

"Momma," said Breanna. "Amber and I are only three years apart. I know Amber spent time with her, but why didn't I meet Aunt Aubrey?"

Momma looked away from Breanna and gulped down the last sip of wine from her glass. She chuckled, then stared at her with squinted eyes. "Because Aubrey was wrong."

"Wrong for what, Momma? What did she do?"

"She was just wrong, okay," Momma huffed. She stood from the island, placed her wineglass in the sink, and walked out the kitchen. "Just go to bed, Bree."

Breanna scoffed, watching her mother step toward the staircase as if she were walking a straight line. Following her, she stared at the pictures on the wall and spotted a picture of Momma and Aunt Pauline standing next to Great Aunt Vivian. She was a little taller than the two of them. Her light brown skin resembled that of honey and caramel swirled into one, and her body was curvy in all the right places. Great Aunt Vivian's auburn brown hair sat on her shoulders in glorious curls, like she was an old-time movie star. Her smile seemed prideful yet alluring, just like Aunt Pauline and Momma's smiles.

Breanna looked above the picture and noticed a smiling, dark-skinned woman with thick, kinky hair sprawling over both her shoulders. It was longer than Aunt Pauline and Momma's hair combined. She held a laughing baby girl in her arms; her skin tone nearly matched the woman's complexion.

The woman favored both Momma and Aunt Pauline; she was just darker than they were. Breanna frowned. Was that the only picture Momma had of Amber? Was that the only time she honestly loved her sister? As she looked to the left of the picture, Breanna saw nothing but photos of herself throughout her childhood and teenage years.

Mom was right. Great Aunt Vivian chose who she wanted to love based on their skin tone. That's why Grandma Zora didn't talk about Great Aunt Vivian much because she was dark-skinned like Amber. She was probably mistreated the same way Aunt Aubrey and Amber were. This shit had to come to a stop; she couldn't allow something this stupid to continue to choke her already strained relationship with her sister.

"Momma?" Breanna peered at Momma she stopped in her footsteps and turned toward her. The frown on her face showed more than just disdain. It was attempted murder by thought. "Is that Aunt Aubrey holding Amber in that picture?"

One by one, Momma gingerly stepped down each step until she made her way back toward her. She stood beside Breanna and peeped at the pictured as she sighed.

"Momma," Breanna said. "Is that Aunt Aubrey holding Amber in that picture?"

Momma gawked at her and then started up the steps again without saying a word to Breanna.

"Momma?"

She stopped in her steps again. Her shoulders slumped as she threw her head back and took a deep breath. "You don't know when to leave well enough alone, don't you? You got that mess from your damn father."

Breanna scoffed as she shook her head. "I just asked you the same question twice, Momma. I know you heard me."

"You best watch your tone, little girl."

"I'm not a little girl anymore, Momma. The last time I checked, I was full grown."

"That's your problem. You done got stupid like your damn daddy."

"At least he tried to tell me the truth, Momma. And like you, I was too pigheaded to listen to him."

Momma marched down the few steps she went up and stood in front of Breanna. "You're about to lose your bed if you keep this shit up, Bree."

"I don't care about where I sleep tonight." She scowled. "I just want you to answer the question you've been dodging to answer."

Momma pursed her already tightened lips. "Why do you want to know so bad, girl? That woman didn't love you. I did."

"She was my Auntie, Momma. You never allowed me to spend time with her."

"That's because she was too busy trying to be a boy than the girl my mother, your grandmother, raised her to be. I didn't want you around that."

Breanna frowned, then shook her head. "You didn't like her because she was gay?"

"I didn't like her choices," Momma retorted. She placed one hand on her hip while pointing her finger at her with the other. "I couldn't support Aubrey."

"So, that's why you hate Amber too, isn't it?"

Momma scoffed. "That stupid girl followed Aubrey's footsteps and did the same thing she did."

"Being gay doesn't change who you are, Momma. It's just a preference."

"It was a preference my mother and father supported. Hell, I can't forget how they lost sight of Pauline and me when we needed them more than her."

"How so, Momma? They paid attention to all of you."

"Because she always cried about people picking on her. Aubrey always wanted their attention. And she got it," Momma said, sniffling.

She wiped away a fleeting tear. "She got everything Pauline and I ever wanted from our parents."

Breanna stared into her mother's tear-filled eyes. Her chest heaved up and down as if she ran a five-k marathon without stopping. The two people Momma spoke of didn't seem like the people she had grown to love as a little girl. Why would Grandma Zora and Granddaddy Edward ever neglect them?

She contemplated what Mom and Daddy told her about Aunt Pauline and Great Aunt Vivian. If there was one thing she understood from both her parents about those two women, it was the fact that neither of them was happy with themselves. And they for damn sure didn't want to see others smiling and enjoying themselves.

Besides, whenever she and Amber visited Grandma Zora after Momma and Daddy finalized their divorce, she never made them feel insecure or wrong for being the way they were. Grandma Zora knew Amber was gay. She'd never treated her or Breanna any differently. Those were lies Momma let spill from her lips. Whomever Momma spoke of, it sure as hell wasn't Grandma Zora.

"So, did that happen because Great Aunt Vivian didn't love Aubrey and showered you and Aunt Pauline with the affection you both craved?"

"Of course not," Momma blurted out. "Aubrey couldn't take a joke, let alone advice from Aunt Vivian. She was just too damn sensitive."

"Too sensitive?" Breanna glared at Momma. The look of pity stained her face. "It sounds like they ostracized her for being dark-skinned and sexually wrong."

Momma chuckled nonchalantly; it reverberated from her throat like a dog's low growl. "You sound just like your grandmother now. It was Aubrey's fault Great Aunt Vivian didn't like her."

"How was that her fault, Momma?"

"Because nobody told her to run off and fall in love with some white girl she met in high school. Nobody told them to elope secretly. And nobody for damn sure told them to move out on their own when neither of them had a pot to piss in. Still, your grandmother and grandfather bent over backward to help them."

"That's because they cared about all of you. Not just one of you," Breanna said.

"Well, they should have only cared about me and Pauline," Momma blurted out.

"How could you even say something like that, Momma?"

"Because the little bitch took everything from us," Momma huffed. "The house Daddy left for me was given to Aubrey. The trust fund he and your grandmother saved up for us, he gave it to those two freaks."

218

Breanna shook her head. "But Grandma Zora said you didn't want the house when Grandaddy Edward offered it to you."

Momma stared at her with squinted eyes, then made her way back up the steps. "Get out of my house."

"So, it's true." Breanna scoffed as she shook her head once more. "Why didn't you take the house Granddaddy Edward offered you?"

"Get out, Breanna."

"Was it because it was too small, Momma? Was it because you thought you were worth more than that piece of wooden shack?"

"Get out of my house, Breanna."

"I'm not leaving until you tell me why you refused the house Granddaddy Edward tried to give you, Momma."

The sounds of pounding feet against solid oak flooring rushed down the steps toward her. Momma's labored grunts echoed through Breanna's ears as witnessed her mother's hands claw at the skin on her face and neck. Pushing Momma away from her, she ran toward the front door. The clanking and clashing of wine glasses against her body and the floor made her pant in fear of the very woman who gave birth to her.

Now, she honestly couldn't tell what was worse anymore. Being strangled by a man she thought was her end-all, having her own flesh and blood scream to the heavens she hated her, listening to the very man yell at her to leave a home they once shared, or witnessing Momma's rage unfold before her eyes. Life was funny tonight. Maybe she should have taken the easier way out.

Breanna fell to her knees and covered the back of her head with her forearms. Momma's fists slammed away at the back of her extremities. She closed her eyes, letting tears stream from them.

"Momma!" Breanna cried. "Please, stop!"

Momma's blows continued. Growl like grunts emitted from a deep-seated frustration within her soul.

"Please, Momma! Stop!"

"Get the fuck out of my house!" Momma yelled. She stood to her feet, gasping for air as she glared at Breanna.

Breanna stood to her feet, staring at Momma with wide eyes. The very woman she called Momma was no longer that woman. She was gone.

"Momma! Why can't you see you hurt me and Amber—"

Another slap to her cheek stopped her lips from moving. Breanna held it as she eased away from her.

"Everything I did, I did to protect you. And what did you do?" Tears streamed down Momma's cheeks. "I should have listened to Aunt Vivian and aborted both of you."

Breanna covered her mouth and cried. "You don't mean that, Momma."

Momma glowered. "It would have saved me this heartache and pain. Now, don't you ever step foot in this house again, Bree."

Breanna opened the front door and ran out of it. Rain doused her hair and clothes as she stepped onto the pavement. Fumbling to get her car keys out of her pocket, she leaned her head against the car door and cried to herself.

A clap of thunder jolted her from her tears. Breanna quickly pulled her keys out her pocket, unlocked her car door, and slipped inside. She locked the doors and examined her soaked surroundings. She rested her head against the headrest, closed her eyes, and took a deep breath. There was only one more person she could try.

As she cranked the car, Breanna grabbed her phone from her pocket and dialed a set of numbers. She listened to the phone ring, praying to God he would answer.

"Breanna."

"Daddy," she sobbed. Breanna grabbed the steering wheel and held it tight. "I need you."

"What's wrong, Bree?"

"You were right, Daddy."

He took a deep breath and exhaled slowly. "I'm sorry you had to find out about your mother this way."

"She didn't care, Daddy. She didn't care at all."

He sighed. "Your mother—" he stopped, then took another deep breath. "Your mother doesn't think about the people around her most times until something forces her to, Bree."

"I'm so sorry I didn't listen to you... I didn't listen to Elijah."

"I heard about what happened to him. Is he okay?"

"He is," she sniffled.

"Where's Isabella? Is she okay?"

Breanna covered her mouth, trying to silence her tears. "She's okay, Daddy. They both are."

"What happened, Bree?"

Breanna took a deep breath as she eyed a streak of lightning dance across the night sky and swallowed hard. "Elijah and I broke up, and I no longer have shared custody of Isabella." She sniffled. "Oh! I forgot to mention that I have no other place to stay since Elijah and Momma don't want to have anything to do with me anymore."

"Then, come home, sweetheart," he said. "Regina and I will be waiting for you when you get here."

"Are you sure, Daddy? I don't want to make you angry."

"Come home, Breanna," he said. "We'll talk more later."

220

"I love you, Daddy."
"I love you too, Breanna."

Chapter Thirty-Seven

The rain seemed to like Breanna tonight. No matter where she went, it was right by her side, like a puppy waiting for his new owner to pick him up and nuzzle his head. She parked her car in Daddy's driveway, then rested her head against the steering wheel and took a deep breath. The last thing she wanted to do was ruin her last chance with the only set of people who continued to love her when she didn't deserve it. But with her luck tonight, that was probably going to be easier done than said.

"Here I go again," Breanna mumbled to herself as she stepped out of the car and pushed the door closed. The rain appeared to have let up some as she ambled toward the front door. Though, it wouldn't stop Mom from asking her why she didn't use an umbrella to cover her head.

Breanna remembered how she hated to hear Mom go on and on about her walking through the rain. She hated it so much she used to hum to drown out Mom's nagging until the woman would sing louder than her humming. God! That woman's voice was like butter on toast; it was so smooth. But she didn't mind the nagging, now. It was probably going to be the only source of comfort she would get. Not that she deserved it, but it would have helped soothe the wounds she imposed on herself.

The front door opened before she could knock on it. Breanna noticed Mom standing in the entranceway with a half-smile tugging at her full lips. She wore a thick pink cottony robe that made Breanna's shoulders slump from seeing it. That was her pillow, away from her pillow. Mom used to wear it whenever she combed her and Amber's hair to prepare for church every Sunday. The soft fluffiness of the robe against the back of her head made her instantly sleepy, sending her back to an unconscious state before she had to let go of her pillow. She wished she were there right now.

Breanna returned her gesture with a half-smile and stepped inside the house. She didn't deserve her kindness at all.

"Breanna," Mom said, locking the front door. "You're soaked, sweetheart. Why didn't you use an umbrella?"

"It's no big deal, Mom. I'm okay."

"It's a big deal to me, Breanna. You can catch a cold," Mom watched Breanna walk closer to the picture of Isabella hanging on the wall inside the foyer and press her fingers against it. "Are you okay, Bree?"

She stared at Mom for a moment. One by one, tears slipped down her cheeks as she shook her head. "I'm not okay, Mom. Not at all."

Breanna slumped to her knees as she covered her face and cried. Nothing could repair the hole she left gaping in Elijah's and Isabella's hearts. And no matter how hard she tried, there wasn't anything she could do to fix it. What was done was done.

Mom wrapped her arms around her shoulders as she pulled her into her embrace and held her tight. Breanna slumped to her lap and rested her head on Mom's thighs as she continued to sob. "I don't deserve your love."

"Shh." Mom moved several strands of Breanna's hair from her face. "We all make mistakes, Breanna, but that doesn't mean we don't deserve love. This is the time we need it the most."

"Why would someone love me for what I did, Mom?" she sobbed. "I don't blame them for hating me."

"They don't hate you, Bree. They're in distress right now. A lot of it," said Mom. She rocked her slowly as she rubbed her head. "That doesn't mean you can't mend what you've broken."

"Elijah asked for full custody of Isabella, Mom," Breanna said through tears. A stinging burn lingered in her throat with every breath she took. "I'm never going to get her back."

"Breanna, you've really messed things up between your daughter and your boyfriend. That doesn't mean you can't stop trying to fix what you broke."

"But Elijah doesn't want to have anything to do with me, Mom."

"Right now, he doesn't, Bree," she replied. "Elijah's confused and hurt. He's trying to figure out why things went wrong the way they did, yet he's happy that this stress is off him now. In the end, he's still going to figure out who and what he wants in his life."

Breanna closed her eyes as she sniffled. Morgan was right where she needed to be for Elijah. She was there to pick up the pieces she had left

223

strewn all over the floor. All she had to do was beckon Elijah and Isabella into her arms, and Breanna was no longer a figment of their imagination, let alone a person they wanted back in their lives. And regardless of their relationship, he and Morgan had history—a far better history than the one she shared with Elijah.

The more Breanna thought about it, the more it made sense. Morgan wasn't just trying to create a business partnership with Elijah; she was trying to find her way back into his life. She was just too stupid to realize the door she'd opened for her.

"So, what do I do now, Mom?" Breanna asked, sitting up from her lap. She stared into Mom's eyes, trying to muster a smile, yet tears welled in them instead. "What do I do?"

"As your mother said to you before, you need to forgive yourself first before you apologize to Elijah and Isabella," Daddy said, sitting on the floor next to them.

"Daddy." Breanna stared into his eyes before throwing her arms around his neck and holding him tight. She loved how he always made himself present when she didn't know he was around. She had to account that to the quiet steps he took or the fact he loved to eavesdrop first before putting in his two cents. Regardless, Breanna had to go with the latter.

"Your father is right, sweetheart," Mom said. "You need to forgive yourself first before you can attempt to make amends with the ones you love."

"That's the only way you're going to heal, Bree," he said.

Healing. That was such a big word for her to conquer. With the way she felt, nothing seemed like it would heal the wounds she inflicted on herself, especially the ones she inflicted on Elijah and Isabella. This wouldn't be an easy road to travel down. It was going to be the roughest. Yet, she was willing to take every bump, bruise, and scrape to fix what she had broken.

"Daddy," Breanna said, staring into his brown eyes once more. "Can you forgive me for everything I ever said and did to you?"

He smiled and then pulled her back into his embrace. "I forgive you, Bree," he whispered in her ear.

"I love you so much, Daddy."

"I love you too, Bree."

Mom's warm embrace wrapped around her body again. She closed her eyes and whimpered against Daddy's shoulder. Her tears splashed onto his shirt. They loved her. Despite the mess she'd drug them through, they loved her. They loved her more than she loved herself. But how? How could someone love someone else who only wanted her

224

needs and wants to be met? How could they love someone who refused to listen to the whole truth?

Breanna remembered how Mom and Daddy would ask her and Amber to help them settle simple disputes between them. She remembered how they wanted them to think about the other person's feelings—how they needed to consider both sides of the stories before making a final decision. All of that flew out the window when she moved in with Momma permanently. She remembered how Momma used to tell her they brainwashed her into believing some new Feng Shui shit when all they needed was a simple truth. Yet Momma couldn't even give her the simple truth. The woman lied to her for years.

She broke apart her and Amber's relationship, and she made her believe Mom and Daddy were the worst people in the world when, in fact, she had been living with the devil the entire time. Hell, she even let the woman ruin her relationship. She frowned, holding Daddy tighter in her embrace. As mad as she was with Momma for lying to her, Breanna knew she had to forgive her, too. This was the very process they spoke of. It just wasn't going to be an easy one.

"Breanna," Daddy said. "I got a call from Mrs. Bryson a while ago. She said she tried to call you several times, but she couldn't reach you."

"I had spoken to her at the hospital before I left, but...." Breanna hesitated. Numbness and pain danced about the base of her neck as it swelled. "I was too embarrassed... to speak to her."

Breanna swallowed hard. Knowing that Mrs. Lori wasn't the kind of person to put fluff up someone's ass, she knew for a fact she told Daddy about what happened to her at Soul Bistro. "What did she tell you?"

"What, you already know what I'm about to ask you, Bree," he said, sitting back from her. He cupped her chin, then moved it upward, revealing the inflamed, red marks on her neck.

Mom covered her mouth as she glared at her with wide eyes. "When did this happen, sweetheart?"

"More importantly, why didn't you tell me that man you had been seeing did this to you?" Daddy folded his arms across his chest.

"Because," Breanna darted her eyes away from the both of them. "I didn't want to upset you."

"So, you were just going to come into my house and act like I wouldn't find out about this man attacking you... twice."

Breanna sighed, closing her eyes. Hearing the groggy gruffness in Daddy's voice made her feel like a teenager getting caught coming into his house late again. Though she missed it, it was the last thing she wanted to hear. "I thought I could solve this problem between me and Nathaniel, but that didn't happen."

225

"Ya' damn right it didn't happen," Daddy huffed. "If the bastard wants to come around here, I got somethin' for his ass."

"Daddy, it's my fault—"

"That asshole put his hands on my baby girl. Twice," Daddy said. "I'mma put his ass six feet under if he thinks he got balls bigger than a bull's."

Breanna sobbed as she looked away from him again. "This was my fault. I caused all this mess I'm going through right now."

"That you did, Bree," said Daddy. He cupped her chin once more and stared into her eyes. "That doesn't constitute his irrational actions against you. That man has no right putting his hands on you."

Breanna looked away from his eyes. She was the spitting image of Momma now. She was no better than the woman she swore by. "Daddy, why did Momma stay with a man that beat her?"

"Because he threatened to end her life if she ever left him," Daddy replied. He scoffed. "Peter Oswald. He was her former boss at the ad agency she used to work at. I would never forget the smug look on his face when I walked into her office and saw the two of them having sex."

Breanna closed her eyes. Momma never told her any of those things Daddy told her about their relationship. All she did was make it seem like it was his fault for not trying hard enough for their love. She always blamed him for not going the extra mile for her, Amber, and herself. "So, what happened after you caught her?"

"She played that shit off like nothing ever happened."

"Really?!"

"In Gwendolyn's defense, I made the biggest mistake in the world. But when I found out that she had been cheating on me before I ever messed around with Pauline, that's when I knew our marriage was done. I couldn't erase the fact she didn't want to be a mother."

"She told me that before I came here."

Daddy chuckled. "I'm surprised she didn't say that it was my fault too."

"She did."

"That's the Gwendolyn I know," he replied. "I asked your mother countless times if she wanted to go through with the pregnancy, but she never talked to me. She just moped around like I was supposed to read her mind."

"Then, how could you tell she didn't want either of us?"

"When she threatened to put you up for adoption after a nasty argument we had."

Breanna's eyes widened. Momma was truly full of surprises. "Why, Daddy?"

226

"Because she thought you were Peter's child instead of mine." He sighed. "Thankfully, the DNA test I took matched your blood instead of that arrogant white asshole she called herself being a sidepiece to."

"He was white?"

Daddy nodded. "If you ever wondered why she didn't like Elijah, now you know."

Breanna shook her head as she stared into Daddy's deep brown eyes. "Why did she make it seem like it was your fault, though?"

"For one, she said I never allowed her to be herself when we were married," he replied. "That Peter gave her all the reasons to be herself, but when he didn't get what he wanted from her, he started beating her."

"And why was that?"

Daddy chuckled, trying to maintain his composure. "He wanted her to leave me and put you and Amber up for adoption so she could have children with him. According to this crazed bastard, he saw how submissive she was to him and wanted more of it."

"And that's where you stepped in, right?"

He nodded once more. "That was the night Peter held your mother at gunpoint. He threatened to shoot me in the head if I tried to come to her aid. The bastard didn't know how good of a shot I was."

"Did she even thank you for saving her life?"

"Just like I told Regina, Gwen just decided to end it all rather than work things out. When we went our separate ways, she tried coming back into my life, but by the time she had pulled that little stunt, Regina and I had been seeing each other for more than a year."

"That's why Momma called Mom the other woman."

"Your mother allowed those witches, Vivian and Pauline, to come into her life and fill her head up with some mumbo jumbo shit about deserving better—"

"When she already had something good at home." Breanna knew that all too well. Momma had done a fabulous job in distorting her mind and making her believe she needed a man better than Elijah. Yet Eli had been there from the moment she pleaded with him to help her with her statistics course to the day her water broke in his truck. He was there. She had to fight for his love. The time for waddling in her own pity had to stop. She had to deal with the shit she created and change it. No matter how hard it would be, Breanna couldn't let Elijah and Isabella waltz out of her life.

Breanna rested her head on Daddy's shoulder and closed her eyes as she held on to Mom's hand. She couldn't let them slip through her fingers, either. She couldn't keep fighting them and pushing them away from her. Breanna needed the people she loved the most surrounding

227

her. She needed—the sounds of jingling keys sliding into a keyhole made her heart sink into her stomach. Not wanting to fight with her sister, she knew Amber wouldn't be thrilled seeing her in her territory.

"Are you fucking serious right now?" Amber stared at the three of them sitting on the foyer's wooden floor. She closed the door behind her and walked past the three of them, shaking her head and mumbling under her breath.

Daddy rose to his feet and followed Amber into the great room. He took a seat on the gray sectional couch and grazed his hand over the smoothness of his salt and peppered hair. "Amber, I need you and your sister to sit down and talk."

"Why? That heffa doesn't like me." She turned on her heel and pointed in Breanna's direction. "Why should I waste my breath talking to her?"

Breanna stood from the floor, pulling Mom up with her. She took a deep breath and walked inside the great room. "I know I did you wrong, Amber—"

"Don't give me that bullshit, Bree," she said, cutting her off. "You're just like Momma. Bitchy and self-centered."

"You're right, Amber," Breanna said, fighting back the tears. "But I know now she was wrong. I know that I was wrong."

"I'm glad you've finally learned that," she replied, placing her hand over her heart. "You want a cookie."

Mom stepped inside the great room and took a seat next to Daddy. "Girls, you two need to talk this through and not tear each other's heads off."

"Then, tell her to leave." Amber folded her arms across her chest. "I refuse to live under the same roof with this bitch."

"That's enough, Amber," Daddy said.

Amber shot him a stern glare, then rolled her eyes in Breanna's direction. Breanna returned her gaze, then looked away from her. Amber had all the right to call her out of her name. The pain she endured from her and Momma's mistreatment over the years damaged her, and she understood why she hated her. But she couldn't let that be their relationship now. She had to change that regardless of if Amber refused it or not.

"Momma lied to me too, Amber," Breanna stated. "She wanted me to stay with a man who hit me rather than work out my relationship with Elijah."

"You mean your ex."

Breanna sighed, feeling the sting of those words rush through her ears. "Yes. My ex."

"You know all this shit is your fault, right?"

"I know, Amber." Breanna stepped closer to her. "But I want to make things right with my big sister."

"Well, that's going to be a waste of your time because I don't want to hear it."

"Amber, please just give your sister a chance to talk to you," Mom pleaded.

"You two may have fallen for her crap, but I know what it is like to live with this little—"

"Don't you even say it, Amber," Daddy said, folding his arms across his chest.

Breanna reached for Amber's hand, then witnessed her snatch it away before she could grasp it. Asking for forgiveness was much more challenging than she assumed it was. "I love you, Amber. What happened to me tonight taught me I needed my genuine family; a family that loves and supports me despite my bullshit. You don't have to love me, Amber, but I'll always love you."

Breanna noticed the tears welling in Amber's eyes. All that hurt and anger played at the corner of her tear ducts. All that bottled-up rage was ready to lash out at her. Momma had done a perfect job in separating the two of them. But Breanna was tired of fighting with the ones she loved. She had to take back what she allowed their devilish Momma to take from her.

As she reached for Amber's hand again, Breanna grabbed it and squeezed it tight. "I love you, Amber. More than you would ever know."

"Sure, you do."

"I do, Amber."

"Momma chose who she wanted as her real daughter, and she made sure I knew who that daughter was."

"And she was wrong for what she did to both of us; she had no right to come between our sisterhood."

"You sound fake as hell right now, Breanna."

"But I still love you just the same, and nothing's going to stop me from needing my big sister."

"Sure, Bree," Amber said. "I'm listening to your sob-ass stories."

"You don't have to believe me, Amber. You really don't. But what I know is that Aunt Aubrey would have been so proud of you if she saw you today. I only wished I knew her like the way you did."

A tear slipped down Amber's cheek. "You saw the picture at Momma's house?"

"I did," Breanna nodded. "Amber, I don't expect you to forgive me overnight, but that doesn't mean I won't stop until I make things right with you."

Amber narrowed her eyes. "I won't ever let you get close to me again."

Breanna stared at Mom and Daddy, then took a deep breath. "Maybe I should get a hotel room for the night. I don't want to make matters worse."

Amber nodded. "Finally, something that we both can agree on."

"No one is going to be leaving this house tonight," Daddy said. "Either you learn how to deal with each other for the time being, or you both will be without a bed to lie on."

"That's not fair, Dad," Amber retorted.

"I think it's pretty fair," Mom chimed in. "If neither of you is going to work on getting along with each other, then there's no need for either of you to stay in this house."

"Fine," Amber huffed. "But don't you dare get in my way, Breanna."

"I won't, Amber." Breanna kissed her sister's cheek, then stepped away from her. "I hope you can forgive me for everything that I ever did to you, big sis."

Chapter Thirty-Eight

The sounds of muffled sobs and whimpers caught Amber's attention as she strode past Breanna's old bedroom door. She frowned, shaking her head. The heffa was putting on the biggest show she'd ever seen, and Mom and Dad lapped that shit up like it was the best last drop of gravy dripping off their biscuits. But whether it was real or not, she deserved every little kick to the ass and slap to the face she got. Her niece shouldn't have ever endured the mistreatment her flesh and blood put her through.

What mother would ever pick her selfishness over her child's needs and wants? Oh! She had forgotten. Momma was the queen of desire. Breanna was taught by the best in the business. And just like Momma, Amber couldn't wait to watch Breanna burn, too.

Amber heard Breanna sob again and shook her head once more. She rolled her eyes as she stepped away from the door. Leaving her ass was the best thing Elijah could have done. Her sister didn't deserve a man as loving and faithful as he was. Hell, she didn't deserve the patience he had given her. Even after she cheated on him, Elijah still wanted to marry her. But brother-in-law came to his senses, thankfully. There was so much better out there for him.

The familiar sounds of a melodic piano drifted from underneath Breanna's closed door, forcing Amber to step back toward it. She pressed her ear against the decorative wooden slab and listened to her sister sing along with Smokie Norful's "I Need You Now". She couldn't remember how long it had been since she heard her sister sing, let alone that very song.

Breanna was only nine-year-old when she sang this at church. For her to have been so young, she belted out those lyrics like she was a full-grown woman—a woman going through the stresses and strains of life. Amber closed her eyes and then took a deep breath. That was during the time Momma and Dad called the quits. Even though she was happy Dad left Momma, Breanna didn't know how to deal with it. Unlike her, she needed them both to feel happy; she needed them both to feel complete. Momma had taken that away from her.

A tear rolled down her cheek as she listened to Breanna sing. Her voice was reminiscent of a raspy jazz singer that could hit a soprano but naturally sung in alto. Amber closed her eyes and listened to her hit the song's highest note. Breanna's voice fell back to its natural, smooth rasp. She hummed along with Breanna's vibrato.

She remembered how Momma hated them singing around the house. The woman often complained they kept up too much noise. Yet, whenever Grandma Isabella came over, she and Breanna would always sing with her. Momma knew they were happy when Grandma Isabella came around. Grandma would bust out into a song, and Breanna would sing right along with her. Momma hated that all their good traits came from their father's side of the family. She even threatened to take away their possessions if they kept singing throughout the house.

Momma's threats didn't seem to faze Breanna much. Well, that was because she was the favorite daughter and all. But when Grandma Isabella passed away, Breanna stopped singing. Sure, Momma was happy about that. She was overjoyed they weren't running around the house singing at the top of their lungs anymore. But rather than asking Breanna why she stopped singing, Momma didn't so as much try to talk to her about handling her grief.

"God," Breanna said from behind the closed door. "Please forgive me for what I've done to my family. Forgive me for the anguish I've caused them."

Amber wiped a tear from her eye as she listened to her.

"I just want my daughter back. I want my husband back. I want my sister back, oh, father," she whimpered. "But I've hurt them so badly; I've shredded their hearts into pieces."

Amber covered her mouth, trying to muffle her sobs. It had been so long since she heard her sister pray. Was this the Breanna she remembered before Momma ruined her? Was this the Breanna she loved when they stayed with Mom and Dad for the summer of 2002?

"Please, God! Even if it's just for a moment, I want Amber's love again. I wish I never broke her heart. I miss my sister so much."

Amber tapped on her door, hoping she didn't wake Mom and Dad with her knocking. "Breanna, can I come in?"

The creaking sounds of clicks graced Amber's ears as she watched the door swing open, revealing a tear-stained Breanna. She watched her little sister wipe her eyes and sniffle. Breanna glanced into Amber's eyes, then darted them toward the floor.

"I'm sorry if I woke you up, Amber. I didn't—"

Amber pulled Breanna into her embrace, holding her tight. "I miss you too, little sis."

Breanna's body trembled in her arms as she cried against her shoulder. "I love you so much, Amber."

"I love you too, Bree," she sobbed, hugging her tighter. Tears flowed onto her sister's hair and shoulder. "Promise me you'll never leave again."

"I promise, Amber," Breanna cried. "I'll never let that woman tear us apart again. I promise."

Amber sobbed, hoping she didn't wake Mom and Dad from their slumber. This was the Breanna she remembered. This was the little sister she dreamed would return to her one day. And by the grace of God, she had. Momma did a hell of a job screwing over Breanna's logic; she ripped the very bond they shared apart. But as Grandma Zora always professed, Breanna was going to start thinking on her own two feet again, and it wouldn't be long before she realized Momma's ways.

As much as she didn't believe Grandma Zora, Amber should have seen this coming. Amber smiled against Breanna's shoulder, remembering how they used to sit on Grandma Zora's stoop and eat the blueberry muffins she made for them when they were little girls. She and Breanna would smile at each other to see who had the bluest teeth and tongue. They would laugh their hearts away until Breanna heard Momma's horn honk in the background and witness her smile dissipate into a pitiful pout.

Amber never wanted to discuss how Breanna felt when Momma used to pick her up from Grandma Zora's house, but that one Saturday afternoon stood out like a bright red stop sign in her mind. For it to have been late June, the summer's breeze kept them comfortable in the heat. She watched Breanna get up from the stoop and run through Grandma Zora's French doors after hearing Momma's horn. She recalled standing to her feet and watching Breanna hug their grandmother, begging her not to let Momma take her home yet.

Amber always thought Breanna didn't want to go home because she wanted to stay with Grandma Zora for the rest of the week like she was. Yet, it didn't dawn on her that she wanted to be with her sister. Grandma Zora was right.

"I'm so sorry for all the pain I've caused you," Breanna whispered in her ear. "I don't know where to begin to make things right between us."

233

"This is a good start, Breanna," Amber replied. She took a deep breath. "I forgive you, little sis."

Breanna's sobs melded with Smoky Norful's voice in the background as she cried again. Amber held her sister tight in her embrace, not wanting this moment to ever end. This was the Breanna she longed to have back in her life again.

Chapter Thirty-Nine

Two days of lying in a hospital bed, and Elijah was ready to break free from his confines. The numbing aches and tingles shooting up and down his back and legs made him want to jump from the window next to his bed. The impact would indeed send him straight off this earth, knowing his luck, but at least his ass would thank him for the stretch.

He gazed at Morgan sprawled about on the too tight sofa positioned near the window and smiled. Elijah was so thankful she was around to find him; he was thankful Isabella had someone to support her during the incident. He narrowed his eyes, examining the couch. Breanna would have liked it since it had white and yellow chrysanthemums scattered about its jaded green hue. That woman's sense of style was nowhere to be found. Breanna. She had the audacity to come into this very room and pretend like she could push her way back into his life.

After all the bullshit she'd put him and Izzy through, Breanna needed to be shoved out that window Morgan slept next to. Hell, if he could have, Elijah would have pushed her out the window with his foot and watched her fall to the ground until she bounced a couple of times before settling in one place. Sure, he knew the fall would kill her, but he didn't care what happened to her. All he cared about was regaining his happiness. All he wanted was to make his daughter smile again as she deserved to.

"Hey, Sunshine," Morgan said, sitting up on the couch. She rubbed her neck as she winced. "How are you feeling this morning?"

"Much better, Morgan." He smiled. "Did my mom take Izzy with her last night?"

"Lori." Morgan sighed. "Yeah, she took Isabella with her."

He watched her stand from the ugly piece of furniture, then inhaled and exhaled slowly. Those two never got along. No matter how hard he tried to get Mom to understand Morgan, she never gave her the opportunity to speak with her peacefully. And Morgan was the same way. She never allowed Mom to finish her sentences. Morgan always assumed Mom thought of her as another no good for nothing black woman. But that was far from the case. Those two needed to come to a moot point if they were going to make this work. And Izzy didn't need any more drama in her life. She had been through enough shit already.

"You know," Elijah said, moving to his side and allowing his butt bone to get a breather. "Mom isn't a bad person."

"Like hell, she isn't, Sunshine," Morgan said. "I'm surprised she loves Isabella."

"Mom doesn't care about the color of your skin, Morgan."

"Are you sure about that?"

He frowned, nodding his head. "I'm sure about that."

"Well, maybe she liked Breanna because the bitch acted white."

"That's not true, Morgan. Mom didn't care if Breanna was black or not. Besides," he said, trying to calm her down. "Mom knows I'm attracted to black women. I always have been, and I always will be."

Morgan placed her hand over her heart. "That's sweet of you to say, Sunshine, but your mother is an undercover racist."

Elijah sighed, rubbing his temple. Mom wasn't racist. She was just unnecessarily picky over the women he dated. Even when he dated Kylie, the beautiful brunette with the hazel brown eyes and porcelain skin who played on the soccer team back in high school, he knew Mom didn't like her either. That was because Kylie was generously open to her male counterparts on the baseball and soccer teams. He would never forget how Mom used to call her K-Mart Kylie. There was no telling how many kids she had by now.

"Mom's not racist, Morgan," Elijah said. "She only wants the best for me and Kat."

Morgan stared at him with a side-eye and smiled as she nodded her head. "Oh! I almost forgot about Katrina. She's another one that doesn't like me either."

"And do you believe Kat's racist too?"

"Naw," Morgan shook her head. "She throws shade whenever she feels like she's being threatened, but other than that, she's just spoiled."

He lifted an eyebrow. "Then what do you think of my dad?"

236

"I like Mr. Jonah. He knows how to stay out of the way, unlike your sister and your wanna be startin' something momma."

Elijah took a deep breath without the urge to cough festering in the back of his throat. It had been a long time since that phenomenon occurred. "Listen, Morgan. I can't change how the way you feel about my mom and sister, but what I can do is thank you for saving my life."

She grinned, shrugging her shoulders. "No problem, Sunshine. Besides, I didn't want to see the only man who gave a shit about me hurt. It was the least I could do."

"What are you talking about, Morgan? There are plenty of men that care about you."

"Not like the way you do," she breathed, gazing into his eyes. Morgan sat next to Elijah, letting her fingers brush against his. "You've always made me feel... you know... special."

"How so?"

Morgan leaned closer to his lips, then bit her bottom lip. "Because you never forgot about me."

Elijah cupped Morgan's chin and drew her lips toward his. He kissed her, savoring the sweet remnants of chocolate on them. A subtle moan emerged from her throat like a low growl. Her lips were so sweet, so delicate, so soft. Just like the way he remembered them. He ran his fingers through her curly hair, letting his hand slink its way to the middle of her back. Elijah deepened the kiss, losing himself in listening to her moans and tasting her lips until the sudden bothered yet scratchy clearing of one's throat in the background made him pull from them.

He stared at Dr. Holly and Mom for a moment, taking in the surprised look of one and the near assassination of the other.

"Um," Dr. Holly stammered, fumbling his chart around in his hands in search of his pen. His white lab coat covered his plaid red and white button-down shirt. The khaki pants he wore seemed as if they were going to shoot off him from how tight they looked. "I've got great news for you, Mr. Bryson."

"What's that?" Elijah kept his eyes trained on Mom.

"You're going home today."

"That's some good news, Sunshine," Morgan said, kissing his cheek. She rolled her eyes in his mom's direction and smiled.

"I've got your prescription ready for you as well," Dr. Holly continued, rubbing his hand over the circular bald spot in the middle of his head. The rest of his hair decided it wanted to part the area like vinegar was splashed into a cup of water. "And oh! I'm going to need you to go easy on the heavy lifting for about a week or two. This way, the nebulizer can work its magic on your lungs and get you feeling like yourself again, or more like improve them, might I add."

Elijah turned his attention from Dr. Holly's and recaptured his gaze with Mom's unsettled eyes. It seemed like every fiber in her being was lit on fire. That was because she and Morgan were too busy playing head games with each other.

"I'll be back with your discharge work, Mr. Bryson, and then you'll be good to go."

"Morgan," Mom said, stepping closer to them. "I would like to speak with my son alone, please."

Morgan flashed her a wry smirk, taking in the frustration drawn all over Mom's face. "Whatever you need to say to him, you can say in front of me."

Mom took a deep breath and glared at him with narrowed eyes before directing them back toward Morgan. The last time he witnessed Mom look like that was when Dad went out and bought that motorcycle. But it was even worse when Dad fell off it and broke his wrist. That motorcycle was gone before he even got home from the hospital. "Morgan, I'm not asking you. I'm telling you to step out, please."

Morgan chuckled, then stood to her feet. "Sure, Lori. I don't mind stepping out for a minute."

Mom eyed Morgan as she walked out the room. She turned toward Elijah and then sat next to him. "What the hell are you doing, Eli?"

"Mom, please don't start with that—"

"Don't start. Son, I know I raised you better than this." The vein in her forehead looked like it was about to pop. "You're going to leave one woman and jump into another woman's arms. You're not thinking straight, right now."

"I am thinking straight, Mom. Morgan has been there for me and Izzy when Breanna wasn't around."

"So, you're cheating too, right?"

"I'm not cheating on her, Mom," he fussed. "Breanna had been laying in another man's bed for the past two months."

"Then why in the hell did you still propose to her, Eli?"

"Because I thought we could work out our relationship."

"Son," Mom said. She took his hand in hers and patted the top of it with her other one. "Don't you remember when your grandmother used to accuse me of stealing your father's money?"

Elijah shook his head, not wanting to remember those moments when Grandma made Dad choose his money over Mom. Those were moments he tried to erase from his memory. Instead, they happily remained unwelcomed in his mind. "I do, Mom."

"Do you remember when my brother came and took you and Kat to the fair the day your grandmother came over for the weekend?"

238

Elijah nodded, noticing her frown lines deepen. "I remember Mom."

"That was the very day I decided to end our marriage for your grandmother. I left the house that day knowing I wouldn't be around to see my children like the way I used to."

"But that's different, Mom. You never cheated on Dad." The sight of tears welling in her eyes made Elijah shake his head. His heart drummed against his chest, not wanting to hear what she was about to say. "Mom, you never cheated on Dad, right?"

"I did, son," she answered solemnly. "It was a mistake I made out of anger."

"Not you, Mom."

"I'm not perfect, Eli," she said. "Your grandmother is fully to blame, but I'm the one who laid up with a man who I had just met."

"You never told me this." Elijah glared at her before looking away from her and pulling his hand from hers. "How could you do that to Dad, Mom?"

"Because the woman whom your father loved dearly made her own son choose his money over me, and that drove me insane. I couldn't believe he was willing to divorce me to please a woman who nearly killed your sister and me."

Elijah's shoulders slumped as he hung his head. A tear fell onto the top of his hand and rolled over to his thumb. Ms. Gwendolyn did the same thing to him and Breanna. Though her reasons were far different from his grandmother's, Ms. Gwendolyn had come in between them like Grandma did. Still, that didn't give Breanna the right to go out and lay up with some man she thought was going to restore what she lost. That didn't give Breanna the right to find comfort in another man when she could have talked to him. Another tear slipped down his cheek as he looked up at his mom.

"Why didn't you fight for your love for Dad, Mom? Why did you let Grandma do that to you?"

"Because I knew if I placed your father in a position where he had to choose, I knew he wouldn't forgive himself for how your grandmother reacted if he chose me over her," she sighed. "After your grandfather passed away, Beverly went on a mission to destroy everything he gave his blessing to. Why do you think your uncles stopped coming to Tennessee after your grandfather passed away?"

He stared into Mom's eyes for a moment with furrowed eyebrows, knowing what Mom was about to say would be far worse than he heard before. "Grandma ran them away too?"

Mom nodded. "Your Uncle Pete and his wife Stacy didn't want her ruining the private practice they built from the ground up, and your

239

Uncle Mike and Bethany didn't want her around their kids after they had bought bonds totaling over $500,000."

"Wait. So, you're saying that grandma was money-hungry."

"Your grandmother was a jealous, greedy bitch who wanted her children to take care of her despite them having lives of their own. Your father stuck around to make sure your grandmother got around. Instead, she nearly ruined us."

"But what happened between you and Dad? Did you ever tell him you cheated on him?"

"I did. And we talked it over. Of course, he wasn't happy with me, but he understood why, Eli."

"But I never recalled you two ever separating," Elijah said, raking his fingers through his hand.

"Your father and I didn't want that to spill over into your and Kat's lives, so we worked it out. It wasn't easy, but we learned to forgive each other. We learned what was more important to us. We wanted each other. We wanted our children to be happy."

"But it's not that simple with Breanna, Mom. She cheated on me for two months."

"And I had a one-night stand," she retorted. "Don't make the same mistake she did with you, my son."

"I can't forgive her for what she did to Isabella; I can't forgive her for what she did to me."

"I know, Eli. It hurts," Mom said, standing from his bed. "But please consider the decisions you make before you find yourself in Breanna's shoes if Morgan decides she wants to step out on you again too."

"I'll be careful, Mom."

"You better be because I don't like her. That woman's greedy and jealous like your grandmother."

"I don't think she is, Mom."

"She waited for you to drop Breanna so she could hop into your bed again. There's something that she wants, my son, and it's way more than what you think it is."

Elijah watched his mother leave out the room. Morgan wasn't that person anymore. He knew that for a fact. Hell, she saved his life when Breanna wasn't around. Yet, Mom's words lingered about in his brain like a nightmare. Morgan wouldn't do that. He knew she wouldn't, or would she?

Chapter Forty

Thirty minutes and no sign of Leslie. Breanna glanced at the other patrons sitting and talking with their companions inside the naturally lit dining room and sighed. She sunk into the booth where she sat and took another sip of her lemonade, hoping she didn't waste her time waiting for Leslie to appear. It had been a week since she responded to her message, but she replied, nevertheless.

Maybe this was her way of getting back at Breanna. If it were, she couldn't blame Leslie. She would have struck at herself, too.

The sounds of Najee's saxophone hummed through the diner's sound system. She closed her eyes, thinking back to when Elijah brought her here after her volleyball game. And the night they shared after sharing a slice of chocolate cake was far more thrilling. That was their third time having sex, and her first time coming home late to Momma's house.

Breanna stared at her clock and then looked at the door. Still no sign of Leslie. She wished she could have convinced Amber to come with her instead of going out with Leilani. She needed her big sister to hold her hand like the way she had when she got her ears pierced when she was ten years old.

"Is this seat taken?" a young man asked, smiling at her. His ivory skin seemed like it needed more sunlight, and the slew of pimples on the side of his face told her more of a story than he may not have wanted to relay. "You look like you can use some company."

"I'm good, thank you," she responded. His blue eyes resembled Elijah's. They just didn't have that hint of gray in them. "I'm waiting for someone."

"Oh, okay," he said. "I'm John, by the way. If you change your mind, I'll be sitting with some friends of mine."

"Thanks, John, but I'm fine."

"That you are," he said, walking away from her.

She scoffed as she looked down at her phone. No other man could take the place Elijah left vacant in her heart. No other man could come close to the way he touched her, kissed her, and pleased her. Now, he was with another woman—another woman that was willing and ready to make her the laughingstock of Kentfield.

"Is there anything else you want to order, Ma'am?"

Breanna looked up from her phone and stared into Leslie's eyes. A smile pulled her lips and tears welled in her eyes. "Leslie... it's been—"

"A while since we spoke. I know."

"How have you been?"

"I've been doing well," Leslie replied, sitting across from Breanna. As Leslie beckoned for the waitress to come her way, she turned her attention toward Breanna and flashed a half-smile. "I'm not as stressed out as I used to be now that I work with Dr. Ackers at the pediatric clinic."

Breanna nodded as she smiled at her. Breanna noticed Leslie peck away at her cellphone, then looked in John's direction before returning her attention toward the front door. This was a mistake. What she had done to the people that loved her wouldn't change the fact they couldn't stand the sight of her. The only reason Leslie showed up was so she wouldn't look like the bad guy.

"Leslie," Breanna said, clearing her throat. "I'm sorry for wasting your time. I should probably go."

"Breanna," she said, placing her hand on top of Breanna's. "You're not wasting my time. I'm just surprised and happy you called me. It's been some months since we've sat down and talked to each other."

Breanna quickly swiped away a tear sliding down her cheek. "It has, hasn't it?"

Leslie nodded. "There were times I wanted to reach out to you, but I didn't want to risk saying or doing something stupid that would ruin our friendship further."

"Well, nothing didn't stop me from ruining our friendship." Breanna wiped another fleeting tear away from her cheek.

"Breanna," Leslie said. She took a deep breath. "I was wrong too."

"How so, Leslie?"

242

"Because I didn't take your feelings into consideration," she replied. "I was too busy trying to tell you what you had done wrong versus seeing the whole picture."

Breanna stared into her big, deep brown eyes. Another tear slid down her cheek. All she ever did was blame Elijah for keeping her from living her life, yet she remembered the many times he went back and apologized to her. She remembered how he used to lie on the bed next to her and rub her stomach when she didn't feel well. Breanna remembered when he used to run her bath water and place her inside the bathtub after they had done all they could to stop the surging cramps ripping from her stomach to her thighs.

"I really appreciate you for saying that, Leslie," Breanna said through the now flowing tears cascading down both her cheeks. "But you don't have to apologize for what you thought was right."

"And that didn't give me the right to tell you how to run your life either, Breanna," said Leslie. "I knew Elijah had his fair share of wrongs too—"

"But he apologized for them too, Leslie. You can't overlook that."

Leslie looked away from her, wiping away a tear from her eye. "I can't, but that still gives me the right to tell you what you should and shouldn't have done with your boyfriend."

"You were only looking out for your best friend. Just like when I looked out for you when you first met AJ. I thought he was too good to be true."

Leslie smiled as she nodded. "I remember your exact words too."

Breanna chuckled. "Damn, he fine, but he better not be lyin'."

She and Leslie laughed aloud together, making the other patrons look at them sideways. Breanna took hold of Leslie's hands and squeezed them tight. It had been a long time since they sat down and laughed with each other. She missed that.

"Breanna," Leslie said, squeezing her hands tighter. "I'm happy you called me."

"I'm glad you came out," Breanna said, taking a deep breath. She hesitated for a second. "I knew I messed up our relationship. That was my fault, Leslie. I let another man and some thirsty ass heffa who claimed she was my friend come in between us. I honestly hope you can forgive me."

"I forgive you, Bree," said Leslie. "You know I love you like a sister, right?"

"I know." Breanna nodded as she closed her eyes for a moment. Tear stains covered her face. "I love you like a sister too, Leslie."

Getting up from the booth where they sat, Breanna and Leslie embraced each other, not caring if the other patrons were gawking at them or not. It was these little moments she and Leslie cherished. That was something Tessa never did. Hell, she probably didn't know what the definition of kindness was. Though the damage had already been done, she realized Tessa was only a leaf in the wind, ready to be blown wherever the wind took her.

Breanna remembered how they used to cut cartwheels and backflips in Daddy's backyard and fall to the ground in laughter when he came running outside, attempting to do a backflip only to bust his ass and groan in agony through his laughter. Breanna smiled. How could she have let all that pass her by? Why was the better question that needed to be asked?

"Bree," Leslie said, pulling away from her. She stared into her eyes, then looked away from her, trying to avoid what she was about to say next. "AJ told me that Morgan's been staying with Elijah since he got out of the hospital."

Breanna took a deep breath, trying to digest the information she just heard. Though she didn't put the thought past her, she knew that would happen in their relationship. She just had to roll with the flow now.

"Is he happy?"

Leslie stared at her with a raised eyebrow. "Are you serious right now with this ish, Bree? You've got to talk to him."

"Elijah has nothing to do with me anymore," Brenna replied. "He's probably better off with her than dealing with the shit I put him through."

"Breanna," Leslie said, grabbing her by the hand and leading her out of the diner. "You fucked up. There's no getting over that. But if you let that man and little girl walk out of your life forever, you'll never know what could have been."

"Maybe it's better this way, Leslie."

"No, it's not, Bree. It just isn't," Leslie fussed. "Morgan is out to suck Elijah dry and rip their company from underneath them."

Breanna stared into Leslie's eyes, seeing the frustration in them, and sighed. "Leslie, I know you don't like her, but Morgan saved his life."

"And she's about to take his breath away again too if she sinks her claws in deep enough."

"What are you talking about, Leslie?"

The laughter of kids riding on bikes and skateboards on the sidewalk and barking down running behind him drew her attention away from Leslie's eyes. She knew Leslie meant well, but what she had done to Elijah sealed her fate. There was no returning to normalcy with him and Isabella anymore. That ship sailed months ago.

"I'm talking about the fact that Morgan's trying to buy their company from under them and make Elijah and AJ work for her."

Breanna furrowed her eyebrows. "AJ told you this?"

"He did." Leslie nodded. "Right before Elijah went into the hospital, AJ spoke with some of her employees, and they weren't happy working for her. They're overworked and underpaid. Yet when they're working solely with AJ and Elijah, they're happier. That's because she knows she can't compete with them."

Breanna folded her arms across her chest as they strode away from the diner. Spring's breeze slowly shifted into the sweating season as she realized the cardigan she wore was making her sweat. "Leslie, I get why you're trying to urge me to call him, but he won't listen to me."

"Then he'd better get used to seeing you around," Leslie said with a smirk.

"Leslie." Breanna eyed her with a raised eyebrow. "What's going on in that brain of yours?"

"You said your shift ends at 8 p.m. tomorrow, right?"

Breanna nodded. "Yeah. I did. Why?"

"Swing by my house after your shift, okay."

"Leslie," Breanna pleaded. "What are you up to?"

"Just trust the process, sis."

Breanna glanced at Leslie and smiled at her hesitantly. Whatever was about to happen, she had to fasten her seatbelt tight.

Chapter Forty-One

Of all things holy, why in the hell did Leslie invite her when she knew Elijah would be here? Breanna sat in her car, fumbling the keys around in her hand. This man had nothing to do with her, and now, a week and a half later, she was stalking him so she could talk to him again. She took another deep breath. This wasn't going to go well. She just knew it wouldn't.

Breanna emerged from her car and brushed a few stray crumbs and residual cake batter away from her work uniform. She pulled off her stain ladened apron and slung it to the backseat of the Honda. Nightingales chirped their beautiful lyrics behind the leaves of dogwood trees. The red sky touched her skin as she walked toward AJ and Leslie's front door. The sight of Elijah's pickup truck beside AJ's Camry made her take a deep breath. She hoped Leslie was right about this.

Before Breanna could even fix her hand to knock on the door, Leslie opened it. "Come on in, girl. I've been waiting for you to arrive."

"Um...," Breanna scratched her head for a moment. "Do you guys have hidden cameras or something?"

Leslie pointed to the hidden camera above her head. "It gives me the peace of mind I need when I'm here by myself. Plus, I can listen to Mr. Stanley and his wife, Mrs. Emma, fuss over who won the 1974 episode of Jeopardy."

Breanna closed her eyes and snickered. "That is so wrong on so many levels."

"I know," Leslie replied, gesturing for her to step inside the foyer. "But I get it honest."

"By the way, how's your mom doing?"

"She's been doing well. She's supposed to be coming in town sometime this month," said Leslie.

Breanna followed Leslie toward the family room and stood behind her. Her heart raced against her chest, hearing Elijah's voice. He sounded so peaceful, so content. It wouldn't last long after she showed her ugly mug.

"Who was at the door, sweetheart?" AJ glanced at Leslie, spotting Breanna standing behind her. He turned his attention to Elijah and continued his conversation like he never saw her.

Why in the hell did she even come here? Breanna closed her eyes and took another deep breath.

"Eli," Leslie said, walking into the family room. "There's someone here who wants to speak with you."

He turned in Breanna's direction and stared into her eyes before turning away from her.

"I thought you said that Aaron and his little sister, Leah, were coming over for a while."

"I may have lied a smidge bit, Eli," Leslie said, gesturing for AJ to come her way. "Instead, we thought it would be a good idea for you and Breanna to talk."

Breanna watched Elijah as he rolled his eyes and turned from her. She stepped into the family room and sat in the recliner across from him. As she noticed AJ and Leslie tip out of the room like they were in church, Breanna heard their footsteps on the wooden floor fade in the distance.

"Elijah—"

"Save it, Breanna. I don't feel like going back to the hospital at your expense."

"Elijah, please," Breanna pleaded. "Let's just try to talk, okay."

He chuckled. "Whenever I tried to just talk to you," he said, making the quotation fingers. "Yo' ass jumped down my throat about what I'd done to you."

"You're right, Elijah. I did that to you," she said. "But I was wrong for what I did to you and Isabella."

"You keep Isabella out of this, Breanna."

"She's my daughter too, Eli."

"Oh, so now you want to act like a mother now. Where was this energy when she needed it the most, Breanna?"

Breanna swallowed hard, fighting back the tears. His words ripped into her core like a knife to a watermelon. She closed her eyes for a

247

moment. "I wasn't there for her when she needed me most. I know what I did to her was wrong."

"So, you're just not realizing this? You're just not realizing you had a good man at home, yet you still took your ass to another man who only wanted to treat you like a fucking punching bag. I feel sorry for you."

A tear slipped down her cheek. "You're right, Elijah. I was only focused on what I wanted, not what I needed."

"You know," he said, standing from AJ and Leslie's black leather sofa. "You need to take your crazy ass back to ole dude."

The utterance of the words spilling from Elijah's lips sent a pain shooting down her spinal cord. She closed her eyes again. Several tears stream down her cheeks. "Where did you hear that from?"

"I've met Nathaniel before," Elijah said with a smirk. "He ran into me when AJ and I were at the park playing a pickup game of baseball during our lunch break."

"I'm so sorry, Elijah."

"Stop wasting your breath. What's done is done. Deal with it."

"If I could take this all back—"

"You wouldn't," he retorted, cutting her off. "Don't even fucking pretend like you would change anything because you wouldn't."

"I would, Elijah. I honestly would."

He laughed sarcastically. "You need an Emmy for this performance, Breanna."

"I would die for you and Isabella, Eli," she sobbed. "But even if I died, that still wouldn't mend your broken heart. I know it wouldn't. At least all your problems would disappear, though."

Breanna stood from the chair and walked toward the room's opening. She turned toward Elijah and stared into his narrowed eyes. There was so much pain and anger behind them. She couldn't blame him for how the way he felt. She couldn't forget that this was her fault.

Breanna darted her eyes away from him again and wiped away her falling tears. Now she knew how he felt. "I'm sorry I wasted your time."

"Breanna," Elijah said, sitting on the sofa. He ran his fingers through his hair. "Why tell me this now?"

"Because," she paused, trying to stop her voice from trembling. "At least you would know how I feel about you and Isabella."

"I still think you're full of shit, Breanna."

"You're right." She nodded, wiping away another tear. "I'm all fucked up inside, and I waited until now to realize that I am."

"Are you asking for some kind of pity party or something like that, Bree?" He frowned.

"I'm not. I'm just living with my consequences now."

248

Elijah chuckled. "That's the second smartest thing I've heard you say."

Breanna took a deep breath. She let her head slump backward as she sighed. "All I want is your happiness."

"Then why didn't you fight for it, Breanna."

"Like you said, Elijah," she said, turning her back toward him. "I'm full of shit."

She walked out the family room and stood in front of Leslie and AJ, who were too busy bickering among themselves about how they could get her and Elijah back on stable ground.

"Thanks for inviting me over," Breanna said, sniffling. "I better get going before Daddy calls me."

Leslie walked toward her and wrapped her arms around Breanna's shoulders. "I thought this was going to work, Bree. I'm sorry if I caused more trouble for you."

"You didn't, Leslie," Breanna said, holding onto her best friend tighter. "At least I have closure now."

Pulling from Breanna's embrace, Leslie strode behind her and followed her out the front door.

"Did Leslie put you up to this, AJ?" Elijah stared into AJ's eyes as he walked back into the family room.

"Naw, man," he replied. "Leslie and I both thought this through."

"Then do me a favor."

"What's that, E?"

"Keep her away from me. I ain't got shit to do with her anymore."

"And what about Isabella?"

"She won't miss her anymore either."

Chapter Forty-Two

"Breanna, sis," Amber said, staring at her little sister from the corner of her eye as they stood outside Margo's Honda Dealership. "I commend you for doing this, but do you honestly expect me to be your chauffeur after you sell your car?"

Breanna gawked at Amber and chuckled. That was Amber. No matter how awesome or horrendous the idea sounded, she would question it, especially if that meant she had to burn unnecessary gas. There was no wonder Leilani said she was cheap. "No, big sis. Daddy and Mom already have me covered."

"So, you're really going to go through with this?" Amber asked, entering the dealership behind her. Its brightly lit room showcased every pristine detail of the glistening cars parked inside the building and every smashed bug against the black marbled showroom floor.

Breanna gave a half-smile. It had been two and a half weeks since she'd seen her little girl. The least she could do was lighten the load on Elijah and provide the medication their daughter needed. God, Breanna wanted to see those little pink lips turn upward into a smile. She wanted to hear her little voice sing along to the tunes of Duck Tales. She wanted to hug and kiss Isabella before putting her down to bed again.

Life was going to be difficult without seeing her daughter anymore. But as long as Morgan did right by her, she had to accept that Isabella would be happier with her, like the way she was more content with Regina than her own biological mother at the moment.

"Yeah. I'm going to go through with it," Breanna replied.

"You know that Howard's going to put your newfound understanding to the test, right?"

"I know," Breanna responded. She stared at the salesman walking in their direction, then glanced at her sister before putting on a fake smile.

"Okay, little sis," Amber said. "If Howard tries anything cute, I'mma rip his pink pants wearing ass a new one, you hear me."

"Loud and clear, big sis."

"How can I help you two beautiful ladies today?" His hazel eyes and perfect white teeth gleamed off his mocha latte-toned skin. The curly hair on his head made her think of Nathaniel for a moment. There was no doubt the man before them was sexy as hell. But it was his type that always had a hidden agenda—an agenda to have his every desire fulfilled regardless of how the woman he hooked up with felt about it.

"I'm looking to sell back my car."

"Oh, really now?" he responded. "Is there something wrong with it?"

"Nothing except the fact it's sucking my pocketbook dry," Breanna said.

She noticed how he kept making eye contact with Amber and flashing his flawless smile back at her. She knew her big sister was going to have a fit if he tried to ask for her number, not knowing that Amber only preferred beautiful black women that emerged from the south. This was going to be a sight to see.

"Well, that's not good," he said. "But I can surely help you out. Is there anything you would like to replace it with? Something a little more affordable?"

"No. I just want it off my hands until I am stable enough to afford another car."

"I understand," he said, smiling at Breanna and Amber. "I'm Tyson, by the way. And you two beautiful ladies are?"

"Not interested in men," Amber said, walking away from him.

"Okay." He scratched his head for a moment, then turned his attention to Breanna. "Did I say or do anything to offend her?"

"No," Breanna answered. "My big sister's in a relationship with a woman whom she loves dearly."

"Well, now that I know," Tyson said, tidying up his bowtie. "What's your name?"

"I'm Breanna," she said, extending her hand to shake his. "And I've got a shift in the next hour at the Soul Bistro Restaurant. Can we make this quick?"

"My God!" Tyson looked away from her. "Today just isn't my day today, isn't it?"

Breanna smiled. "No, Tyson. It is your day; it's just not with us."

251

Thank God AJ kept his promise to him. After he and Leslie started hanging around Breanna again, Elijah avoided them like the plague whenever they were around her. She was the last person he wanted to run into. Besides, this was the best he'd been in the last two and a half weeks. He didn't want to constantly duck and dodge from her like he was in permanent stealth mode.

Elijah made a right turn onto his parent's street and glanced into the rearview mirror, noticing Isabella look out the window with pouty lips. He frowned. Izzy never pouted about going to his parents' house. Something must have been bugging her.

"Hey, Shortcake," he said. "Do you want to listen to Jill Scott or India Arie?"

"Oh, come on, Sunshine," Morgan said, staring at him with a "Sir, are you for real face". "I see why she's angry. "You've got that child listening to Jill Scott and India Arie when she needs to be on some Queen B, some Nicki Minaj, some Lil Boosie, and some Cardi B. Give her something to bob her head to."

Elijah sighed. "We don't let her listen to music that's too vulgar."

"But you let her listen to Jill Scott, of all people. The bitch is the queen of vulgar the last time I heard," Morgan said with furrowed eyebrows. "And who's we?"

Elijah bit his bottom lip, remembering how Breanna and Izzy sang along to "There's Hope" by India Arie every time they heard the song play on the radio. He had forgotten how beautiful their voices blended whenever they sang that song. Though it was far and few between, it was always a delight hearing them sing together.

"Nothing," said Elijah. "Still, Jill Scott's music is much better for her tender ears than Cardi B and Nicki Minaj."

"Are you serious with that, Sunshine? She's going to hear it eventually. You might as well expose her to it while she's young."

"And have my daughter trying to learn how to twerk. No thanks."

Morgan chuckled. "Alright, boy scout. I hear ya."

Elijah drove into his parents' driveway and brought the big pickup truck to a halt in front of their three farm-styled garage bay doors.

"Are you ready to go see Grandpa and Gigi?"

"I guess so," Isabella said, shrugging her shoulders.

"You need to handle that before she gets out of control," Morgan said, turning in Isabella's direction and shaking her head with pursed lips.

"I've got my daughter," he said, getting out the truck. "Just take in the ice and that jug of lemonade we got and help Kat set up the table."

"Alright," Morgan slipped out the passenger seat and made her way toward the truck's tailgate. "You best handle that, though."

He watched Morgan walk toward his parents' front door with a bag of ice in one hand and the jug of lemonade in the other and tapped her foot against it. The sound of her huffing and sucking her teeth made it clear she didn't want to wait too much longer. Elijah opened Isabella's door and kissed her forehead as he unbuckled her from her booster seat.

"What's wrong, Shortcake?" He stared into her eyes as he smiled. "What's making you so sad?"

She shrugged her shoulders once more, then looked away from him. "I don't know, Daddy."

"There's gotta be something wrong, Izzy." He lifted her from the booster seat and placed her feet on the ground. "You know you can tell Daddy what's bothering you, right?"

The child nodded, then looked away from him again. He heard Mom talking in the background as she walked toward them and noticed Isabella perk up. At least that put a smile on her face. But for how long?

"Sweetheart," Mom said. "You're a pastry genius. I just wish you could've come over before the dinner started and showed me how to ice this cake you helped me bake."

As Mom neared them both, he heard Breanna's voice on the phone. Mom didn't know how to take a hint. He absolutely had nothing to do with her, yet she kept appearing in his life unwanted by proxy.

"Okay, sweetheart. Make sure you take a break today, okay. Please don't let your foolish boss work you until you can't stand on your own two feet like you did last night."

"Mom," Elijah said, frowning. "Why are you still talking to her?"

She glared at him, continuing her conversation. "I love you too. Talk to you later, sweetheart." Mom ended the call. She frowned at Elijah. "Because I love her like she was my own daughter."

"You've got Kat, Mom," he said, holding Izzy's hand as they walked toward the massive house's entrance.

"I know I do, my son. But I've always thought of your ex as my second daughter."

"I don't see why."

Mom stopped in her footsteps and stared at him as if she were a mercenary laying on a rooftop, waiting to take the perfect shot. Mom kept her eyes trained on him, then slowly looked in Isabella's direction, taking remnants of his soul with her. She smiled at the child. "Hey, Izzy. Go ahead and run inside. Grandpa has a surprise waiting for you."

Elijah watched his daughter's eyes light up as she gleamed at his mom. "Okay, Gigi."

Uneasiness crept down his spine as he watched his daughter skip inside the house without him. He didn't want to see or hear the beast festering behind Mom's calm demeanor. Hell, a part of him wanted to hold on to his daughter's hand just so he wouldn't experience Mom's wrath. Then again, it was going to find him, no matter how hard he tried to run from it.

"Mom, I would appreciate it—"

She held her hand up, stopping him in mid-sentence. "First of all, Elijah Christian Bryson, how dare you question who I can and cannot converse with."

"Mom, I just wished you would—"

She cleared her throat. "I wasn't done with you," she retorted, cutting him off again. "If I want to talk to Breanna, then that's on me. If it bothers you that bad that I still talk to her when you refuse to, then maybe you still love her."

"Mom. I would appreciate it if you would stop speaking with her. That's all I am asking of you. Besides, you know Morgan and I are dating now. That's kind of disrespectful what you're doing."

"Disrespectful?" She looked away from him and took a deep breath. "Son, I love you to the moon and back, but you dating Morgan again is one of the stupidest mistakes I've ever seen you make. And she's staying with you from what I understand."

"She's been helping around the house since I'd been off the job."

"And you've gone back to your job, and she's still there. What kind of sense does that make, Eli?"

"It makes perfect sense to me, Mom."

She scoffed. "Then she must have one hell of a coochie because I can't seem to make any sense of this."

"Okay," Elijah said, folding his arms across his chest. "Then, out of all the women I've dated in the past, why did you like Breanna so much?"

"I liked Breanna because I saw something she was willing to do than them other chicken heads you brought clucking around my house would never attempt."

"And what's that, Mom?"

"That she was willing to own up to her mistakes when she learned she was wrong."

"It took her five years to realize she was wrong, Mom. That doesn't seem like change to me."

She chuckled. "Change doesn't happen overnight, Elijah. Do you remember who told you that?"

He stared at his mom, taking in a deep breath. Granddad was right. Change didn't happen overnight. But stupidity could last a lifetime. "I remember, Mom. But that still doesn't detract from the fact she cheated on me."

"Then, tell me what the hell you're doing so that I can make sense of this," Mom huffed. "Because you shacking up with Morgan seemed like you thought about cheating, too. Breanna just beat you to it first."

"That's not the case, Mom."

"Oh, it isn't, huh?" She laughed as she placed her hand over her chest. "You wouldn't have taken up with Morgan again if the idea of you stepping out on Breanna wasn't lingering on that brain of yours, son. You're a Bryson. Remember that."

He watched Mom walk back into the house and sighed. As much as he wanted to point out that Mom was only defending Breanna because she loved her, the idea hadn't occurred to him that maybe he was waiting for Breanna to mess up so he could revisit what he and Morgan did have back in college.

Hearing a rumble in the near distance, he glanced at the few stray gray clouds passing through the sky and raked his fingers through his hair. As hard as Mom and Katrina prepared for this dinner, he hoped it wouldn't rain. Just as he hoped Mom and Morgan's discontentment for each other wouldn't blow through their family dinner like a monsoon.

A lasting reminder of spring's breeze brushed against his skin. He understood why Mom loved Breanna so. She was, in fact, the mother of his child. Yet, it was more than that. Breanna and Mom had similar tastes. They both loved watching old Kung Fu movies, especially anything of Bruce Lee and Jackie Chan. They couldn't get enough of watching those slap-stick comedy sketches, and they loved getting their hands dirty when it came to cooking. She was Mom's altered version. Still, that didn't give Mom the right to make Morgan feel less than. She saved his life. But was that all he was dating her for? Had he jumped too quickly into a relationship with Morgan?

Elijah closed his eyes. For the life of him, he saw himself like Breanna, and he couldn't shake the feeling off him.

"Earth to big bro," Katrina said, standing in front of him. "Mom told me to come get you so you could put a leash on Morgan."

"A leash?" Elijah frowned. "What happened?"

"You mean what did your girlfriend just say to your daughter."

"Fuck me," Elijah mumbled under his breath as he rubbed his temple. This day couldn't get much worse than what it was now. It just couldn't.

"I heard that, big brother."

"What did Morgan say, Kat?"

Katrina scoffed. "Does she want children of her own?"

"She hasn't said she wanted children. Why?"

"Because I get the feeling she doesn't want to have anything to do with Isabella since she has Breanna's blood flowing through her veins too."

Elijah took another deep breath. Did he make the right choice dating Morgan again?

"Katrina," a male voice called in an alto-tenor-like tone. His Columbian accent was prominent throughout every word he spoke. "Your mother sent me out here to collect the both of you just in case you got stuck in conversation."

"Okay, Miguel," Katrina said.

Elijah stared at Miguel as he came closer to his view. He watched him hug his sister and smiled. Kat honestly liked this guy. He just hoped Miguel didn't pull any stunts with her heart like Breanna had with his. Kat's boyfriend would find himself as a set-piece inside one of his and AJ's new houses.

"Oh! Before I forget," Katrina said, dragging Miguel by the hand toward Elijah. "Eli, this is Miguel. Miguel, this is my big brother."

"It's nice to meet you, Eli," Miguel said, extending his hand to shake Elijah's.

Elijah stared into his fiery brown eyes, noticing that his hair was just as vibrant as his eyes. He smiled while shaking Miguel's hand. "It's nice to meet you too."

"Okay, great. Now that's over with, let's get inside before Mom decides she wants to barbeque us all."

"That is a good idea, cariño," Miguel said, smiling back at her. "Tu madre nos cocinará enteros si le damos la oportunidad."

"Nosotros no podemos correr ese riesgo," Katrina replied, smiling.

Elijah stared at his little sister with a cocked eyebrow. "So, you speak Spanish now?"

Katrina glanced back at him and smiled, winking her eye at him as she caught up with Miguel. "Pues sí, Hermano. Hago."

As he followed Katrina and Miguel inside the house, Elijah heard Isabella whimpering from the kitchen. Mom and Morgan must have gotten into an argument in front of her. She must have told them to stop arguing, and one of them must have said something to hurt her feelings. Had this been him and Breanna, they would have kept the

256

argument from her prying ears so she wouldn't freak out over the two of them not getting along. But their relationship went way past reconciliation in front of Isabella; it went straight nuclear.

Elijah stepped inside the kitchen and saw Dad holding Isabella in his arms. He rocked her from side to side, trying to stop her from crying. Yet all she did was rest her head on his shoulder and whimper. He hadn't seen his daughter like this since he and Breanna—maybe this had something to do with her. Perhaps, Isabella was still hurting from what happened and didn't know how to express it. Regardless of the matter, Elijah had to make sure his little girl could grow from this.

"It's okay, Shortcake?" Dad said, still rocking her in his arms. "Your daddy's here now. He's got you."

Elijah took Isabella into his arms and looked into her eyes. "What's wrong, Shortcake?"

She shook her head, still wiping away the tears from her eyes.

"Come on, Izzy," Elijah said, kissing her on the forehead. "You can't keep negative words or actions inside because it will do is—"

"Eat you up from the inside out," Isabella responded. She rested her head on Elijah's shoulder. "I don't think Ms. Morgan likes me. She told me that I was in the way when she was trying to put the ice in the icebox."

"Did you ask her if you could help her?"

She nodded. "She didn't say anything. That's when Gigi told her to let me help her, but when Gigi left, she told me to get out the way."

"Okay," Elijah said, frowning. "I'm going to make sure Ms. Morgan apologizes to you, okay."

"Okay." Isabella nodded.

He placed the child on her feet and gestured for her to go outside. He knew it would take some time for Morgan to get accustomed to Isabella, but it was going to be the last damn time she would treat his daughter that way.

"Son," Mom said, walking back into the kitchen. "I promise you, if Morgan says something cute to or about Isabella or her mother, I'm going to sit that woman straight on her ass. Do I make myself clear?"

Elijah stared at her with wide eyes. He hadn't seen Mom this angry since Grandma was alive. The fire resting behind her ocean blue eyes hadn't festered like this in a long time. He knew those two couldn't get along, but he had to get the two of them to talk peacefully. Elijah just didn't know where to begin in that process.

"I understand, Mom," he replied. He watched as Dad, Katrina, and Miguel went out into the backyard. He peered at them like a little kid getting scolded by his mother in front of the classroom.

257

"Good," she said. "Let's go sit down as a family and fellowship with each other."

Elijah watched his mother walk out the French Doors as he followed her. He took a deep breath, hoping God heard his silent prayer. If there was one thing he needed right now, it was clarity.

"Mr. and Mrs. Bryson," Miguel said, sitting next to Katrina. "I appreciate you all inviting me here today."

"You're more than welcome, Miguel," Dad said, sitting at the table. "And Miguel, since you're new to our family, I think it would be good for you to say grace."

Morgan scooted closer to Elijah's ear. "Your family makes the guest pray at the family dinner?"

"It's a tradition," Elijah whispered.

"OMG! You all are like one of those sucky Lifetime movies I find myself watching, but I end up regretting it, anyway."

"Morgan," Mom said, staring in her direction. "Is there something you want to say too?"

"No, Lori. There isn't" Morgan crinkled her nose at Mom and focused on her nails.

Miguel looked around the table and smiled. "Okay. Let us go into prayer," he said, closing his eyes and bowing his head. "Gracious Father, thank you for the many blessing you've bestowed on us. May we continue to uplift and praise thy holy name. Amen."

"Amen," they all said in unison.

"So, Mom and I have whipped up the best home-style Italian feast this side of Kentfield," Katrina said, sneaking a glimpse of Miguel and smiling.

"Yeah. In white people's terminology, that means little to no seasoning," Morgan said, smirking at Mom. She took a sip of her lemonade, then crunched on a piece of ice.

"Is there something you want me to know, Morgan?" Mom eyeballed Morgan with pursed lips before turning her attention to Elijah. "Because I've just got this feeling you've been trying to tell me something since you've got here."

"I have nothing to say to you, Lori."

"Come on, Morgan. Let's not fight among each other, okay." Elijah glanced at Katrina and Miguel, noticing their raised eyebrows.

"Please, let's not," Dad agreed. "I would like it very much if I could eat with my family in peace."

"Sure, Mr. Bryson," Morgan replied, shooting Mom a smirk as she chuckled. The silent duel between Mom and Morgan was far from over. This was just the beginning.

"Gigi? Did you make the meatballs to go with the spaghetti like you did last time?"

"I sure did, Shortcake," Mom smiled. "Eli, hand me Isabella's plate so I can fix it for her."

Elijah nodded. He stared at Morgan for a moment, then drew his attention back to his mom. Bringing Morgan here was a bad idea. She waited for Mom to slip so she could sink her claws into her skin. He never understood why those two couldn't clear the air, but it had to be done if they were going to move further into this relationship.

"Mrs. Bryson," Miguel said, handing the platter filled with garlic bread toward Katrina. "This Chicken Alfredo is delicious."

"That it is, dear," Dad said, taking another bite of the pasta.

"Dad, have you tried the ravioli yet. I had a little help making it," Katrina said, smiling at Miguel. They stared at each other while slurping up their fettuccine off their plates.

Elijah stared at the two of them and smiled. They reminded him of how he and Breanna used to act with each other before she cheated on him.

"Eli," Mom called. "Do you want some Chicken Parmigiana? I made it just for you?"

"Thanks, Mom. I appreciate that." Taking the plate Mom fixed for Isabella, he set it before her and watched the child dissect her Italian Meatballs like a surgeon.

"I must admit," Morgan said, taking a bite of the Chicken Parmigiana. "This is pretty damn tasty, Lori. You honestly seasoned this."

Mom stared at Morgan with squinted eyes. "I actually like to season my food, Morgan."

"So, what do you do for a living, Elijah?" Miguel looked at him while taking another bite of his chicken and pasta.

"I co-own a real estate and construction business with my best friend. We build and renovate houses."

"Wow! I probably should get you to come look at my home," he replied. "I'm in need of some home improvement."

"I'll give you my number after—"

"Elijah forgot to mention that he and his best friend are currently working on a major project in the Myers District."

"Oh, yes. I know exactly where you all are building," Miguel said. "There's some tough competition out there. My cousin and his wife are building houses in the same district, but it's in a different subdivision."

"Do tell," Morgan said, taking another sip of lemonade. "Who do I need to look out for?"

259

"Well, my cousin, Hadrian, and his wife, Chloe, have been building houses for over fifteen years."

"Wow! I can't wait to get there myself," Morgan said.

Mom cleared her throat. "You do know that my son and AJ are in this business for themselves. They're not working for you."

"Lori, I don't feel like listening to you right now, okay."

"Daddy, why do Ms. Morgan and Gigi always argue?"

"It's okay, Shortcake," Elijah said. "They just don't agree all the time, but they're getting better at it." He kissed her on the forehead, hoping that would calm her down.

"Well, you took over the answer like it's your company when it isn't."

"I didn't say any of that. However, if things go well for us, we can become one solid company."

"What? Wait a minute." Elijah stared at Morgan with wrinkled eyebrows. "AJ and I haven't talked about consolidating our business with yours, Morgan."

"I know, Sunshine. But that's what I'm hoping we eventually do."

"Well, I'm glad you're telling me this now," Elijah said, lifting a brow.

"Lo siento. I did not mean to start argument." Miguel said.

"Miguel, you started nothing." Elijah held his hand out toward him, trying to keep dinner as peaceful as possible.

"But you said you've got a cousin who does the same work as I do. Why don't you use them instead of Elijah?" Morgan asked, peering into his eyes as she took another bite of her chicken.

Miguel chuckled. "Sorry. I should have explained that they only build new homes. They stopped renovating years ago."

"Oh, so you're hoping Elijah does the work for the low since you know him, right?" Morgan sat back in her seat, keeping her eyes fixed on Miguel. "Sounds like you're trying to get my services without shelling out the cash for it."

Elijah frowned at Morgan. "Morgan, this isn't your company."

"I'm just saying it theoretically."

Mom chuckled while taking a sip of her sparkling water.

"Okay, so you obviously have something to say to me, Lori." Morgan folded her arms across her chest. Clouds slowly covered the beaming sun as Elijah watched the two jab at each other, taunting the other to make the other flinch.

"I only laughed, Morgan."

"You're laughing at me, Lori. I don't appreciate that."

"You appreciate nothing."

"Oh, I am so sorry, Lori, but I refuse to be like Breanna's weak ass."

"Please don't curse around Izzy." Elijah rubbed his temple and sighed.

"Oh, my God! You all are such fucking goodie two shoes. That little girl sitting across from me is half the woman that went out and screwed some other man all because she was unhappy."

"Didn't you do the same thing, Morgan?" Katrina stared at her with a frown. A few droplets of rain fell upon their heads.

"What I did was different."

"That's a load of bull, and you know it, Morgan." Mom said, chuckling as shook her head.

"I guess it must be hard for you to see a strong black woman who can stand on her own two feet rather than bow down like Breanna did. That's probably why you love her so damn much."

"Morgan, please stop," Elijah pleaded.

"No. I will not stop until this bitch sitting across from me admits that she's a racist pig attempting to love a little girl that's going to grow up to be like her skank ass momma."

Isabella wiped the flowing tears away from her eyes. She reached into Elijah's pocket and slid his phone out of it without him noticing. Isabella stared at Morgan and ran from the table.

"Morgan, as God as my witness. If you call me a bitch one more time, I will see to it to give you the ass whooping that your parents failed to give you."

"Oh, so now you want to whoop my ass because I'm black. You ain't nothing but a racist bitch."

Mom stood from her chair and slammed her hand down upon the table, causing everyone's glass and plates to shudder. "Don't you ever come to my house and tell me I don't recognize you. My granddaughter is a little precious black girl that I love dearly."

"I'm sorry, Lori. It's hard to believe anything—"

"You shut that shit up," Mom hissed. "I saw Breanna's skin, and it didn't matter to me at all. She was human, just like my granddaughter. The problem you'll forever have is that you'll never be on Breanna's level. Ever!"

"You bitch—"

"Get out!" Dad said, glaring at Morgan and Elijah. "Both of you leave now."

"But Dad!"

"But nothing, son," he said. "You've got to learn that mistakes are easy to make but hard to fix when you don't think there's a problem."

"Mom? Dad? Eli? Where's Isabella?" Katrina stood from her seat. A nervous frown rested on her brows.

Elijah shot up from his seat and ran into the house. He panned the kitchen, then walked into the family room, hoping Isabella was sitting on the couch. He closed his eyes and cursed under his breath. His little girl was still a casualty, and he didn't understand how she was still in harm's way.

Elijah walked up the steps and peeked into every room until he heard crying emerge underneath his old bedroom door. Opening the door, he looked at Isabella curled on his old bed with his phone in hand and sighed. She cried louder when he walked inside and sat next to her.

"What's wrong, Shortcake?"

"I can't find Mommy's number anymore. Why did you get rid of it?"

"Because," he swallowed hard as he rubbed her back, trying to soothe away her tears. "She and I are going through some tough times at the moment."

"I want my Mommy back, Daddy."

"That's going to be a little hard to do right now."

"Why?" She stared at him as she wiped her eyes with the backs of her hands.

He sighed once more. "Because we're trying to make sure we do right by you, Izzy."

"But I didn't do right by Mommy, Daddy." She cried once more, wiping away more tears. "I told Mommy that I hated her and made her cry."

Elijah closed his eyes and sighed. And there it was. Those words were tearing her up inside, and she had no way of telling Breanna she was sorry. He glanced at the door and peered into Mom's eyes. This was a tough pill to swallow. But he had no other choice than to do what was best for Isabella.

Chapter Forty-Three

Elijah glanced into the rearview mirror and gave a half-smile. His little girl had finally dozed off to sleep after a tornado swept through her life over at his parents' house. He brought the pickup truck to a halt at a red light and watched the rain cascade across the windshield in drizzles. Maybe the rain had a hand in helping ease her mind. Or perhaps she grew tired of Morgan's constant neck rolling and lip-smacking nagging she had about his mom, Katrina, and her boyfriend, Miguel, and now his dad.

The constant sounds of scrubbing rubber against glass drowned out Morgan's voice as he switched on the windshield wipers. The last thing he needed or wanted was for her to go on another tirade about how he still had feelings for Breanna. Elijah didn't want either of them in his life right now. All he wanted was silence.

He sighed, listening to Morgan's voice go up another octave. She had gotten to her boiling point now and he was tired of hearing her shit.

"I know you heard me, Elijah."

"Morgan," he said, glancing at her while making a right turn onto Walgreen's parking lot. "I heard you, and honestly, I think you need to apologize to my parents."

"Apologize!" She stared at him with furrowed eyebrows and arms folded across her chest. "Are you fucking serious about this shit right now?"

"I am, Morgan, and for the last time, please stop cursing around my daughter."

"Fine," Morgan huffed. "I'll stop cursing around your daughter, but don't you dare expect me to apologize to Lori and Jonah."

As Elijah backed his truck into a parking space and shifted it into park, he stared at her. He raked his fingers through his hair and chuckled to himself.

"What's so funny?"

He scoffed. "It's pathetic how you act like you can't get along with my mom. Why do you have such a grudge against her, anyway?"

"Pathetic? Elijah, you've got some balls to even dare say something like that when you know your mother has never liked me."

"Mom never liked you because you never liked her."

"Oh! So, you're saying this is my fault, right?" Morgan looked away from him, shaking her head. She flipped down the visor, opened the lid to the mirror, and ran her fingers through her wavy tresses, trying to style it with her hands. "You know, sometimes I think you want me to act like Breanna."

He stared at her for a moment with parted lips and paused. Breanna. He hadn't seen her since AJ and Leslie tried to get them to talk. He hadn't thought about her either. But at this moment, he found himself just wanting to talk to her again, despite all the shit she'd put him through. At least Elijah knew Breanna would have put their daughter first whenever they argued.

"I don't want you to act like Breanna, Morgan," he replied. "I would appreciate it if you took the time to talk to my mom, dad, Katrina, and her boyfriend like a sensible person."

"People like them don't listen to people like me," she said, squinting at him. "You have to make them listen to you."

"You make them tired of you, Morgan."

"You know what, Sunshine. It's people like you that's too naïve to even see when people like your family are trying to make a fool of people like me."

"I think it would be a good idea if you went back to your apartment tonight," Elijah said. He unlocked the driver's side door and opened it. Rain drizzled onto one of his pants legs. "I just want to give you some room to breathe."

"So, you don't want me to stay with you tonight?"

"I think Izzy and I will be okay for tonight."

"I can't believe that you're siding with your racist mother, Elijah," Morgan huffed. "I just honestly can't believe you right now."

He shook his head. "Mom's not racist. Yout won't allow her to show that, Morgan."

"I still can't believe you would—"

"I'll be back, Morgan," he said, closing the driver's side door. He walked through the drizzling rain, allowing its cooling splash to calm his festering anger.

You got what you wanted, Elijah.

He took a deep breath as he walked inside the store. Did he think things through before getting back into a relationship with Morgan? Hell, did he pull the same shit Breanna did to him before he called the quits with her?

Maybe Mom was right. Perhaps he needed to talk to Breanna again—no. He wouldn't put himself through that dance routine again and find himself back in the hospital. He just needed Morgan to think before she spoke. Though that was hard for her to do, it wasn't like she couldn't try to change. Breanna didn't try to change until she knew she fucked up. He was better off with Morgan.

He glanced at a bottle of Jergens Almond Cherry lotion and frowned as he walked into the pharmacy area. That was Breanna's go-to lotion. He had to stop thinking about her.

"Hey, Mr. Bryson," the clerk said, smiling at him. "How are you doing today?"

"I'm doing alright, Ms. Evangeline." Elijah sat seat next to an older black couple in the waiting area. He smiled at them, noticing they were holding onto each other's hands.

"Just alright?" she asked. "What's wrong with ya, honey?"

"Let's just say it's complicated at the moment." Elijah gazed into her deep brown eyes before she stepped away from the cash register. The salt and pepper hues of her gray hair shimmered under the ceiling lights as he watched her move from one drawer to the next in search of the customer's medication in front of him. Her brown skin resembled Breanna's.

Why was everyone and everything reminding him of Breanna? Why couldn't he go one moment without thinking about her name? Breanna meant nothing to him anymore; she was everything—that Isabella needed in her life right now. Just hearing his daughter wail uncontrollably about how she told Breanna she hated her made him think about his decision to take full custody of her.

But even if he allowed her the opportunity to come back into Isabella's life, Elijah didn't want her to experience the letdown she had before all over again. He couldn't take those chances with Breanna anymore. He feared his little girl was going to hate him for not allowing her to apologize to her mother, though.

"Mrs. Emmerson," Ms. Evangeline said, holding a white bag in the air. "I finally found your medication, hun."

265

Elijah watched the older woman stand to her feet and step to the counter. She placed her purse on it and breathed a sigh of relief. "Thank you so much, sweetheart. I knew that wig wearin' fool misplaced my Stanley's medication again."

"Mrs. Emma, you better stop with that name-calling."

"Do you think I care, child? Hell naw. Had she not been too busy trying to get attention from them little musty ass boys walking in here earlier, we wouldn't have had to come back out in all this rain."

Elijah chuckled as he shook his head. Someday he would have love like that. He and Breanna would have had several grandchildren and great-grandchildren running around the house. They would have been just like—God! Why couldn't he stop thinking about her?

"Excuse me, young man," the older woman said, standing in front of him. "You're my neighbor's friend, aren't you?"

Elijah's eyebrows wrinkled as he stood to his feet to help her back to her husband. He'd forgotten AJ and Leslie lived next door to an older couple that always gifted them peach cobbler for the holidays. "If you're talking about AJ and his fiancée, Leslie, then I know exactly who you are, Mrs. Emma."

She wrapped her arm around his waist and pulled him closer to her. "I should have known that was you."

"It's good to see you, Mrs. Emma," Elijah said. He waved at Mr. Stanley. "How are you doing today, Mr. Stanley?"

"Ya say what now, son. Speak up." Mr. Stanley said, getting up slowly from the chair.

Elijah stepped toward him and helped him rejoin hands with his wife. "How are you doing today, Mr. Stanley?"

He smiled. "I got a good woman by my side. I'm still using my limbs to walk. And I still got my driver's license too, so I can drive my Buick downtown now and then."

"I hear ya on that, Mr. Stanley."

"How's Mrs. Bryson?"

Elijah sighed. "Well, let's just say she's doing okay from what I know."

"Whaddya mean from what you know?" Mr. Stanley asked, glaring into Elijah's eyes.

"Mrs. Bryson and I haven't spoken to each other in two weeks."

"No shit!"

"Emma!"

"What, Stanley," she said, shrugging her shoulders. "I only said what was on my mind."

"You could be a little more sensitive."

266

"A little more sensitive?" Mrs. Emma huffed. "First, you say I'm too sensitive. Then, you say I'm not sensitive enough. "That's the reason you can't remember that Marcus Higgins won the last clue in Jeopardy back in 1985."

"That wasn't Higgins that won in 1985, sweetheart. That was Kenneth Stovall."

"Stovall won back in 79, not 85."

"That's not right, darling," Mr. Stanley responded with a wry smile. "I think you just wanna be right, so you don't have to make them rutabagas and hot water cornbread like you promised me five years ago."

"And have your doctor fussing at me again, mister. I think it's time for your nap."

"You two are so cute. That's what I want with my husband," Ms. Evangeline said. A grin pulled at the corners of her lips. "What's the secret ya'll hiding."

"Talking ain't no secret, honey," Mrs. Emma said, smiling. "When you and your husband get our age, ya'll will do the same thing, too. Just keep talking to each other."

Elijah nodded. Communication was the key to a happy relationship. But did he allow Breanna to communicate with him?

"You're right," Ms. Evangeline said. "We just gotta keep living."

"Sounds like your husband's a good one," Mr. Stanley said, carting Mrs. Emma by the hand. "Ya'll take care now."

"Alright now. You two be safe out there."

Elijah watched the older couple walk through the store until they disappeared through the sliding double doors. He turned his attention to Ms. Evangeline and sighed. "I was hoping to get one inhaler of Isabella's medication today."

"Are you sure you only want one?"

He frowned. Something about that didn't sound right. "What do you mean?"

"I thought she told you."

"Told me what, Ms. Evangeline?" Elijah cocked a brow. "And who are you speaking of?"

"Ms. Ellis," she replied. "She came in this afternoon and bought twelve inhalers for Isabella today."

Elijah frowned. How did she afford that many inhalers? She would have had to tap most of her savings account just to afford this many. Then again, she probably kissed and made up with Nathaniel and suckered him into paying for the inhalers. Either way, he couldn't be angry with her for doing what she did.

"Ms. Evangeline, how did Ms. Ellis afford all these inhalers?"

267

"All I know is that her sister was with her, and she said she was going to need a ride to work for a while."

Breanna sold her car? That damn thing meant the world to her since Howard bought it for her. Hell, he even made her pay that high-ass car note. That's all she went on about was how her boss, more like a bestie, bought her a new car when he wouldn't. Maybe she was changing.

"Do you want me to call her and inform her you want to make any changes?"

Elijah shook his head quickly. "No. You don't have to."

"Alrighty then, Mr. Bryson," Ms. Evangeline said, handing him the inhalers. "You have a good night."

"You too, Ms. Evangeline."

Elijah took in a deep breath as he made his way out the store. This wouldn't change a thing about what Breana did to him and Isabella. It just wouldn't. Still, he couldn't fathom why she would do this. He walked outside, allowing the rain to plop on his head. This was the Breanna he came to know over the years; this was the Breanna that he longed to be around again.

Chapter Forty-Four

Just two more hours and Breanna could finally go home and get some sleep. She stared at the clock ticking away on the break room wall and yawned. Since Tessa was on vacation, yet again, Howard made it his business to work her until she couldn't stand on her own two feet anymore. But at least tonight wasn't like last week.

All she could remember was holding a plate in her hand one minute and then waking up to the horrified expressions and gasps of shocked patrons who helped her off the ground after she face-planted it the next.

Howard nearly had a conniption after seeing how angry some patrons were when Breanna went down for the count. Yet she couldn't understand why he was so mad. She was the one that had to suffer from the knot on the side of her head. Still, Howard made it his priority to make sure she paid the price for exhibiting how tired she was. Either way, big sis was right.

After she sold her car to get Izzy's inhalers a month ago, Howard had been going in on her like she was a platter of honey gold chicken wings, waiting to have the meat sucked off them, then thrown to the side in a pile. And no matter how much she pleaded with Howard not to overwork Kelvin and Latasha for the little mistakes she made, he made it his business to see that all three of them reaped what she had sown.

Breanna needed to vacate the premises like two years ago. Howard would never give her the promises he said he would. She rubbed one of her shoulders as she closed her eyes and took a deep breath. Elijah was right, too. Yet, she refused to listen to him because she only wanted people to cater to her like Daddy used to cater to Momma.

You're really dumb, Bree.

"Ms. Breanna," Latasha said, knocking on the door as she entered the break room. "Your sister's out-front talking to Howard."

"Amber's here?"

"Mmm-hmm." Latasha nodded. "And she's about to give the diners a dinner and a movie."

"Should I just let her deck his ass one?" Breanna smiled, tiredly.

"I'll go make us some popcorn if you wanna watch with me," Latasha giggled.

As Breanna stood to her feet, she stumbled backward, then steadied her balance as she held her arms out.

"Ms. Breanna, I've only been here for about six hours now, and I have watched you nearly fall to your face all day. You need to go home."

"I'm okay, Latasha," she said. "Besides, I don't want Howard trying to force you to work the hours that I'm working."

"Breanna!" Amber's voice trailed in the background.

Breanna cocked an eyebrow as she glanced at the break room door. "Is my sister back here?"

"I promise you, Amber." Howard's voice trailed off in the distance behind hers. "I will call the cops."

Breanna watched the door swing open as Amber marched inside.

"Then, call the cops, Howard. Hell, I call them for you." Amber beckoned for Breanna to follow her as she stepped outside the door and stood in front of him with her arms folded across her chest. "Bree, come on so you can go home and get some sleep."

"Amber, I'm okay."

"Daddy told me you didn't come home last night."

"I had to fill in for another co-worker who's on vacation."

"That woman's been on vacation for the past three damn weeks now," Amber fussed. "Had I not spent the night at Leilani's last night, I would have brought you home then."

"Breanna's a big girl," Howard stated, sticking his chest out. "She knew what she was getting into, and she can damn sure handle herself."

Amber laughed, cracked her knuckles, then stomped at Howard, sending him falling to the ground on his butt. "That's what I thought."

"Amber," Breanna said, walking out the door behind her big sister. "You're going to get me fired."

"I wish this prick would try to fire you," Amber huffed. "I guess I need to call my lady, who, by the way, is the lead investigator with the EEOC and let her know my sister needs to file a complaint."

"Amber," Howard said, standing from the ground and dusting his backside off. "Listen, there's no need to make threats like that."

"I'm just making sure you won't try, Howard." Amber glared at him. She turned to look at Breanna and shook her head. "You can't keep letting that man treat you like this, Breanna."

"I know, Amber, but—"

"But nothing, Breanna," she fussed. "You've got people that love you and want to see you doing well. Do you hear me?"

Breanna stared at Amber and nodded, seeing fear and anger jumbled together in her brown eyes. The last time she saw that look Amber had, Momma separated them from each other. She looked away from her big sister and closed her eyes, trying to stave away the tears playing at her tear ducts.

Amber was right. Mom, Daddy, Amber, Grandma Zora. They all wanted to see her doing well. But the people she wanted to see were the ones she abandoned for a man who put her in the hospital once. And even he disappeared from the picture. Thank God Nathaniel left her alone. The last thing she needed was to go through the lengthy process of trying to put a restraining order on him.

"Ms. Breanna," Latasha said, handing her, her purse. "Please go home and get some sleep."

"I need you here bright and early tomorrow, Breanna," Howard fussed.

"I'll be here in the afternoon, Howard." Breanna took her purse from Latasha's hand and smiled at her. "Besides, you owe me for making me work through my break last week."

As she followed Amber down the hallway and through the double doors into the main dining room, she locked eyes with Morgan as she walked toward the customer ordering area. The smirk that pulled her lips and the glimmer that gleamed in her eyes made the hairs rise on her arms. Something wasn't right. Of all the people she wanted to see, Morgan wasn't one of them. Then again, she was probably trying to make her presence known. She and Elijah had been together for a month now, and there was nothing more the heffa wanted to do than to let her know about their relationship in the most public of ways.

Morgan leaned against the counter and rang the bell, waiting for someone to come to the counter. She kept her eyes on Breanna and her sister as they made their way out the door.

"Morgan," Howard said, straightening up his shirt while flashing a wide smile. "It's been a minute since I've seen you. How have you been?"

Morgan placed her hand on her hip and smiled. "You know I'm good."

"And what about the mister?"

"We've had some difficulties, but we're back on good terms again. His brat of a daughter gets on my fucking nerves, though."

"Kids." Howard laughed. "Who wants them anyway?"

"Crazy ass people who ain't got nothing else better to do than procreate senselessly."

"What you said, honey," Howard said, snapping his fingers with every word he spoke.

"Hopefully, I can convince him to let his racist ass momma keep her for a while."

"You think he'll go for it?"

"With the red and black teddy doll I got waiting for him, all Elijah's going to do is say yes, honey."

They laughed and danced about together, causing some patrons to stare at them with raised eyebrows.

"But anyway," Morgan said, pulling a strand of her wavy hair behind her ear. "My crew has a banquet happening this Friday, which I know is only three days away, but I need the function to be catered. Can I count on you to come through for me, Howard?"

"Is the sky blue and the grass green?"

Morgan nodded with a smile. "Thank you so much, Howard. I knew I could count on you."

"For you, honey, you know I got your back. Just like when I set you with Brian back in college."

"Oh my God! He was screwed up in the head, but the brotha knew how to throw down in the bed," she said, rolling her hips.

Howard danced with her as he giggled. "How many people will be there?" He grabbed a pen and a small white pad.

"About fifty to seventy-five people," Morgan replied. "And oh! Could you get Ms. Ellis to work that event?"

"Why would you want her around for?"

"For one, the bitch can bake like nobody's business. And two, I want her to see how happy her man is now."

Howard's lips curled into a sly smile. "Done. But you gotta make sure you tell me everything that happens, okay?"

"Don't worry, honey." Morgan smiled. "I got you."

272

"Come on, Shortcake," Elijah said, glancing at his watch. He smiled, watching Isabella run with her kite in the middle of the grassy field. "You've got ten minutes, young lady, and then Daddy's gotta take you Gigi's so he can get back to work."

"Okay, Daddy," she replied loudly. She twirled in the middle of the field. That smile on her face was something he missed seeing.

She needed this. She needed to focus on something else other than the last words she spoke to Breanna. Even though it was wrong for Isabella to have said that to her mother, Breanna deserved every spiteful annunciation of those words. The sun beamed on his skin, forcing him to put on Dad's old baseball cap.

"Well, if it isn't the infamous Elijah Bryson," a tenor like voice spoke from behind him.

Elijah turned, meeting Nathaniel's cognac brown eyes up close. "What do you want?"

"Is that how you're gonna greet me, Eli." Nathaniel chuckled. "Man, I thought we shared some commonalities, considering we both dated Breanna."

"And?"

Nathaniel smirked, then nodded as he chuckled once more. "I thought you'd seen your lady again."

"Naw man, she's all yours." Elijah turned his attention to Isabella, keeping his left hand close to his concealed weapon. The last thing he needed was for this fool to try something while he had his daughter with him.

"It's funny you say that because it seems she can't keep her pussy away from you."

Elijah turned toward him slowly. A frown pulled his eyebrows. "Whatever you two have got going on, please don't get me involved."

Nathaniel laughed. "Man, it's funny you say that too because ole girl never gave me any of the cookie she gave you."

"What the hell are you talking about, Nathaniel?"

"I'm talking about the woman who I proudly took off your arm never shared with her body with me like the way she did with you."

Elijah's frown deepened. As often as she found herself in his bed, she'd never had sex with him. The both of them must have been playing games with him. "Listen, if you want her, you can have her."

"Well, damn!" Nathaniel smirked as he turned his attention to Isabella. "Tessa told the truth. You and ole girl broke up, huh?"

"Listen, whatever you're trying to do, I don't want any part of it."

Nathaniel smirked once more as he chuckled. "Then, the next time you see ole girl, she won't be the same again."

"I could care less," Elijah said. "Now, do you mind? I'd like to take my daughter home."

Nathaniel turned his attention to Isabella again. "She's beautiful. Just like her mother."

Elijah stared at him, keeping his hand close to his gun. "You keep my daughter out of this."

"Don't worry, my guy," he replied. "All my plans are for Breanna. I'll see ya around." He nodded at him once before walking away.

Whatever Breanna got herself into, Elijah hoped she could work her way out of it. But that was her problem. That was all her problem. But for the life of him, he just couldn't understand why he couldn't shake the eerie feeling creeping up into his chest and throat.

Chapter Forty-Five

Lifelessness. That's what every moment of Breanna's life felt like now. What she'd done to them couldn't be excused with a simple apology. It just couldn't. Yet she would have given her life to prove she regretted her choices. She would have given her life to see their smiles and hear their laughter again.

Breanna frowned as she stared at the pocket-sized picture of her, Elijah, and Isabella playing in a field of leaves. She slid her index finger over the glossy paper and wiped away a tear playing at her. She didn't need Latasha getting herself all riled up because she was crying. That young woman had come to her aid more than Breanna could count. She and Kelvin both. Breanna closed her eyes and inhaled the aroma of lemon zest, parsley, rosemary, and garlic lingering in the back of the van she rode in, savoring memories on her tongue. She cooked this very meal for Elijah once for their one year anniversary. Izzy hadn't made herself to the world yet. They were so in—he didn't love her anymore. He loathed her. Hell, she didn't blame Elijah for ending their relationship a month ago. She shredded their hearts into pieces. It just hurt like hell knowing she wouldn't see them again.

Tears welled in her eyes again. A month ago. Breanna hadn't seen or heard from Izzy for an entire month. She wiped away a fleeting tear before Latasha caught a glimpse of her crying. It was a month ago when the man she claimed she loved told her to get her ass out the house they shared. It was an entire month.

"Ms. Breanna?" Latasha looked back at her with wrinkled eyebrows. "Are you okay?"

Breanna mustered a smile and nodded. "I'm good, Latasha. I'm just... still a little tired. That's all"

Raising an eyebrow and tilting her head to the side, Latasha leaned closer to her. "Are you sure, Ms. Breanna?"

"Yeah," Breanna breathed. "I'm good."

Latasha nodded hesitantly. "Alright, then."

Breanna turned away from Latasha's gaze. She could still feel her eyes burning her skin. Even though she was eighteen, quick-tempered, and had a mouth like a sailor and pirate combined, Latasha was one of the sweetest young ladies she ever met and worked with. After Leslie left, Howard was desperate to find an employee stupid enough to work for little pay, do double shifts, and bend over backward for him if it meant his restaurant remained open for high profile and common customers alike.

But Latasha needed the work to take care of her fourteen-month-old baby and three-year-old little brother after her mom left them. Latasha reminded her a lot of herself, in a way. They both worked harder than most people around them and had fickle mommas who expected the world from them.

Breanna closed her eyes again and sighed. This was one of those favors Howard needed her to do since he claimed he couldn't trust anyone else to do the job she was the best at. She frowned. She was tired of his bullshit lies.

After helping the man Breanna called friend open Soul Bistro, her role never settled to the head pastry chef. Instead, she was the pastry chef, hostess, waitress, and cashier.

"We're here," Kelvin spoke. He whistled as he surveyed the building. "This is a fancy-looking place."

Breanna unbuckled her seatbelt. "Let's get to work, you two."

She slid the door open and stepped out of the van. Breanna looked around the parking lot and shook her head at all the cars there. It had to have been over fifty people. Howard was going to pay for this one.

"Gawd damn! This a lot of folks," Kelvin said, gawking at all the cars in the parking lot. He stepped toward Breanna and began taking some items out of the van. He smiled. "I'm glad this is an afternoon banquet."

"Who said it wouldn't be nighttime by the time we get back home?" Breanna watched Kelvin's wide smile fade to a sullen scowl. His neatly trimmed mustache and wavy hair made him look like a teenager for a twenty-two-year-old. The sun beamed on his light brown skin, festering a couple of droplets of sweat beads on his forehead. Latasha met up with them and smiled at them both. Her brown skin meshed with the dark auburn curls scattered about in her pixie cut.

"There's no time like the present, right, Ms. Breanna?"

"It sure isn't," she said, pulling out one of the foldable carts from the vehicle and placing its wheels on the ground.

Breanna watched the two of them catch each other's eyes and smile while they unloaded the food from the van into the cart. She gave a half-smile. They were like her and... Elijah. She needed to talk to him. She needed to see him. Breanna needed to be back in his embrace again.

She looked away from them and continued loading the cart. Dad was right. She needed some time to sit down and relax. She needed... she wanted... Breanna couldn't have the people she gave up for the man who used her body like a punching bag.

"Yo, Master Chef," Kelvin asked, placing the last box inside the cart. "Where do the people want us to enter to get this food set up?"

"Howard said somebody was supposed to be waiting for us when we got here, but as usual, there's nobody out here waiting," Breanna said. She dug her phone out of her pocket and dialed Howard's number. Listening to it ring until it went to voicemail, she sighed. That was like Howard. Send them on assignment and leave them high and dry without a map in sight. Great! This was all she needed. "Looks like I got to bang on the door. Wait for me just in case we came to the wrong location."

Latasha and Kelvin nodded as they watched her walk toward the white stone-structured building. As she neared the door, Breanna overheard a familiar voice laugh from behind it. She knocked on it and waited, folding her arms across her chest. Still hearing the same voices, she knocked on the door harder, then waited.

"Oh! Come on. I know you heard me bang on the door," Breanna muttered to herself. She banged on the door one more time. Somebody had to have heard her knocking, but she still stood there in silence. She scoffed. Why in the hell didn't she see this coming? Howard may have sent them to the wrong place just to mess with them. As Breanna made her way toward the van, she heard the door open.

"Breanna," a woman's soft voice said. "Is that you?"

She turned around and noticed Leslie standing in a one-shoulder black dress that flowed to the midpoints of her calves. The black open-toe pumps she wore accentuated her pinned back natural coils. White and pink crystals shimmered on the pins, holding her hair back. Breanna smiled. "Leslie! Oh! my goodness. You look so beautiful."

"Thank you," she said, touching her coils. Leslie pulled her into her embrace and squeezed her tight. "I try my best, girl."

"That you did, Leslie," Breanna said. She stepped away from Leslie and walked around her, admiring her beauty.

277

"I didn't think Soul Bistro was catering for the banquet today, but I'm so glad you're here. At least I know the food will be on point."

Breanna nodded as she smiled. "Well, I'm glad to be of service."

Leslie peeped at Latasha and Kelvin, waiting by the van. "Howard only sent the three of you?"

Breanna gazed into Leslie's eyes with the "now what do you think look" and chuckled. "We're it, Leslie."

"Okay. I'm going to find you all some extra help," said Leslie. "There are about seventy-five people inside the banquet hall. And all of them are hungry, Bree. Howard was wrong for this shit he pulled."

"Well, just think of it as Howard sending his over glossed hugs and kisses," Breanna said. She beckoned for Latasha and Kelvin to make their way to the building.

"The shit still isn't right, Bree," Leslie said. She walked beside her until they stood outside the kitchen's double doors. "It just seems like he always had it out for you."

Breanna tightened her lips. Elijah used to tell her the same thing. She never listened to him. That was all her fault. She stared into Leslie's eyes, then gave a half-smile. "Maybe I need to change that for once."

Leslie smiled. "He won't like it a bit, but he'll survive as he always says."

"He sure will," Breanna said. "Without me holding him up."

Leslie grinned as she nodded, giving her that "you go girl" look. "You all can start setting up in the kitchen straight ahead."

"Thanks, Leslie."

"No problem, girl," Leslie said. "I'm going to let these folks know that the food has arrived, so they can calm their hangry asses down."

Breanna smiled. "Don't worry, Leslie. We got you covered."

She watched Leslie flash a wide smile and a thumbs-up as she walked down the hall. She disappeared into the double door entry of the dimly lit banquet hall. Incoherent talking and laughter escaped through the slow closing doors. This was going to be significantly longer than she thought before.

She made her way back down the hall and stood at the front door. She watched the three young men Leslie sent to help Latasha and Kelvin bring the other boxes of food to the door. Thank God for her best friend.

"Hey, Master Chef," Kelvin said, entering the building with another cart. Latasha and the other three gentlemen followed him inside and stood next to him. "Where are we taking the carts and boxes of food to?"

"Down the hall to your right. You should see the double doors as you get closer to the kitchen."

278

He saluted her as he pushed the cart toward the kitchen's direction. Breanna covered her mouth and chuckled as she watched Kelvin gesture for the others to follow him. Latasha stared in Kelvin's direction and scoffed. She could barely contain the smile on her face.

"You're so extra, Kelvin," Latasha exclaimed, shaking her head. She rolled her eyes as she followed behind him with a box of food in her arms. "What are you going to do with him, Ms. Breanna?"

"Let Kelvin do what he does best," Breanna said, still smiling. "Be himself."

One of the young men turned toward Breanna and flashed a wide smile. His hazel brown eyes nearly matched his brownish-red hair. "You must be Breanna Ellis," he said with a thick Columbian accent. He extended his hand toward hers.

"I am," said Breanna, shaking his hand. "How do you know of me?"

"I'm Miguel Matias," he answered. "Katrina Bryson is my girlfriend. She told me so much about you."

"Oh! Well, it's a pleasure meeting you."

"Likewise," said Miguel.

"Um, Miguel," Latasha called from a distance. "Stop talking to everybody you see and come on."

He grinned. "I must go now."

Breanna nodded at him with a smile and watched him run toward the others at the kitchen's double doors. Katrina had a boyfriend. It was about time. She couldn't let Elijah continuously scare her away from dating. Katrina couldn't... Elijah... God! She longed to be near him again. She just... needed to maintain herself until the banquet was over with.

She watched the five of them vanish into the kitchen and sighed. At least the tears seemed to have stopped flowing for the moment. Although the distractions only lasted for a little while, she was glad she had something to occupy her mind from slipping into nothingness.

A familiar voice lingered in the background. It resembled Elijah's almost perfectly. Breanna closed her eyes and took a deep breath. She must have been tripping or desperate to see him again. Still, she couldn't shake the fact the more the speaker talked, the more she noticed his similar ebbs and flows in his speech pattern.

"Get a grip, Bree," she whispered to herself.

Breanna made her way into the kitchen and saw Leslie and AJ helping place the food on the tables before them. Miguel stood beside Kelvin, sorting the chicken and pork plates apart from each other. Latasha helped the other two set up serving trays. If only Howard had treated his employees right, they would've been happy rather than ready to key up his BMW. That's if his partner didn't beat them to it first.

"Breanna," AJ said with a smile. "How are you doing?"

"I'm doing good. I wasn't expecting to see you here."

"I wasn't expecting to see you here either, but I'm so glad you're here." AJ walked over to her and hugged her. "I would love to stay and chitchat, but I've got to get back to the crowd. They're going to eat my brother alive if I don't help manage the crowd."

Breanna smiled. "Then, you better get back out there and help him."

"Will do. Besides, I wouldn't want our business partners and potential home buyers to wage a small war out of hunger," he said.

Breanna frowned. "Wait. I thought this was a company luncheon for Leslie."

Leslie stared at her and AJ with wide eyes. "Um, Bree... This is for—"

"What are you doing here?"

Breanna closed her eyes and swallowed hard. She released a staggering breath, feeling Elijah's presence behind her. She turned slowly and met Elijah's scowl. His steel-blue eyes seemed cold. The last time they were this cold, he was in the hospital.

"Elijah—"

"—Why are you here, Breanna?" Elijah demanded. "And how did you find out about this banquet?"

Breanna stiffened, hesitating to answer his barrage of questions. "I'm... I'm... here as part of the catering crew Howard sent at the request of a customer."

He shook his head, then left the kitchen.

"I'm sorry about that, Breanna," AJ said. "I'll speak with him." He walked out the double doors.

A tear streamed down her cheek as she stood in the same place Elijah left her standing. Leslie stood in front of her, pulled her to the side, and wiped the tear from her eye. "I don't know if Howard told you, but the high-profile customer is Morgan Everly."

"He didn't," Breanna whispered, fighting back the tears.

"God! I wished I could have told you he was going to be here," Leslie said. She rubbed Breanna's back. "Are you going to be okay?"

Breanna nodded. "I have no other choice but to be. Besides, I'm the one that fucked up."

"Breanna, please don't start beating yourself up. You've got a lot on your plate to worry about today than blame yourself."

She nodded. This was the very moment Breanna dreaded. She longed to see Elijah happy with her. Not him wanting to post her head on a spike.

280

"Listen, I'm going to come back and check on you," she said. "I got your back, Bree."

"Thank you, Leslie," Breanna said. She stared into her brown eyes and smiled. She didn't know what she would have done without Leslie. Knowing she didn't deserve any of her kindness, Leslie was still there for her like they never had a falling out. She only accounted for their falling out to a time for healing. Breanna never saw it as anything worse than that. Leslie was a far better person than she ever could have been.

Leslie hugged her once more. "I'll be back, okay."

"Okay," Breanna nodded.

Leslie made her way out the kitchen. The double doors continued to swing until they settled into their stationary position. She stared around the stainless-steel chef's kitchen and took a deep breath. She remembered the day Elijah took her inside an old bakery for lease. Its kitchen resembled the one she stood in. Each cabinet was sleek in its bright, modernized white and black contrast. The island before them reflected the stars nestled within the darkness of the universe. It glistened from the light hovering over it. The cherry oak vinyl floors were reminiscent of the floorings in the kitchen she once shared with Elijah.

Latasha stood beside Breanna and watched the tears flow down her cheeks. "Ms. Breanna, what's wrong?"

"Remember when I told you I caused a lot of pain to two very special people in my life?" she said, looking at Latasha.

"I do." She nodded.

"He was one of them."

"Really?" Latasha stared at her with wide eyes. "Have you tried talking to him since the breakup?"

"I haven't," Breanna said. "I didn't try because I knew he didn't want to hear it."

"But does he know you still care about him?"

"All he knows is that I wounded him and our daughter." She wiped away the tears. "I got myself into this mess. I need to get myself out of it."

Latasha smiled, then pulled her into her embrace. "This is why I admire you so much," she whispered in her ear.

"Why? I'm no better than your mother, Latasha."

"Don't say that. My mother didn't have the nerves to admit to her faults, let alone learn from them. You've grown."

"Thank you for saying that, but I've still got a long way to go," Breanna said, rubbing her shoulder blade.

"I know you'll get there," Latasha said.

281

Breanna heard the double doors creak as they swung open. Two young men entered the kitchen in front of Leslie, then joined the others.

"I brought two more gifts," she said. "This is Daniel and Jason. Their two college students from that prestigious university in East Kentfield."

Breanna stared at Leslie and smiled. "What do I owe you, sis?"

"Some apple fritters with that special glaze of yours, and I'll call it a deal."

"Are you sure?"

"Girl, yes," Leslie said. "Besides, I've been craving for them like crazy since I left Soul Bistro to work at the children's clinic."

Breanna mustered a smile. "Then, I got you, sis."

"Excuse us," one of the young men asked. "Where do you want us?"

"Help Kelvin and Miguel get those plates onto those serving trays by the specific type of protein, and let's get these people fed."

"Sure thing, chef."

"Thanks, Leslie."

"You're welcome, girl." She replied, pushing one of the double doors open. "I've got to make my way back out to the crowd for a few minutes."

Breanna nodded. "Alright."

"What do you need me to do, Ms. Breanna?" Latasha stared into her water-filled eyes.

"You can take out those black and white plates for the deserts."

"Sure thing, Ms. Breanna."

Breanna watched Latasha sway her way over to the stack of boxes they sat on the kitchen's countertops and mustered a smile as she peeped inside each box in search of the plates. She pulled them out and sat them in three stacks on the island in front of her. Breanna used to do the same thing whenever she and Grandma Isabella used to go to the state fair for the pie competitions. She took a deep breath and then released it slowly through her mouth. This day wouldn't get any better, but she had to get through it no matter the hate she got. All she could do now was wear her fuck up on her sleeve and own up to it like Hester Prynne.

Leslie ran back into the kitchen and peeped her head through the door. "Hey guys, are you all ready?"

"In about three more minutes, and we'll start serving."

Leslie nodded and pranced out the kitchen.

"Yo' master chef," Kelvin called. "Do we have any extra garden salads just in case we run out of the Caesar salads?"

"We do, Kel."

"Alright, Master Chef," Kelvin said. "I think we're ready over here."

"Good. Let's do a quick check of the proteins by serving tray, wash your hands, and put on your serving gloves."

Breanna folded her arms across her chest as she smiled. She watched the young men prep themselves before putting on their gloves and standing in a line. Miguel glanced back at Breanna and smiled, flashing her a thumbs up. His long white-sleeved shirt and black slacks made him fit in well with Kelvin's black vest and slacks. His white shirt wrinkled from his constant movement as Kelvin pretended to act cool in front of the others.

Howard would have lost his mind had he seen them smiling and talking to each other before serving the patrons. Had that been him, Howard would have marched around them and yelled at them in his attempt to make himself look like a respected leader when he only made him look like a buffoon. Thank goodness he didn't come with them today. Breanna would have punched him in the face had he wrinkled his nose and fixed his lips to say something cute.

"Are we good, Master Chef?" Kelvin asked. He stood tall with his shoulders broad.

"You guys are perfect."

A smile tugged at Kelvin's lips as he tried to maintain his professional charm. "Thanks, master chef."

"Alright, you all," Breanna said, standing by the door and opening it. "Let's move out."

She watched them leave out the kitchen. They looked so confident as they strode down the hall. She couldn't have been prouder of them. She heard them hype each other up as they made their way to the banquet's double doors. The sounds of clapping erupted from the banquet hall as she watched them disappear into the room one by one.

Breanna stared at Latasha while rubbing her chin with her thumb and index finger. "You know what I'm thinking."

Latasha nodded. "That we better start on the dessert just in case someone asks for theirs first."

"That's why I love you so much."

"You've taught me well, Ms. Breanna."

As Breanna walked alongside Latasha, they lifted a box filled with desserts from the cart and placed it on the island. She dug into another container and pulled out her favorite icing piper, already pre-filled with lemon cream. Since she was a teenager, she had that icing piper. And whenever she used it, she always tried to impress her parents with her baking and pipping skills. Even though Momma hated watching her mess up the kitchen, Daddy partook in every moment she baked. From helping her prep to taste testing, Daddy never turned her away from baking.

283

She closed her eyes for a moment. Why couldn't she tell the difference between Momma and Daddy back then? Was she that stupid? Breanna sighed. Whenever Daddy told her to pursue her dreams of being a baker, Momma would tell her she needed something more tangible than serving people, that she didn't want to waste her life slaving away at a stove. But baking was her passion. Baking was ingrained in her from both Grandma Zora and Grandma Isabella. Hell, Grandma Isabella was the very force behind everything she did when making pastries. She was the reason Breanna named her daughter after her and nicknamed her Shortcake. She never wanted to forget where her dreams began. Instead, she allowed Momma to kill them and persuaded her to get a degree in business. She was stupid for letting Momma do that to her.

She watched Latasha take out the tarts from their covered platters and place them in the center of black and white designed square plates she sat on the countertop. Breanna followed behind her, drizzling each lemon and strawberry tart slice with the sweet icing.

"Breanna," AJ said, walking into the kitchen. "There's a Mr. Marcus Devereaux wanting to know what's for dessert."

Breanna rose an eyebrow and pursed her lips. "That name sounds familiar."

She paused for a moment. That couldn't have been renowned Marcus Devereaux, who created the famous chocolate and cinnamon souffle and vanilla bean sorbet. She couldn't tell if the day was getting any worse or better. All she knew was that she had to make a good impression. "Tell him it's a lemon and strawberry tart topped with a lemon cream with a ginger zest."

"Thanks, Bree," AJ said. He ran back out the kitchen. The door swung for a moment until it slowed into its stationary position again.

"Ms. Breanna, do you think you'll ever get your culinary degree?"

She smiled. "One day, I will."

"I hope you do."

Breanna stared and smiled. "Why?"

"Because you'll be the first woman I know who went after her dreams."

"And what about yourself, Latasha? What dreams do you have?"

"Honestly, I don't know," she said, shrugging her shoulders. "All I know is that I'm good at creating things."

"Things like what?"

Latasha's cheeks reddened as she continued setting the tarts on the plates. "I love interior design. I've even helped Kelvin set up his apartment."

"Really?"

284

Latasha nodded. "I have. I just don't know where to start."

Breanna looked away from her. If Elijah didn't hate her guts so much, she probably could have convinced him to let Latasha design the interiors of some of their homes. Sure, he was good. But having another interior designer would take the heavy load off his shoulders. "I think you should pursue it."

"I don't know, Ms. Breanna."

"Nothing will happen if you don't try."

Latasha stared at her and smiled. "Thanks, Ms. Breanna. I guess I—"

"He wants you to bring him a plate," AJ said, busting through the kitchen's double doors again. He held up a finger, trying to catch his breath.

"Right now?" Breanna stared at him with wide eyes.

He nodded. "He's waiting for you as we speak, Bree."

She paced the floor as she shook her head and mumbled under her breath. The more she thought about stepping inside the banquet hall, the more she thought about being cursed out by Elijah in front of Mr. Devereux. "I can send Latasha in with the plate."

"Breanna," AJ said, standing between the double doors. "He wants you to bring it."

"But... what about... Elijah?"

"He's going to have to deal with it, for now, Breanna," said AJ. "Besides, this guy's a big-time buyer for us. I can't let my brother from another mother screw this up because y'all can't get along."

"AJ... I can't—"

"Bree, please. You've got to do this." He looked out the door, then directed his attention back to Breanna. "Look, I've got to get back out there. I'm going to tell him you're on your way. I'll be waiting for you."

Breanna watched AJ run out the kitchen. She couldn't go into that room. She just couldn't. Sure, she could have put on a brave face and moved her ass in and out of the area within seconds but knowing both Elijah and Morgan were out there made her head swim and her heart drum against her throat.

"Ms. Breanna."

Breanna jumped. She stared at Latasha with wide eyes. Water welled in them.

"You've got this," she said, handing her a pair of white gloves.

Breanna wiped away a tear as she washed her hands. She took the gloves from Latasha's hand, then took a deep breath. Sliding them on one by one, she took a plate from Latasha's hand and stared into her eyes once more. She couldn't believe she was going to do this. But it was either having AJ breathing down her neck for leaving him hanging

285

or watching Elijah and Morgan visually murder her with their gaze. She was going to take the latter.

Breanna pushed past the swinging double doors and descended the hall. Every step she took seemed like she was Indiana Jones hopping from one stone to the next, trying to avoid falling face-first into a pit of molten lava. She stood in front of the banquet room's double doors and took another deep breath. It was now or never.

As she pushed one of the banquet doors open, Breanna stepped inside and stood by the door for a second. Her heart thumped against her throat as she swallowed hard. Everyone's eyes seemed to have reverted to her as she walked through the intimately lit room toward Mr. Devereaux's table. AJ saw her and smiled, beckoning her to follow his direction. Breanna trekked behind him and stared at Mr. Devereaux. He was sitting at the same table where Elijah sat. She noticed him holding Morgan's hand as she neared them.

Her heart drummed harder against her throat. Her right eye twinged with pain. Elijah's eyes seared the skin exposed from the black and white tuxedo she wore. His frown yelled in her face. God! Why couldn't she have stayed inside the kitchen?

"Here you go," Breanna said, sitting the plate in front of Mr. Devereaux.

He smiled, then raised an eyebrow. Mr. Devereaux held his fork up as if he were trying to make a bid and slid the back end of the utensil against the cream drizzled on the plate, tasting the pastry. He stared at her with his gray eyes, then smiled, flashing his wide his gapped tooth smile.

"Elegant," Mr. Devereaux said. He sliced the fork through the tart, inhaled the aroma of the piece of pastry, and placed it into his mouth. He moaned, tilting his head to the side as he chewed. Mr. Devereaux shimmed in his seat as he consumed the pastry.

"My dear," he said, still savoring the tart. "Are you the pastry chef at Soul Bistro?"

"I... I... I am," Breanna stammered.

"This is exquisitely done. Are you classically trained or self-taught?"

"I'm self-taught, sir."

"Please, call me Marcus or Mr. Devereaux whichever you choose. Just don't call me, sir. It's too formal."

Breanna glanced at Elijah for a moment. His steel-blue eyes seemed black. Morgan stared at her with a smirk and snuggled closer to him. If she could have just slapped the bitch in the face one good time, that would have taken some of the edge off. If only, though, Breanna.

"My dear," Mr. Devereaux said. He furrowed his eyebrows and leaned closer toward her. "You seem shaken. Are you okay?"

Breanna nodded, mustering a half-smile.

Mr. Devereaux stared at her, then turned and glanced at Elijah and Morgan. "Ah! I see." He rose from the table and beckoned for her to take his hand. "Let's walk. I would like to get to know you better. Away from green eyes, of course."

"Excuse me? Who has green eyes?" Morgan asked, glaring at Breanna and Mr. Devereaux.

He turned toward Morgan and chuckled. "She just spoke."

Breanna watched Morgan roll her eyes and shake her head as they walked away from the table. She felt so light as she stepped away from the table.

"I've been keeping an eye on your work," Mr. Devereaux said, leading her toward the banquet doors.

"You have."

He nodded. "Mmm-hmm. A few months back, I visited Howard's restaurant and came across your vanilla and caramel spiced ice cream you served with fudge crumble brownies. It was exquisite. It was as if southern charm and gourmet had a love child from a one-night stand."

Breanna smiled. "Thank you, Mr. Devereaux. My grandmothers taught me how to make pastries."

"Let me guess. One is from the south, and one was an actual pastry chef."

"How did you figure?"

"Because baking like that comes with a lot of experience, and for someone your age, you've been in the kitchen with them."

"Grandma Zora, my mom's mother, was a pastry chef back in Chicago for a while before moving back to Tennessee. And my dad's mother, Grandma Isabella, wasn't trained, but she knew how to burn. She lived in Mississippi all her life. Those two were like best friends whenever they were around each other and baked pastries."

Mr. Devereaux nodded. "And that's where you gained such skills. Marvelous."

"They always taught me how to bake from the heart."

"I see, but does Howard allow you to do that?" Mr. Devereaux stared into her eyes. "From what I can understand, he has you working multiple positions. Am I correct?"

"He does, Mr. Devereaux," Breanna replied. "I helped him open the restaurant some years ago, and he trusted me since he knew I would get the job done."

"Sounds more like he trapped his competition. What friend would keep his business partner extremely busy and not solely focus on what her expertise is?"

287

"A friend who promised that I would see my due share in the restaurant once it rose from the ground up."

"And have you?"

"No."

"Mmm-hmm," Mr. Devereaux smiled at her, pulling a card from his pocket. He handed it to her. "Do you know about Straus and Culler Culinary Arts College?"

"I do," Breanna answered, smiling. "Some of the best pastry and gourmet chefs have graduated from there."

Mr. Devereaux pushed open the kitchen door for Breanna to walk inside and followed her. She watched Latasha drizzle the last few tarts.

"I see that you have trained this young lady well."

Latasha looked up from her last plate and waved at Mr. Devereaux with a wide smile, flashing her slightly gapped front teeth.

He stared at Breanna and smiled. "I would love for you to come down to the college one day when you're not too busy and show you around the place."

"I would love that," Breanna said. Examining the card, she tapped her index finger on the number. "Is this the number I can contact you at?"

"Yes, my dear." Mr. Devereaux walked around the kitchen, surveying the desserts. He held his hands behind his back as he proceeded throughout the kitchen. "And when you come, be prepared to make a dish. I would love for the students to see your work."

"Yes, Mr. Devereaux."

"Very well, then. I will be expecting your arrival," he said, opening one of the double doors. "I hope soon."

Breanna watched Mr. Devereaux leave the kitchen and placed her hand on her chest. God was funny. Even though she was walking to her guillotine, he guided her past the knife's edge. She closed her eyes and leaned against the refrigerator.

"Was that Mr. Devereaux, Ms. Breanna?" Latasha beamed at her with a bright smile.

"That was him." Breanna nodded.

"Please tell me you're going to take that opportunity."

She raised an eyebrow as she watched Latasha pick up several serving trays and place them on the island next to the desserts. "What do you mean opportunity, Latasha?"

"From what that sounded like, I think he just recruited you for his college."

Breanna pulled off her gloves and leaned against the industrial sink. The thought of leaving Soul Bistro ran across her mind more in the past month since she'd been staying with Mom, Daddy, and Amber. Howard

288

wouldn't give her a share of the restaurant. She knew that now. All he was going to do was force her to work at both restaurants or pull double shifts whenever Tessa was out. Maybe this was the leap of faith she needed to take.

"Master Chef," Kelvin said, walking into the kitchen. The food's a big hit. "Oh! And people are asking about that tart you brought to Mr. Devereaux a few moments ago."

"Really?" Breanna smiled. "Already?"

Kelvin nodded. "Yep. There's even a lady out there who wants you to recreate that pastry for a baby shower she's throwing three weeks from now."

Latasha looked at Breanna and smiled. "Ms. Breanna, you really should consider Mr. Devereaux's offer."

Breanna stepped toward the island. Her smile made her cheeks flush. "Well, let's get these people served and make them happy."

Breanna grabbed a serving tray and began placing plates on it. "Latasha, you can follow me and take one side of the room if you like."

"I sure can, Ms. Breanna."

"Kelvin, have one of the young men serve some champaign."

"On it, Master Chef," he replied, making his way out the kitchen.

"Master chef? Really?" Morgan walked into the kitchen. Her purple halter top dress made her cinnamon touched skin glimmer. She stood in front of Breanna. Her long leg peeped through the thigh-length slit in her dress. "The only thing I can see you being the master of is fucking other men."

Breanna closed her eyes and took a deep breath. "I didn't come here to start with you, Morgan."

"Well, why did you come then?"

Latasha stood beside Breanna with the serving tray in hand. "Ms. Breanna. Who's this heffa?"

Morgan widened her eyes. "You've got some nerve, little girl."

"I ain't ya' little girl, Scary Spice wannabe."

Breanna placed her hand on Latasha's shoulder. "Latasha, you don't need to defend me."

"Ms. Breanna, I got you."

"Thanks, sweetie. I got me too."

"Sounds like somebody's grown some balls. Or more like been sucking on them."

"Morgan." Elijah stepped into the kitchen. He watched Latasha eyeball Morgan on the way out of the kitchen. "This isn't the place nor the time."

Morgan stared at Breanna and frowned. "I didn't ask for this piece of shit—"

289

"—You best watch your mouth, Morgan," Breanna interrupted her. She stood before her, looking into her eyes.

"Just wait for me, okay. Go back to the banquet," Elijah said, frowning at Breanna.

"Okay," Morgan huffed. "I'll be waiting for you, Sunshine."

Breanna watched her leave out the kitchen. She stared into Elijah's eyes with drawn-together eyebrows.

"Did you come here on purpose, Breanna?"

"I didn't, Eli. Howard has me catering events now on top of other duties I can barely fulfill."

"Sure, he does."

"You don't have to believe me, Eli."

"I don't."

Breanna looked away from his gaze, trying to fight back the tears she had been battling most of the day. "Eli... I know I hurt you and Isabella badly. I know sorry isn't enough, either. But I am. I just want to straighten things out with the two of you."

"Straighten things out, Bree," Elijah retorted. "You should have thought about that before you started fucking Nathaniel."

"I never slept with him," she sobbed. "You won't believe me."

"It's hard to believe a slut."

Breanna's eyes widened. "Did you just call me a slut?"

"It's what you answered to, right?"

"E... Elijah," Breanna stammered. "I did you and Isabella so wrong. I fucked up in the worse way, and I don't blame you for not wanting to believe me. But—"

"—You were the last person I wanted to see, and I hope this banquet ends quickly so I don't have to see you again," Elijah interrupted her. "When you're done here, get your shit and leave."

"Eli... please. If you would let me talk to you—"

"I said get your shit and leave, Breanna."

Leslie and AJ stood inside the kitchen and stared at the two of them with wide eyes. Breanna watched as Elijah pushed past AJ and Leslie and walked out the kitchen. She covered her face with both hands and sobbed. Why did she even listen to them in the first place? Had she stayed inside the kitchen, this exchange wouldn't have happened.

"Breanna," Leslie said, taking her into her embrace. "What just happened?"

"I happened," Breanna sobbed.

"Do you want me to talk to Elijah?" AJ asked.

"You don't need to. I deserved it. I deserved all of it." Breanna said. "I need to leave."

"Breanna, you can't leave yet," Leslie said. "We still need you around, and the people are raving about your dessert."

"That's great, Leslie, but I've done more damage in the past hour than I ever have in my entire life."

Kelvin ran into the kitchen. "Yo', Master Chef," he said breathlessly. "Mr. Devereaux wants you to come back into the banquet."

Breanna stared at him for a moment and shook her head. "I don't think I should."

He scoffed. "Come on, Master Chef. This is the moment you've worked your ass off for."

Breanna took a deep breath. She worked for this opportunity, but at the cost of throwing herself further into a burning house, she'd rather stay inside the safest place in the building. Still, they were right. If she didn't take this opportunity, she was only going to hate herself more than she already had. "Only for you all."

Leslie took her by the arm and walked her back into the banquet hall. She saw Latasha placing a plate of dessert in front of an older woman who reminded her of Grandma Zora. If she were here, she would have told her to stop waddling in her own bullshit and correct the mess she made. That's what Breanna had to do.

"Ladies and gentlemen," Mr. Devereaux exclaimed. "Please give Chef Breanna Ellis a round of applause."

People stood from the seats and clapped. Their smiles. Their raised champaign glasses. The scowl resting on Elijah's face.

"Please, chef. Come, make a speech." Mr. Devereaux held the microphone out to Breanna.

This was it. This was the moment she should have run out of the room and back into the van, where no one else could see her. Instead, she walked to the center of the raised platform, took two steps upward, and received the microphone from Mr. Devereaux's hand. Why the hell was she doing this? Why?

She closed her eyes. This was the moment Breanna knew she had to start over. Not only for the family she abandoned but for the woman she mistreated. Herself.

"Good afternoon, you all," Breanna said. Elijah's glare burned through her soul. "I would like to say thank you to the Harvey and Bryson Company for allowing me and my team to showcase our work. These people have been behind me through my best and worst, and I want to thank them for their continued support. Please support them as they continue to make this community better with their luxurious yet eco-efficient homes."

As she left the stage, Breanna caught Elijah's frown. She knew she had to leave before she made shit even worse. For his sake and her own.

Chapter Forty-Six

The redness of the sun meshed with the blueish grays of the evening sky as it set. Breanna tilted her head backward, closed her eyes, and took a deep breath. The stabbing echoes of Elijah's vindictive words rushed through her veins like a dangerous drug. She opened her eyes and gazed at the straggling guest leaving the building with to-go plates in their hands. At least she got one thing right. The sounds of their laughter and smiles made her cringe a bit. Happiness was no longer something she could grasp anymore, not with Elijah and Isabella, anyway.

She peeked at Elijah's truck, still parked next to AJ's car, then placed the last of the containers into a box and slid it inside the van's trunk. Thank God she had enough dessert and food to feed a hundred people. Had Howard been there and run out of food, he would have blamed her without hesitation. He was some friend alright.

Breanna frowned. Maybe it was time for her to leave that place behind. Besides, he had his bestie, Tessa, there to keep him company whenever he wanted to get drunk and rant about how his partner had a stick rammed up his ass. Had she just listened to Eli—what was done was done. She had to get that through her skull.

Not too long ago, Brenna was in the same boat with those. She often complained about how Elijah never allowed her to be independent, how he kept her from living her life, and how he wanted to control her. All he did was protect her and his unborn child. That's all he did. She was too stupid to see that.

Now, all she wanted was her boyfriend and daughter back. No. Breanna wanted her husband back. That's what he was to her. But that no longer mattered. She wouldn't get them back in her life. They hated her.

"Ms. Breanna," Latasha said, walking behind her with a box in her arms. "I think this was everything from the kitchen we brought with us."

"Good," she nodded. "I think you guys have worked hard enough today for you two to take the rest of the day off."

"What about you, Ms. Breanna?"

"I'll probably stay for another shift and take off tomorrow."

"But you've been at the restaurant since seven this morning," Kelvin said, closing the trunk to the van. "You've got to get some rest too, Master Chef."

Breanna sighed. "Howard won't let all three of us off at the same time. Somebody's gotta stay behind and man the fort."

"Tessa should be there, shouldn't she?" Latasha stared into her eyes.

Breanna looked at her. Her frown and tight lips spelled out the frustration on her face. "She may be gone for the day since she doesn't work a full six hours on Fridays."

"Ugh," Latasha grunted. "I can't fucking stand Howard for that. Why does she get all this special treatment? She caused all this shit we're going through now."

Breanna rubbed her shoulder. "Because everything can't always be justified. I've just learned that one myself."

She watched as Latasha shook her head as she hopped into the passenger side of the van.

"That ain't right, Master Chef," Kelvin said, slipping into the driver's side of the van. "Howard needs to come up off that. Seriously."

"I'll be okay, guys," Breanna said, getting inside the van. She slid the door shut and rested her head against the headrest.

She noticed Elijah and Morgan walking out of the building together as they held hands. The smiles on their faces were that unmistakable joy she used to have with him. A joy she handed to Morgan on a silver platter tinged with rhinestones on the lining of it.

She would never have that with him again. She had to live with that fact. What Breanna had done to Elijah and Isabella was etched in stone, never to be removed.

She watched the two of them. They stood in front of his truck and kissed. She looked away from them. Her chest and throat burned with every breath she took. This was her fault. The arguments, the guilt, the hurt, the dishonesty. She did all that to Elijah and Isabella.

294

She closed her eyes as Kelvin drove the van off the parking lot. She lost the best things in her life because of the wants she longed to have fulfilled. Wants her momma believed were the best for her. And even she, too, couldn't stand the air Breanna breathed because she didn't want to get her ass beat by a man who only wanted her body to begin with.

"Hey, Master Chef," Kelvin said, looking into the review mirror at her. "Would you be mad if I left Soul Bistro?"

"I can't be mad at you for searching for something better." Breanna watched the signal lights dance from yellow to red, slowing the van to a stop.

"I ask because Mr. Devereaux asked me if I would be interested in attending that culinary school he works at. I really want to, Master Chef."

"Kelvin," Breanna smiled. "You don't need my permission. We're in the same age bracket here."

"Well, Ms. Breanna," Latasha said. "You are older than both of us. You got more wisdom than me and Kel over here."

"I'm not that wise." Breanna chuckled.

"You're wise enough to know how to keep me from letting my mouth get me in trouble. My momma couldn't even do that."

"And know how to keep Howard from trying to bombard us with crazy hours and unfair treatment."

"That's because you two were the breath of fresh air I needed when I didn't have any help in sight," Breanna said. "But if you think you need to move on, you're not hurting me at all. I would be thrilled for you."

"Well, maybe we should all leave together. Howard ain't trying to change no time soon, and I got Pampers I gotta buy for my baby. That little chump change ain't doing shit for me."

"Latasha. Kelvin." Breanna looked into the rearview mirror, glimpsing into both their eyes. "You two can't stay around because of me. You two need to move on and grow."

"Then, can you promise us you'll take that offer Mr. Devereaux has for you at Straus and Culler Culinary College, Ms. Breanna?"

Kelvin raised an eyebrow. "So, does that mean that you'll be my instructor if I attend?"

Breanna smiled as she shook her head. She watched several mustangs zip past them as they switched lanes, heading for Pelter Street. "I'm not sure, Kel, but I'm still thinking about it."

"Come on, Master Chef," Kelvin said. "He must see something in your skills that he wants at the college. You gotta take that offer."

"What you said," Latasha said, chiming in. "I can't wait to see the look on Howard's face when you take that offer."

After noticing several cones and off-limits signs cutting off the intersection of Pelter Street and Jones Drive, Kelvin made a U-turn. One by one, the streetlights lit up as Kelvin made a sharp right onto Washington Cove. She closed her eyes again. Breanna had about five more minutes of peace before Howard started breathing down her neck again.

Her phone vibrated in her pocket. It was either Howard wondering if they were trying to play hooky after the banquet or someone who still loved her. She dug it out and peeped at the screen. She smiled, seeing Amber's and Daddy's names scroll across the screen.

Amber: Hey, little sis. Could you please show me how to make those lemon bars so I can hush Leilani up? She keeps complaining that I couldn't bake if I tried. I can bake... a little bit.

Daddy: Hey, baby girl. Don't forget to call Leslie when you're done. I'll be on my way at eight-thirty, whether Howard likes it or not. You've been there too long.

Her smile widened as she replied to the text messages. Despite all the bad she had gone through in the past month, she had to think about the people she gained in her life. Mom, Daddy, Amber. She never thought a day in her life she and Amber would ever be this close again. Hell, she never thought she would ever see eye to eye with Mom and Daddy. It was funny how God worked. When one bad thing happened, something good came along.

Breanna stared at the sign on the top of Howard's building and sighed. Back to Soul Bistro again, where getting breaks weren't meant for her. Yep. She was so glad to be back. An odd rush of butterflies fluttered in the pit of her stomach as the van came to a stop. She frowned. Something didn't seem right.

"I can't make any promises I can't keep, but I will try my hardest, okay."

Latasha turned to her and smiled. "I'll take that."

"Me too, Master Chef."

As Breanna got out of the van, she noticed something move from the corner of her eye. What looked like a figure moving back and forth behind the bushes made her heart race. She surveyed her surroundings. Something just didn't sit well with her. She rubbed her shoulder and sighed. That must have been the effects of pulling two double shifts for the past few weeks.

"Master Chef," Kelvin said, opening the van's trunk. He pulled out the cart and sat it on the ground. "Are you okay?"

She nodded. A cool gust of wind unraveled her hair from its bun. "I'm good, Kelvin."

"I swear you need to go home and get some sleep, too. Howard will be alright tonight," Latasha said, standing next to her. She pulled out a couple of boxes and sat them inside the cart Kelvin laid out for her.

"I'm fine," said Breanna. "Besides, my dad will be here in another hour to pick me up."

"It's a wait, but it's better than nothing," Latasha said.

She noticed the bushes move from the corner of her eye again. Breanna looked around as she frowned. It either had to have been a cat playing around in those bushes or some drunk college kids passed out over there. Whatever it was, it was unnerving her.

"Hey, guys. Start taking the equipment inside the restaurant. I've got to make a quick phone call to my best friend, so I can watch the materials." Breanna said, reaching into her pocket.

"Are you sure you don't want Kelvin to stay with the van, Ms. Breanna?"

Breanna shook her head. If Howard saw her and Latasha walking into the building, he would fire Kelvin without hesitation. She didn't want Howard's irrational thinking weighing her already heavy conscience down. "I'll be okay, Latasha."

"Okay, Ms. Breanna."

She watched the two of them walk toward the restaurant. They wouldn't let her stay long enough for Howard to force her to work another shift. She stood before the opened trunk and woke her phone. Noticing that she pulled her picture out along with her cellphone, Breanna stared at it. She wanted them back in her life so badly. She wiped away the tear before it fell. Breanna didn't need Latasha to see her cry again. She'd already come to the rescue once tonight.

Her hair fell off her shoulders, forcing her to turn around and survey the parking lot again. Nothing was there. She swore there was a hand on her shoulders, but as usual, Breanna's mind was toying with her. Her phone buzzed in her hand, begging for her attention. She looked at it. An unknown text notification lit up the device. The words "Hey, Beautiful" sat before her eyes.

She stiffened. "Nathaniel?"

Breanna examined the parking lot once more, checking every car she saw. Her heart drummed against her chest, forcing her to breathe faster. She wished she would have listened to Mom and got that restraining order against Nathaniel, but even with the court order in hand, that didn't mean he would follow the rules. Then again, she was overthinking and overworked. She took a deep breath and looked at the pocket-sized picture in her other hand and smiled. Their smiles were the only things that calmed her overactive mind.

As she dialed Leslie's number, Breanna reached inside the van and grabbed a box. A pair of hands wrapped around her mouth and waist. Her eyes widened as she was ripped from the vehicle. Breanna struggled against the hold, fighting to get away from the tight grip. A fairly large hand muffled her screams, squeezing her mouth shut.

The sound of her phone crashing onto the ground made her breathe harder. She stared at it. Her only call for help laid shattered on the pavement. She gripped the picture in her hand, not letting it go, no matter how much he tossed her around. But she had a bigger problem than the picture she held. How was she going to get away from him now without her phone? She had to improvise.

That old black pickup truck with the for-sale sign in the window was the only thing Breana saw as she struggled harder to get out of his hold. Breanna braced herself as he threw her to the ground next to the vehicle. The smell of gas and a dead animal lingered in the area as she watched a shadow loom in her direction. "Nathaniel?"

"Hey, Beautiful."

She heard his gruff panting as he neared her. This couldn't have been what he was about to do to her. It just couldn't have. She knew Nathaniel only wanted to have sex with her, but not to this extent. This wasn't the man she knew back in high school. This wasn't—maybe that was his true nature all along. He probably hid it long enough to stalk her until he got her into his bed, and when he wasn't successful, he was going to get it anyway he wanted to.

She eased away from him. Tears streamed down her cheeks.

"Did you miss me, Beautiful?"

"Nathaniel," Breanna whimpered. "Please, don't do this."

"Don't you dare act like a victim," he hissed. "It wouldn't have come down to this if you gave me what I wanted."

As Breanna tried to move past him, Nathaniel stomped at her, forcing her to press her back onto the oil-stained door of the old pickup truck. "Please, don't come any closer."

"And where's the fun in that, Bree?"

Breanna watched him as he stood in front of her. He kneeled beside her and stroked her cheek with his index finger. She trembled as she panted. She closed her eyes tight and then swallowed hard. "Please, Nathaniel. Don't do this to me."

"Though I find your pleading sexy, that shit ain't enough anymore," he said. "You all outta luck now, especially since white boy ain't no longer in the picture."

Breanna noticed the door to the restaurant open from the corner of her eye and turned as she watched a couple holding hands walk out the building. It was now or never. She kicked Nathaniel in the shin and shoved him to the ground. Making a beeline toward the couple's direction, she found herself back in his grasp again. His hand squeezed her mouth tighter, keeping her from screaming. He pulled her out of their sight and threw her to the ground once more. "You're pissing me off, Breanna."

"Good," she said, standing to her feet. Breanna watched him move around her slowly. The smile on Nathaniel's face made her ease away from him. He was sizing her up, waiting for her to run and scream from him. For once, she had to think like the man before her. She had to make him writhe in pain like he did to her.

As Nathaniel lunged at her, Breanna jumped out of the way, then kicked him in the balls. His staggered breathing and deep coughing gave her a small window to get away from him. His tearful groans turned to malicious growls as he held his groin while trying to collect himself. Breanna ran toward the van, hoping this nightmare would be over with. She wanted him to stay on the ground.

But that wasn't in Nathaniel's character. No matter what the situation was, he always got the last laugh. The sudden grasp of his hands on her shoulder made her scream. She grabbed his hand and flipped him over her shoulder with all her strength.

He coughed once more as his body smacked the ground. Just a few more seconds. That was all she needed to get to safety. Nathaniel's loud groans gave her the okay to run further from him. She had to stay focused—she had to get back to Elijah. She couldn't stop now.

Breanna scooped her phone off the ground as she ran past several cars in the parking lot. This was the farthest she'd gotten away from Nathaniel. She illuminated Elijah's name, then paused in her steps, hearing his laugh nearby. Breanna stared at how far she still was from the building and cursed under her breath. Usually, she loved parking further away from the restaurant since that lessened how fast she had to deal with Howard, but this was the one time she hated it the most.

With the sudden painful grasp around her arm, Nathaniel jerked her into his embrace and witnessed her own feet lift off the ground. She braced herself as Nathaniel tossed her to the ground like a rag doll. The world spun around a bit from her impact with the cold gravel. Her eyes widened as she watched him stand before her.

"Try that shit with me again, Bree," Nathaniel growled. He grabbed her by the hair, pulling her onto her feet. He punched her hard in the stomach, forcing her to cough and gag simultaneously. Breathing in deep became the most challenging task to perform.

He threw her onto the ground again. She held her head as it swam from hitting the gravel yet again.

"Move one more time, and I'll break yo' ass in half, bitch."

Nathaniel smirked at her, then kicked her forcefully in the spine. Breanna screamed. His foot had more punch than a horse's hoof with the horseshoe on it. Pain surged and burned through her body as she tried to stand on her feet. She fell, panting harder as she watched him come for her again. Her picture of Elijah and Isabella lay before her. As Breanna reached for the glossy piece of paper, Nathaniel slapped her in the face, sending her body back to the ground. She held her cheek and cried as she curled herself into a fetal position. Her entire body pulsated. Nathaniel got his chance to hurt her. Wasn't that enough?

"Shut the fuck up and give me what you owe me." He grabbed her by her hair again and dragged her back toward the old black pickup truck. Pushing her against the vehicle, Nathaniel punched her in the face. He watched as blood trickled down the side of her face and smiled. "Beautiful."

He pressed his body against hers and jammed his hands into her pants. Her panties tore from his clawing fingers as he gripped them and ripped them from their original shape.

"No!" she screamed. "I don't want this."

"You owe me, bitch." He punched her in the face again. Her bottom lip stung like hell from his last hit. She had to get away from him.

"Please, Nathanial."

"Shut up," he growled. He punched her in the stomach again, causing her to double over and fall to the ground. She held it, groaning in pain as she rolled around.

Breanna grimaced from the second blow to the gut. She hoped he would stop, but at this point, hoping was useless. His fingers entangled themselves with her hair and yanked her onto her feet. She stared into his eyes. His pupils were constricted. Never in her life had she seen so much lustful rage flow through someone's eyes and veins. It was as if seeing her pain was the drug that kept his hard-on intact and firmly erect.

"I take what I want," he said, standing in front of her. He ripped the black vest she wore away from her body and tore open her white button-down shirt, exposing her black bra. The corners of his lips curled up even further.

He slid his tongue up her neck until he got to her lips and kissed her. Breanna bit his bottom lip, making him grunt in pain. She watched him back away from her as he grunted louder this time. He held it, then stared at her. The Nathaniel she knew was gone. This was the devil she was dealing with now.

Breanna ran from him, hoping she could get to safety. But as he grabbed her waist again, she knew it was only going to get worse from here. Nathaniel clutched a handful of her hair again and slammed her head against the truck. Her head bobbled as she tried to stay up on her feet. She couldn't let him win. He ripped her shirt from her body, then pressed his own against hers again.

"You like that, don't you?" Nathaniel huffed in her ear. He wrapped his fingers around her neck and squeezed.

Her vision blurred as she struggled to breathe. She couldn't let him do this to her. As Breanna came to her senses, she stomped his foot with the heel of her shoe and scurried from his grasp.

Nathaniel grunted, then smiled. "That's added interest, Breanna."

Aching muscles and electric-like jolts flowed through her body as she tried to run from him. The pain surged in waves as she hobbled toward the van. Breanna needed Elijah. She needed to feel the warmth of his arms wrapped around her; she needed to see his smile to soothe her pain. Breanna needed to see Isabella's smile and hear her laughter to make her feel better. She gasped for air while running as fast as she could. She couldn't let him take her life.

"Gotcha!"

He tackled Breanna, slamming her body to the ground with a thud. The weight of his body knocked the breath out of her, but it didn't stop her from moving. Breanna wiggled away from him, turned on her back, and punched Nathaniel hard in the face. He smiled as he grabbed her forearm and slammed it onto the ground. The sound of splitting skin and cracking bones filled the night air. Breanna belted out a guttural scream as she glanced at Nathaniel, licking his lips at her pain. His smile turned her stomach. A thousand knives felt like they entered her body all at once.

She panted, seeing the midpoint of her forearm bent from the rest of its counterpart. His smile continued growing into something far more malevolent. He was proud of what he'd done to her. He was about to conquer his conquest.

Nathaniel dragged her from the area she got to and tossed her back toward the pickup truck. He yanked off her shoes, then yanked her black slacks off her legs. Trying to kick him off her, Nathaniel gripped her thigh, nearly sinking his nails into her skin. He slapped her hard in the face. The sounds of her panties ripping apart made her struggle from him as he held her down.

She watched him unbuckle and unzip his pants. He exposed himself, letting her watch his length point at her as it taunted her. He laid on top of her and covered her mouth with his free hand. The smile on his face curled into something non-human.

"Now, tell me you're mine," he whispered in her ear.

Breanna fought against his body weight again, then bit his hand. "I'll never be yours!"

301

A frown distorted Nathaniel's already frightening image. She watched him cock his fist back and lunge his knuckles into her eye and cheek. Pain surged through her eye into her mouth and down her neck. Over and over, Nathaniel's fist connected with her face. Each hit was harder than the last. His hand gripped her throat and squeeze it tight. A distant scream in the background alerted her for a moment before everything swirled before her eyes. Breanna coughed and gasped for air as his grip tightened. The darkness welcomed her into its embrace. It wouldn't let her go; it didn't want to let her go. She thought of Elijah. His smile faded into a scowl. No one could save her anymore. She had gotten what she wanted for so long. Her eyes closed. This is what she asked for. This is what she deserved.

Chapter Forty-Seven

"Dad, has Breanna called you yet?" Amber hopped out of her car and bumped the car door closed with her hip. She stared into the night sky and frowned. Breanna was probably working another double again after she told her not to. "It's almost nine o'clock."

"No, Amber," Dad responded. "She hasn't, but I'm about to pull into Soul Bistro's parking lot in another two minutes and wait for her, okay."

"Okay, Dad," Amber said. "Do you want me to warm up your dinner Mom cooked earlier?"

"No, sweetheart. I can do that when I get home with your sister."

"Okay, Dad. I'll see you soon."

"See you soon, Amber."

As Amber ended the call, she slid her key into the lock and twisted it, opening the door. The smell of fried chicken, mashed potatoes, and mac and cheese casserole wafted up to her nose. The ending credits of "Something New" could be heard from the great room.

She walked through the foyer into the great room and smiled. Mom fell asleep on the couch again. She shook her head, noticing she was still in her blue and white scrubs while wearing her favorite fuzzy white slippers. It was about time for Mom to retire. That woman dedicated nearly twenty-five years of her life to Highland Memorial Hospital.

Stepping closer toward Mom, Amber gazed at the picture Mom held in her hand. It was the one of Isabella, Elijah, and Breanna playing in a field of leaves. She sighed. Amber knew Mom missed seeing her grandbaby. Hell, she missed seeing the little munchkin, too.

Her phone rang in her pants pocket, causing Mom to stir from her slumber.

"I'm sorry, Mom," Amber said, grabbing the phone and answering it. "Dad. Hello." The loud whirring of sirens pierced her ears. "Dad, I can't hear you. Are those sirens going off in the background?"

Mom jolted from the couch with a frown. "What's going on? Is he okay?"

Amber shrugged. "I'm not sure, Mom."

"Amber," Dad said, frantically. "Oh, God!"

"Dad! What's wrong? Dad!"

"Amber, it's your sister. She's being transported to the hospital."

"What happened, Dad?"

"Nathaniel," he growled. "That asshole raped my little girl."

"Raped?" Amber shook her head as the phone slipped from her fingertips. She sat on the couch where Mom sat. Tears welled in her eyes. How could that have happened to her?

"Marvin," Regina said, picking the phone up from the floor and placing it to her ear. "What happened to Breanna?"

"Nathaniel raped her," he sobbed. The sounds of his fist hitting the horn of his car jumbled with his incoherent yelling and curses. The clash of noise rung in her ears. "Her co-workers found her, but they said she was unconscious by the time they got to her. The bastard ripped her clothes off her and left her on the ground when he saw them coming his way."

"My baby was raped," she said, trying to keep calm. Tears slipped down her cheeks. She sat next to Amber and pulled her into her embrace.

Amber held Mom tight as she stared at the recent picture she and Breanna took while shopping at the outlet mall with Mom and Dad a few Sundays ago. Echoes of Dad's sobs filled the silence in the room.

Her little sister was violated, and Howard let that shit happen to her. That little bastard was going to pay for everything he had done to her. Everything.

304

Chapter Forty-Eight

W as this a cruel prank God pulled on her, or was this the lesson she hoped Breanna would learn from? Amber pulled into the hospital's parking lot and parked next to Leilani's blue Nissan Rogue. Mom's hand grace her shoulder knocked some of the edge off for the moment. She placed her hand on top of hers and took a deep breath. Amber wasn't ready to deal with this. Hell, she didn't know how to deal with this.

One by one, tears cascaded down her cheeks. "Mom," Amber sobbed. "Did I cause this?"

Mom pulled Amber into her embrace and ran her fingers through her smooth black curls. "No, baby," she said, rocking her. "You didn't."

"Then why does it seem like every time I get my little sister back, someone takes her away from me."

Mom wiped away Amber's sliding tear and kissed her cheek before cupping her chin. "When one person's happiness causes another person's anger, that person would do anything to take away the other person's happiness. Even if that means losing a bit of themselves."

"Like Momma did to us," Amber replied.

Mom nodded. "Gwendolyn couldn't come to terms with what she did to you and Breanna. Still, that doesn't mean she destroyed your lives. You're both still here."

Amber sighed deeply. "What if she doesn't make it through the night?"

"Don't talk like that, Amber," Mom whispered through tears. "She's going to pull through this. I know she will."

Mom was right. Still, there was that little voice in the back of her head that kept saying otherwise. Its hissing nags and raspy jeering made Amber suck in a breath. It forced its way through her ears as they rang from the silent humming inside the car.

"Amber," Mom grabbed her hand tighter. "Don't you dare let negativity infest your mind right now?"

Amber stared into Mom's eyes, watching as she fought to hold back the tears. "I won't, Mom."

"You better not," she retorted sternly. "Your sister needs you now more than ever. Do you understand me?"

"I do," Amber whispered through tears.

Opening the car door, Mom stepped out and took a deep breath. Amber watched her run her fingers through her hair as she closed the car door. Never in her life did she ever think someone would hurt Breanna like this. Sure, her little sister needed to learn a lesson, but this wasn't how she thought it would happen. This wasn't—the sight of that woman's black Mercedes Benz pulling up next to her car and parking made Amber frown. Why the fuck was Aunt Pauline here?

"Oh, Amber," Aunt Pauline said, getting out of her car and running toward her with her arms wide open. "Your father told me what happened." She held Amber tight in her embrace.

Amber stared at the still running Mercedes Benz, looking for her ungrateful mother, but the woman wasn't there. "Where's Momma?" Amber pulled from her embrace and stared at her with wrinkled eyebrows.

"She told me she couldn't make it at the moment, but she'll be out here later to see Breanna."

"Is that what she said, Aunt Pauline?"

The woman crossed her heart with her index finger and smiled. "Would I ever lie to my favorite niece?"

Amber kept her eyes trained on her aunt and gawked at her prancing about the parking lot while wailing like she honestly wanted to be there. Why in the world did Dad call this buffoon? Neither she nor her crazy momma needed to be there. Then again, Amber didn't deserve to be there either. After all, she told her sister she needed to get her ass beat. Perhaps that was what God sought to teach her. Maybe that was what she was hoping would happen to Breanna all along.

But what if her little sister succumbed to her injuries? What would happen to Isabella? What would happen to Dad? Would any of them look at her the same anymore after she confessed to them what she told her sister?

Amber covered her mouth, trying to contain her sobs.

"Amber," Mom called.

Amber stared into her mother's eyes with her wide watery ones. She frowned as she watched her aunt walk toward the building, fanning herself as she continued to wail.

"You're not the cause of this, Amber," she said. "Just be strong for your sister, okay."

Amber nodded. She needed more than strength right now. She needed body armor, weapons, and extra vitality to get her through this night.

Her heart raced against her chest as she walked toward the hospital's sliding doors. The rush of warmish cool air blew through her curls as she stepped inside the sterile whiteness of Highland Memorial's lobby. Amber noticed Dad sitting next to Leilani and stopped in her treks, watching him twirl his thumbs and stare off into the distance.

Tears slid down her cheeks at the sight of Dad's tears. She couldn't force her feet to move. Aunt Pauline's voice carried on like a broken organ that wouldn't stop playing its recorded tunes. She closed her eyes and sobbed. "I can't do this."

"I got you, honeybee," Leilani said, embracing her tight. "You ain't gotta do this by yourself, okay."

Seeing a young man and woman walk in their direction, Amber noticed their uniforms. They must've worked with Breanna. They must've been the ones who found her lying on the ground.

"Mr. and Mrs. Ellis," Latasha said, holding onto a small pocket-sized picture in her hand. "I wish there was something more we could've done."

"You found my little girl," Dad said. "You two did more than you think you've done."

"Sir," Kelvin spoke, hesitantly. "Latasha and I found this picture that Master Chef kept in her pocket."

Mom covered her mouth as she sobbed, then walked away from the group. Amber watched Kelvin hand the picture to Dad, then noticed him nod before another tear slipped down his cheek.

"Is that what you all you called her?" Amber stared at them, noticing the welling tears in Latasha's eyes. A single tear slid down her cheek as she tried to catch her breath. "My little sister always bragged about you two."

"Ms. Breanna is like a big sister to me. I would've been fired from this job if it weren't for her."

Amber swatted away a fleeting tear as she stared at Kelvin and Latasha once more. "Please stay with us. You two are family."

"We would love to, but Howard will rip us a new one if we don't go back to work," Kelvin said.

"I wish he would try." Amber frowned. "He hasn't done anything but torture you all."

"Besides, my little girl needs all the love and support she can get right now," Dad said. "She needs—"

"Mr. Ellis," a soft female spoke behind him. Her tight black coils were highlighted with gray streaks. Her glasses made her hazel brown eyes shine even more. "My name's Dr. Logan. I wanted to let you know your daughter is finally out of surgery, but she's still unconscious."

Dad took a deep breath. "What does that mean?"

"That means," Dr. Logan said, pausing for a moment. "That Ms. Ellis is in a coma."

"A coma?" Amber stepped closer to them. Her heart raced faster against her chest. "You mean to tell me that bastard beat my little sister into a coma."

"It does, unfortunately," Dr. Logan replied. "Honestly, we don't know when she'll wake up."

Amber placed her hand over her chest and slowly sat in a chair. Her head swam from the information floating through her ears. Breanna was on the verge of death, and there was nothing she could do about it.

"Before we take her into her room, Mr. Ellis," Dr. Logan said. "I need your permission to have the rape kit performed on your daughter."

He nodded. "I need to know what he's done to my little girl."

"I can't promise you anything, Mr. Ellis," Dr. Logan said. "But as God as my witness, I will do all that I can to make sure she wakes up to her family again."

"When will we be able to see her?"

"In two more hours," she replied. "We need to gather every picture, sample, and swab of what happened to Breanna tonight."

"You better make sure you find that asshole," Dad hissed.

"I will, sir."

Amber watched Dr. Logan board the elevator and then disappear from her sight. Her head swam from their exchange of words.

"Marvin," Grandma Zora called, walking as swiftly as she could toward them. "What have the doctors said about Breanna?"

Amber watched her father slump into a chair, nearly missing the seat. Tears streamed down his cheeks as Mom and Grandma Zora rushed toward him.

"Please tell me that my baby is okay," Grandma Zora said, taking her son-in-law into her arms.

"Oh, my God! Why in the hell did you have to come here, Momma?" Aunt Pauline asked, twisting her neck from side to side and rolling her eyes. "You always show up when you want to be seen."

"Little girl," Grandma Zora said. "You still ain't too young to take no whooping now."

"Whatcha going to do? Take your hand and spank me. I'm too old for that, Momma."

"Have some respect, Aunt Pauline," Amber stated firmly.

"I know you ain't trying to talk, lesbo."

"Who the fuck you think you—"

Mom pushed Amber aside and stood in front of Aunt Pauline, glaring into her deep brown eyes. Her long jet-black hair hung in waves to her shoulders. The hospital lights beaming down on both Mom and Aunt Pauline made their skin shimmer. Even though Mom was darker-skinned than Aunt Pauline, the light made her skin glisten like diamonds.

"Don't you say another word to Amber," Mom said, stepping closer to her. "Don't give me any reason to commit vehicular homicide tonight, Pauline."

"Excuse you—"

"You heard me," Mom retorted, cutting her off again. "If you want to be underneath the tires of a Dodge Challenger, keep talking."

Sitting next to Leilani, Kelvin, and Latasha, Amber kept her eyes trained on Aunt Pauline. That woman didn't come here to see about her little sister. She came here to bask in her demise.

"Has the doctor said anything about Breanna yet?" Grandma Zora paced the floor while wiping a tear from her eye.

"She has Mrs. Marshall," Dad replied. "I gave them permission to perform her rape kit recently."

Amber watched Grandma Zora take a deep breath as she placed her hand over her chest. Her dark skin resembled hers in every way. Her short salt and peppered colored hair sat in a subtle mohawk.

She watched Grandma Zora tighten her black and white cardigan as she bit her bottom lip, trying to hold back her tears. The people who were here never gave up on Breanna, except those who needed Breanna more than anything. Somehow, despite all the bullshit her little sister put her through, Mom, Dad, Grandma Zora, and her co-workers all saw past it. Amber sighed. Although Mom told her not to blame herself, she couldn't help thinking she helped put her little sister in this hospital.

She glanced at the elevator, watching it open and close for visitors trying their hardest to see their loved ones. As Amber took another deep breath, she closed her eyes and released it. All she wanted now was a little glimmer of hope.

"Mr. Ellis," Dr. Logan said, standing in front of him.

Amber jumped in her seat and immediately turned toward the doctor.

"We've made room for you and your family to go to the floor that she'll be residing on for a while."

"Thank you," he said.

"It's the least I can do until we finish her rape kit."

Amber reached for her phone and stared at it as they all stood from their seats. Elijah needed to know what happened to Breanna. He needed to know for their daughter's sake.

"Have you called him yet, honeybee?" Leilani grabbed her hand and held onto it as they walked toward the elevator.

"I haven't," Amber said. "But I'm going to call him."

"He may not care, but." Leilani sucked in a breath. "Their precious little girl needs to know."

Amber nodded. God, she hoped this night wouldn't get worse. Yet every time she tried to calm her core, her muscles tensed up like she had just run a 400-meter relay during the peak of her athletic collegiate years.

Amber took another deep breath as the elevator thrust them upward. Once it came to a stop on the fourth floor, Amber stared into Dr. Logan's eyes. There was so much care in them, so much reassurance.

"The lobby area is this way," she said, leading them off the elevator and down the hall. Stale white lights, an irritating hum, and a single red flashing light made the hair on her skin raise as they followed the doctor.

"What wing is this?" Mom glanced at the half-closed doors. "I don't recall seeing this area before."

"About two years ago, a very loving mother and father of a young rape victim gave a generous donation to us after their daughter succumbed to her injuries," Dr. Logan said. "They wanted to make sure victims like their daughter had all the care they needed."

"So, this is the Kerri Heathers ward, correct?"

Dr. Logan nodded. "It sure is. We've been able to do great things for these victims."

"As long as I've worked here, I've never known about this ward."

"Many doctors and nurses don't know about it, unless they were assigned to this area."

"Then how do I get assigned to this area?"

"Mrs. Ellis, I don't think that's a good idea—"

"That's my baby that's about to be laying in one of these rooms. I want to see about her."

Dr. Logan stared at Mom, then at the rest of the family as they finally arrived in the silent lobby. Sounds of a ticking clock and humming soda and snack machines blared into their ears as they walked inside the room.

"Then I'll speak with your supervisor and make some arrangements for you so you can work in this area for a while," Dr. Logan said.

Amber looked around the room, still holding onto Leilani's hand, and sobbed.

"It's okay, honeybee." Leilani pulled her into her embrace. "It's okay to cry."

The sound of Aunt Pauline's chuckles lingered in the background. Amber pulled away from Leilani and watched her take a seat next to one of the snack machines.

"What's so funny?" Amber's eyebrows furrowed as she listened to her aunt continue to cackle.

"You know how to put on a show, don't you?"

"My sister's in a coma, Pauline," Amber hissed. "I know you don't expect me to be all smiles and giggles right now."

"First of all, little girl, I didn't say that," she retorted, rolling her neck. "You just remind me of my late sister. She was always full of drama."

"Aunt Aubrey wasn't full of drama, Pauline. That was you and your stupid sister who I call mother."

"Enough, you two," Grandma Zora said. "We've got too much going on right now to be fighting amongst each other."

"You're right, Momma," Aunt Pauline said. "But you and I both know my poor niece acts like Aubrey."

"At least Aubrey had common sense, Pauline."

"Oh, so now you're going to agree with my niece too, Momma."

"Sure, I am," Grandma Zora said, glaring at her daughter. "You and Gwendolyn had always acted like you were entitled to more when all of you had to same afforded liberties."

"Are you bullshitting me right now, Momma?" Aunt Pauline rose from her seat and stood in front of her mother, pointing her finger in her face. "You are the last person who should be talking."

"Sit yo' ass down, Pauline," Marvin said, stepping closer to them.

"Then make me, Marvin," she chuckled. "Like you did years ago in that hotel room."

"That's enough, Pauline."

"Shut the hell up, Momma."

"You need to apologize to Grandma Zora."

"Oh really, lesbo." Aunt Pauline placed her index and middle finger on both sides of her mouth and flicked her tongue at her. "Go sit your gay ass down."

"That's enough, Pauline," Grandma Zora said, slapping her hard in the face. The sound echoed throughout the small lobby. "You've said enough. Now, it's time for you to leave."

Aunt Pauline held her cheek, then nodded her head as she smiled. "You stupid bitch."

Before her hand could connect with Grandma Zora's face, Amber pushed her aunt into one of the snack machines, causing her to hit the back of her head.

"You're going to pay for that bitch."

"Then come get this lesbo, you stupid heffa."

Watching Aunt Pauline run in her direction, Amber dodged her attack, then grabbed a hand full of her hair, slinging her onto the ground.

"I need security here, ASAP," Dr. Logan said, running toward the front desk.

Dad, Mom, and Leilani scuffled to pull her and Aunt Pauline apart.

"Let me go, Marvin," Aunt Pauline yelled. "I'm going to teach my niece a little lesson."

"It looks like she already taught you that, Pauline." He pushed her toward the two police officers' direction. Her muffled cursing and screaming could be heard down the hall as they dragged her.

"Ma'am," one of the police officers stood in front of Amber and Grandma Zora. "Do you want to press charges?"

Amber stared at Grandma Zora, watching her nod her head. "Yes. I want to press charges."

"We can take your statement over here."

"Please, let's try not to fight among each other anymore," Dr. Logan stated. "You have way more important things to deal with than pettiness."

Amber noticed a nurse wheeling a bed into an empty room next to them and stared at the woman lying in bed. Tears filled her eyes once more. Dr. Logan was right. There were way more important things they needed to be concerned about because the very person lying in that bed meant more to her than Aunt Pauline and Momma ever had in her life right now.

Chapter Forty-Nine

Breanna. She was all Elijah could think about. The woman ripped his heart from his chest and tap-danced on with a big smile. Not to mention she fucked up Isabella's belief of what a good mother was supposed to be. She had some nerve showing up at the banquet today. She had some—she—he couldn't understand why he wanted to be near her again. He scoured his phone's photo album, swiping through selfies of Breanna and Isabella doing their best puckered lips and inflated cheeks poses. They must've stolen his phone while he slept. A slight smile tugged at the corner of his lips before slipping into a frown.

He closed his eyes. Morgan had proven she could change; she had even shown she was a much different person than she was in college. Though, she still demanded people to fall at her feet whenever she strode by them. Hell, if they didn't follow her way the first time, they didn't stand a chance with her. So why did Morgan give him another chance?

Elijah sighed, opening his eyes. Confliction was a bitch. He had a beautiful woman lying next to him in bed, and he couldn't so much as touch her. Not like the way he used to touch Breanna. The way her toes would curl whenever he kissed the nape of her neck. The way she would bite her bottom lip whenever she straddled and rode him. The way she—he couldn't let her back into his and Isabella's lives.

Elijah put his phone on the nightstand and stood from the bed. He coughed. His chest tightened, forcing him to rub it. He hadn't had an asthma attack in a month. Why now? He continued to rub it as he walked out the bedroom door.

"Hey, Sunshine," Morgan said, smiling. She rolled onto her stomach. Her black boy shorts hugged her ass tight. She wore his white button-down shirt like a nighty; it barely covered her black and white polka-dotted bra that hugged her C-cup-sized breasts. "I thought you wanted to commemorate our one month together."

"I'm really not feeling like it tonight," Elijah answered. "Besides, Izzy may still be up. I wouldn't want her to hear us."

She scoffed. "Elijah, you've said the same thing for the past three nights now. What's wrong with you?"

"Nothing, Morgan."

"There's gotta be something wrong with you because you've passed me up three times, and I'm fucking hot." Morgan got off the bed and stood before him.

"That you are." He smiled, admiring her half-exposed curves. Elijah walked back into the bedroom and pulled her into his embrace and kissed her lips. "But I'm not ready yet."

She wrapped her arms around his neck. "I bet a can make you shiver like the way I used to back in college."

Morgan nibbled his earlobe, then lured her hand into his sweatpants. Elijah swallowed hard as he closed his eyes. He pulled her closer to his body, deepening the kiss. Elijah flicked his tongue inside her mouth, enjoying the subtle moans she made. She moaned against his lips once more as he swept her up from the floor, kicked the door closed behind him, and placed her on the bed.

"That's much better, Sunshine."

Elijah trailed her neck with kisses and then pulled her leg around his waist. Breanna's giggles and moans echoed in his ears. He kissed Morgan once more, hoping rid of his of Breanna, but her moans never stopped flowing through them. Elijah couldn't do this. He couldn't see himself with—his cellphone rang. She placed her fingertip against his lips and shook her head.

"I thought you turned off your cellphone." Morgan pushed him off her and sat up.

He scoffed. "I like to keep my phone on in case of emergencies."

"Well, tonight was supposed to be special. No cellphones."

"Morgan," he said. "You know I have a daughter, right? If something happened to her, I would need to get to my cellphone quickly. Not wait for it to load while it's booting up."

"Are you pranking me or something?"

"No. I'm not, Morgan." Elijah leaned toward her and planted a kiss on her cheek. "I'm trying to be responsible."

His cellphone rang again. He frowned. Maybe it was Katrina trying to get in contact with him about something. Elijah grabbed the phone

314

and looked at it. Leslie called. A rush of butterflies flooded the pit of his stomach. It was 11 p.m. Leslie and AJ were like an old couple. They were in bed by 11: 30 most nights.

The phone rang again in his hand. Leslie's name scrolled across the screen. He swallowed hard as he noticed Morgan get off the bed. Her eyes burn the side of his head as disappeared into the bathroom and slammed the door shut behind her.

"Hey, Leslie—"

"Elijah," she sobbed through labored breaths. "She's... she's.... Oh my God!"

He frowned. He'd never heard Leslie sound so distraught, except for when her father passed away in front of her some years ago. He closed his eyes, then opened them. "Leslie, what's wrong. Leslie—"

"Hey, Eli," AJ said.

"What's up, man?" Elijah could still hear Leslie crying in the background.

"It's not good." AJ took a deep breath.

Elijah's heart raced; his chest tightened again. He couldn't shake the thought of Breanna from his mind. It was as if she was trying to reach out to him or something. Like she needed him. Maybe that was the former bond they once shared with each other. He shook his head. Perhaps he was overthinking. "What's not good?"

"It's Breanna." AJ paused. He heard Leslie's cries fade into the distance. "She was attacked and raped in the parking lot of Soul Bistro earlier tonight."

Elijah's eye grew wide. He coughed, then cleared his throat as he rubbed his chest, trying to stave away the asthma tugging on his lungs. "Raped?! This must be a joke or something."

"I wished it was Eli. Leilani called us a little while ago. She said she would have called sooner, but Amber and her aunt got into a scuffle at the hospital."

Nathaniel. That was the only person Elijah could think of. When he ran into him at the park, he just thought Nathaniel was trying to get under his skin. The asshole was all talk and no show; he was just trying to... Oh! God! Nathaniel told him she wouldn't be the same after he had a little chat with her. Elijah frowned. He let this happen to her. "Did she say who found her?"

"Leilani said that Latasha and Kelvin found her in the parking lot," AJ replied. He took another deep breath. "She said Latasha and Kelvin spoke with Breanna's father at the scene of the crime before Breanna was transported to the hospital."

"Which hospital?"

"She's at Highland Memorial East," said AJ. "Leslie and I are about to go out there now."

"Okay. I'll see you two out there soon," Elijah said.

"Alright, E," AJ said. "See ya soon."

The call ended. Tears welled in his eyes as he looked around the room. The way he spoke to her earlier. The way he looked at her. He ran his fingers through his hair. Every single word he said to Breanna played back through his mind. Had he wished this upon her? Had he wanted to get back at her so badly?

Morgan stopped in her steps as she walked out the bathroom. Her eyebrows furrowed. "What's wrong, Sunshine?"

He stared at her. He couldn't force anything out of his mouth.

"Elijah." Morgan waved her hand in front of his face. "Talk to me. You're scaring me."

"I need to get to the hospital."

"Are you okay? Are you having another asthma attack?"

"No," he answered. He stared into her eyes. Another tear streamed down his cheek. "I... I need to go."

"What about Isabella?"

"Could you stay here and watch her? I don't want to alarm her."

"Yeah. Sure," Morgan nodded. "Wait. Does this have something to do with Breanna?" She folded her arms across her chest and watched him pull on some blue jeans and a black t-shirt.

Elijah stared at her. He knew if he told her Breanna was in the hospital, Morgan would have lost her proverbial shit. She was the last person Morgan wanted to hear about. But this was the mother of his child. This was the love of his—he needed to support her family. "I need to go."

"You never answered my question." Morgan watched him pull on his light brown steel toe boots.

"It's not," he answered. "I've gotta go."

Elijah grabbed his inhaler from the dresser and jetted out the bedroom door. As he ran down the steps, Elijah noticed a picture of him, Breanna, and Isabella playing in a field of leaves he forgot to take off the wall. He sighed. How was he going to tell Isabella what happened to her mommy? How was he going to look into his daughter's eyes and utter those words? There was a real possibility she would hate him for what happened to her.

She was already losing sleep at night and could barely focus at school because she told Breanna she hated her. Now, this.

He snatched his keys off the dining room table and ran to the garage door. Why was he even rushing to the hospital, to begin with? She cheated on him with Nathaniel for two months. Maybe this was what she had coming to her. Perhaps she needed to be taught this lesson. Maybe she deserved—no matter what Breanna had done, she didn't deserve to be... raped.

She was raped. Elijah backed out of the driveway quickly, then sped down the street. His phone rang again.

"Hello," Elijah answered sternly.

"Elijah," Mr. Marvin spoke. "Have you heard from AJ and Leslie yet?"

"Yes, sir," he said. "They told me what happened."

"Are you on your way here?"

"Yes, sir. I am."

"Good," said Mr. Marvin. "I need to talk to you, son."

The butterflies flooded the pit of his stomach again. He held his breath, hoping Mr. Marvin wouldn't say what he feared most. He hesitated, then said, "Mr. Marvin? Is she okay?"

He sobbed, then cleared his throat. "Dr. Logan says that my little girl is in a coma."

Elijah gripped the steering wheel tighter as he pressed his foot on the gas pedal. He drove through the yellow light before it turned red and got on the ramp to merge onto the expressway. This couldn't have been happening. The sound of Mr. Marvin crying reverberated through his ears. Elijah took a deep breath, trying to stave off his tears. Nathaniel must have beaten her unconscious. That son of a bitch. "Is it induced? Is she in a lot of pain?"

"Elijah, son. Dr. Logan said she was unconscious when she arrived at the hospital a couple of hours ago."

Elijah drove toward the I-40 exit, closing his gap toward the hospital. The speedometer neared ninety-seven miles per hour as he raced down the expressway. If any police officers were out tonight, he was going to have a hell of a time explaining why he was driving so fast.

"Mr. Marvin," Elijah bit his bottom lip to keep from crying. "Have you seen her yet?"

"I... I have." Mr. Marvin stammered. "My little girl—I need you here, son."

"I'm almost there, sir."

"We're on the third floor. Room 315. I'll see you when you get here."

"Yes, sir."

The call ended in silence. Elijah merged onto the exit for Highland Memorial Hospital and drove toward Pelter Street. He glanced at the surrounding houses, spotting the place he and AJ flipped three years ago. Its tropic green and ocean blue paneling made the dwelling stick out. That was the first home they sold and brought home a profit of $45,000. He remembered how excited Breanna was when he told her

317

about the sale. Now, she was lying in a hospital bed, unresponsive. Nearing the illuminated sign for Highland Memorial, he drove toward the visitor's entrance and entered the parking lot. He saw AJ's black Toyota Camry and parked next to it. He noticed Amber's red Dodge Challenger and Mr. Marvin's black Lincoln Corsair alongside a blue Nissan Rogue.

He jumped out the truck, closed the door behind him, and ran toward the hospital's entrance. Just a month ago, he was here. Now Elijah found himself here, hoping the woman he used to—no still loved would pull through her injuries.

"Can I help you, sir?" The young woman behind the receptionist's desk stared at him with big, doe brown eyes. They were the same kind of eyes Breanna had.

"No, ma'am. I know where I'm heading to," Elijah replied.

"Okay. Just let me know if you need any assistance."

He walked toward one of the elevators and pressed the button. A rush of static overcame him as one of the floating rooms opened to him. He stepped inside, then pressed the third-floor button. He leaned against the wall and wiped away a fleeting tear as he took a deep breath.

As the elevator came to a stop, he wiped his eyes once more and stepped into the hall. His chest tightened as he neared the room Breanna was kept in. Amber's wails touched his ears. His heart pumped hard against his chest.

He watched AJ rub Leslie's back as she held onto his shirt and cried on his shoulder. Amber paced the floor with her arms folded across her chest. Mrs. Regina looked at him, sprung from her seat, and ran in his direction. She hugged him tight.

"I'm so glad you came," Mrs. Regina whispered in his ear. "My baby's fighting for her life in there."

He eyed Amber as she leaned against the wall and covered her face. Her body trembled as she slid to the floor. Leilani kneeled beside her and wrapped her arms around her. The Amber he knew didn't cry. She was the one dishing out heavy-handed pats on the back and man-checking men who tried their best to outwit her. Seeing her cry made the rush of butterflies swell in the pit of the stomach even more.

"Is Amber going to be okay?"

Mrs. Regina looked at him, then shook her head. "Before you got here, she and her Aunt Pauline got into a heated confrontation. Ms. Zora was here to help break up the mess, but the doctor had to call the security guards after Pauline tried to slap her own mother."

"Really?"

Mrs. Regina nodded. "She was just starting shit because that's in her nature. I'm glad you never had to deal with her foolishness."

318

Elijah watched her get up from the floor and walk away from Leilani. "I'm going to talk to Amber and Leilani."

"Please do," Mrs. Regina said. "Amber needs all the comfort she can get right now."

Elijah walked behind Leilani and touched her shoulder. She turned toward him and smiled. "How are you doing, Leilani?"

"I'm good," she replied. She rubbed her temple. "I can't believe this happened."

Elijah stared at her and nodded. Tears fought with his tear ducts as he heard Amber cry. "It's hard for me to believe too."

"She needs you right now, Eli." Leilani took him into her embrace. "She needs her brother-in-law."

He nodded, then made his way toward Amber. Elijah placed his hand on her shoulder as she placed her hands against the wall and cried.

"Brother-in-law," Amber sobbed. She turned toward him and wrapped her arms around his neck. "My baby sister won't wake up. She won't wake up."

"She will, Amber. We have to pray that she will."

Amber's body trembled in his arms. "I just got my sister back. I can't lose her again. I just can't."

He held her tighter, letting a tear slip from his eye. "You won't, Amber. Breanna will still be here with you."

"Then help her come back to me," Amber sobbed. "Please, Elijah. Help bring my baby sister back to me."

Mrs. Regina came over and took Amber into her embrace. She rubbed her back as she wailed. "I've got her. You should go see Breanna before the doctor tells us to leave."

He nodded. As he walked to the door, the sound of the heart rate monitor beeped in the distance. Its slow yet steady beeping was the only thing that could be heard. Elijah stepped inside the room and lost his breath. A rush of tears flooded his eyes as he walked closer to her.

Breanna laid in the bed motionless. One of her eyes was purplish-black and swollen. Her forearm was wrapped in a thick white cast with red tape surrounding it. Breanna's fingers were barely visible from the thickness of the covering as it laid on several pillows to keep it elevated. Several red, purple, and black finger-sized marks lined her neck. A bandage was placed near her hairline, barely hiding a gash that still oozed with blood. Elijah stared at the breathing tube placed in her nose. With every breath Breanna took, the oxygen machine gave her supplemental air to help her breathe.

"Oh, God!" He said, trying to swallow back his tears. "Why were you out in the parking lot by yourself, Bree?"

319

Elijah touched her cheek. Its coldness graced his fingers. Tears streamed down his cheeks. This was Nathaniel and Tessa's work. Those two were out to manipulate and destroy every good thing Breanna had. And she allowed it to happen. No. He allowed this to happen to her. Had he tried to talk to her rather than breathe fire down her neck, she probably would have been okay. She would have been... he wiped away another tear.

He sat next to her and listened to her breathe. Her eyes were closed tight. Her hair laid about both her shoulders. Elijah sat beside her and grabbed her uncovered hand, intertwining his fingers with her limp ones.

"I didn't think I would talk to you like this." He sniffled. "Breanna... I'm... I'm... so sorry for how I treated you earlier. Please forgive me."

Mr. Marvin knocked on the door. "Can I come in for a second?" He stared at Breanna and wiped a tear away before it fell. "Dr. Logan is going to let one person stay out here with her tonight. Amber said she wanted to stay with her tonight."

"Is she sure?"

"Yeah. She doesn't want to leave Breanna's side." Mr. Marvin sat on the couch next to the window. A flat-screen T.V. hung on the wall not too far from him. "I won't stop her. Those two grew close after she and you broke up."

Elijah gave a half-smile and nodded. He wiped away another tear. "I'm glad they started talking again."

"I finally got my girls back," Mr. Marvin said. "I know I haven't been the best father, but these two are my life. Just like Isabella is Breanna's life."

Elijah closed his eyes. Isabella didn't know what had happened to her mommy. Right now, she could have been crying herself to sleep because of what she said to Breanna a month ago. He couldn't let her live with that if something happened to her.

"You need to let her see her mother, Elijah." Mr. Marvin sat up from the couch. "She needs to see her—if my baby girl doesn't... pull... through—Isabella needs to see her."

Elijah nodded as he wiped his eyes. "Yes, sir."

"I know she hurt you and Isabella badly, but she's taken this time to change. Breanna's grown up from the person she used to be. Breanna's... It wouldn't be right if she didn't see her."

Elijah looked away from him, then took a deep breath. Mr. Marvin was right. The pain she caused them both was searing. She left Isabella motherless and him without a wife. His wife. Elijah still wanted her to be his wife. But how were they going to overcome this? How were they going to make things right?

320

"Did Ms. Gwendolyn ever come out here to see Breanna?"

Mr. Marvin laughed. "That woman hung up the damn phone when I called her. She has nothing to do with her or Amber."

Elijah shook his head. "Doesn't she know Breanna's in the hospital?"

"Gwen knows. She just doesn't care. After she and Breanna had a little talk, she's told me countless times that I destroyed the only loyal daughter she had left."

"What made her like that?"

"Her devil of a sister, Pauline. That woman is the embodiment of misery."

Elijah stared at Breanna. He watched her chest move upward and downward. "What about Ms. Zora? Did she get a chance to see her before Pauline's rampage?"

Mr. Marvin nodded. "She did, not too long ago. She had to press charges on her daughter."

A tap on the door alerted them both. Elijah stared at the doctor standing in the doorway and stood from his chair. She smiled at him.

"Mr. Ellis," she said, walking inside the room. "I should know the results soon from the rape kit we performed earlier. Thank you for giving us that permission."

"You're welcome, Dr. Logan."

Dr. Logan clasped her hands together. "The police are still conducting their investigation as well. I'm going to do all that I can to make sure your daughter goes back home with you."

"I appreciate that, Dr. Logan." Mr. Marvin rose from the couch and made his way toward Dr. Logan. "Is it almost that time?"

"Yes," she replied. "But unfortunately, I can't let anyone stay tonight. My team and I have decided to observe her for the night. Her injuries are rather grave."

"Have you told my other daughter this?"

She nodded. "I have. Besides, she needs the rest. I'll allow overnight visitation tomorrow."

Elijah stared at Breanna again. Everything they had been through boiled down to this. He followed Mr. Marvin and Dr. Logan out of the door. He didn't want to leave her; Elijah couldn't leave her. She needed him. He needed her... he needed her to wake up to him again.

Chapter Fifty

Why did this have to happen to Breanna? Why couldn't they work things out between them? Elijah took a deep breath, then struggled to release it without coughing. His chest tightened, forcing him to take a pump of cooling forced air into his lungs. The very woman he saw himself marrying one day was laid up in a hospital bed, unresponsive, bruised, and violated.

Had this happened to her because she wanted to get his attention? Was she that desperate to get back to him? He took another deep breath as he stood beside his truck. A warm breeze played with the ends of his hair. Breanna would never do that herself. She wasn't that type of person. Yet what he knew about her was he had to force Breanna to tell him things like this. He nearly had to shake her down to get her to talk. But that wasn't the case tonight.

Elijah watched the others walk to their cars, then stared at Amber. Her eyes were so red and puffy. Black tear stains trailed her cheeks from where her mascara ran. She waved at him as she got into the passenger seat of her car. Mrs. Regina cranked the vehicle, then pulled Amber into another hug. God, he prayed his wife would make it through the night. He needed her to.

His wife. That was the second time he thought that tonight. The woman lying in their bed didn't belong there. Morgan didn't deserve to lie in the spot Breanna occupied for years. Hell, she didn't earn the right to be there in the first place. Still, he let her inside his home with their daughter and ignored every sign of how she treated Izzy.

He fucked up. Elijah knew he had. When she tried to apologize to him a month ago, all he did was tune her out. He grew tired of her bullshit. He was tired of being hurt by her. All Elijah wanted was for Breanna to feel the same pain he felt every night when she didn't come home. He wanted Breanna to suffer for laying up in another man's bed. And she did, at the high cost of refusing to have sex with a man who only lusted after her body to begin with.

Elijah closed his eyes as he leaned against his truck and raked his fingers through his hair. Nathaniel literally told him he would do something to her, and he did nothing. Another tear slid down his cheek. He did nothing at all.

Elijah placed the back of his head against the door of his truck and gazed at the stars. He remembered how he and Breanna used to sit in the baseball stadium at night and gaze at the stars. He smiled, wiping away another tear. On the night they saw a shooting star soaring through the night sky, Breanna told him she was pregnant. The fear and joy that nestled inside him couldn't be described. All he knew was that he was going to be a father, and the very woman he fell in love with was going to be such a wonderful mother and wife.

There was that word again. But she couldn't be that if she... he couldn't think like that. He couldn't.

"Elijah," Mr. Marvin said, standing beside him. "Are you okay?"

He frowned, then shook his head, trying to keep from crying. "I'm not sure how I'm feeling right now."

Mr. Marvin sighed. "Same here." He took a deep breath. "I want to know why he did this to my little girl."

Elijah clenched his fist, breathing harder. "Mr. Marvin," he hesitated to speak, not wanting to know the outcome of his reaction to what he was about to say. "Nathaniel approached me at the park some days ago."

Mr. Marvin nodded as he chuckled. "I'm assuming the bastard got some balls to talk to you."

Elijah nodded. "He told me Breanna wouldn't be the same the next time I saw her."

"And you never warned her about what he said."

Elijah faced the truck's door and jabbed it, pressing a dent into its exterior. Tears slid down his cheeks. "I didn't warn her at all."

"And you think this is your fault, right?"

"It is my fault," Elijah yelled. He jabbed the truck's door once again, bruising his knuckles in the process. "It's my fault."

Several people walking from the building watched him as he continued to yell. Noticing a woman carrying a little girl who resembled Isabella in her arms, Elijah kicked the door with one of his steel toe

323

boots, putting another dent into the truck. Mr. Marvin stood beside him with his arms folded across his chest and leaned against Elijah's truck as he continued to jab at it.

"Son," Mr. Marvin said, watching his wife and Amber stare at them from afar. "That's not your fault. You didn't know what he was going to do to her."

"I could have at least told her to be careful," Elijah huffed through tears. "I could have kept her from getting hurt."

"I know, Elijah," he replied. "But what I want you to understand is that this isn't your fault."

Elijah groaned as he cried. His chest tightened, forcing him to take deeper breaths. "I don't know how I'm going to tell Isabella this. I don't think that I can."

"You can. It will take some time, but you'll tell her," Mr. Marvin said, placing his hand on Elijah's shoulder.

He coughed harder this time as he forced himself to breathe through the wheezing.

"Besides, you need to be strong for her."

Elijah jabbed the door of his truck one last time, then stared at Mr. Marvin. "Mr. Marvin... I hope you can forgive me."

"Elijah, you're not at fault for this," he replied. "But don't expect me to trust you with my daughter's life once she pulls through this."

Elijah looked away from him, then nodded. Another tear slid down his cheek.

"Breanna wasn't the only person who fucked up in this relationship," Mr. Marvin said. "I understand you were hurting, but you replaced one woman for another so quickly, you didn't give yourself or your daughter time to adjust to the change. And you allowed this woman to mistreat my grandbaby from what your mother has told me."

"Mr. Marvin, I can explain—"

"Save it, Elijah," he said, cutting him off. "I've been there and done that. But before everything fell, I tried my hardest to talk to Gwen, even when I was ready to walk away from her."

Elijah took a deep breath again, then jabbed the truck's door. "I understand, sir."

"Good," he replied. "Keep your relationship amicable from here on out. I don't want either of you putting yourselves in harm's way again. Do I make myself clear?"

Elijah nodded as another tear slipped down his cheek. Every word Mr. Marvin spoke pierced his soul. The one man who always supported him, no matter the situation, was now the very man who no longer trusted him. He didn't blame Mr. Marvin. Had he watched Izzy go through the same thing as his wife did, he would have lost all trust in the young man she loved, too. Still, it was difficult for Elijah to fathom that.

"Yes, sir," Elijah said, resting his hands against the door of his truck. He watched Mr. Marvin walk away from him and get into his car. Now he understood the desperation, dread, and despair Breanna endured when he told her he wanted full custody of Isabella. She must have been beside herself. She may have even tried to harm herself.

Elijah closed his eyes while taking a deep breath. He remembered the first time she told him when she had gotten that low. When the only thing she wanted was peace between Amber and their mother, Breanna took it upon herself to take a knife to her wrist to stop the two of them from fighting. She was fifteen then.

As he got into his truck and slammed the door shut, Elijah took his phone out of his pocket and dialed Mom's number. This wouldn't be easy. Hell, he might as well put a bed beside Breanna's. At least he would have been with the actual woman he loved. That was if he could even be in the same room with her after Mr. Marvin laid down his ground rules.

"Eli," Mom said, answering the phone. "It's 12:30 in the morning. What's wrong?"

"I'm fine, Mom, but," he paused, not wanting to hear his Mom's response to Breanna's current diagnosis. "Breanna isn't doing so well."

"What? What's happened to her?"

He swallowed hard. "She was... attacked and raped in Soul Bistro's parking lot."

"What? That can't be. I spoke to her yesterday morning when she had gotten to work."

"It's true, Mom."

He closed his eyes once more as he listened to his mother sob. He heard Dad stir from his sleep as he grumbled.

"When did this happen, Eli?"

"Around seven or eight o'clock last night."

"This is all Howard's doing," she said through sniffles. "He forced her to work that event you all had."

Elijah frowned. Breanna told him the truth. God, he felt even stupider for attacking her the way he had. "So, she didn't know she was working at our event."

"No. She didn't know. Why?"

Elijah frowned as he closed his eyes. Wiping away another tear, he took a deep breath. "I said some things to her I shouldn't have said."

"Then, have you had the chance to talk to her since the incident?"

He cleared his throat. "She's not responsive, Mom."

"Elijah, I don't understand what you're talking about."

325

Another tear slid down his cheek. "Breanna's in a coma. Her attacker beat her unconscious, Mom."

"Oh my God!" Mom sobbed once more. "What hospital is she at?"

"Highland Memorial East."

"Elijah, I know the two of you have been through a lot. But now is the time you need to make amends."

"I'm not sure if I can do that anymore either," he replied. "Mr. Marvin doesn't trust me anymore."

"I don't blame him."

"Mom, I wasn't the one who put her in that situation. She did that on her own. She's responsible for what that man did to her."

"My son, you may not have put her in that situation, but Breanna didn't deserve what happened to her."

"I know Mom, but—"

"But nothing, Elijah," she retorted. "You gladly brought another woman into your home—a home your father and I worked hard to help you get when Breanna was four months pregnant."

Elijah clenched his fist once more. "I know what I did. But she had no reason to cheat on me."

"You're right. She didn't. But you didn't have any reason for bringing that monster of an ex-girlfriend back into your life, let alone your daughter's life in such a rush."

"Then what was I supposed to do, Mom? Was I supposed to sit there and let her continue to ruin my life and Isabella's?"

"No, my son," she replied. "You should have walked away from her when things got worse, not rush into another relationship. Had you taken some time to think things through, you would have been better off."

He held his head down and sighed. Mom was right. He rushed into this relationship with Morgan and didn't think twice about how it would affect his daughter. He was no better than Breanna. "I wanted her to hurt the way I had been hurt, Mom," he said, sniffling. "But I didn't want this to happen."

"I know, Eli. I know exactly how you feel," she said. "When I cheated on your father, I knew he was ready to leave. But I let him have his space so he could breathe."

"Then, how did you two work things out?"

"We didn't rush into our relationship again. Instead, we took things slowly, and we overcame the challenges that held us down."

"You make that sound so easy, Mom."

"It wasn't, Eli," she replied. "But it was worth it."

"Mom," he said, noticing a pocket-sized picture slipping from his visor. He grabbed it and stared at the beautiful black angel smiling back

326

at him with their daughter in her arms. "How do I work through this with Breanna, then? How do I get my wife back?"

She sniffled, then said, "First, you two need to learn how to communicate. That's the key to all your problems. Second, pray, my son. Pray for her healing, pray for her understanding, and pray for her heart."

He nodded. If there was anything Mom was right about, it was prayer. At first, he didn't understand why she always went to faith. That was the last thing to enter his mind, but things always got better whenever Mom prayed for them. It never happened when she wanted it to, but it always happened when she needed it to. "I will, Mom."

Chapter Fifty-One

Elijah walked inside his home and closed the garage door behind him. He leaned against the door and rested the back of his head against it. He gazed at the picture of Breanna he held in his hand and smiled, running his thumb over the glossy piece of paper. He couldn't fathom the thought of her being in a coma. He just couldn't. After all the bullshit they put each other through, it was time for them to stop fighting over who was right and work out their differences.

But the opportunity for that realization may never happen since she was in a coma. The one woman who he told Mom and Dad he would marry was slipping away from him slowly. A tear slid down his cheek. God, had he known what Nathaniel truly meant about Breanna not being the same anymore, he would have driven her home despite Morgan's protests.

He would have held her tight in his embrace until... Elijah wanted her back in his arms again. No. He needed her back in his arms where she belonged. He needed his family whole again.

He walked down the hallway, then made his way up the stairs. Elijah took a deep breath as he neared Isabella's door. The sounds of whimpers and sniffles caught his attention.

"Isabella," he said, opening her bedroom door. He watched her wipe her eyes with the backs of her hands. Her favorite bedtime storybook set in her lap. "What's wrong, Shortcake?"

She stared into his eyes and sniffled once more. "I asked Ms. Morgan if she would read this book Mommy used to read to me, and she told me to leave her alone."

He sat on the bed next to her and beckoned for her to come into his embrace. "I'm so sorry I put you through this, Isabella," he said, planting a kiss on her forehead as she nestled herself onto his lap. "Daddy should have thought things over before bringing Ms. Morgan here."

She looked up at him, noticing a tear sliding down his cheek. She wiped it away with her thumb. "Why are you crying, Daddy?"

Elijah sighed deeply. "Because Daddy needs to tell you something that I'm not sure if you can handle."

She wiped her eyes again. "But I'm a big girl, Daddy."

"I know you are, Shortcake." He held her tighter in his arms. "But this was something that Daddy didn't want to hear either."

"Did it make you cry?"

He nodded. "It did, Izzy."

Isabella moved from his embrace and grabbed her Princess Tiana doll. She hugged it as she nestled back on his lap again. "I got Princess Tiana for you, Daddy. She always makes me smile whenever I'm sad."

He smiled before taking a deep breath. "Thank you, Izzy. I appreciate that."

He wiped away another tear. This was the hardest thing he ever had to do in his life. God, he couldn't do this, but he knew he had to.

"Isabella," he said, holding her tighter. "I saw Mommy tonight."

"You did." The smile on her face wiped away her lingering tears. "Where is she? Is she coming home soon?"

"She's," he hesitated for a moment, not wanting to see her beautiful smile fade from her lips. "She's in the hospital, Shortcake."

Her little lips quivered as she fought to keep from pouting. "Why, Daddy?"

"Because someone did something horrible to her."

Her heartbeat drummed against his abdomen. "Is she okay?"

"Yes and no, Shortcake," Elijah replied. "Mommy's asleep, and the doctors don't know when she'll wake up."

"Mommy won't wake up?" Isabella stared at him with water welling in her eyes.

"No, Izzy. She won't."

"Why can't she wake up, Daddy?"

"Because she's hurting really bad, Izzy."

Isabella sobbed as she rubbed her eyes. "Daddy, can you kiss her and wake her up?"

"It's not the simple, Izzy."

"Why isn't it?"

"Because Mommy," he swallowed hard, trying to keep his composure. "Needs to heal, and her healing will take some time."

"I want Mommy to wake up, Daddy. Why can't you wake her up?"

"Because I can't, Shortcake. Mommy's in the best place right now." The warmth of his tears graced his cheeks as his daughter's body tremble against his. Elijah held her tight, listening to her whimpering. He rocked her as he closed his eyes tight. Tears streamed down his cheeks as he breathed deeply. Every argument he and Breanna had rummaged through his mind. Why couldn't they communicate? Why didn't they try to communicate?

Elijah placed the back of his head against the wall and sobbed. Mom was right. Communication was key, yet neither of them tried to use it. Instead, they battled each other like they were contenders on American Gladiators, vying to see who was going to come out on top when their daughter was caught in the middle of their war.

He took another deep breath, then cried. Isabella's little fingers latched onto his shirt as she whimpered. She coughed, trying to compose herself. Breanna had to wake up. She just had to. They needed to work on each other and set aside their differences. They needed... to communicate. He knew what he had to do.

"Izzy," he said, wiping away his tears. "I promise I'll do all that I can to help Mommy get better, okay."

She nodded her head against his chest. "Okay, Daddy." She wiped her eyes with the backs of her hands.

"What's going on?" Morgan stood in Isabella's doorway, yawning. "The two of you are loud, and I've got to go to work in the morning."

Isabella snuggled closer to Elijah, hiding from Morgan's glare.

There was no time like the present to start cleaning house. The first thing he had to do was get rid of the monster he brought into his home.

"Okay, Shortcake," he said, beckoning her to get back into bed. "Daddy needs to talk to Ms. Morgan."

Isabella nodded. "Okay."

"I promise you I'm going to make things right."

She wiped away her tears with the back of her hands and nodded. "I know you will, Daddy. You're brave like Aladdin."

He looked at her and gave a half-smile. Elijah kissed her forehead, then tucked Isabella back into bed. "Thank you, my little, Shortcake. Daddy needed to hear that."

Morgan folded her arms across her chest and rolled her eyes as she looked at a picture of Isabella and Breanna dancing together. She scoffed, then rolled her eyes again. "Oh my God, do you have to turn my stomach at this hour?"

Elijah stared at her and frowned. "I need to speak with you."

"Anything you have to say to me you can—"

"Not in front of my daughter, Morgan," he said, cutting her off.

She folded her arms over her black robe and stepped out Isabella's bedroom. She watched him close the door behind him. "What's your problem, Elijah?"

"You're the problem, Morgan."

"Excuse you—"

"Did you tell Izzy to leave you alone after she asked you nicely to read to her?"

She looked away from him, rubbing her neck. "I told her I didn't have time to."

"Don't lie to me, Morgan?"

She frowned. "You're going to believe her over me?"

"That's my daughter, Morgan. I'm going to put her word first until I have all the facts straight," he said. "Now, did you tell her to leave you alone?"

"I didn't tell her that," Morgan retorted. "She's such a little drama queen. She's like her skank ass momma."

Elijah looked away from her and took a deep breath. Now wasn't the time to lose his cool. "Leave her mother out of this, Morgan."

"But it's true, Elijah. You just don't want to face the fact that your little girl is just like her skank ass—"

"Don't you ever talk about her mother like that," Elijah yelled, slamming his fist into the hallway's wall.

Morgan stared at him with wide eyes as she eased away from him. "Elijah, why are you so upset?" She nodded, squinting her eyes at him. "She's the one you went to go see, isn't she—"

"Not now, Morgan," he said, looking away from her once more. "You lied to me. I can't keep letting you do the shit you've done to my daughter."

"She's gotta learn somehow, Sunshine," Morgan said. "And yeah, I told her to leave me alone. I'm tired, Elijah. I didn't want to be bothered after you left to go attend to an issue."

"You need to leave."

"What? I need to leave? The fuck's wrong with you, Elijah?"

"Get your things out of my house and leave, Morgan."

Morgan frowned. "I get it now. Breanna's the one that's in hospital, right?" She scoffed. "The bitch is in the hospital, and now you wanna run back to her? Don't forget she cheated on you, Elijah."

"And so did you, Morgan," he replied. His frown deepened. "You even brought the guy to my apartment and fucked in him my bed. Remember that, Morgan? Remember how I walked in on you two? You nearly had his dick and balls down your damn throat."

"Oh! So, now you're comparing me to Breanna?"

331

Elijah stared at her and chuckled as he shook his head. The last thing he needed was to go to jail for sending Morgan through his bedroom wall. "That bitch that's in the hospital just so happens to be the mother of my child. And that woman did something you never have, Morgan."

Morgan scoffed as she shifted her weight from one leg to the other. She placed her hands on her hips as she rolled her eyes at him. "And what's that, Elijah?"

"She apologized for what she had done to me and Isabella."

Morgan scoffed. A smirk pulled the corners of her lips. "Aww. You wanna give her a cookie."

"No," he retorted. "I should have listened to her instead of allowing you to waltz your uppity, money-hungry ass back into my life."

"Don't forget who saved your life, Elijah."

"I won't forget that, Morgan," he said. "I'm grateful that you did, but you had a motive I failed to see because I was too hurt."

She laughed. "There it is. Now, I'm the bad guy," she said. "But you're just as wrong as I am. You left me to see a woman who brought this shit onto herself."

"She didn't ask to be raped, Morgan," Elijah huffed. "She didn't ask to be beaten into a coma."

The crease in Morgan's eyebrows deepened. "Sounds like a setup to me."

He walked toward her, forcing her to back away from him until she bumped into the wall with her backside. "The mother of my child was raped and beaten, and all you can say is she brought this on herself? Mom was right about you."

"Really, Elijah! You're bringing your racist mother into this—"

"Get the fuck out of my house, Morgan. And whatever you do, don't you come back."

"I'll see you at work tomorrow, Elijah."

"It won't be too much longer that I will be seeing you there too."

She stopped in her footsteps. "What are you trying to say?"

"That I want you gone, Morgan. Now, get the hell out of my house."

He watched her go into his bedroom, gather her things, and march out of there like she was a soldier on a mission. She stomped her way down the stairs, mumbling incoherently as she went. This wasn't the end of Morgan. The woman was a nuclear time bomb waiting for her moment to drop. He knew he had to be ready for her every move. Thank God he listened to AJ and Leslie about Morgan's motives for their company.

Still, it was only just a matter of time before she stalked them like prey in the wild. He needed to make sure his and AJ's deal with the

Johnsons wouldn't fall through. But more than anything, he needed to make sure his wife lived.

Chapter Fifty-Two

"Come on, Shortcake," Elijah said, leading Isabella by the hand as they entered Breanna's hospital room. The beeping of the heart rate monitor clashed with the neighing of Prince Phillips's horse as he fought through a hoard of Maleficent's minions in his plight to find Sleeping Beauty. Elijah glanced at the television, then back at his sleeping wife. If he could wake her up like Prince Phillip woke Sleeping Beauty, he would in a heartbeat.

But that was only a fairytale. Nothing like that would ever happen. He took a deep breath, fighting back the lump building in his throat and tears lingering in his eyes. Why would something so childish give him hope during a time like this? He wiped away the sliding tear before Izzy had the chance to see him and lifted her off the ground. He sat her on the bed next to Breanna. "Be careful, Izzy. You don't want to hurt, Mommy."

He watched her stare at Breanna for a moment, then her doppelganger eyes stared back at him. Tears welled in them as she nodded.

"It's okay, Izzy," he said, kissing her forehead before he sat in a chair next to Breanna's bedside.

"Daddy?"

"Yes, Shortcake."

"Can Mommy hear me?"

He smiled. "She can hear you, Izzy. You should talk to her."

"Do you think she'll wake up if I keep talking to her?"

"It wouldn't hurt to try," he said. "You may be what she needs to wake up."

He watched their daughter lay against Breanna's side, then nuzzled her nose into Breanna's cheek before kissing it. "I'm sorry for what I said to you, Mommy." The child sniffled. "I didn't mean those mean words."

Elijah took a deep breath, trying to hold back the tears forcing their way past his tear ducts. He took hold of Breanna's limp hand and held it. Listening to Isabella hum through her sobs made him sit back in the chair and close his eyes. Tears emerged from under his closed lids as he rubbed his temple.

Just come back to me, Bree.

"Mr. Bryson," Dr. Logan said, knocking on the door as she stood in the entryway.

Elijah stared at her, wiping the tears from his eyes, and gave a half-smile. "Hi, Dr. Logan."

"I was just coming by to check on my patient," she said, walking closer to Breanna's bedside. She stared at Isabella lying next to her and smiled. "And who is this beautiful little girl?"

"This is Isabella," Elijah answered. "She's our daughter."

"Oh, my goodness!" Dr. Logan peered at him, smiling, then darted her eyes to Breanna and Isabella. "I can see the resemblance of both of you in this precious little girl."

"Izzy? Don't you want to say hi?"

Isabella nodded, wiping away a tear with the back of her hand. She waved at Dr. Logan. "Hi."

Elijah knew his daughter had shut down. Dr. Logan wouldn't get too much out of her. He remembered when he came to and stared into her red puffy eyes when he was in the hospital. Izzy didn't so much as a peep, let alone move from his side. It was as if she was guarding him until he could stand on his own two feet again.

Dr. Logan pulled up a stool next to Breanna's bedside and sat on the rolling seat. She placed her chart on the tray next to her and looked into Isabella's blue eyes. She smiled. "I remember when my Mommy was in the hospital for some time."

"Was she asleep like my mommy?"

"She sure was." Dr. Logan nodded. "She was asleep for five long days, and each day, I brought her flowers."

"Did they wake her up?"

Dr. Logan smiled. "I believe they did," she answered. "When she woke up, she told me she had a dream that her favorite flowers surrounded her like plushy pillows on a bed."

"Do you think my mommy would wake up if I brought her flowers?"

335

"I'm not sure, Ms. Isabella," Dr. Logan said. "Flowers were my mommy's favorite thing in the whole wide world. What's your mommy's favorite thing."

Isabella smiled. "My mommy's favorite thing in the whole wide world is Disney movies."

"Really?"

Isabella nodded. "Mmm-hmm. Mommy loves "The Lady and The Tramp", "101 Dalmatians", "The Princess and The Frog", "Sleeping Beauty", "Robinhood", "Hercules", and "Big Hero Six.""

Dr. Logan smiled. "That's funny, Ms. Isabella because her mother and father told me the same thing when they were here earlier."

"Granddaddy Marvin and Grandma Gina!" Isabella beamed. "They told you that too?"

"They sure did," Dr. Logan replied. "They wanted her favorite movies to play while she slept so that she can have pleasant dreams."

Isabella turned toward Elijah. The smile on her face made her glow. "Daddy," she said. "Did you hear that?"

"I did, Shortcake," he said, returning her smile.

"Ms. Isabella," Dr. Logan called. "Is there a Disney movie that you and your mommy love to watch together?"

She nodded. "Uh-huh. "Lilo and Stitch" and "Aladdin" are our favorites," she said. "We love to sing the songs together."

"Oh! So, I have two songbirds on my hands, huh?"

Isabella nodded once more. "Did Granddaddy Marvin and Grandma Gina tell you that too?"

"They sure did," Dr. Logan replied. She peeked at Elijah for a moment. "How about, if it's okay with your daddy, I bring those two movies here, and the both of you can stay overnight with her tonight and watch them?"

Isabella stared at Elijah with wide eyes. "Can we, Daddy? Please."

He nodded. Elijah wouldn't take Isabella away from her mother again. "We sure can, Shortcake."

"Thank you, Daddy." Isabella smiled as she snuggled closer to Breanna's side.

"Okay, Izzy. Can you give Daddy a few minutes to speak with Dr. Logan?"

He watched her nod her head slowly. She was fighting a battle with sleep and wasn't fairing very well. But Elijah understood why. Isabella hadn't slept this well in quite some time. Now that she was back in her mommy's presence, she was going to catch up on some much-needed z's.

"Dr. Logan," Elijah said, walking toward her. "Did you learn anything about the rape kit you performed on her last night?"

336

She sighed, beckoning him to follow her outside the room. "As I told Ms. Ellis's mother and father this morning, there's good news and bad news."

He nodded. These kinds of situations always made his stomach bubble. The fact he ignored Nathaniel's warning was sickening enough. Surely, he knew he wouldn't be able to handle the idea of Breanna getting pregnant or contracting a sexually transmitted disease from this asshole. "I'd rather have the bad first."

"Well," she said. "Ms. Ellis put up a real fight with this guy before he finally took her down. He broke her forearm and bruised two of her ribs. He also left a nasty bruise on her inner thigh from where he grabbed her."

Elijah stepped away from her, raked his hand through his hair, and took a deep breath as he stared at their daughter lying by her side. Had her co-workers not found her, Breanna probably would have been dead by now. A tear slid down his cheek as he stepped toward Dr. Logan again. "How bad is the bruise on her inner thigh?"

"It's worse than the bruises on her face and neck, Mr. Bryson."

"Fuck," Elijah hissed under his breath. "What about his bodily fluids?"

"Well, this is where the good news comes in," Dr. Logan replied. "Though there was semen on the same inner thigh, Ms. Ellis had no vaginal tearing, bruising, or bleeding."

"So, he didn't penetrate her?"

Dr. Logan nodded. "That's the good news. There was no sign of penetration. However, Ms. Ellis was still sexually assaulted. That fact will not change."

"So," Elijah swallowed hard. "Breanna will still be considered a victim of sexual assault, correct?"

"Unfortunately, Mr. Bryson, that's accurate." Dr. Logan took off her glasses and put them inside the pocket of her white lab coat. She ran her hand over her salt and peppered coils. Her chocolate skin glistened from underneath the ceiling lights. "Ms. Ellis's mother and father already spoke with two detectives this morning when they were here. I'm not sure what their conversation was about, though."

"Do you think they've found anything?"

"Maybe. But it would be in your best interest to speak with them regarding the investigation, Mr. Bryson."

He nodded. Elijah understood how Mr. Marvin felt about him now. He knew he couldn't press his luck too much. But for Breanna's survival, he was going to take those body blows and uppercuts. Hell, they were worth it. "Thanks, Dr. Logan."

"You're welcome, Mr. Bryson," she said, stepping away from him. Before she entered the room again, she turned toward him. "Mr. Bryson."

"Yes, ma'am."

"I understand why her parents said you were the one for her."

He frowned, cocking his head to the side. "Why did they say that?"

She smiled. "Despite the crap couples often put themselves through, there's a time and place when to know to call for a truce, Mr. Bryson. You knew when to end trivial matters when Ms. Ellis needed you most. Good men do that, Mr. Bryson."

As he watched her walk back into the hospital room, Elijah walked toward the waiting room and stepped inside. The hums of the drink and snack machine graced his ears as he sat in a chair. He leaned forward and placed his face in the palms of his hands as he cried.

The very thought of Nathaniel approaching him in the park and telling him what he was going to do to her infested his mind like a hoard of zombies sprinting and salivating after the last survivor. It was so hard for him to believe that Breanna's parents still thought of him as a good man when he failed to keep her from harm's grasp. He coughed, trying to catch his breath through the sobs. Elijah let this happen to her. He wasn't a good man; he was a monster.

"Brother-in-law," Amber said, sitting beside him. She placed her hand on his shoulder blade. His body trembled underneath the palm of her hand. "It's okay."

"Amber," he sobbed. "I let this happen to her."

"Elijah. You can't take the blame for something you didn't know was going to happen," she said.

"The man was bold enough to approach me at the park while I had Isabella with me."

"The bastard's got balls, but you had no clue he was going to do something like this, Elijah."

"But I ignored him, Amber. What kind of person does that make me?"

"Normal," Amber replied. She watched him sit back in the chair. "I don't blame you for what transpired at the park. You were hurt, brother-in-law."

"I couldn't stop thinking about all the bullshit Breanna put me and Isabella through."

"I know. My little sister ain't no saint. But over time, she's grown to recognize her sins. Hell, she's even begun correcting them."

"Mr. Marvin told me."

"Speaking of my mom and dad, they wanted to know if you wanted to meet them at the precinct at about 12:30 today."

338

"I can," he said, sitting forward. He stared into her eyes. "Have they found more evidence to arrest Nathaniel?"

"I'm not sure, brother-in-law. But this has his name written all over it. I'm not sure if they've pointed all the arrows to him. It's only been a day since this has happened."

Elijah peaked at the watch on his wrist. He had about another hour and a half before meeting Mr. Marvin and Mrs. Regina at the precinct. He prayed to God the detectives found evidence to throw Nathaniel in jail. The last thing Elijah wanted was for him to attack her again, let alone get itchy and try to attack Isabella.

"I can stay here with my little munchkin and watch some more Disney movies with her. That's if she isn't still asleep."

Elijah smiled. He knew Izzy wouldn't win that battle. "She'll love that, Amber."

Elijah watched her wipe a tear from her eye as she sat back in her seat. She sighed deeply, turning her attention toward him again. "You know, brother-in-law, Breanna wasn't always like this."

"I know," he said. "Ms. Gwendolyn made it her intention to get me away from her."

Amber chuckled, wiping away another tear. "When Breanna was in the tenth grade, she dated this Korean guy by the name of Daniel Tsai."

Elijah chuckled. "Is he the one that dressed up as Inuyasha for the school's Halloween Ball that year?"

Amber nodded as she giggled. "He's the one," she replied. "The only reason he liked Breanna was because she loved to watch anime."

"Then why did they break up?"

"She started watching Outlaw Star, and he wasn't going for it."

"Are you serious, Amber?"

She laughed. "Yep. That was the only reason he dated her," she said. "But Bryant wasn't any better. She dated him in the tenth grade too."

"What did he do?"

"Well, they were playing Marvel vs. Capcom 2, and he lost. Several times. I only recall him winning once or twice."

"And he broke up with her over that?"

She nodded. "Bryan Harper was the president of the robotics club back in high school, named one of the top fifty hottest guys in his twelfth-grade year, and was the only Black guy inducted in the Rutherford B. Jenkins Epsilon Mathematics Honor Society. He never lost until he met my sister."

"God, her taste in men wasn't great at all when she was younger, huh?"

"Not at all," Amber said. "But there was this white guy named Lucas Oliver she really liked. They began dating two months after she and Bryant call the quits. I honestly thought those two were going to go far."

"What happened to him?"

"Well, he knew his parents didn't want him dating outside of his race, so he kept Breanna his little secret."

"Damn. He must've liked her."

"He did until our mother saw the two of them kissing after school one day and decided to give his parents a delicate explanation of what their son was doing."

"Wait. She didn't do this with the other guys, right?"

"She didn't. She only pulled that mess with you and Lucas."

Elijah scoffed. "Sounds like she has a thing against white guys."

"She does."

"That explains a lot." Elijah stared at Amber. "But why, though?"

"Well," Amber sighed deeply. "Our mom cheated on our dad with a white guy. The man was obsessed with her, and she thought nothing of it. She just brushed it off to him being highly in love with her."

He nodded. Breanna thought nothing of Nathaniel's obsession with wanting to have sex with her, too. Ms. Gwendolyn had honestly taught her daughter well. "Do you know why she didn't think nothing would come of his obsession with her?"

"Because Mom thought she could change him from what Dad told me," Amber responded. "She told our dad that Peter was a great guy until he began stalking Breanna at school. Dad wasn't having that."

Elijah raked his hand through his hair as he stared at the wall. Their mother had put their family in harm's way on several occasions, and she still thought nothing of it. Even worse, she raised Breanna to be just like her when she ostracized Amber. "How old were you two when this happened?"

"Breanna was about nine or ten years old when this happened," she said, wiping away a fleeting tear. "And I was about twelve or thirteen."

"That's crazy, Amber."

"I know," she replied. "Peter made her choose who she wanted to be with, and if she made the wrong choice, he was going to end her life. Hell, he probably would have ended our lives too. Thank God, our dad is crazy."

Elijah frowned. That explained Breanna and Amber's mother well. Ms. Gwendolyn assumed the worst for Breanna dating him. The woman even filed false charges against him to get him arrested because Breanna gave birth to a half Black and half White baby. He shook his head. God! He couldn't fathom trying to talk any sense into her, let alone understanding.

340

All Ms. Gwendolyn wanted to do was steer Breanna clear of him. Well, she did. But she led her daughter into the hands of a man who would take her body regardless of if Breanna complied or not. And, the woman pegged Nathaniel as the better man. What kind of mother would do that to her own flesh and blood?

Elijah stood from his seat and took another deep breath. "I'm heading back to sit with Breanna and Isabella."

Amber nodded. "I'll be there shortly. I just need to gather myself too."

"Take all the time you need, sister-in-law," he said.

Amber smiled, wiping away a fleeting tear. "Breanna's happy ass needs to marry you ASAP."

"Yeah. Well, I gotta see if Mr. Marvin will let me ask first."

"He will, Elijah," she responded. "Dad's hurting badly. In a matter of nearly two months, he gained his youngest daughter back and lost her again in the blink of an eye."

Elijah nodded as he made his way toward the door. They all had. Just when Breanna was beginning to change, someone pulled her back.

Elijah's mind swam as he pulled into the precinct's parking lot. He gripped the wheel tighter, not wanting to go inside the tiny building. Grey clouds covered the beaming sun. Droplets of rain plopped onto the truck's windshield. He wasn't sure if he was ready to see the evidence of Breanna's attack, let alone sit beside her parents and watch it if it were captured on video. Hell, Elijah didn't think he could push him to walk inside the building.

But after Amber mentioned she couldn't stomach the idea of seeing evidence of how Nathaniel hurt her little sister, he didn't think he could either. That last thing he wanted was to see video footage of him attempting to rape Breanna. But he had to know. No. He needed to know how her attack went down. He needed to get to the bottom of this shit and put an end to Nathaniel's crazed sexual obsession with her.

God, he hoped the detectives had gathered good evidence. He needed to make sure Breanna wouldn't be hurt again. He needed to make sure their little girl was safe.

As he got out of his truck and closed the door behind him, Elijah walked toward the building. Everything in his body protested for him

341

not to go inside. The headache developing over both of his eyes. The tightness squeezing his chest as he breathed. The knot developing in his stomach. The urge to want to break Nathaniel in half. The need to kick himself in the ass. He could no longer think straight. But he had to. Elijah needed to see how Breanna suffered. He needed to help get justice for the woman he still loved.

He noticed Mr. Marvin and Mrs. Regina sitting in the lobby as he walked inside the precinct. A small wave of relief washed over him, seeing Mrs. Regina's smile.

"I'm glad that you could make it," Mr. Marvin said, standing to his feet.

"Thanks for asking me to come out."

"You're welcome," Mr. Marvin replied. "Besides, Amber hardly slept last night, and her mother and I didn't want her to worry more than what she already is."

Seeing two detectives walk in plain cloths toward them, Elijah swallowed hard. This was the moment he dreaded and had been waiting for.

"I'm Detective Valeria Monroe," the woman said, shaking each of their hands. Her jet-black hair was pulled into a braided bun. Her light brown skin somewhat resembled Breanna's, except for the dark birthmark covering a small portion of her collarbone and the base of her neck. She smiled, beckoning her partner to introduce himself.

"And I'm Detective David Bradford," the man said, shaking all their hands too. He stood beside his partner, placed his hands in his pants pockets, and sighed. Beads of sweat rolled down his chocolate, clean-shaven head until it disappeared into his bountiful beard. "We would like for you all to come with us to the back room."

Detective Monroe smiled at all of them, motioning them to follow Detective Bradford. Elijah closed his eyes as he walked behind Mr. Marvin, Mrs. Regina, and the detective. His asthma squeezed his chest tighter.

You can get through this, Elijah. You just have to.

"Please, have a seat at the table," Detective Bradford said. He closed the door behind them.

"Well." Detective Monroe sighed. "We got a witness's statement and video footage."

"You all have video footage of my little girl's attack?" Mr. Marvin held his wife's hand tighter. Elijah stared at the two of them and swallowed hard. Knowing how cheap Howard was, he was surprised the man even had a camera out in the parking lot. He knew for a fact Howard didn't do that willingly.

342

"Kelvin Eastman, Breanna's co-worker, installed a camera in the parking lot two days after he started working there. After someone tried to break into his car, he took it upon himself to set up the camera."

"Praise God for small miracles," Mrs. Regina said.

"It is a small miracle for us," Detective Monroe said. "But it is limited."

"When you say limited, do you mean the clarity of the picture or the precision of the sound?" Mr. Marvin stared at Detective Bradford, watching his every move.

"The video is a bit fuzzy, but it is clear enough to see faces. However, there is no sound."

"Before we begin this video," Detective Bradford said. "I must warn you about the graphic nature of it."

Elijah breathed deeper, trying to keep himself calm. He noticed an already teary Mrs. Regina. He knew she wouldn't be able to withstand the footage. "How long is the video?"

"Five minutes long," Detective Monroe answered. "Which is why I wanted to know if you all wanted to know about the witness's statement first before we start the video?"

Mr. Marvin sighed as he stared at Mrs. Regina and Elijah. "What do you all want to do first?"

"Let's see the video first," Mrs. Regina said. "I want to make sure that the witness's statement coincides with the footage."

Detective Bradford nodded. As he lowered the screen, he flicked on the projector.

Elijah watched Breanna stand behind the van's opened doors. Boxes from the banquet they catered sat inside the vehicle. She held her phone in one hand and what looked like a picture in the other. As she wiped away a tear, she looked around her surroundings after her hair fell to her shoulders. She must have been paranoid out there by herself.

He took a deep breath as he watched her glance at her phone, then survey her surroundings again. Watching her lips form Nathaniel's name as she looked around, he took another deep breath. Why didn't she just go inside with the others? She would've been safe.

Elijah took another deep breath as he watched Breanna return to the van. With her phone and picture still in hand, she reached inside and grabbed a box. As an enormous shadow loomed over her body, he watched as Nathaniel grabbed her by the waist and mouth and dragged her away from the van. She fought against his hold as much as she could before he pulled her toward a black pickup truck.

"Oh my God!" Mrs. Regina covered her mouth, trying to control her sobs.

They all watched as she was thrown to the ground next to the vehicle. Elijah clenched his fists at the sight of Breanna crying and pleading for her life.

Mrs. Regina turned her attention away from the screen as she watched Breanna run away from Nathaniel, only to be snatched away from help.

A frown pulled Mr. Marvin's calm demeanor into a solemn scowl as he watched his daughter fight back against Nathaniel. Once Breanna got to the van again, Elijah watched as she flipped the bastard over her shoulder and ran out of sight. He dug his fingers deeper into his clenched fists, not wanting to watch the remainder of the video.

Elijah watched Breanna scoop her phone from the ground and wake it up. Nathaniel was just fucking with her; he was stalking her like she was prey waiting to be taken mercilessly. He waited for her to fall into his trap. They all watched Nathaniel slam her body against the ground. He hovered over her, pulled Breanna to her feet, and punched her in the stomach before throwing her onto the pavement again.

"I can't sit here and watch my baby get abused like this," Mrs. Regina said, rising from her chair and leaving out the room.

"Do you want us to stop the video, Mr. Ellis?" Detective Bradford asked.

"No," he replied. "Keep it going. I need to see what this bastard did to my little girl."

Detective Bradford motioned for Detective Monroe to see about Mrs. Regina after she exited the room, leaving the three of them behind. Her wails could be heard from a distance as the closed slowly behind her.

As they watched Breanna curl into a fetal position after Nathaniel plowed his foot into her spine and slapped her hard in the face, Elijah shook his leg, trying to contain the anger festering in his veins.

Another tear streamed down his cheek. With all the beating she endured, Breanna still reached for the picture she once held in her hand. That was the last time she thought she would see their faces. That was the last wonderful memory she would remember before Nathaniel ended her life. She thought she wasn't going to come through this nightmare alive.

You allowed this to happen to her, Elijah.

He took a deep breath as he closed his eyes for a moment. He couldn't think like that. Not with Breanna still fighting hard to get back to her family. He couldn't beat himself down if he was going to be there to help his wife heal.

He wiped the falling tear away as he continued to watch Nathaniel's assault on Breanna. Witnessing him rip her clothes off her, he noticed

Mr. Marvin clench his fists. His chest heaved upward and downward. The video was only going to get worse from here. Elijah knew he had to brace himself for it.

Nathaniel forced himself upon her several times, but with every attempt, she fought back harder and harder until he tackled her to the ground and slammed her arm against the pavement, breaking it. As Elijah watched Breanna scream in agony, he heard Mr. Marvin breathe harder. He didn't know how much more her father could take before losing his proverbial shit.

Elijah watched Nathaniel unzip his pants and lay on top of her. Just the sight of Nathaniel forcing himself on Breanna made him want to punch his fist through the screen. He watched Mr. Marvin walk out the room. The echo of his screams and thuds against the wall echoed throughout the small room. He swallowed hard, fighting the urge not to leave the precinct and hunt Nathaniel like the deer he and Dad used to hunt for dinner when he was a teenager.

Watching Breanna fight against Nathaniel's weight, Elijah lost his breath as he witnessed Nathaniel punch her in the face relentlessly before grabbing her throat and choking her unconscious.

"Mr. Bryson," Detective Bradford said, stopping the video footage. "If you need a little time before we recount the witness's statement, you can step out if you like."

Elijah stared at the detective. Tears welled in his eyes. The allotted time he needed wouldn't be enough for what he wanted to do to Nathaniel. "Thanks, Detective Bradford."

"Mr. Bryson," the detective said, looking into Elijah's eyes. "These things are never easy, but you'll get through them."

Elijah stared at him, then looked away from him for a moment. "That woman in that video is the love of my life, even though we went our separate ways a while back. The man she cheated on me with spoke to me before this happened, detective. This is—"

"—Not your fault, Mr. Bryson," he said, cutting him off. "My wife and I went through something similar, but we survived the bullshit. It takes time. A lot of it. But it can be done, Mr. Bryson. You have to trust the healing process."

Elijah nodded. Mom said the same thing, too. "Thanks for the advice."

"When people choose to stay the same, ain't no need for you to stick around, but when people choose to change for the better, that's when you gotta start listening. No matter how much it hurts, there may be something you'll miss if you don't listen."

Elijah nodded once more. Of all the things Breanna did to him to find happiness, it took several beatings and losing joint custody of their

345

daughter to get her to wake up. He never understood why it took people so long to learn from the shit they put themselves through. Yet, what Elijah knew was that she learned from her mistakes. Breanna fought to get her family back. She fought to be reunited with her sister again. She fought to be a part of Isabella's life again. Breanna fought to start over with him again. Now it was time to fight for her.

Chapter Fifty-Three

Elijah parked his red chevy Pickup Truck next to the old black pickup truck sitting on Soul Bistro's parking lot and gripped the steering wheel tighter as he panned the area where Breanna was attacked. Elijah knew it wouldn't be much effort in questioning Howard, but he needed answers to calm his raging mind. He needed answers to keep him from doing something stupid.

He took a deep breath, watching patrons walk in and out of the restaurant. He had to keep his hands to himself and not try to squeeze Howard's head off his neck if he dared say something cute.

Elijah got out of his truck and walked toward the restaurant. He panned the area closer, noticing several bushes and two trees where the van was parked. Elijah frowned. Nathaniel must have lurked in the bushes and waited for the moment Breanna was alone. He must have—how in the hell did he know she was working that night. He remembered the detectives stating that the witness saw a white Mercedes Benz pull into the parking lot about ten minutes before they returned to the restaurant. Someone must have told him she was going to be there at a certain time.

"Excuse me, sir," a young woman said, bumping into him. She stared into his eyes. "Have I seen you before?"

Elijah examined her face, remembering a young woman with dark auburn curls in a pixie cut, downturned brown eyes, heart-shaped lips, and chocolate skin. "Are you the young lady that works with Breanna Ellis?"

"I am," she said. "My name's Latasha Mathews." She pointed at him, trying to pinpoint who exactly he was. "Aren't you Ms. Breanna's husband?"

Elijah sighed. "We broke up a while back."

"Oh!" she said, covering her mouth. "I'm sorry for the assumptions."

"It's alright," he replied. "Do you know if Howard is in today? I wanted to speak with him?"

"He should be here. Since Ms. Breanna's been in the hospital, he's been working me, Kelvin, and Mr. Vaughn, an older gentleman he hired yesterday, like slaves."

That sounded just like Howard. When he couldn't milk the only cow that produced the sweetest milk in the barn anymore, he had to find several others to pump clean until they had nothing left. That was typical of him.

He followed Latasha inside and saw Tessa smiling and winking her eye at a customer. The two of them looked as if they were going to strip their clothes off where they stood until she caught sight of him. Her smile faded from her lips as she backed away from the man she was about to poison. Tessa darted across the dining hall and pushed through the double doors as if she ran the last stretch of a home run. Elijah frowned. Her run made his final home run for the team back in college look minuscule. Hell, he even bruised his thigh like he rubbed up against a cheese grater for the win. But why did Tessa run instead of accosting him like she usually did? Something wasn't adding up.

"That's the first time I've ever seen her move that fast," Latasha said. "You should probably come around more often."

He chuckled. "I guess there's a first for everything."

"I think you're right, Mr....." Latasha hesitated, not wanting to call him by the wrong name.

"Elijah."

"That's right. Ms. Breanna said that was your name," she said. Latasha noticed Howard dart his squinted glare in her direction as if he were a ninja and halted her in her steps. "I know this isn't any of my business, but I understood why you didn't want to have anything to do with Ms. Breanna at the banquet. My mother left me the same way she left you are your daughter."

"Has your mother ever tried talking to you again?"

"Nope. And the bitch never will either," she replied, twisting her neck from side to side. "But if it weren't for Ms. Breanna, I would still have trust issues. She helped me overcome what my mother did to me. It didn't happen overnight, but I am so grateful for her."

Elijah gave a half-smile as he nodded, trying to hold back the tears fighting their way out. "It sounds like she made an impact in your life."

348

"She did, Mr. Elijah," Latasha said, wiping a fleeting tear from her eye. "That woman taught me that it's okay to be angry, but I need forgiveness to make me better."

Elijah closed his eyes for a moment and sighed. Breanna learned how to forgive. She learned how to think things through. She learned how to let things go. "I'm happy to know she did that for you. That means a lot to me, Latasha."

She wiped away another tear. "Just make sure she pulls through this, Mr. Elijah. I wanna see her smile again. I wanna be in her presence again."

"I will."

"Um," Howard said, walking behind the two of them. He stared at her with pursed lips and narrowed eyes. "Is there something that Ms. Mathews can do for you?"

"There isn't," said Elijah. He watched Latasha rush through the kitchen's double doors and nodded his head at her as she waved at him. "I was hoping to get a moment of your time instead."

"Wait!" Howard got closer to Elijah, making him step away from him. "Aren't you Breanna's husband?" He folded his arms across his chest and tapped his foot on the ground. "Why hasn't Breanna come back to work yet? I needed her to fill in for someone today."

Elijah stared at him. His already solemn stare glazed over into a "don't get fucked up stare". God, he wanted to deck him in his eye so badly. He could feel his knuckles connect with Howard's face. But if he did that, Elijah would've found himself sitting in jail for the first time in his life. It probably would have been worth it, though. "Breanna's still in the hospital, Howard."

"Oh! I thought she would have been out by now."

"Howard," Elijah said. "She's in a coma."

"Oh, my God! I didn't know it was that serious," Howard said, covering his chest with his hand. "I guess Morgan overworked the poor girl."

Elijah cocked his head to the side, narrowing his eyes. "What does Morgan Everly have to do with this?"

"Um." Howard looked at the patrons talking among each other and several others who gawked at the two of them and smiled hesitantly. "Can we take this to the back?"

"The world is your stage, Howard," Elijah said, staring him down. Noticing Howard ease away from him, Elijah followed him slowly, watching sweat perspire on his forehead. He didn't care if someone called the cops or not. He wanted to know how Morgan was involved in Breanna's attack. "I've got all the time in the world."

349

Howard twiddled his thumbs about each other. "I thought you knew Morgan requested Breanna to be part of the crew for the banquet."

"She didn't tell me anything."

"Shit."

Elijah cracked his knuckles. "Did you even know that someone attacked her in your restaurant's parking lot?"

Howard shrugged his shoulders with a shaky smile. "Honestly, Elijah. I couldn't tell you what was going on. All I knew was that she was supposed to cover a shift for Tessa that night."

Elijah noticed Tessa from the corner of his eye as she crept through the dining area. He watched her dodge his sight again and then turned his attention back at Howard. "Was Tessa here that night?"

"She left before Breanna, Kelvin, and Latasha got back. Why?"

Everything made sense to him now. After Breanna and Tessa got into a fight a while back, Howard forced her to work Tessa's shifts as punishment. And one of them must have been keeping Nathaniel in the loop. The only way Nathaniel could have known about her working that shift was from Howard, Morgan, or Tessa.

"Howard," Elijah said through gritted teeth. "Do you know of a Nathaniel Morrison?"

"Not really," he said, shaking his head. "I don't talk to him. The guy's a total creep-fest. But I've seen him and Tessa sucking each other's face off a few times in the parking lot."

As Elijah panned the large dining area, he saw a glimpse of Tessa as she ran out of the restaurant. How could he have been so stupid? Both these women played him. While one aimed to tear their relationship apart, the other sought to take his and AJ's company. And all they wanted was the treasures someone else worked their ass off to have.

"Are you done harassing me, Elijah?"

Elijah stared at him. "For the moment, I am."

"You have nothing else better to do?"

"Besides waiting for Breanna to wake up, I have all the time in the world, and I can spend that time talking to you a little more."

Howard swallowed hard once more. "I'm looking forward to that."

"Good, cause we have a lot more to discuss." Elijah dug one of his business cards out of his pants pocket and handed it to Howard. He never broke eye contact with him. "I'll be waiting for your call tonight unless you want me to pay you another visit and entertain your paying customers,"

Howard back away from Elijah once more. "I'll call you when I take my first break for the day. I normally take about three since I'm—."

"I need you to call me as soon as you can, Howard," Elijah said, sternly.

Howard nodded. "I won't make you wait, Elijah."

"I'm looking forward to it."

As he turned away from Howard and made his way out of the restaurant, Elijah dug his cellphone out of pocket and dialed a set of numbers. His head swam with the overload of drama surrounding him and Breanna's broken relationship.

God, if you're listening, I need your help.

"What's up, E?" AJ answered.

"Go ahead and meet with Mr. Johnson today."

"Are you sure? He's going to want to talk to you too."

"AJ, this is as much of your business as it is mine," Elijah said. "Besides, if it weren't for you meeting up with him at the banquet, we wouldn't have any other options."

"Alright," he said. "E? Is everything okay?"

"Naw, man. It isn't, but I, at least I have a starting point in solving this shit."

"Listen, man. Don't go doing something stupid."

Elijah chuckled. AJ knew him too well. "I won't, AJ. Oh! Are Morgan's employees still there?"

"Yeah. And I've got their contracts ready too."

"Nice. I'll probably be out there tomorrow."

"E," AJ said. "You need to stay close to Breanna. She needs you."

"Are you sure, AJ?"

"For my sister from another mother, I'm positive."

"Thanks, AJ."

"Just make sure she gets better."

"I will, man," Elijah said. He had to because he needed Breanna, too.

Chapter Fifty-Four

"The view is so beautiful here, Aunt Aubrey." Breanna smiled, watching a flock of sparrows fly through the crisp blue sky. Never in her life had she seen trees so vibrant with green leaves and filled with plump red apples hanging from the branches. The sun shined its rays upon her skin, letting her bask in its subtle warmth. If she could stay here forever, she would. There was no peace for her where she currently was.

Aunt Aubrey turned toward her and flashed a wide smile. She was the spitting image of Amber, all except for her hair. It sat in black waves on both of her shoulders. "That's why I love it here; it's so beautiful, so calm."

She stared at her aunt with tears welling in her eyes. "I hate that Momma kept me from spending time with you."

Aunt Aubrey cupped Breanna's cheek. Her beautiful smile still graced her glowing face. "But you're here with me now, Breanna."

"And I want to stay here with you, Aunt Aubrey."

"You can't stay here, Breanna. You know it isn't your time yet."

"There's nothing but pain and anger and jealousy back home." Tears slid down her cheeks.

"And there's love, support, and forgiveness there too, Breanna." Aunt Aubrey wiped away her tears with her thumbs, then pulled Breanna into her embrace. "There are people who long to see your beautiful smile grace their presence again."

"But Aunt Aubrey," Breanna sobbed. "I caused all of their pain. My family hates me for what I did to them."

"Your family still loves you, Bree."

"How do you know that, Aunt Aubrey?"

"Come with me," she said, taking Breanna by the hand. She led her toward a lake. Its blueish green waters shimmered from the sun's rays shining upon it. A pair of swans and their two cygnets swam together as a family.

"You see those swans, Breanna," Aunt Aubrey said, pointing at them. "That's you and your family."

Breanna frowned as she stared at the birds. There was a second cygnet when there only should have been one. "I only have a daughter, Aunt Aubrey."

"And that'll soon change."

"How, Aunt Aubrey? I can't even—"

"Others may say otherwise, but the final say isn't theirs."

"I don't understand."

"Do you have faith, Bree?"

Breanna glanced at the family of swans swimming together and smiled. A tear trickled down her cheek. They looked so peaceful, so happy. There was no way she could get this kind of happiness again. Not with the past trauma she left behind for her ex-boyfriend and daughter to deal with. Elijah and Isabella were probably ready to burn her at the stake. "I guess I do."

She smiled at her. "It sounds shaky to me, sweetie."

Breanna wiped away another single tear flowing down her cheek. "I've always had faith, but this is a little hard to believe."

"You're still trying to hold on to the world's reasoning. The world doesn't owe you anything, Bree."

"Then what do I hold on to?"

"To the hands of the man God placed in your life seven years ago."

"But he hates me."

"He loves you more than you know. He needs you more than you know."

"How, Aunt Aubrey? I hurt Elijah and Isabella so badly."

"Did somebody just call my name, baby?" A sweet, melodic voice sang from afar.

Breanna panned the area, looking for the owner of that voice. Another tear trickled down her cheek. It couldn't have been her. "Grandma?"

"Yes, my baby," Grandma Isabella said. She walked toward her with arms wide open. Her smile and giggles were just as melodic as her voice. Her mocha-toned skin glimmered under the sun's rays. Grandma Isabella's silver hair sat in a long braid that rested between her shoulder blades.

Breanna let go of Aunt Aubrey's hands and ran toward Grandma Isabella. "Grandma," she sobbed, hugging her tight. "I've missed you so much."

"I've missed you and Amber so much, too," she said, rocking Breanna in her arms. "I had to see you before you left."

"I don't want to leave you and Aunt Aubrey."

"Breanna," Grandma Isabella said, kissing her forehead. "It isn't time for you yet."

"Please, Grandma! I want to stay with you."

"Baby," she said, lifting Breanna's chin with her index finger and staring into her eyes. "You're here because you needed guidance to find your way back."

"Please, Grandma! I don't want to go back."

"You don't think your daughter needs you?"

"She hates me."

"She's lying beside you as we speak," Grandma Isabella said. "And your husband is holding onto your hand. They need you. Cameron's gonna need you too, my baby."

Breanna frowned. "Who's Cameron?"

Grandma Isabella pointed to the second cygnet. "He's waiting to meet you."

"What? I don't understand, Grandma."

"Have faith, Breanna," Aunt Aubrey said. "And tell Amber that I love her so much."

"Please, don't make me go back there."

"Breanna, this is what you needed." Grandma Isabella let her go. "You'll stumble. You'll even fall hard. But this time, you'll know how to get back up and dust yourself off."

Breanna watched them fade from her sight and cried as she slumped to her knees. Why couldn't they take her with them? Didn't they know of the people she'd hurt? "I can't do this without you."

"Yes, you can, my baby."

"I can't, Grandma. I don't know where to begin anymore."

"You do, Breanna. You can't let fear hold you back."

"Grandma, please don't leave me again!" Breanna cried.

"Don't cry, my baby." Grandma Isabella's voice lingered in the distance. "You're never alone, Bree. Never."

"Have faith, Breanna," Aunt Aubrey said, smiling at her. She faded from Breanna's sight.

"I'll try Aunt Aubrey," Breanna said.

"You can, sweetie. You just need to trust yourself."

Breanna nodded as she wiped away another tear. She exhaled as she glanced at the family of swans swimming away from her and smiled.

354

Trust. That was something she had to learn to do if she wanted her family back. But it was a task she was willing to stumble at to have the ones she loved the most back in her life.

Chapter Fifty-Five

Elijah jolted from his sleep and sat up in his chair, wondering if Breanna's fingers truly intertwined with his. He stared at his still unconscious wife and sleeping child and exhaled. He heard Amber mumble in her sleep as she moved about on the overly floral cramped couch and sat back in his chair. The sounds of the heart rate monitor and Tianna and Prince Naveen singing with Mama Odie meshed melodically somehow. A tear rolled down his cheek as he sat back in his seat. Today marked the fourth day Breanna hadn't awakened from her coma.

He stared at her once more, then closed his eyes for a moment. Dr. Logan said there wasn't a guarantee she'd wake up soon, but he shouldn't give up on hope. Hope. Elijah scoffed, massaging his temples. Hope was elusive to him. It was the very thing that dangled before him he couldn't have. Even when Isabella requested he kiss Breanna on the forehead every night before going to sleep, Elijah couldn't force himself to see the rainbow through the clouds.

He wanted her to wake up to him again, and even that was looking farfetched to him now. Raking his hand through his hair, Elijah stood from the chair and stepped closer to Breanna's bedside. He caressed her cheek with his index finger.

"I need you to wake up, okay," he whispered. Another tear rolled down his cheek. "Our daughter needs you. Your sister needs you. Your parents need you, Bree." Elijah bit his bottom lip. Tears streamed down his cheeks as he closed his eyes once more. "I need you to wake up to me again. Please don't let go."

He kissed her forehead. "I love you, Breanna."

Elijah sobbed as he placed his forehead against hers. This was too much for him to bear. He couldn't just sit back and watch her lay lifeless in this bed forever. He couldn't.

He walked out the room, not wanting to wake his sister-in-law and daughter with his sobs. He ambled through the hallway and took a deep breath without constraint. For the past twelve hours, his asthma took a back seat. Even Isabella's asthma seemed under control now. Those were small miracles. But what he truly wanted wasn't happening. Maybe he'd gotten the wish he wanted for Breanna after all. Maybe he'd—he had to stop thinking like this. It wasn't going to get him anywhere.

As he stepped inside the lobby, he stared into the deep brown eyes of a handsome little black boy who held on tight to his mother's hand. She stood in front of the drink machine, mumbling over which soda to choose.

"You still haven't told Momma what you want to drink, Cam," she said, looking down at her son. "You gotta tell Momma so you can get what you like."

Elijah sat in a seat next to an uncovered window and stared out of it for a moment. From the corner of his eye, he noticed the little boy point in his direction.

"Momma," the little boy said, tugging on the tail end of her coral-colored blouse. "That man over there looks sad. Can we get him something to drink?"

Elijah smiled for a moment, then returned his attention to the reddish-golden ball rising from the corner of the semi-dark sky. He closed his eyes and ran his hands through his hair before resting his hand on the back of his neck. Elijah remembered the morning he and Breanna watched the sunrise just days before Isabella was born. Their daughter had kicked Breanna's insides so hard that she nearly knocked her out of bed twice. He smiled.

God, he didn't know what to think or what to feel at this moment. All he knew was that hope was fleeting away from him.

"Excuse me, mister," the little boy said, tapping his index finger against the rough material of Elijah's blue denim jeans. "My momma let me buy this root beer for you."

Elijah stared at the boy's smiling mother, then returned his attention to the small child standing in front of him. His big brown eyes glimmered like he had a new toy before him to play with. "Thank you," Elijah said, taking the soda from the child's hand. "It's been a long time since I've had root beer."

"I hope that cheers you up, mister."

"It sure does," Elijah said. "By the way, my name's Elijah. What's yours?"

"Tell him your name, Cam," his mother said.

The child twisted his shoe about on the white tile floor and giggled. "My name's Cameron, and I'm four years old," he answered, holding up four fingers. His smile made Elijah smile.

"Hi, Cameron," said Elijah. "You have the same name as my grandfather."

"Really?" His brown eyes sparkled. "My momma said that my daddy named me after him, but daddy's—" the little boy looked down at his shoes again and sniffled. "Daddy's sad because my big brother's been asleep for weeks now."

Jesus! It must have taken a lot of strength for the little guy to mention what happened to his big brother.

His mother walked toward them and grabbed her son's hand. "I'm sorry, Elijah," she said. Her voice was soft and melodic. "Cameron will strike up a conversation before you know it."

"My little girl is the same way."

She smiled as she nodded her head in agreement. "How old is she?"

"Isabella is five years old, and in two more months, she'll be the big six."

"They grow up so fast, don't they?" She kissed her son on the cheek.

"That they do, ma'am."

"Ayesha," she said.

"It's nice to meet you, Ms. Ayesha."

"If you don't mind me asking," she said, pulling Cameron closer to her side. "I saw you hug Nurse Ellis about two days ago before she went into the patient's room you came out of. How do you know her?"

"Her daughter—" he looked away from her and took a deep breath. "She's the mother of my daughter."

"Oh," she said. The woman looked away from him. "Has she gotten any better?"

Elijah shook his head, fighting back his tears as he sniffled. "Breanna's in a coma."

"So is my oldest son," she sighed. She swatted away a fleeting tear rolling down her cheek. "Broderick was on the phone with me when I heard a woman call after him. At first, he kept talking to me until she yelled to get his attention. That's when I heard two-gun shots."

"Oh my God! I'm so sorry that happened to your son."

"The bitch thought my son was her ex-boyfriend," Ayesha sobbed. "But when the police got there, they found her trying to—" She gasped for air through her tears. "They found her trying to sodomize my son."

358

Elijah closed his eyes as he shook his head. His attack sounded too much like Breanna's attack.

"What made matters worse was that she tried to deny she did anything to my baby."

"Are you serious?"

"She sure did." Ayesha nodded. "I'm just thankful to God that my husband is one hell of a lawyer because he made sure she wouldn't get out of jail until she turned sixty-five years old."

"That's good to hear," Elijah said. "I hope that the police can find my wife's attacker."

"Oh, my God. I'm so sorry to hear that," she said. "They'll find her attacker, Elijah."

"I hope they do."

"They will," Ayesha said. "And she'll awake from her coma soon. I'm a firm believer that God is intentional. I know I don't like the harshness of the path at all, but he never said that it would be easy. Just don't let go, Elijah."

"I won't, Ms. Ayesha—"

"Ayesha!" A tall black man ran inside the lobby with tears flowing down his cheeks and a smile on his face. His chestnut-toned skin and short waved hair resembled Cameron perfectly. "Broderick's awake, baby. He's awake."

Elijah watched her pick up her son and run toward the lobby door. "Remember what I said, Elijah."

He glanced at her and smiled before she disappeared from his sight. As much as he wanted to give in to the negativity, Elijah knew he couldn't let it slink its way into his head and his heart. All that was going to do was cause him more stress and asthma attacks. He wiped away a fleeting tear as he stood from his seat and walked out the lobby. The trek back down the hall seemed longer than when he first stepped out the room. Ms. Ayesha's son was in a coma for two weeks. There was no telling how long it would take for Breanna to wake from her coma. All he knew was that if it took two weeks or two months, he wouldn't leave her side.

Elijah entered the hospital room the same way he left it. Rays of sunlight shimmered over Breanna and Isabella as they slept. He smiled. *She'll wake to you again, Elijah.*

He stepped closer to her bedside and admired her beauty. The bruises around her neck and eye were healing well. He caressed his index finger along the line of her cheek and smiled.

"I love you, Breanna," he said, pressing his lips against her forehead once more. "I've never stopped loving you."

As he was about to take his seat, he heard a low groan. He stared at Breanna. She hadn't moved. Maybe it was Izzy trying to get comfortable. Or perhaps it was his mind toying with his emotions again. "I love you too, Elijah."

Chapter Fifty-Six

"I missed you so much, mommy." Isabella gazed into her mother's deep brown eyes. She rested her small hand on Mommy's cheek and smiled through her sobs. "I'm so sorry for what I said to you, Mommy. Can you forgive me?"

Breanna nodded. A single tear cascaded over the bridge of her nose and dripped onto her pillow. "I forgive you, Shortcake," she whispered. "I love you so much."

"Little sis." Auntie Amber stood by her bedside and kissed her forehead. A tear streamed down her cheek. "How are you feeling?"

"I'm in a bit of pain, but I feel okay, Amber."

Daddy rushed back inside the hospital room with Dr. Logan by his side. He ran a quick hand over his face and sniffled. Daddy had been crying again. It wasn't often she witnessed him cry. Honestly, she didn't know if Daddy knew how to cry. Sure, he knew how to laugh, frown, and stare at people until they sat in their seats quietly. But she had never seen tears. This was new for him.

He rushed toward Mommy's bedside and caressed her face with the back of his hand. She hadn't seen this in a long time, either. For what seemed like forever without Mommy, she hadn't seen Daddy this happy. Even when he dated Ms. Morgan, he wasn't happy like the way he was now.

"Ms. Ellis, my name is Dr. Beverly Logan. How are you feeling this morning?" Dr. Logan shined a small light in both of Mommy's eyes.

"My inner thigh feels sore, and my left side hurts pretty bad."

"Do you feel dizzy or have a headache?"

Mommy shook her head. "No. This pain I'm feeling is making me feel uncomfortable. What happened to me?"

Isabella watched Dr. Logan nod her head and then focus on Auntie Amber and Daddy.

"Ms. Ellis," Dr. Logan said. "Can you answer a few questions for me?"

"Sure."

"What's your middle name?"

"Leigh."

"And can you tell me your daughter's full name?"

Mommy frowned as she nodded. "Her full name is Isabella Sahara Bryson."

"How about Mr. Bryson's first and middle names?"

"It's Elijah Christian. Doctor," Mommy scoffed, clearly frustrated. "Why are you asking me all these questions?"

"Ms. Ellis, you're experiencing a traumatic response to a very horrible incident."

"What incident? What are you talking about?"

"Breanna," Auntie Amber said, placing her hand on Mommy's shoulder to keep her calm. "Do you remember what happened Friday after the banquet?"

Isabella watched Mommy glare at Auntie Amber and shake her head. The frown on Mommy's face and the tears in her eyes said otherwise. She had no clue what happened to her.

"Breanna," Dr. Logan said. She pulled up the same stool she sat on when she first spoke to her. But this time, she sat at the foot of Mommy's bed. "Can you tell me where you were working last Friday?"

"I had to work an event," Mommy replied. "But I can't remember where the event was."

"Bree," Daddy said, standing closer to her. "Do you recall us separating?"

She nodded. "I do, but I'm curious why you and Isabella are here with me."

"I think it would be a good idea for either you or Mr. Bryson to take Ms. Isabella out the room for a while," Dr. Logan said, gazing at both Auntie Amber and Daddy.

"I can take her," Auntie Amber said, walking in Isabella's direction.

"Okay, Shortcake," Daddy said, planting a kiss on her forehead. "Go with Auntie Amber and behave yourself, okay."

She stared into Daddy's doppelganger eyes and nodded. "Okay, Daddy."

Isabella kissed Mommy on the cheek one last time and smiled. "I love you, Mommy."

"I love you too, Shortcake."

Isabella crawled off the bed gingerly so she wouldn't hurt Mommy. She hoped Mommy would be okay after this. She hoped that Dr. Logan kept her promise and made Mommy whole again.

Breanna stared at Dr. Logan and Elijah and frowned. Their silence and constant staring at her made the hairs on her arms stand. She couldn't understand why they stared at her like that, but the uneasiness that crept into the pit of her stomach sent waves of unpleasant chills crawling over her skin now. "Can someone tell me what happened?"

"Breanna." Elijah swallowed hard. "Do you remember where you work?"

"Yeah. At Soul Bistro."

"That's a good start," Dr. Logan spoke. "Now, let's try thinking back to the events that led to Friday night."

The sudden tapping at the hospital door jolted Breanna from her train of thought. "Dr. Logan," Mom said, peeping her head inside the room. "I hope it's okay for me to come be with my baby."

"Of course." Dr. Logan nodded. "Your presence may help trigger a memory for Breanna."

As Breanna saw Mom walk into the room, she smiled. She needed another calm face surrounding her. With all the hesitant hush-hush going on around her, Breanna knew she needed someone with some common sense to talk to her.

"Bree," Mom stepped toward Breanna's bedside. "Your sister told me you don't remember what happened to you on Friday night."

"I don't, Mom."

Breanna stared at the green scrubs and white clogs Mom wore. They were familiar. They were protection. They saved her.

"Was I here before, Mom?"

Mom nodded. "You were sweetheart."

Breanna frowned. "Why is Friday night so important?"

"Bree," Elijah said. He took her good hand into his and held it tight. "You worked at a banquet for my and AJ's company."

"Was it a catering event?"

"It was, Bree."

She stared at Elijah, recalling his once smiling face covered by a scowl. It was a scowl she would never forget. It was a scowl that tore them apart.

"You were angry with me for being there."

Elijah sighed. "I was, Breanna."

"Why? What had I done to make you so angry with me?"

Tears welled in his eyes before he darted them in another direction. Breanna watched Elijah take a deep breath and frowned. She scarred him gravely, and that wound was still oozing. "Elijah, what did I do to you?"

"Breanna... I—"

"Ms. Ellis," Dr. Logan said, cutting Elijah off. "I know you want to know what happened, but right now, I need you to think about last Friday's events."

Breanna shook her head. "I can't. I don't remember what happened to me after the banquet. I don't remember why Elijah and I broke up. Why do you keep asking me questions?"

The heart rate monitor dinged as her heart rate increased. She breathed deeply. Why were they making her jump through so many hoops?

"I understand why you need to ask Breanna so many questions, Dr. Logan, but aren't we risking overstressing her?" Mom stared at Elijah and Dr. Logan before reconnecting her attention with hers.

"We are, Mrs. Ellis." Dr. Logan nodded. "But I need to make sure your daughter's amnesia is temporary."

"What about the police? Won't they ask her a lot of questions too?" Elijah squeezed her hand tighter as he kept his eyes on Dr. Logan.

"They probably will ask several questions, but before I let them come in and barrage my patient, I need to make sure she can handle it."

Handle questions from the police? Why were they going to question her? What the hell happened to her after the banquet for the police to be involved.

Their voices jumbled over each other as they rummaged through Breanna's ears like an out-of-tune horn. There were so many questions. So many voices going on all at once. Why didn't they just stop and let her breathe for a moment? Why couldn't they let her breathe—those footsteps. Was someone walking behind her?

Breanna closed her eyes. The clumping of those very footsteps against the hall's floor reminded her of someone walking on the pavement. They reminded her of someone lurking behind her. Each step grew louder as they neared the half closed door. Had someone tried to snatch her purse from her? Had someone tried to attack her?

364

"I'm going to pick up dinner on the way home. Is there something you want specifically?" a male voice said from a distance. It was husky yet deep in its sincerity. "Fried chicken it is, then, Beautiful. I'll see you soon."

Breanna opened her eyes wide. She heard that word before—it stalked her like she was its prey. It laid waiting for her to submit to it.

"Nathaniel," Breanna whispered. A tear streamed down her cheek. The heart rate monitor dinged once more as her heartbeat neared 110 beats per minute.

"Breanna." Elijah stared into her wide eyes as he watched another tear slip down her cheek. "What's wrong?"

She stared into Elijah's eyes, remembering how his steel-blue eyes darkened as his once calm demeanor turned into a scowl. She knew why they broke up now. This was all her fault.

"Ms. Ellis." Dr. Logan stared at her. "Are you okay?"

Breanna shook her head, trembling. "Is he here?"

"Is who here, Ms. Ellis?"

"Nathaniel. Is he here?"

Elijah grazed his hand over his beard as he took a deep breath. "He's not here, Breanna. You're safe."

"Mr. Bryson is right, Ms. Ellis," Dr. Logan said soothingly. "You're safe."

Breanna whispered, "I caused all of this."

"Breanna," Mom said, sitting on the bed next to her. She moved a strand of her hair behind her ear and mustered a smile as she tried to keep her tears at bay. "You didn't cause this."

"I did, Mom," Breanna said, breathing harder. "I ruined so many lives; so many people hate me, and I deserve it." Tears flooded her eyes before they ran down her cheeks.

"Ms. Ellis, it's okay." Dr. Logan said calmly. "I'm going to need you to relax."

The heart rate monitor dinged repeatedly, alerting them all that her heart rate reached 130 beats per minute.

Elijah glanced at the machine and cursed under his breath. "Bree, please calm down. You're safe, okay."

"I caused this, Eli. I deserved what happened to me."

"Bree, please don't say that—"

"I may need to give her a sedative if she doesn't calm down on her own."

"Wait!" Amber stood in the doorway as she held Isabella's hand. "I know who can calm her down."

"Who?" Mom turned to look at Amber and Isabella.

As Amber and Isabella stepped out the way, Dr. Shelby entered the room. She peeped at Breanna, then stared at everyone else in the small hospital room.

"After speaking with Amber yesterday, I promised her I would try to get out here and see Ms. Ellis. I hadn't spoken to her since our last counseling session two weeks ago."

Elijah stared at her and frowned. "She's been having sessions with you, Dr. Shelby?"

"She has. But as you know, Mr. Bryson, that's all the information I can share with you."

"I understand," he replied.

"Dr. Logan." Dr. Shelby extended her hand to shake hers. "Is it okay if I can speak with Ms. Ellis for a few moments? Maybe I can lend a helping hand."

"If that means I won't have to use a sedative on her, then please go right ahead," Dr. Logan said, shaking her hand.

Dr. Shelby sat next to Breanna and smiled at her, placing her hand on top of Breanna's good hand and squeezing it reassuringly.

"Okay, everyone," said Dr. Logan. "Let's allow Dr. Hampton to speak with Ms. Ellis for a moment."

Breanna stared into Dr. Shelby's eyes and breathed deeply. The door closed softly behind the last person walking out the room. She closed her eyes and sobbed. "I caused all of this, Dr. Shelby, yet Elijah's here with me. My daughter is here with me. I don't deserve their love."

"Breanna, remember when you told me that all you wanted was to have them back around you."

She nodded. "I do."

"They are back with you now."

"But I'm the one that caused all this mess happening to them. To me."

"Breanna," Dr. Shelby stated firmly. "You did create this mess you're in now, but by no means did you deserve this kind of treatment. That man had no right to put his hands on you."

"But Dr. Shelby—"

"Did you tell him to hit you? Did you tell him to touch you when you didn't want to be touched?"

Breanna shook her head. Tears continue to flow down her cheeks. The heart rate monitor stopped dinging loudly as her heart rate decreased slowly. "I didn't think Nathaniel would do something like this to me."

"I know, Breanna. Mr. Morrison sexually assaulted you. Are you going to live your life as a victim now, or will you get up from this?"

"How do I get up from this?"

"Breanna, you've told me yourself that you were willing to be friends with Mr. Bryson as long as you had the opportunity to be a part of their lives again and improve on yourself. Isn't that what you still want?"

Breanna nodded. "It is, but—"

"But nothing, Breanna. You've come too far to allow yourself to start back from square one."

Dr. Shelby glanced at the monitor and smiled, noticing that Breanna's heart rate was back to normal.

"Dr. Shelby, I've caused so much heartache and pain. I wouldn't blame them if they didn't want to talk to me again."

"Breanna," Dr. Shelby smiled. "You've overcome the stigma your mother hindered you with. You've admitted you were wrong for cheating on Mr. Bryson, and you've even admitted you needed to be a better mother to your daughter."

Breanna wiped away her tears with her good hand. "They even told me I needed to get up and dust myself off."

"Who told you that, Breanna?"

"My Aunt Aubrey and Grandma Isabella."

Dr. Shelby smiled as she nodded. "I see. And did they tell you, you shouldn't give up?"

Breanna nodded. "They did."

"Then it's time for you to get up from this fall, Breanna. Dust yourself off and fight for yourself and your family. They're waiting for you."

Chapter Fifty-Seven

Four days of lying in a hospital bed were not just cruel and unusual punishment; it was freaking insanity. Breanna winced as she sat up in bed and moved her legs around. Her joints argued with her as she reached for the remote to replay Lilo and Stitch. Isabella moved against her side and snuggled her. She looked down at her sleeping daughter and smiled. The sight of her brought back so many memories of when she was a toddler.

As she touched the remote with her fingertips and dragged it closer to her, Breanna moved her broken forearm and closed her eyes tight as she whimpered. This and childbirth were nearly tick for tack.

Sure, not having the use of her left arm wasn't that big of an issue. It was the crawling itch that rummaged up and down her forearm like a gremlin tearing out the parts of a plane during flight. Even worse, the pain would sneak up on her as if it were a thief and knock her on her ass for about thirty minutes.

This wouldn't have happened if you hadn't cheated, Breanna.

Breanna closed her eyes once more, holding back her tears. As much as she wanted to curl into a ball and waddle in her own tears, she refused to give Nathaniel that win. And with the amount of evidence Dr. Logan collected and Detectives Bradford and Monroe secured, Nathaniel had no choice but to turn himself in.

It wouldn't be that simple, though. With no knowledge of his whereabouts and Tessa's sudden disappearance, it seemed as if the bastard got away with sexually assaulting her. Her skin crawled and her stomach turned at the thought.

"Breanna," Elijah said, entering the room and closing the door behind him. "What are you doing up?"

"I couldn't sleep."

"Are you in pain again?"

She nodded. "My forearm and left side are having a wrestling match."

Elijah chuckled. "That sounds pretty bad, Bree."

She watched him sit back in the chair next to her good hand and lean back, resting his head against the back of the seat. He closed his eyes for a moment before glaring into her eyes. "Eli, I really appreciate you staying with me, but you should probably take Isabella and go home so the both of you can rest."

"I'm not going anywhere, Breanna, not until you've been released from this joint."

She smiled as she shook her at his response. God, he could be so corny. "Elijah, I—"

"I love you, Breanna," he said, cutting her off. "I know we hit a tough spot in our relationship, but I want to make things work between us."

"Elijah," Breanna sighed. "I love you too, but—" She paused, grazing her teeth against her bottom lip. "I don't want to put you and Izzy back in the place where I left you two."

"Breanna, you've proven to me you've been fighting to change. You've been seeing Dr. Shelby, you sold back your car to buy Izzy's medicine, and you even reconnected with your family. Do you not trust yourself, Bree?"

She looked away from him. That question rested on her chest like a weighted blanket. Elijah was right. She'd taken the time to change for the better, but the fear of screwing her family over again lingered in her mind. That wasn't something she could just ignore.

"I have changed, Elijah. And I want to keep changing if that means I have the people I love dearly surrounding me. I just—" she hesitated once more. "I can't take that chance of hurting the both of you again."

"Breanna, trust is something we both need."

"I know, Eli. But before you can trust me again, would you be willing to forgive me for all the shit I put you through?" She swatted a tear away from her eye with her good hand.

He smiled. His eyes grew watery as he stared into her eyes. "I forgive you, Breanna. Can you forgive me too?"

She nodded, wiping away another tear. "Yes."

Elijah took her good hand into his and pressed his lips against the back of it. Breanna watched his face beam from his beautiful smile. His

369

steel-blue eyes seem to have gleamed. As much as she wanted to jump back into his arms and be his girlfriend, or wife, someday, Breanna didn't want to make the same mistake twice, not with the man God blessed her with.

"Then promise me one thing, Elijah."

"What's that, Bree?"

"That we'll be friends before anything else."

He frowned. "Breanna, we've always been friends."

"Elijah, I'm talking about us not seeing each other anymore. I know that you and Morgan still have unfinished business, and I won't come in between your happiness."

"Bree—"

"I'm serious, Elijah."

She watched as his body stiffened. A tear slipped down his cheek as he looked away from her.

"All I want is to see our daughter again and talk to the man I still love dearly."

"Breanna, Morgan and I haven't talked since you've been in the hospital."

"That doesn't mean she won't apologize for her actions, Eli."

"Did your father say something to you about us keeping our relationship platonic?"

"He did," she replied. "And I agree with him."

Elijah shook his head as he frowned. He placed the back of his hand against her forehead, then put his other hand on his forehead. "You feel normal."

Breanna chuckled. "I'm fine, Elijah. I know I don't want to hurt either of you again."

He nodded. He cupped her chin as he caressed the smoothness of her cheek with his thumb. "Breanna, that doesn't mean I'll stop loving you."

"I won't stop loving you either, Elijah, but I want to give you and Isabella the best I have to offer."

"Then, can you promise me something?"

"What's that, Elijah?"

"Mr. Marvin told me about the fight you and your mother got into before all this happened. You need to talk to her."

Breanna scoffed. "That woman hurt me in more ways than I can count on all my fingers and toes, Eli. Talking to her is out of the question."

"Breanna," he said, staring into her eyes. "Ms. Gwendolyn did a lot of horrible things to you and Amber. But Amber still tries to have a relationship with her."

"Amber's a much better person than I would ever be."

"You're a good person too, Breanna. But I know you are bigger than your mother's idiocies."

A single tear streamed down her cheek. "I thought she loved me, Eli."

"She loves you, Breanna. She just had some hateful tendencies that she so graciously passed down to you."

"Then why can't I forgive her?"

"Would you want Isabella to hate you for the rest of her life if you treated her like your mother treated you?"

Breanna stared at him, squinting her eyes. Now, he wanted to make sense of her mother. Of all people who deliberately tried to persuade her to stay with a man who beat the shit out of her and attempted to have his way with her, Breanna wasn't going for that. She couldn't. But damnit if Elijah wasn't right.

She had to be the bigger person and try to mend the broken relationship with Momma before it festered into something more.

Breanna shook her head as she smiled at him. "Handsome, smart, and genuine. I'm so blessed to have you as a friend."

"I'm blessed to have you as a friend too, Bree."

"Knock, knock," Dr. Logan's voice sang as she opened the door. She walked inside the room and smiled, looking at the three of them. "How are you feeling this morning, Ms. Ellis?"

"Despite my forearm and left side waging war between each other, I feel okay."

"Okay. I'll get the nurse to give you some medicine before you leave us today."

Breanna stared at Dr. Logan and smiled. "Are you telling me I'm busting out this joint?"

Who's the corny one now, Breanna?

"Yes, Ms. Ellis," Dr. Logan chuckled. "That means you'll be getting out of here soon. And oh! I want you to discontinue taking your birth control until you're done with this medication. I don't want to overload you with too much medicine."

"Yes, ma'am," Breanna nodded. Her smile couldn't be erased from her face.

She stared at Elijah. "Thanks for being here with me, Eli. I appreciate it."

"You're welcome, Bree," he said, gazing into her eyes.

371

"You should probably get some sleep, Bree. Shortcake will understand why you didn't finish the movie with her." Elijah walked toward the construction site, watching AJ and the others place the finishing touches on the roof of the latest house they built.

Breanna yawned. "I don't want to disappoint her, Eli. She's been waiting to watch this movie with me."

"She'll understand. Izzy's just happy to be with you, regardless."

"I know she is, but—" Breanna yawned again. "I promised her I would watch this movie with her, and Amber hasn't come back with the pizza yet."

"Amber's a talker. You know that."

Breanna chuckled. "Isn't she, though?" She chuckled once more as her laughter trailed into another yawn. "Still, she promised Isabella pizza, and I had to eat something with this medicine before taking it."

"Is Leilani with her?"

"Mmm-hmm. She is. Why?"

"I recall Amber saying she was thinking about proposing to her soon. Maybe this is the moment." Elijah smiled. He locked eyes with Morgan for a second, then noticed her wipe a tear from her eye and step away from him. He sighed. This was going to be interesting.

"You think so."

"How long have they been together now?"

"About four or five years, I think." She yawned once more.

"Then she could be getting down on one knee as we speak," Elijah said. He noticed Morgan stand by her car. Her back was turned to him. She embraced her own shoulders as if she were standing in thirty-five-degree weather. Breanna's subtle breathing over the phone made him smile. He needed every bit of the joy Breanna gave him before engaging in this war he was about to get himself into. "Just let Amber do her thing, Bree. Isabella's in heaven right now. She's got you, Granddaddy Marvin, and Grandma Gina under the same roof right now."

"I guess you're right, Eli."

"She'll be fine, Bree. Just get some sleep. I'll swing by later tonight and pick her up."

"Okay. I'll see you then. That's if I'm not still asleep."

"Alright, Bree. I'll see you later."

"Night, night, Eli."

Elijah smiled as he ended the call. The last time she said that to him, Breanna fixed him some chicken noodle soup and gave him a Hot Toddy to help combat the sinuses invading his nose just days before his big game against Hedgewell University in Alabama. Thanks to her, he struck out every batter that stepped on his turf. That was the

372

Breanna he loved more than anything, and she was finding her way back to him.

He took a deep breath, held it for a moment, then released it without the struggle to regain his breath. It had been that way since Breanna got out of the hospital three weeks ago. But as he neared Morgan, the urge to cough tickled the back of his throat. He never understood why the women in his life triggered his asthma. Perhaps God was yelling in his ear again.

"Morgan," Elijah said, standing behind her. "AJ and I—"

"Signed the deal with Mr. Johnson yesterday." She turned in his direction. Tear stains graced the softness of her cinnamon-brown cheeks. "I overheard AJ talking to one of my former employees yesterday."

"Morgan—"

"You don't need to say anything else." She waved him away as she turned her back toward him again. "I got enough of that yesterday."

"You know you brought this on yourself, Morgan."

"That's very sweet of you to say, Sunshine."

"Morgan, I'm not attacking you, but when you played with other people's livelihoods and safety, I wasn't just going to sit back and watch you run amuck."

"My employees were well taken care of. You just so happened to snatch them from underneath me."

"If they were well taken care of, Morgan, why were they complaining about being underpaid and overworked whenever they did jobs for you?" Elijah glanced at AJ and Mr. Glenn as they looked in his direction. The cocked eyebrows and subtle nodding of their heads told him everything they were thinking.

"First, you kick me off the team, then you take my employees." Morgan smirked as she nodded. "Sounds like a true Bryson to me."

"What's that supposed to mean?"

"You sound like your racist ass mother."

Elijah nodded, pressing his lips into a thin line as he looked away from her. Elijah needed to restrain himself before he found himself in jail for throwing Morgan off the rooftop of one of the homes they built. "For the last time, Morgan, my mother isn't racist. She just has my best interest at heart."

"Oh, my fucking God!" Morgan opened her car door and slumped into her car seat. She wiped her eyes with both hands and breathed deeply. "You've got what you wanted from me, Elijah. Just leave me alone."

373

"Morgan." He stood in front of the opened car door, keeping her from closing it. "I didn't come over here to gloat or rub crap in your face."

"Then why did you come over here?"

"Because I wanted you to know that you taught me something very valuable."

"And what's that, Elijah?"

"That not everyone is willing to change."

"What's that supposed to mean?"

"You never tried to change."

Morgan shook her head as she laughed. "I changed way more than you think, Elijah."

"Are you sure about that, Morgan?"

"Oh, I'm certain of it."

Elijah stared into her watery brown eyes. The woman could always talk a good game when her back was pressed against the wall, but admitting her worst qualities and defeat wasn't something she could do easily. Hell. Morgan would go down in flames first before she'd ever admitted that she was wrong. "You had a hell of a way of showing me, then."

Morgan rose from her car seat and stood in front of Elijah, looking up at him. She pressed her index finger into his chest. "You're doing this because of Breanna, aren't you?"

"She's part of the reason."

"Then, what else is it, sunshine. I ain't got all day to stand here and be belittled by you and your—" She motioned her fingers in quotation marks. "Brother from another mother."

"At least AJ didn't lie to me about requesting people to work an event to humiliate them."

"What the—" Morgan paused as she closed her eyes slowly, releasing a stressed breath. She looked away from him and cursed under her breath sharply. "Elijah, I didn't think you'd cared about—"

"She was sexually assaulted after the banquet, Morgan. Did you know that?"

"Elijah, I honestly thought you wouldn't care about her."

"Regardless of how I felt, that woman is still the mother of my child, and if she hadn't awakened from her coma, Isabella would have hated me for keeping her from her mother."

"She fucked someone else, Elijah. That was all the justification you needed to be with—"

"With you again. Right, Morgan?"

A tear slid down her cheek. "These feelings didn't happen overnight, sunshine."

"Well," he said, rubbing his beard. "After having a come to Jesus meeting with Howard, he told me everything that I needed to know."

"What?" Her eyes were wide. "What did he tell you?"

"That you came back to Kentfield looking to make a profit from someone else's hard work," he said. "But you were looking to rekindle something you lost years ago, too. You had to worm your way back in. And like the fool I was, I invited you right back in."

"Elijah, I'm—"

"Sorry? You honestly thought I was stupid enough to let you take a company that my best and I built from the ground up and give it over to you because you flashed your ass and titties in my face." He chuckled. "When I finally learned that even you and Tessa talked, I had to remind myself about the kind of woman you truly were."

"I only spoke to her one time, Elijah."

"I know," he replied. "And that was to find out who she'd supposedly slept with to get to me. But it wasn't until you and Tessa got into an argument during the banquet that you called Nathaniel."

"Elijah, I didn't think he was going to do anything to her. I swear."

"I know you didn't. That was Tessa's last call."

Morgan rested her hand on her chest and stared at him with wide eyes. "Oh my God—I didn't think she'd—what happened to Tessa?"

"The police arrested her this morning," Elijah said. He noticed her eyebrows wrinkle as she rubbed the back of her neck.

"Elijah," she said. She turned her back toward him, letting her risen shoulders slump. "I'm sorry."

"I know you are."

She turned toward him with a frown. "How do you know that?"

He chuckled. Breanna was right. "Someone told me you would be."

"Let me guess." Morgan folded her arms across her chest. "Breanna said that, right?"

He nodded. A half-smile tugged at his lips.

"Elijah, I wanted to be with you again. You were the best person for me, and I didn't realize that until I made a stupid mistake. I won't ever do it again. I promise, Elijah. I won't."

Elijah chuckled once more. The truth in her voice was about as rotten as the old jar of shea butter Breanna used to keep in the pantry for her hair. She pulled this same stunt back in college when she slept with Brian, and he knew she would do it again if he gave her another chance. "You know, Morgan, as much as that sounds like sincerity, I don't believe you."

Morgan wiped her eyes. "Elijah, I'm serious."

"Then, if you're serious, Morgan, prove it."

"I am proving my sincerity to you right now, Elijah. You can't see that?"

He nodded. Mom's suggestion for him to pray more led him to read the Bible more, and out of every book he read within it, King Solomon's decision to split a baby in half made it clear when someone truly loved a person, they would give them up, no matter the situation. Breanna made that clear to him. "Morgan, I need more than that."

"Oh, my goodness!" Morgan laughed as she wiped away another tear. "I can't compete with this bitch anymore. If you want to go back to that skank ass hoe, then go back to her, Elijah," she hissed.

"That's all I needed to know, Morgan," Elijah said. "I'll see ya around."

He walked away from her, leaving her standing by her opened car door. Morgan's grunts made him smile as he listened to her curse from a distance and slammed her door shut. King Solomon wasn't a king for nothing.

"Hey, E," AJ said, walking toward him. "Is she okay?"

"Not really." Elijah shook his head. His smile never left his face. "But she'll be back to her old self in no time."

The screech of tires against rock and dirt caught Elijah and AJ's attention. They watched her car speed off the construction site and down the street.

"I'm grateful to have friends like you and Leslie. You two saved my ass," Elijah said. He watched the Mercedes Benz come to an abrupt stop before making a wild right turn into traffic. Yep. Morgan was herself again.

AJ laughed. "As Leslie would say it, anytime, sir. Anytime."

Elijah held his stomach as he laughed. He could picture Leslie's raised eyebrows and pursed lips as she would look from left to right before answering. Had he kept this relationship up with Morgan, he would have been right back at the starting line trying to figure out which most expensive restaurant she wanted to dine at and watch her eat her meal while he starved.

It wouldn't be an easy road, but he knew he wanted Breanna back. Elijah knew he wanted her to be his wife. All he needed now was patience, and he needed plenty of it if he was going to fight for the only woman he ever loved.

Chapter Fifty-Eight

"**A**m I making a mistake coming here, sis?" Breanna stared at Amber with wide eyes before turning her attention to a nearly filled parking lot outside Culler and Straus Culinary College. Her heart thumped against her chest as if someone drummed the hell out of bongos in their drunken stupor. She inhaled and held it for a moment before releasing it slowly. The last thing she wanted to do was step foot onto the pavement. "I probably should go back home."

Amber looked at her and smiled. "Breanna, you're going to be okay. You're going to knock this demonstration out of the water, honey."

"You think so?"

Amber nodded. "Yeah. Mr. Devereaux would have never invited you to come here if he didn't see something in your skills."

She took another deep breath. The bed was a much better place to be right now. It didn't judge her. It didn't make her feel scared. It didn't—she had to do this. Not just for herself but for Isabella and Elijah. Breanna had to get away from Soul Bistro before she took a butter knife to Howard's throat and made him bleed sprinkles and glitter. "Okay, sis. I think I've got this."

"No, Bree. You got this, girl," Amber said. "There's no think. You're either for certain or not, and I know you're ready for this."

Breanna stared at Amber and smiled, then looked away from her. "You know," she said, taking another deep breath. "When I was in that coma, I saw Aunt Aubrey for the first time. We even talked, and she sounded just like you."

"Really?"

Breanna nodded. "She did. And she told me to tell you she loved you so much."

Amber sniffled, then wiped away a tear welling in her eye. "Breanna, if you're trying to make me cry, then you're doing an awesome job at it, little sis."

"She did, Amber," Breanna said, sniffling. "I was just so happy to see your face when I woke up that I forgot to tell you."

Amber pulled Breanna into her embrace and held her tight. Her sister's soft palm rubbed her back in a circling motion as she held onto her. "You've got this, Breanna," Amber said, letting her go. "With the skills you got in the kitchen, you're freakin' unstoppable."

"I hope you're right, Amber."

Amber flashed a wide smile. "Girl, had it not been for you making that strawberry crème brûlée for me and Leilani, the love of my life wouldn't be with me right now."

Breanna chuckled. "Well, at least I did one thing right."

"And you're going to knock the socks off these people. You just gotta go in there with your head held high, use your one good arm, and bake like you've never baked before."

Opening the car door, Breanna placed one foot on the pavement and took another deep breath. She had to take this trek from Amber's car to the building. The last thing she wanted to do was leave the safety and security of the deep cabin, but Breanna knew she couldn't stay there forever. If she didn't move, she wouldn't move at all.

"Little sis?"

"Yeah."

"Don't be afraid, okay."

Breanna's shoulders slumped. "Thanks, Amber."

As she placed her other foot on the ground, she stared at the calligraphy like sign headlining the building and started her walk. Beat by beat, her heart thumped against her chest. Every little chirping bird and muffled noise lingering in the background made her walk faster toward the college. She already allowed Nathaniel to stalk and attack her; she couldn't let the man run wild in her mind too.

She adjusted her black and white pinstripe pencil skirt and wiped away the lent from the black ruffled blouse she wore as she stood in front of the massive red double doors and grabbed the handle. She closed her eyes and inhaled deeply before letting it go slowly.

Just go in there and show these folks how to make a whisk dance, Bree.

A much needed rush of cool air blow through her tresses as she opened the door and walked inside. Vibrant yellow, blue, and green abstract works of art hung on pristine white walls. They caught her eye

378

as she neared the glass receptionist's desk. A young man and older woman sat beside each other, pecking away at their keyboards.

"How can I help you today?" The young man stared at Breanna with his bright green eyes and subtle smile. His hair resembled Elijah's, except it was blonde.

"I'm here to meet with Mr. Marcus Devereaux."

"Oh!" The woman stared at her with big brown eyes and a wide smile. Her black and silver curls sat about her head like a crown. Her chocolate skin glimmered against the young man's tanned skin. She leaned toward him; her fingers never left the keyboard. "Mr. Devereaux said that you were coming today."

Breanna smiled. "Great. Is there anything I need to fill out?"

"No, ma'am," the young man said. "Marilyn and I can escort you to the kitchen."

"Thank you." Breanna watched the two of them stand from their chairs behind the receptionist's desk and walk toward her. Either the two of them were joined at the hip or nosier than Mrs. McGhee, who swore she'd never gawked at Elijah and Isabella whenever they played outside together with Daisy but complained they were keeping up too much commotion whenever they made Daisy bark. There was no wonder why her children left her by herself most times.

"Mr. Devereaux said you were supposed to be putting on a demonstration, but that doesn't seem like you're going to be able to do that with one arm," Marilyn said.

"Oh," Breanna said, glancing down at her broken arm resting in its comfortable black sling, then catching Marilyn's attention again. "I had an accident three weeks ago, but that won't stop me from showing my skills."

"I hope it doesn't cause Mr. Devereaux said you can throw down Ms. Ellis," the young man said.

"Is thinking with your stomach in mind the only thing you can do, Benji?" Marilyn looked at him, shaking her head. "Please forgive my co-worker, Ms. Ellis. All he does is eat and doesn't gain a pound."

"You gotta get with the program, Marilyn. I've been telling you to stop counting all those calories and start watching your portions."

"So says the man who can wolf down two-foot-long Subways sandwiches in one sitting."

"That's if I skipped breakfast that day, Marilyn."

"Whatever, Benji," Marilyn said. She held her hand close to his face as they continued to walk in front of her. "He just wants whatever you're about to bake."

Breanna smiled. "I'll do my best to make the best pastry you've ever had, Benji."

"And then she can back it up too. God, I hope you make enough for everybody."

Walking through a set of double doors behind Marilyn and Benji, Breanna looked around the massive stainless-steel kitchen. White subway tiles sat underneath a stainless-steel range hood surrounded by rustic dark teal cabinets. A vast, dark teal and white island sat in the middle of the floor. Several round tables were scattered about the large room accompanied by four antique-styled chairs at each of them.

"Is this a classroom?"

"Nope. It's our showroom." Benji walked toward a pantry-like style door and knocked on it. Its frosted glass brought back memories of Grandma Isabella's old kitchen. Daddy had her nickname, Big Mama, engraved on the glass.

"A showroom?"

"Yeah. We often have guests that donate to the school during our dinner parties or whenever a well-known chef rolls through and wants to film an episode for their show."

Breanna stared at Benji with wide eyes. "Wow! I never knew this school was so prestigious."

"Girl, yes," Marilyn said. "And you know Mr. Devereaux's father was none other than the world-renowned pastry chef Lucas Devereaux."

"Oh, my goodness." Breanna smiled as she walked about the showroom. "I didn't know he was Mr. Devereaux's father."

"The one and only, Ms. Breanna Ellis," Mr. Devereaux said, walking out of the office door with his arms opened wide. "I'm so glad to see you're doing better."

"Thanks, Mr. Devereaux," Breanna said. "I appreciate you being patient with me."

"For your skills and talents, I would've waited for two months."

"Again, thank you, Mr. Devereaux."

"Well, let's get the students and the deans on staff today in here, and let's get to baking, shall we?" Mr. Devereaux walked into the kitchen and flipped on the range hood.

"On it, Mr. Devereaux," Benji said, making his way toward Mr. Devereaux's office.

Breanna's heart nearly came out of her throat from how fast and hard it was beating against her chest. This was the moment that would make or break her, and she couldn't let her nerves win over her today.

"Mr. Devereaux, could I use two of your students to help me make this pastry today?"

"I was hoping you would ask," he replied. "This will allow me to see how you interact with them."

She smiled. "Thank you."

"By the way, what are you going to make today so we can get the ingredients together before we start?"

Breanna's smile widened. "I'm going to dedicate this pastry to my daughter and make her favorite. Strawberry-filled beignets with a vanilla bean dipping sauce."

"There is a God," Benji sang as he made his way toward Mr. Devereaux.

Marilyn looked at Breanna and laughed. "Didn't I tell you this man always thought about his stomach first?"

"That sounds scrumptious, Ms. Ellis." Mr. Devereaux sat at the table closest to the island and rested his chin on the palm of his hand as he smiled. "This is going to be quite the demonstration."

The sounds of laughter and footsteps entered the showroom from the opposite side. She smiled, hoping she wouldn't mess up this opportunity because her fingers turned buttery.

"Good afternoon, you all," Mr. Devereaux said, rising from his seat. "This is Ms. Breanna Ellis. She's the one I've been telling you all about."

"It's so nice to meet you," an older woman said, walking toward her. Her grayish blonde hair peeped from under her chef's hat. "My name's Jennifer Fairly."

"It's nice to meet you, Ms. Fairly," Breanna said, shaking her hand with her good one.

"Please, call me Jennifer. I get enough of the ma'ams and misses all day."

"And I'm Jean Luc Benoit," a younger man said as he made his way toward them both. His black hair resembled Elijah's in so many ways. But it didn't have that famous side-swept s curl that he loved to style in one place.

Memories of Elijah rushed into Breanna's mind as she shook Mr. Benoit's soft hand. Just the feel of his palm made her want to be back in Elijah's embrace. No. She needed to be back in his embrace. But that wasn't a risk she would take anymore. She refused to break his heart again because she could no longer trust her own heart.

She chuckled to herself. She hated when Elijah was right about this kind of stuff.

"It's nice to meet you too, Mr. Benoit."

"I'm hoping Mr. Devereaux hires you on, so I won't be the youngest person on staff any longer."

"How old are you, if you don't mind me asking, Mr. Benoit?" Breanna smiled as she studied the barely visible stubble on the end of his ivory chin.

"Just turned twenty-six about three weeks ago."

381

Breanna chuckled. "Well, whether or not Mr. Devereaux hires me, you're still going to be the youngest person on staff."

"Oh, come on!" Mr. Benoit scrubbed a hand over his face. "Man, I was hoping that I was going to be older than someone else on the team."

"Attention everyone," Mr. Devereaux said, clapping his hands. "The ingredients for the beignets have been gathered, and Ms. Ellis will now have the floor." He flashed her a wide smile and a thumb's up as he took his seat.

Breanna's heart pounded against her chest for a moment. *Keep your head in the game, Bree. You've got this.*

"Go get 'em', Ms. Ellis," Jennifer said before taking her seat.

"Good afternoon, everyone," Breanna said, standing in front of her audience. "My name is Breanna Ellis, and today, I'm going to be making home-style strawberry-filled beignets with a vanilla bean dipping sauce. This is one of my daughter's favorite pastries because she loves to bake them with me."

"Aww," Jennifer said, placing her hand over her heart. "I used to bake with my babies when they were little too."

Breanna smiled. "Though she's not here with me right now, I'm going to pretend that I can hear her singing her strawberry song, so I'd know to fill it just right."

She heard several audience members laugh as she made her way toward the island. Two students walked behind her and began laying out her ingredients. The young man to her left reminded her of Kelvin. From the waves in his smooth black hair to his smooth brown skin, the two could have passed for brothers if they wanted to.

"Okay, before we make this pastry, we need to get some warm water and active dry yeast married together, so they have their happy time and become frothy."

"Yes, chef," a young woman said as she smiled, standing to her right. Her silky jet-black hair sat in a French braid that hung to the small of her back. Her almond brown skin seemed to glimmer a golden-yellowish hue underneath the lights.

"Chef Ellis," the young man asked, pouring three cups of flour into a glass bowl. "What would you like for me to do next?"

"How about we get to know each other as we bake these beignets?"

He smiled. "Okay."

"Both of my grandmothers loved to bake, and they would always ask me why I love to bake." Breanna grabbed a pack of powdered sugar and pulled it toward her. "So, can you introduce yourself to me and tell me why you love to bake?"

Breanna noticed the young woman's cheeks turn red as she whisked the active dry yeast with the water together.

382

"My name's Jackson Warner," he said, waving at his classmates and faculty. "My father was the king of the kitchen. He would always appoint my older brother and me as his sous chefs. He was the one that sparked my love for sweets."

"My name is Iraja Gulika Williams. I was born in India, but after my father's tour ended there, my parents moved here to Kentfield," she said. Her cheeks reddened more and more with every glance she made at Jackson. "My mother and I love French pastries, and my father loves good ole fashioned American sweets. They always guided me toward the sweeter side of life."

Breanna smiled. "I love the fact that each one of us shares something in common for the love of baking. As my grandmothers would say, a little love makes the pastry a little sweeter."

She opened the powdered sugar with one hand and pulled a glass bowl toward her. "Now that we know we each other a little more and got our prep started, Iraja, I would like for you to put one cup of flour into the water and yeast mix, and Jackson, I would like for you to get three and a half cups of bread flour, one and one-fourth sticks of unsalted butter and three eggs out so we can marry our dough mixture with our yeast mixture."

"Yes, chef," they both said simultaneously.

"Once the flour is all combined with the water and yeast mix, we're going to cover that with some saran wrap and let it sit for about ten minutes so that it can have a little more fun."

"Ms. Ellis," Mr. Benoit said, raising his hand. "How long do you let your dough and yeast proof after it's been mixed?"

"Well, I normally let it go for about an hour and thirty minutes because my daughter and I like our beignets to be a little more on the flakier side," she answered. "But today, we'll only let it proof for about an hour."

Breanna smiled as she watched Iraja and Jackson set aside the combined mixture to let it rise. They reminded her so much of herself and Amber when they used to watch Grandma Isabella and Grandma Zora working in the kitchen. Breanna grabbed a pack of strawberries sitting on the island next to the sink and opened the lid. "Next, we're going to make our strawberry jam. Because I normally make my family's jam from scratch, I keep the ingredients to three simple items. Strawberries, sugar, and fresh lemon."

"Ms. Ellis," Mr. Devereaux said, sitting forward in his seat. "You don't use any gelatin or pectin to thicken the jam?"

"I sure don't," she answered. "Both of my grandmothers believed the best way to achieve the perfect jam was to use a candy thermometer and allow the mixture to boil until it reached 220 degrees."

Breanna watched Mr. Devereaux speak to the dean quietly as she continued her demonstration. God, she hoped she wasn't screwing this opportunity up.

"Since we have an hour to let hour dough rise, we can start hulling these strawberries and dicing them into smaller pieces. Jackson, could you get those mason jars and soak them in some boiling hot water for about fifteen minutes?"

"Yes, chef."

"Thanks, Jackson. Iraja," she said, looking into the woman's beautiful marbled brown eyes. "Start hulling and dicing those strawberries, please."

"Yes, chef."

Breanna opened a medium-sized jar of sugar and dipped her cup inside to gather the ingredient. Pouring about one and one-fourth cups of sugar into a glass bowl she had next to her, Breanna looked back at the rising dough and smiled. If there was one thing going right in this demonstration, it was those beignets.

"Chef Ellis," Jackson said. "Those mason jars have about thirteen more minutes to go."

"Great. Let's get those square cookie cutters so we can start shaping those beignets in a while."

"Yes, chef."

"Chef Ellis," Iraja stared at her. "Do I need to chop these strawberries a bit more, or is this fine?"

Breanna looked at the chopped strawberries and nodded as she smiled. "That's perfect, Iraja."

"Chef Ellis," Jackson said, running toward her and Iraja's direction. "Do you want me to check on the dough?"

Breanna nodded. "Yes. Also, pull out those vanilla beans so we can get the dipping sauce started too."

"On it, chef."

Breanna turned on one burner, setting it to medium-high heat. As she watched Iraja pour the sugar into the pot, she moved out of the way so she could start stirring the jam until it thickened to the right consistency.

She glanced at the audience. The smiles on their faces and hands rubbing their stomachs looked like a good sign to her. Had Elijah been sitting out there, there wouldn't have been any strawberries to put in the pot. He would have eaten most of them, then fed some to her before pulling her into his embrace and kissing her with his sticky sweet lips.

Just remaining his friend was harder than she thought it would be. The way Elijah's mustache would spread when he smiled. The way the muscles in his arms and stomach would flex whenever he lifted something heavy. The way his steel-blue eyes would gleam whenever he stared at her. All of that and then some toyed with her brain like a little boy poking at an animal playing dead with a stick. This transition was by far the most challenging thing she'd ever experienced. Still, she couldn't forget that this was her fault.

Breanna moved around the kitchen, checking the clock. She had to let go of those shoulda, woulda, couldas and keep her head in the game.

"Chef Ellis," Jackson called. "The mason jars have about eight minutes left."

"Great," she said. "How is the jam coming along, Iraja?"

"The froth is beginning to blend in with the mixture and thicken, Chef Ellis."

"Perfect. Be sure to place the candy thermometer inside the jam to check its temperature."

"Yes, chef."

"So now that we've got strawberry going and the dough rising, we'll start on the recipe for the vanilla bean dipping sauce."

"How many vanilla beans do you normally use for this dipping sauce, Ms. Ellis?" Jennifer asked as she took notes on her phone.

"I like to use two vanilla beans. They not only give the sauce flavor, but I love the presentation they display as well."

"Chef Ellis," Jackson said, making his way toward her with a bottle of heavy cream in one hand and a bottle of milk in the other. "What are the measurements for the milk and heavy cream?"

"Two cups for each one," Breanna answered. "Also, we're going to need twelve egg yolks for this sauce."

"Yes, chef," he replied, placing the bottles on the island, then running back to the refrigerator.

The sweet smell of strawberries wafted through the air as Iraja worked her magic. Breanna switched on the second burner next to her, grabbed another pot, and placed it on the stove. "I couldn't have asked for better help. You two are so awesome right now."

"Thank you, Chef Ellis," Jackson said. He placed a carton of eggs on the island. One by one, he cracked each egg, separating the yolk from the egg white and putting them into a glass bowl.

"Likewise," Iraja said, still stirring the strawberry jam. "From here on out, I'm making jam without the pectin. This is so much better than what I normally do."

Breanna smiled. "I'm glad that I've made a believer out of faithful pectin users."

The audience laughed as they watched them work inside the kitchen. Even if she didn't get this gig, this was the absolute best day of her life. Mr. Devereaux gave her more than just hope; he gave her a passport to fulfill a dream she'd always wanted to do. Share her love for pastries, as Grandma Zora and Grandma Isabella did.

"Alright, you all. It's getting close to the time that we've all been waiting for."

"You said the prize-winning words, Ms. Ellis," Benji said, snapping his fingers together.

Breanna laughed as she poured her milk and heavy cream into the pot she had warming on the stove. "Yes, Benji. Beignets are coming soon."

The audience laughed as she noticed Marilyn staring at Benji. She shook her head with pursed lips and folded arms across her chest. Their laughter brought sweet memories of Grandma Zora and Grandma Isabella baking together in the kitchen. Whenever Grandma Isabella started singing and Grandma Zora tapped her foot and hum along to her melodies while smashing those sweet potatoes for the sweet potato pie, Breanna would bob her head from side to side and smile.

Those very moments were happening before her eyes. As much as she wanted this opportunity to go in her favor, she was okay if Mr. Devereaux passed on her. After all the bull crap she put her family through, she deserved every bit of misfortune falling at her feet.

"Chef Ellis," Iraja said. "The jam's ready to go."

"Perfect," Breanna said, smiling at her. "Jackson, how are those mason jars?"

"They're fully sanitized, and the beignets have about twenty minutes left before we roll out this dough."

"Great. You two are so awesome."

"Thank you, chef." Jackson ran toward Breanna and placed the hot mason jars on some paper towels on the island to let them dry out.

"Okay. The final touches have been made to the jam, and we're going to get that canned shortly. But for now," she said, stirring the milk and heavy cream mixture. "I'm going to get my egg yolks and scraped vanilla beans over into this hot pot so that the sauce can finish up."

"Chef Ellis," Mr. Devereaux said. He held up one hand. "I've noticed that you've got five mason jars on the island here. How many jars does the jam actually take?"

"Well, when I make this at home, I normally have enough jam for two jars. But since I knew you all were going to want to taste the jam, I made more for those who want to take some home with them."

386

"I knew you were thinking about me, Ms. Ellis," Benji said. He held his head high in the air as he inhaled the aroma of strawberries and vanilla.

"If you'd like to get a jar of jam, Benji, you are more than welcomed to," Breanna said.

Her eyes darted back to Mr. Devereaux again as she saw him talk to the dean this time. She sucked in a breath and held it for a second. Every nerve ending in her body wanted to catch on fire, but she kept her cool. She had to at this point. The idea of seeing her future discussed in front of her eyes made her want to run from the kitchen.

It was one thing to be judged by others she couldn't see. Yet seeing the person discuss her every move and thought process was total insanity.

"Chef Ellis," Jackson said. "The dough has proofed, and it's ready to the cutout."

"Wonderful," she said, stirring her vanilla dipping sauce. Stem drifted into the air, letting her know it was ready to plate.

Breanna watched Jackson and Iraja press the square-shaped cutters into the dough and line them on a sheet of parchment paper.

This was it. These beignets were either going to give her the go-to snatch her shit from Soul Bistro's locker or keep her head held down until she found something else better. Regardless, she couldn't have asked for better.

Breanna tapped her foot against the white and gray-streaked vinyl floor, trying to keep herself from twirling her already brittle hair between her index and middle fingers. She grazed her teeth against her bottom lip. God, she wanted to know what was being said behind the closed door before her.

After she, Jackson, and Iraja served the audience, all she could hear was happy moans and lip smacking. Grandma Isabella believed that if food could quiet down the loudest of beasts, it could change the mind of the pickiest eater.

As she heard the door open before her, Breanna stood to her feet. Mr. Devereaux stared into her eyes. A smile tugged at the corners of his wide lips.

"Ms. Ellis." He extended his hand toward hers and shook it. "I have a few things I want to talk with you about."

"Okay."

He smiled. "Those beignets were absolutely delightful."

"Thank you, Mr. Devereaux. I normally don't make those since they're a family recipe."

"A scrumptious one, might I add." He stared at her with his big gray eyes. "How long have you worked at Soul Bistro?"

"It's going on four years now."

"I recall you telling me you helped Howard open that place, correct?"

Breanna nodded. "I did."

"Well, he's going to have to say goodbye to you, Ms. Ellis, because your talents are far beyond that restaurant."

Breanna swallowed hard. "What are you saying, Mr. Devereaux?"

"Ms. Ellis, I would love for you to be the head pastry chef here at Culler and Straus Culinary College."

Breanna's eyes widened as she shook his hand. His words flowed through one ear and out the other. "You want me to be a head pastry chef?"

"That I do, Ms. Ellis," he said, smiling at her. "From the moment I stepped inside Soul Bistro and tasted your pastries, I knew I couldn't let your talent pass me by."

"Oh, my God! I can't believe I'm hearing this."

"Believe it, Ms. Ellis. So, are you interested in taking this offer?"

Breanna nodded. "Of course. I've always loved sharing my skills with those around me."

"Well, now is your time."

"Thank you, Mr. Devereaux. I appreciate you for offering me the opportunity."

"You earned it, Ms. Ellis," he replied. "And oh, how does fifty-eight thousand annually sound?"

"Oh my God! That's amazing. It's way more than I make at Soul Bistro."

"Well, Ms. Ellis, I try to treat my people right when they treat me right."

"That I understand."

"Also, this is a Monday through Friday engagement except for the first Saturday of every month when we have our market days," he said. "And those only last for about two to three hours."

"I love it, Mr. Devereaux. I can't wait to start."

"Well, I'm glad that you said that too because I'd like for you to start next week, if you are up to it."

388

"I would love that very much."

"Great," he said, shaking her hand once more. "I'll see you next Tuesday."

"I'll see you then, Mr. Devereaux."

Breanna watched the door close behind Mr. Devereaux as he disappeared back into the conference room, then held her head back and shimmied. She couldn't contain her wide smile as she pranced. If she kept this up, she would have to see Dr. Logan again for re-injuring her arm from dancing too hard.

Breanna pulled her phone out of her pocket and smiled as she dialed Amber's number. She couldn't contain this happiness any longer.

"Hey, little sis. How did it go?" Amber answered.

"I got it, Amber," Breanna squeaked. "Mr. Devereaux offered me the position."

"Yes! I knew it, little sis."

"Amber," Breanna said. She sniffled. "Thank you for being there for me when I didn't know I needed you the most. I love you so much."

"I love you too, Bree," Amber replied, sniffling. "Girl, you're going to have me crying a river in front of my clients."

"Oh, I'm sorry, Amber."

"No worries. I'm so proud of you," she said. "Plus, you know Mom and Dad are going to want to purge you of every sweet that you bring home from the school."

"I know, right. They're going to clean me out."

"Oh, Bree. Before you ask, I'm letting you know I won't be able to pick you up."

"That's okay. I can call Grandma Zora to pick me up."

"There's no need to. Your ride's waiting for you in the parking lot as we speak."

"Okay," Breanna said, hesitantly. "Should I be worried?"

"Nope."

"Okay, sis."

"Trust me, Bree," Amber said. "You're in great hands."

"Alright, Amber. I'll see you back at home."

"Okay, little sis. I love you."

"I love you too," Breanna said, ending the call. Her heart sank to her stomach with every footstep she took toward the exit. Maybe it was Mom or Daddy. But both of them had to work crazy hours today. There was no way they could pick her up unless she sent Leilani to get her. God, she hoped Leilani wasn't her ride today. As much as she loved the woman, she couldn't stand riding in the car with her, knowing there was a possibility she could go flying out the window even if she had her

389

seatbelt on. That woman was more than a freaking speed demon. She was the Flash times two.

Breanna noticed a big red Chevy pickup truck parked near the front entrance and smiled. It seemed like Amber began playing matchmaker again.

"Hey, Bree," Elijah said. He got out of his truck and opened the passenger side door for her. "How did the demonstration go?"

She stared into his steel-blue eyes and smiled, trying to keep herself from blushing. "It went great, actually. Mr. Devereaux offered me the job."

"Are you serious, Bree?" The smile pulling his lips begged her to kiss them.

She nodded. "I'm serious, Blue Eyes. This chick is finally kicking Soul Bistro to the curve."

Elijah draped his arm around her shoulder as he escorted her to his truck. "I'm very proud of you, Bree."

"Thanks, Eli," she said, smiling."

"So, Amber called you."

"Yeah. I was close by."

"What about the houses you all have been working on? I'm pretty sure either you or AJ need to be out there to help Morgan."

He sighed. "AJ's good. I told him I would take my break early."

"What about Izzy? Do you want me to beg Amber to pick her up from school?"

"Nope. She's in the truck," he replied. "She couldn't wait to see you today, so I got her out of school early."

"Aren't you full of surprises today?"

He smiled wryly. "I guess I am."

Breanna stopped in her footsteps and stared into his eyes. The man that stood before her deserved better than what she did to him, yet there he was in all his sexy glory.

"Elijah—"

His lips pressed against hers before she could finish her sentence. She needed more than the Lord's strength. She needed an armored chastity belt with three locks and four keys.

Chapter Fifty-Nine

The sun had done him a favor today and graced Breanna's caramel brown skin just right. That yellow sundress she wore clung to her curves before extending outward like a 50s style pleated skirt, forcing Elijah to take a deep breath. Her hair was pulled into a messy ponytail, with loose strands lying about her shoulders. He had to remind himself they were just friends now. Elijah had to repeat that over and over again to himself, not wanting to admit he still very much wanted to hold Breanna in his arms, run his fingers through her hair, and inhale her scent of lavender and gardenia, like she used to wear when they dated.

Yet, she graciously reminded him three weeks ago that all she wanted was to be his friend. He knew the kiss he planted on her lips took her breath away, but it wasn't enough for her to let go of their new relationship status. Still, he couldn't let her walk away from him that easily. Even if he had one last attempt, Elijah had to get Breanna back in his arms again.

"You okay, big brother?" Katrina asked, standing beside him under the dogwood tree. She glanced at Breanna talking to Leslie near a table where her students stood, then stared at her brother, squinting her eyes. "You look like you can't keep yourself together."

"I can keep myself together, Kat," Elijah huffed, trying to maintain his collective cool. "Besides, shouldn't you be over there with your boyfriend?"

Shading her eyes from the sun with her hand, Katrina nodded, flashing her brother a wide smile. "I should be, but right now, he's over there grubbing on Bree's chocolate loaf cake." She giggled. "Miguel won't be saying a thing to me until he's had his fill. Which reminds me, I've got to get that recipe from her to keep him coming back."

"You really like him, don't you?"

"Just like the way you can't keep your eyes off of Breanna."

"This isn't about me, Kat."

She glanced at Breanna again, watching her converse with her students as they added pastries to their respective tables for patrons to sample. The sounds of laughing kids riding their bikes through the park's bike trail lingered in the distance. "If you want to know the answer to that question, Eli. Yes. I do like Miguel. I think he might be the one. But as for you, big brother, I see a man who's still in love with a woman he never stopped loving."

Elijah peeped at Breanna for a moment, then drew his attention back to his little sister. "We're only just friends. We're keeping it that way for Izzy."

"Oh my God! Eli, stop lying to yourself. You know you still love her." Katrina peeped at Breanna and smiled. She turned her attention back to Elijah and folded her arms across her chest. "Besides, she still feels the same way about you. It's so obvious, Eli."

"Really, Kat?" He watched Kat stroll her way past the other patrons circulating the outdoor market after walking through the park. She looked back at him and waved, giving him a wry smile as she continued her trek forward. Though he didn't want to admit it, Kat was right. He couldn't help but to long for her, to want to be in her presence again. After their split nearly two months ago, Elijah didn't so much as want to see her face, let alone want to be in the same room as she was. But all of that changed when he thought she wouldn't wake up from the coma Nathaniel beat her into.

He took a deep breath, then released it slowly. It was funny how God brought her back into his life. The very woman who ruptured his and Isabella's hearts was the same woman working on improving her own heart so she could get back to their daughter. Honestly, he admired that about her. That took real strength to admit she was wrong. That was something Ms. Gwendolyn would never do in her lifetime.

What took more strength, though, was owning up to the fact she was a victim of sexual assault and not letting that shit break her down. Whether she knew it or not, he was proud of her for leaving the hospital, not wanting to live her life in utter fear.

He stared at Breanna once more, catching her eye. Elijah saw her smile as she waved at him. It seemed like he was back in college again, seeing her for the first-time playing volleyball alongside Leslie. Though they officially became an item after she ran into him in the library, he had seen her weeks before Morgan went on her sex spree with Bryan.

Breanna was so beautiful; she was so genuine. He'd never met another woman like her.

"Hi, Daddy!" Isabella yelled from across the market. She waved at him as she helped Leslie and Amber place more pastries on the table for the new patrons visiting the market.

He smiled, waving at his daughter. She wore a yellow and black polka-dotted sundress, nearly matching Breanna's ensemble. A smile graced his lips as he watched the two of them walk side by side.

Kat was right. He still loved Breanna. It wasn't just her change; it was because she fought to be the woman he fell in love with seven years ago. It was time one of them made a move, and he damn sure wouldn't wait for her any longer.

As Elijah walked in their direction, he noticed Katrina and Miguel staring at him. The wide eyes and wide smile his sister flashed him was the same pestering gaze she used to give him when he proved her right. He was just going to have to take that walk of shame with Kat later and set his sights on making Breanna his wife once and for all.

"Elijah," Breanna said. A smile pulled her natural brownish pink lips. "I'm glad you came over. I saved you a slice of one of my student's Dutch Apple Pie."

"Thanks." He watched her hair flow with the direction of the late spring breeze. "I appreciate that."

"Hey," she said. "Thanks for coming out."

"You don't have to thank me, Bree."

"I do," she replied.

He admired the radiance of her caramel brown skin as she handed him the plate. Gripping it, Elijah let his index finger brush against hers. She gazed into his eyes, letting her index brush against his before moving it away.

"Why?"

"Did you forget you were supposed to meet Morgan at Soul Bistro today?"

"I didn't forget." He took the plate from Breanna's grasp, still wanting to feel her touch. "I wanted Isabella to spend some time at the park today, so this was a no-brainer."

"Daddy." Isabella squinted, looking up at him. "Can Mommy come over and watch a movie tonight instead of going to Granddaddy Marvin's house?"

Breanna stared at him for a moment, then darted her attention to Isabella. "Daddy may have other plans, shortcake."

Isabella looked at her. Her smile mimicked Breanna's. "Nuh-uh. Daddy's not doing anything tonight. He said so himself."

"And when were you going to tell me you've been eavesdropping on me, young lady?" Elijah kneeled next to her. "You should've asked me first before assuming Daddy didn't want to sleep in."

"But I overheard Auntie Amber saying that it would be a good idea if we all watched a movie together like the way we used to. She even said you and Mommy wouldn't mind if I asked."

"Izzy," Breanna said, taking her by the hand. "You should have asked us sooner rather than waiting until now."

"But Auntie Amber said you had nothing else to do after the pastry sale, so she said I should ask the both of you today."

"Izzy," Elijah said. "You can't go making decisions for everyone else at your leisure."

"But Daddy—" She stopped in mid-sentence and pouted. She sniffled, trying to stop her tears from falling. "I really wanted to spend some time with you and Mommy together."

Elijah sighed. Isabella was right, too. He wasn't doing anything special. Hell, after listening to Morgan plea over the phone to him about how much she wanted to be in his presence again, Elijah nearly hung the phone up in her face. The last thing he wanted to hear her do was beg, so he said he'd meet her at Soul Bistro for lunch today. Well, he hoped she wasn't warming his seat for him.

Elijah stood to his feet and saw Amber smiling and waving at him wryly before darting between the red and white striped table covers where the pastries sat. In her defense, she was trying to keep her niece happy. But he knew she was trying to play matchmaker too. She wasn't alone in her efforts, though. Katrina, Leslie and AJ, and their daughter were in the mix. They were all in this matchmaking game together. It was as if they were vying for who got them to sit down and talk first to win the ultimate prize awaiting them.

Though, all he wanted was to spend time with his family. He wanted the love of his life snuggled up in his arms tight again. He wanted to smell her essence mingled with his own again. He wanted—*snap out of it, Elijah.*

Breanna kneeled next to her and planted a kiss on her forehead. "How about, if it's okay with Daddy, I come over for the movie night you suggested, Izzy. I'll bring pizza." She stared into his eyes, smiling.

Elijah lost himself, staring into her brown eyes. "Um... sure. That's fine with me," he said, hoping the sound of desperation wasn't present in his voice.

"Okay," Breanna agreed. "I'll see you both around seven o'clock, tonight."

"That sounds like a plan," Elijah said. "Oh! Who's choosing the movie?"

"Since Shortcake is the one who made this date, how about we let her choose?"

He stared at Isabella, who returned his doppelganger glare with a wide smile. The sheer happiness on her face couldn't be erased at that moment. "Did you hear Mommy, Shortcake?"

"I sure did, Daddy." Isabella nodded as she smiled.

He watched her walk away from him, blending with the patrons surrounding her. God! She was still just as alluring as the day he first met her. But not only that, her demeanor was lighter. Breanna talked more. She smiled more. She was the Breanna he remembered before her mom pumped her head full of bullshit.

"Can I go help Mommy finish up the pastry sale?"

He nodded. "Sure thing, Shortcake." He watched her slink past the patrons, sampling the pastries from Breanna's students, and smiled. It's official. He honestly couldn't say if he was ready for this date tonight, yet what he knew was that he was ready to have his family surrounding him again on the couch. It was a good thing Isabella begged him to come to the park today.

Chapter Sixty

The dong of the doorbell made Elijah stare at the clock on the wall. Seven o'clock didn't waste any time getting here. He fluffed the last pillow and placed it back on the couch next to the blanket he laid there just in case Isabella fell asleep. He smiled. It had been a while since Breanna had been inside this house with him and their daughter. It had been a little too long.

As Elijah walked to the front door, he straightened out his gray sweatpants and blue muscle shirt, trying to remove Daisy's fur and lent that found its way onto his outfit. He knew Breanna wasn't too hung up on appearances like that, but he at least wanted to look like he knew how to groom himself.

"Hey," Elijah said, opening the door. He smiled, noticing Breanna wore the same colors he did. They were just in the opposite directions. The way her blue sweats clung to her hips made junior shift in his boxer briefs. Yet the gray tank top she wore exposed her navel, making junior grow a little more than he wanted him to do. It was a good thing she wore a jacket. The aroma of pepperoni and sausage with an extra hint of banana peppers wafted up to his nostrils, making his stomach growl. He placed his hand over his stomach and chuckled. "Come on in."

"Thanks for having me tonight," Breanna said, walking inside. She stopped for a second as she looked around the kitchen and family room. She smiled. "Where do you want me to put this?"

"You can set it on the island, if you like," Elijah replied as he watched her walk into the kitchen. He had to jam his hands into his pants pockets to keep himself from pulling Breanna into his arms. He closed his eyes and took a deep breath. This was going to be a tough night if he didn't compose himself now.

"Eli," Breanna called to him. "Do you have a spare charging block lying around? I just realized I left mine at Daddy and Mom's house."

Hearing her refer to Mr. Marvin and Mrs. Regina as her parents made him look at her in a different light. She had truly changed. It was as if she had wrapped herself in a cocoon and came out even more beautiful inside than outside. "I should have another one lying around here somewhere," he said.

"Mommy!" Isabella held the rail as she ran down the steps with Daisy by her side. "You're here." She held her arms out, running into Breanna's embrace.

"Hey, Shortcake." Breanna kissed the child on the forehead as she held her tight in her arms.

Daisy barked and wagged her tail at Breanna, waiting for her to rub her head. "Hey Daisy, girl," Breanna said, rubbing the smiling dog's head.

Isabella ran into the family room and hopped onto the couch. She kicked her legs as she smiled. "I chose a movie for us to watch."

"Awesome!" Breanna sat next to her, pulling her close to her side. "Whatcha got for us, Shortcake?"

"A favorite of yours, Mommy." Isabella beamed. "Date with An Angel."

Breanna stared at her with widened eyes and a bright smile. "How did you know this was my favorite movie?"

She giggled. "Cause Auntie Amber told me."

Elijah chuckled, shaking his head. Now, it was official. They had been plotting this moment for the longest. He was going to have to call his sister-in-law out for this one. Still, they were just friends, though. He closed his eyes and shook his head again. Why in the hell did he have to keep reminding himself they were friends. Sure, they agreed to it; it was what she wanted, but it wasn't set in stone for him.

Even though Elijah didn't want to admit it, Morgan was a great comfort to him at that moment in his life. He didn't think we would have made it as a single father without her. But he had. Besides, Morgan didn't want to have anything to do with Isabella. If she had it her way, Morgan would have shipped Izzy off to some boarding school so she could have him all to herself.

Elijah knew who he wanted in his life. And it damn sure wasn't Morgan Everly. He watched the two most important women in his life laugh and gush over the movie they were about to watch. This was what he wanted; he had to show her now.

"So, are you two going to keep going on about this movie, or are we going to watch it?"

"Really, Eli?" Breanna asked as she giggled. "You're the last one that needs to be talking. You used to always add extra fixings to your popcorn before the movie started. Whoever puts lemon pepper seasoning and hot sauce on popcorn has a twisted sense of taste or either pregnant."

"Oh! So, now you're saying that I have weird taste, and I eat like a pregnant woman." Elijah covered his heart with his hand. "Well, I never."

Breanna and Isabella fell over on the couch in laughter. Elijah listened to them giggle and smiled as he shook his head. He walked toward the couch and gathered Isabella into his arms, tickling her stomach as he picked her up from the soft cushion she sat on. Her squeals and laughter made him smile.

"I refuse to be the butt end of your jokes," he chuckled.

"Then stop making yourself the butt end, Eli," Breanna said through giggles.

"You've gone and done it now, lady." Elijah kissed Isabella's forehead, then placed her back on the couch. He leaned toward Breanna and pulled her into his embrace, tickling her sides. She threw her head back, belting out the loudest snorts and giggles. "You hear that, Izzy. Mommy sounds like one of those farm animals from your book."

He watched her nod her head as she giggled. He hadn't seen their daughter smile and laugh this hard in a while. But what he adored the most was seeing Breanna's smile and hearing her giggles close to his ear. He had his family back again.

"Come on, Eli," Breanna said, trying to catch her breath from laughing so hard. "Let's watch this movie. I haven't seen it in ages."

He stared at her, losing himself in her brown eyes. "Alright, then." He kissed her cheek, reveling in its softness against his lips. Even though this night had to end, it would never end in his heart and mind. It was going to be on constant replay.

Elijah watched her smile at him as her cheeks turned red. Breanna looked away from him, covering her smile with her hand. "Come on, Eli," she said. "I really want to watch this movie."

He smiled. "Okay. You don't have to be so pushy, Bree."

"I'm not being pushy. You're stalling." She smiled.

Isabella giggled as she watched the two of them. "Come on, you two. Let's watch the movie." She rubbed her stomach. "Besides, I'm hungry."

"Uh-oh," Elijah said. He leaned toward her and tapped her on the nose with his index finger, making her giggle. "I've played around long enough."

As Elijah opened the disc cartridge and fed the disc into the DVD player, he heard Breanna get up from the couch and walk into the kitchen. He sat next to Isabella, placed his arm around her shoulder, and pulled her closer to him. This night would never end for him.

Breanna watched Isabella snuggle tiredly against her daddy's chest and drift back to sleep. Her head moved up and down as Elijah snored loud enough to harmonize with the music rolling with the ending credits. It had been a long time since she'd seen them fall asleep together. Breanna picked up the blanket and covered them both, then picked up the destruction of paper plates they left behind while watching the movie. She missed this so much. Even if this were the last time she had to spend with them, Breanna would never forget this night.

Breanna walked into the kitchen and threw away the paper plates. The last time she stood inside this kitchen, she contemplated taking her own life; she had nothing else to live for. Thank God she hadn't. She wouldn't have been able to see this very moment again. She wiped away a streaming tear as she turned on the faucet and let the water run until it warmed to the temperature she liked.

She hummed as she allowed the water to soak the dish towel so she could wipe down the island. Humming, she closed her eyes. She hadn't sung since the first night she got to Mom and Daddy's house.

"Breanna," Elijah said, walking behind her. He rubbed his eye, then stretched, watching her jump. "I'm sorry, Bree," he chuckled.

Breanna looked back at him and smiled. "It's fine. Are you okay?"

"Yeah," he stretched again. "I'm good."

"Good," Breanna said. She stared at the clock on the wall, seeing 11:37 pm staring back at her as she covered her mouth and yawned. She didn't need to overstay her welcome, or more so not make Daddy place an APB out on her for not coming home. Living with her parents again came with its fair share of restrictions, but it sure beat the idea of having to pay for a hotel room every night.

"What time do you need to head out?"

"Probably around midnight," she answered. "I don't want Daddy losing any sleep."

"He knows you're with Izzy and me, right?"

"He does," she nodded. "But I don't want him to worry, considering what happened to me a while back."

Elijah stepped closer to her and took her arm into his soft grasp. "Does it still hurt since you got your cast removed?"

"Not much." She stared into his eyes. Her nipples pressed against the sports bra she wore. She hoped they didn't want to make a grand appearance and embarrass her.

He cupped her chin, losing himself in her eyes. "Please stay tonight. I'll let Mr. Marvin know you stayed with me and Isabella for the night."

"I shouldn't."

His torso pressed against hers, making her knees wobble like jello. He cupped her chin once more, then let his lips press against hers.

She moaned against them, savoring the sweet tanginess of the pizza sauce and robust flavor of the Italian Sausage lingering on his lips and tongue. "Eli..."

"Let's put Isabella to bed," Elijah said against her lips. "Then, maybe we can go to bed too."

"I probably shouldn't," Breanna said. "Daddy's probably going to be worried about me."

"Trust me. He won't be worried."

"Why would you say that?"

"I've got my reasons, Bree," he said, stepping away from her. "I'm going to go get Izzy so I can put her to bed. You can help me if you like."

She watched him walk out the kitchen, then took a deep breath. That man knew how to turn her on. But Breanna wouldn't go back on her word. She still wanted to be friends with Elijah. It was hard as hell for sure. On top of that, the man had a hard-on like no other. She couldn't leave him like that, but tonight she had to.

Breanna heard his footsteps go up the stairs as she walked into the family room and saw Elijah carrying a sleeping Isabella. Her head rested on his shoulder; their daughter never woke from her slumber. Breanna followed them into Isabella's bedroom. She stood in the doorway, watching Elijah lay her in the bed.

"Mommy," Isabella grumbled as she snuggled her head against her pillow. "Can you come back in the morning?"

Breanna walked into the room and sat on the other side of her bed. She kissed her cheek. "As long as Daddy says it's okay, I'll be here, Shortcake."

"Do you have to go now?" She pouted. Tears welled in her little eyes.

"I would love to stay, Izzy, but Granddaddy Marvin is going to get worried if I don't go back home."

"But I want you to stay, Mommy," she said, yawning.

"Maybe next time, Shortcake." Breanna kissed her forehead one last time. "But I promise I'll be back in the morning. Bright and early, okay."

Isabella nodded as she drifted back to sleep. "Okay."

"I got her from here, Bree," Elijah said, pulling the cover over her shoulders.

Breanna nodded, then made her way out of Isabella's bedroom. She wanted to stay the night with them. But she couldn't let Daddy worry his already unstable heart. The last thing she wanted to do was make him worried about her. After Nathaniel assaulted her in the parking lot of Soul Bistro, she hadn't walked into a parking lot alone without thinking he was right behind her since. Every creek and rustle in the background kept her on high alert. She knew Nathaniel was probably still watching and waiting on her every move. Yet, she couldn't live in fear for the rest of her life. She guessed that was why Dr. Shelby wanted her to mentor other young women who had fallen victim to rape and sexual assault like she had.

"Breanna," Elijah said, pulling Isabella's door closed until it made a small crack.

"Yeah." She caught sight of his steel-blue eyes.

"I want you to reconsider and stay tonight."

"Why, Eli?"

He pulled her into his embrace, holding her tight. "Because I want you back with me. I need you back with me."

"I need you too," she whispered.

"Then, don't leave me."

"Elijah... I can't."

"You can." He kissed her lips, allowing his tongue to dip into her mouth, teasing her. "I already called Mr. Marvin before Amber dropped you off earlier."

"When were you going to tell me this?"

"When the time was right." He swept her off her feet and carried her into the bedroom she once shared with him. "I've missed you."

"I've missed you too, Eli."

"Let me make love to you," he said, placing her feet on the floor near the bed. He put his hand against the small of her back and caressed it. "Please."

As she pulled him into a kiss, Breanna moaned against his lips, wanting his hands to caress her body the way he used to. Elijah's hands traveled around her waist, making her suck in a breath. She loosened the drawstring to his sweats and let them fall to his ankles, exposing the blue boxer briefs he wore.

She watched him stand back from her and pull off his muscle shirt. The muscles in his arms and torso seemed to have flexed as she ran her fingers across them. She stared into his eyes and smiled.

Elijah kissed her lips once more as he pulled Breanna back into his embrace. He swept her off her feet, then laid her on the bed. Breanna watched him untie her drawstring to her sweats. His hand slid inside them, slinking its way toward her clit.

Breanna grasped his forearm and sat up to meet his eyes.

"Are you okay, Bree?"

She swallowed hard. "I'm okay... I'm just—"

"I can stop if you want me to—"

"Please don't," she said, cutting him off. Breanna caressed his face with her fingers. She wasn't about to let what Nathaniel did to her come between her and the man she loved. She had done that enough already. "I'm just a little frightened. That's all."

"Please don't be," he said, kissing her lips. "I won't hurt you. I promise."

She nodded as she laid back on the bed. She watched Elijah remove her socks, then slide her sweats down her legs, followed by the black French Cut panties she wore. Elijah kissed his way from her toes to her lips, then straddled her, helping her out of her tank top. He unclasped her bra and threw it to the floor. He caressed her nipples with his fingertips as he kissed her deeper, forcing them to stand to his attention.

Breanna ran the tips of her fingers against his chest and abdomen. He closed his eyes, sucking in a breath. He took her hand in his and kissed the back of it before rubbing it against his cheek. "I love you."

"I love you too, Bree." He whispered. "I never stopped loving you."

Breanna watched him stand from the bed and slide off his underwear. His length pointed at her, begging her to play with it. She watched him scope her body out from her hair follicles to her lavender colored toenails. He smiled at her, letting out a staggered breath.

"Remember our first time," he said, lying next to her.

"I remember," she whispered. Breanna gazed into his steel-blue eyes, feeling his fingers slide down her torso until they found their stopping point. Her clit.

"Close your eyes and relax." He pressed his lips against her forehead. "Let your mind drift away."

The caress of his fingers against her clit made her suck in another breath. "Eli," she breathed. His fingers massaged the part of her body

402

that hadn't felt his touch in a while. Intertwining her fingers with his, Breanna moaned as she arched her back against the softness of the bed. She felt his pace quicken, forcing her to moan louder. She gripped the bedsheet with her free hand and pulled it closer to her body.

"Do you like that?" he whispered in her ear.

Breanna stared at him, seeing his wry smile. She moaned louder as he slid one of his fingers inside of her. "I do."

"Good," he said, slowing his pace.

"Elijah."

"Yes, baby," he whispered.

"I want to feel you inside me." Breanna sucked in another breath. "Please."

"Is that what you want?"

She nodded, watching him move from her side. He parted her legs with his hands, then rested himself in between them, rubbing his length in the wetness he created. He moaned, sliding his length back and forth against her vagina. He kissed her forehead once more, then stared into her eyes. "Are you sure this is what you want, Bree?"

"Yes," she breathed.

Breanna closed her eyes, then parted her lips, feeling his length tease her still. He was so damn thick and long. Elijah wasn't even inside her yet, and Breanna could feel him pressing on her G-Spot. She intertwined his fingers with one of hers as she watched him use the other to guide himself inside her.

Breanna sucked in a breath. She had been without Elijah for nearly two months. She had been without his touch, his taste, his smell, his look, and his sound too long. All of them, which he recreated perfectly in the bedroom.

"Eli," Breanna moaned aloud.

"I'll be gentle," Elijah whispered against her forehead as he kissed it once more.

As Elijah thrusted slowly within her, he rested his body weight on top of her, still holding onto her hand. He kissed her, keeping his rhythm slow and steady.

She closed her eyes as his length slid in and out of her. Breanna buried her face in his shoulder, trying to keep herself from moaning so loud. His steady breathing brushed against her neck, making her bite his shoulder lightly.

"Sounds like you like that?"

Breanna moaned in agreement, feeling him quicken his pace gradually. She moaned his name in his ear, forcing him to bite his bottom lip and moan aloud.

403

Elijah propped himself on his knees and pulled Breanna up from the bed, forcing her to straddle his hips. He held her close to his body as he kissed her. She ran her fingers through his hair as he slid back inside her and thrust slowly within her again.

"Hold on to me," Elijah said, gazing into her eyes.

Breanna nodded. His hand caressed the small of her back as he thrust faster. She bit her bottom lip, trying to keep from moaning aloud again, but he wasn't making it easy for her to stay quiet. All she hoped was that Izzy didn't come knocking on the door because she heard her parents groaning and screaming God's name.

She threw her head back as she closed her eyes tight. The ebbs and flows of his length traveled through her body, making her quiver.

"Eli," she breathed in his ear. "I'm all yours."

"And I'm yours," he responded, slowing the pace of his thrusting. He gazed into his eyes and smiled. "I don't want to live another day without you, Breanna," he said, pulling her into a kiss. "Please be my wife."

"Elijah," she paused. Tears played at her tear ducts. "What about us taking our time? What about us remaining friends?"

"You'll always be my best friend, Breanna," Elijah said, removing a strand of hair from her face. "You'll always be the love of my life, and the woman I deem my wife."

"Eli... I can't—"

He placed his index finger on her lips, stopping her from talking. Removing his finger, he kissed her lips once more. "I love you so much, Bree. I love all of you despite the hard times we went through and are going to through. I don't want to miss the chance of marrying the one-woman God made specifically for me."

A tear slipped down Breanna's cheek. Even with all the shit they had been through, she knew she didn't want to let him go. But she was willing to do it because she wanted him to be happy. She wanted their daughter to be happy. She didn't want to lose him or Isabella again because of her foolishness. But she sure as hell didn't want to ruin his life again, either.

"Breanna," Elijah said, peering into her eyes. "I want you to be mine, and I yours until time fades away. Please be my wife."

Breanna closed her eyes for a moment, thinking back to the times when they used to stare into each other's eyes and smile, waiting to see who was going to give in first and kiss the other. And before Isabella was born, she remembered how they used to lie in their underwear together and watch reruns of The Real World together to see who was going to argue over whose wallet was bigger.

Those were the moments Breanna didn't want to let go of. Those were the moments she wanted to create more of, but she didn't know how, especially after what she had done to them. She didn't want to put their hearts in limbo again. Yet Breanna knew what she needed. Her family. She needed them more than she ever realized. For them, she would go through every up and down as long as she had Elijah and Isabella in her life. As Breanna opened her eyes, she stared into his and nodded. A tear slid down her cheek. "Yes."

He smiled, then pulled her into another kiss. He flicked his tongue into her mouth while slowly thrusting his length in and out of her. "I love you, Breanna."

"I love you too, Blue Eyes."

Feeling him quicken his pace, Breanna closed her eyes again as she threw her head back once more. He wrapped his arms around her torso as he rested his head against her chest. His growl like moans made her moan aloud. The deeper he thrust within her, the more she ground her hips against his pelvis. Every thrust within her core made her bite her bottom lip.

"I wanna save a horse," she said, gazing into Elijah's eyes. She smiled at him wryly as she placed her hands on his chest and guided him to the bed until he was flat on his back.

"I'm ready for this ride, baby," he said, holding onto her hips.

"Good." She rocked her hips, making him harder inside of her.

"Bree," he moaned, biting his lower lip. "God, you feel so good."

Breanna smiled at him, rocking her hips slowly in a rhythmic motion. His hands gripped her waist tighter. He was nearing his peak. But he was going to have to work for that release.

"Oh, God! Please don't stop, Bree!"

She moaned louder as she closed her eyes. Breanna gripped his chest tighter, digging her natural French Tip nails into his skin. She rocked her hips faster as he matched her pace with his thrusts.

"Eli," Breanna breathed. "I love you."

"I love you too, Bree."

His hands guided her hips as she rocked her hips. Every roll of her hips and every thrust of his hips made them moan aloud together. If they woke up Izzy, she knew they had some explaining to do. But it was so worth it. Breanna was with the one man that would never give her less than a five-star orgasm. Better yet, it was more of a ten-star, she mused to herself.

"I'm so close, Eli," Breanna moaned.

He gazed into her eyes. "Cum for me, Bree," he breathed. "Please don't make me wait."

Breanna closed her eyes tight as she dug her nails further into his chest. Every little vibration and tingle exploded in her pelvis, surging its way throughout her body. Breanna savored hearing Elijah moan her

405

name as he climaxed. He wrapped his arms around her as he sat up to meet her. She kissed him deeply.

"I can't wait to spend the rest of my life with you, Mr. Bryson." She stared into his eyes, admiring his beautiful smile.

"Neither can I, Mrs. Bryson." He pulled her into another kiss. "I love you so much, Breanna."

"I love you too, Elijah. I always will."

Chapter Sixty-One

Watching Mommy and Daddy snuggled together under the blanket she and Gigi got them for Christmas last year was a dream come true. They laughed in sync every time Hammy failed horribly at trying to steal food to help RJ feed a ferociously lazy bear. What was the most adorable was when every time Mommy giggled, she would bury her head in Daddy's shoulder. She smiled. Isabella didn't want the fairy godmother to tell her that her time was up if this was a fairy tale. She wanted this to last forever.

"You've seen this movie so many times, Bree, and you still watch it like you're watching it for the first time." Elijah popped a couple of pieces of popcorn into his mouth before kissing her cheek.

"That's because this is an awesome movie, Eli," she replied. Mommy snuck a couple of pieces of Daddy's popcorn and popped them into her mouth. "Besides, this movie doesn't require me to fill in the blanks or complete puzzles like the one we watched last weekend."

"Oh, come on, Bree," he said. "Inception is a thinking man's must-watch."

"Whenever I have to use a guide to help me understand the movie while I'm watching it, Blue Eyes, there's a problem."

He shook his head. "If Izzy understood the movie, then I know you can too."

"Shortcake." Mommy smiled as she stared at her. "Did you understand the movie we watched last week?"

Isabella nodded, glaring into each of their eyes. "They were sleeping and began having nightmares, and they were floating."

Mommy stared at Daddy with a cocked eyebrow and pursed lips. "Does that seem like she understood that hot mess of a movie, Eli?"

Daddy nodded. His smile widened. "It does, Bree. And she probably liked it too. Didn't you, shortcake?"

"Can we watch Robinhood Men in Tights next weekend, Daddy?" Isabella placed her hands together while staring at him with her big doppelganger eyes. "Can we please?"

"You got your answer, Eli," Mommy said, laughing.

"I see where this is going. You two have been plotting."

"The only thing we've been plotting was trying to figure out what Cobb was trying to do while he was jumping and playing around in people's minds."

"Whatever, Bree," Daddy said. He stared at Mommy and kissed her on the lips.

Isabella covered her face with both her hands as she giggled. "Mommy. Daddy. You two have been kissing all day."

"That's what mommies and daddies are supposed to do when they're in love, Shortcake." Breanna leaned over, removed Isabella's hands from her face, and kissed her cheek.

"Speaking of being in love, Shortcake." Daddy paused. He stared into Mommy's eyes, then back at hers. "Mommy and I have something we want to talk to you about."

"Okay," she replied, snuggling closer to her parents. She watched how they smiled at each other before directing their attention back to her again.

"Well, four weeks ago, Mommy and I had a long talk about us being a family again, and we decided we want to make things official."

"What do you mean, Daddy?"

"Well, what your daddy is trying to say is that we've decided to get—"

"Married?!"

"Yes, Shortcake," Daddy said. "Mommy and Daddy are getting married."

"Really?" Isabella beamed. "You two are getting married?"

Mommy nodded. "Yes, shortcake. We are. But since your birthday is two weeks away, we're not sure if we'll be able to get married then."

Isabella's big, bright steel-blue eyes welled with tears. "Why not?"

"There's so much planning that we've got to do, Shortcake," Mommy replied.

"Don't worry, Shortcake," Daddy said, smiling at her. "Mommy and I are going to give you the best sixth birthday celebration ever."

"Okay," she said, wiping her eyes with the back of her hand. Isabella stared at her mommy and daddy and smiled. They were getting

408

married. Mommy and Daddy were finally getting married. Her dream had come true. Gigi and Grandma Gina told her that if she kept praying every night for her Mommy and Daddy, something good would happen.

Mommy's cell phone rang for the fifth time tonight. Isabella watched her pick up the device and frown. It must have been Yaya again. When Mommy tried to talk to Yaya earlier today, she took Daisy for a walk through the entire neighborhood. For Mommy, walking Daisy was more than a workout. It was a high-stakes mission that only secret agents could fulfill.

"Breanna." Daddy stared into Mommy's eyes once more. "You need to talk to her again."

"I don't need to talk to Momma again if she's going to snatch my head off like she did earlier."

"Bree, please. She's just trying to connect with you."

"She's trying to convince me not to marry you, Elijah."

"Why doesn't Yaya want you to marry Mommy, Daddy?"

The phone continued to ring as she noticed Mommy take a deep breath and look away from her. Daddy beckoned for her to sit in between them under the blanket.

"Yaya doesn't want Daddy to marry Mommy because—" Mommy paused, swallowing hard. "Because she doesn't like the color of his skin."

"Why not?"

Daddy took Mommy's hand into his and squeezed it tight. "Because someone who shared my skin color did something terrible to Yaya a long time ago."

"But it wasn't you, Daddy."

"I know, Shortcake," he said. "But Yaya was deeply affected by what happened to her years ago."

"Doesn't Yaya know Daddy didn't do that bad thing to her, Mommy?"

"She does, Izzy," Mommy replied. "She's just... she only wants what's best for Mommy."

"But that's not fair, Mommy." Isabella stared into each of their eyes. "Daddy did nothing to her. Doesn't she know how to forgive people?"

"People deal with pain differently, Izzy," Daddy said, kissing her on the forehead.

Mommy's phone rang once again. Yaya wouldn't stop calling until Mommy did what she wanted her to do. Leave Daddy again. Even though Mommy and Daddy said Yaya couldn't handle the pain she endured years ago, she sure didn't mind hurting Mommy and Daddy

409

for her own needs and wants. Didn't she know how much they loved each other? Didn't she even care?

"Hey, Shortcake," Daddy said. "How about you and I go refill this bowl of popcorn and get some more fruit punch, shall we?"

She nodded, smiling at him. "Okay, Daddy."

Isabella knew exactly what Daddy was trying to do. She just hoped that Daddy wouldn't let Yaya break them apart.

Breanna watched Elijah take Isabella by the hand and lead her into the kitchen. She smiled. Those two people meant the world to her. She couldn't let Momma fuck with her head again like she did before. She flat-out refused. The last time she allowed Momma to infest her mind, she was left lying in a parking lot half-naked and nearly beaten to death.

As she dialed Momma's number, Breanna listened to the phone ring. Momma probably sat there and watched the phone ring. She hated to be the one with lesser power.

"Hello," Momma answered.

"Momma, we need to talk."

"You took the words right out of my mouth, Breanna," she said, sharply. "Please tell me why you're marrying this man."

"Because he cares deeply about me."

"That man doesn't care about you, Breanna. He only wants to control you. Don't you see that?"

"He's not Peter, Momma," she stated. "Elijah has always treated me right, and he's done nothing to hurt me."

"He cheated on you, Breanna."

"No. He didn't, Momma. I was the one who cheated on him, and I'll regret that forever." Breanna frowned, feeling a cramp like pain surge through her stomach and pelvis. She took a deep breath, then rubbed her stomach as the pain waxed and waned. "Momma, why can't you see that I'm the one that messed up."

"Oh, I can see that, honey. You made one of the biggest mistakes by not apologizing to Nathaniel as you should have."

"Momma, that man sexually assaulted me. I wake up every morning and go to bed every night knowing that man hurt me."

"You should have apologized to Nathaniel."

410

Breanna sighed, trying to keep her calm. "Momma, I apologized to the right man, and that's Elijah. He and I are going to get married soon, and if you don't want to have any part of it, then don't come to the wedding."

"So, that's your final answer, huh?"

"It is, Momma," Breanna said, still rubbing her stomach. "You don't have to like it, but you will respect my choice."

"And now you're telling me what you're going to do. Sounds like your father fucked you up worse than I did."

"No, Momma. He taught me I needed to change my ways for the better before I ruined the greatest thing in the world."

"Well, go ahead and marry Elijah, then. You won't see me at your shit show of a wedding."

"Fine, Momma. You don't have to come, but I still love you. I always will love you."

"I wish I could say the same for you, Breanna," Momma said.

"Now, I see why Daddy left you. You had a wonderful man, and you cheated on him with a man that threatened your life and your children's lives. I guess you like that kind of attention."

"You little bitch," Momma hissed. "I hope you have a happy life with your slave owner."

Breanna listened to the phone hang up. Momma's words resounded in her ears. The woman knew how to screw people over when she didn't get what she wanted, but she refused to fall for Momma's shit again.

Pain surged through her stomach once more, forcing her to wince aloud.

"Breanna," Elijah said, walking back into the family room. "Babe, are you okay?"

She rubbed her stomach and tried to stand from the couch. Slumping back into the soft cushion, Breanna shook her head. "I don't know what's wrong."

"Daddy," Isabella said, running into the family room. "What's wrong with Mommy?"

"I'm not sure, Shortcake," he said, pulling his phone out of his pocket. "I'm going to call Mrs. Regina, okay."

"Mom's probably asleep by now."

"It's only eight o'clock, Bree. I bet she's awake watching something on the Sci-Fi channel."

"Mommy," Isabella said, sitting next to her on the couch. "It's going to be okay."

Breanna stared into Izzy's eyes and smiled. The last time she felt pain like this, she was—that couldn't have been what was happening.

411

She overheard Elijah talking to Mom on the phone as she leaned over and kissed Isabella on the forehead. "Mommy's going to go to the bathroom, okay."

"Okay, Mommy. Do you need me to help you upstairs?"

"I got it from here, Shortcake."

Breanna stood to her feet and made her way toward the stairs as she held her stomach. There was no way she could get pregnant again. After the doctors warned her it wouldn't be in her best interest to get pregnant again, she started taking birth control to avoid the risk.

Shit. Breanna hadn't taken her birth control in weeks since Dr. Logan didn't want her mixing all those medicines together. That couldn't have been that, though, she thought. It had been nearly four weeks ago since she and Elijah had sex. It was their so-called attempt at trying to abstain from intercourse since they said they were going to get married soon.

She switched on the light inside their master bathroom, opened the cabinet door, and pulled out the only pregnancy test she had. Before Nathaniel came into the picture some months ago, she thought she was pregnant then. But the tests proved her wrong.

"Hey, my old friend," Breanna said, taking out a testing strip and unwrapping it. She sat on the toilet and let the test do the rest of the work.

"Breanna," Elijah ran into the bathroom. His eyes darted to the box lying on the countertop, then widened as they landed on her. "Mrs. Regina said she'll be here in another fifteen minutes."

"Okay," she said, sliding the top onto the testing strip and setting it on the toilet's tank lid. She flushed it, then washed her hands, trying to keep herself from looking at the testing strip.

"Bree," Elijah swallowed hard. "Are you—"

"I'm not sure yet, Eli. But we'll find out in another minute."

"Have you missed your period?"

Breanna's eyes widened. She hadn't seen that thing in two weeks. Without fail, her flow would make its presence knowingly every mid-month until now.

"How long does it take to tell if you're—"

"In a few more seconds, we'll know." Breanna twiddled her thumbs around one another as she sat on the countertop. This wait was torturous.

"What does it say, Bree?"

Breanna took a deep breath as she grabbed the testing strip. Her heart beat hard against her chest as she looked at the piece of plastic.

"Oh, my God!" Breanna covered her mouth. Aunt Aubrey and Grandma Isabella were right. "Eli... I'm pregnant."

Chapter Sixty-Two

"How far along are you, little sis?" Amber posed, as she admired herself in the three mirrors in front of her. She peeped her leg from underneath the flowy asymmetrical line of the one-shoulder marigold dress she wore.

"Dr. Harrison said that I'm two weeks in." Breanna walked from the dressing room in the white dress Mom chose for her and stared in the mirror. A single tear slid down her cheek as she held her stomach and smiled. She and Elijah weren't only just making Shortcake's day one to remember, but they were bringing another life into their world. Nothing could take that away, except for the odd individual running past the storefront every ten minutes, she noticed as she glanced out of the floor-length windows.

As she watched several people walk past the store they were inside, she focused her attention on the people walking by. For the life of her, Breanna couldn't stop the hairs on her arms from standing every time the tall figure ran by. Her heart pounded against her chest.

If Nathaniel attacked you once out in the open, he wouldn't give two shits about attacking you here.

Breanna took a deep breath. She didn't need that kind of stress on her body. She had a little life inside of her to focus on now.

She looked in the mirror once more and admired the embroidered lacework on the back of the dress she wore. It appeared as if someone painted the beautiful artistry on her bare caramel skin. And the halter neck and waistline cinched to her body like a leather glove, revealing portions of her sides where the embroidery continued.

"Oh, my goodness. Look at my baby," Mom said, getting up from the chair. "The embroidery on the back is fire. Is that how ya'll young folks say it now these days?"

Breanna and Amber looked at each other and laughed.

"It's lit, Mom, and you will not be saying that anymore," Amber said.

"Listen here, chitlins," she said, trying to stop herself from smiling while pointing at them. "I may not have birthed the both of you, but I'm going to give the both of you some good old fashion butt whippings if you two keep messin' with me, you hear."

Breanna laughed. "Mom, you wouldn't have the heart to spank us. We're the awesomest of awesome children."

"Girl, what you said!" Amber held her hand up and high-fived her little sister. "Mom wouldn't dare, especially not in front of my fiancé, anyway."

Mom's eyes widened as she covered her mouth. She turned and looked at Leilani and beckoned for her to come into her embrace. "So, now I've got two weddings I've got to plan."

Breanna turned toward Amber and mouthed the words, "Told ya' so."

Amber rolled her eyes as she shook her head. The redness of her round cheeks deepened as she fought hard not to smile.

"Mom. Leilani and I were thinking about going to the Justice of Peace to get married."

"Not under my watch, you don't."

"But Mom—"

"Not another word, Amber," she said, hugging Leilani tighter. "Your father and I will handle this."

"Mom," Breanna said. "You and Daddy are already making this impromptu wedding happen for me and Elijah in the next week. Amber and I aren't trying to sap you and Daddy out of a house and home."

Mom glanced at each of them and smiled. "Your father and I will be okay. Besides, you two are my world. When I learned I couldn't have children of my own, God blessed me with you two." Mom sniffled. "You girls are the best children a woman like me could ever ask for."

Breanna walked toward Mom in her white dress and hugged her and Leilani. Tears streamed down her cheeks. "I'm blessed to have you as a mom, too. I love you so much, Mom."

"I love you too, Breanna," she whispered against her ear.

"I love you too, Leilani," Mom said, sniffling.

Amber stood in the middle of the showroom floor and wiped both her eyes with her index fingers. "I love you too, Mom."

"I love you too, Amber."

The consultant stood next to her and swatted a tear away. "Okay, you guys are going to make my mascara run," she said, swatting away another tear.

"And Amber," Mom said, staring at her. "You better work that dress."

Amber swayed her hips from side to side, then placed her hands on her hips as she posed. "Oh, I'mma work this dress."

"Breanna," Mom said, looking in her direction. "Is Leslie still coming?"

She nodded. "Yes, ma'am. She said she was running a little late."

"My God, you're beautiful, Bree," Elijah said, walking inside with Mr. Jonah and Daddy behind him.

She smiled, then walked toward him. His eyes seemed to beam as she drew closer to him. He pulled her into his embrace and kissed her.

"Do you like the dress?"

"Bree, you've never looked more gorgeous."

Her cheeks flushed a reddish hue. "Eli, are you trying to make me blush more than I already am?"

"Is it working?"

She nodded.

"Then, my work here is done."

They all laughed. Breanna looked around at her family and smiled. What she wanted before could never give her this. It could never give her this kind of happiness.

"Well," the consultant said, standing among them all. "Is the beautiful, expecting bride going to choose this dress?"

Breanna stared into the young woman's big green eyes and nodded. "I think this is a definite yes."

"Perfect." The young woman clapped her hands as she jumped about. "I also have a single-tier floor-length veil that has the same embroidery on the back of your dress."

"She'll take it," Mom said quickly.

Amber turned her attention toward Breanna and mouthed the words, "I knew I was right."

Breanna shook her head as she giggled before rubbing her stomach and taking a deep breath.

"Are you okay, Bree?" Elijah took her by the hand and guided her toward the couch.

"I'm okay, Blue Eyes," she said, sitting down. "I probably should have eaten a bit more than what I did this morning."

"Bree, you need to eat."

"I know I do," she replied. "I didn't want to make a mess on the floor if I felt the urge to lose my breakfast."

415

"You need some crackers and a Sprite."

Breanna smiled as she waved her hand at the consultant. "I'm okay. I just feel a little weak."

"As soon as we leave here, Breanna, you're going to get something to eat," Mom said.

"We were going to pick up Isabella from Grandma Zora's house," Elijah said. "I know she said that she was making some fried chicken, biscuits, mashed potatoes and gravy, and some green beans with bacon."

"Momma said she was making all that?" Daddy stood beside Elijah and rubbed his stomach. "Why come she didn't tell me that when I called her earlier?"

"Because she knew you were going to tell her not to make all that food." Mom smiled at Daddy wryly.

"Hey everybody," Leslie said, walking inside as she held onto AJ's arm. "I'm so sorry we're late."

"You're fine, Leslie." Breanna pulled her into her embrace and held her tight. "Thanks for coming."

"I wouldn't have missed this for nothing, sis."

"I almost forgot that I still have the jacket you left from the other night," Breanna said.

"You're the best, Bree. I honestly thought I would have to buy my little sister a new jacket. Thank God for small miracles."

"Let me go get out of this dress, and I'll go get it for you."

"Are you sure?"

"I'm sure," Breanna said. "I can get some fresh air, so little one inside won't get angry."

"Aww! How far along are you?"

"Two weeks."

Leslie's smile widened. "Does Isabella know she's about to be a big sister?"

"Not yet." Breanna smiled. "We're waiting for her birthday to tell her."

"OMG! Girl, she doesn't even know you and Elijah are getting married on her birthday."

"Shortcake is going to be elated."

"Girl, she's going to cry."

Feeling a twinge of hunger pain mixed in with cramps, Breanna rubbed her stomach once more. "I better go get out of this dress before I make a mess for real."

Breanna walked toward the dressing room and entered the small area. The consultant followed in behind her and closed the door.

"Ms. Ellis," the young woman said. "You look so beautiful in this dress."

"Thank you. I really appreciate you helping my mom find it for me."

"You know," the young woman spoke. "When I got married two years ago, my mother had five different dresses for me to try on."

Breanna chuckled. "How did you know you found the one?"

"When she had nothing else to say, I knew that was my one dress."

Breanna smiled once more. Mom sort of did the same thing to her, too. It was too bad, though Momma didn't want to be a part of this. It would have been perfect if everyone she loved dearly were here to celebrate this moment in her life. But that wasn't how her life worked.

The hairs on her arms rose once more as she pulled on her jeans and t-shirt. She couldn't shake the feeling that Nathaniel was out there waiting for her. Hell, for the past few weeks she'd been working at Culler and Strauss Culinary College, Breanna hadn't walked through the parking lot without thinking someone followed her.

Breanna took another deep breath. She had to get over this. She couldn't live her life in fear. Still, she couldn't stop her body from reacting to the unsettled things happening around her.

"Thanks for helping out of the dress, miss."

"You're so welcome, Ms. Ellis."

Breanna walked out of the dressing room and toward Elijah. God, he was a pleasing sight to the eye. His silky short brownish-black hair, beautiful steel-blue eyes, and an even more beautiful smile made her nipples press against her bra. That was either the hormones kicking her tail or her attempt at being abstinent wearing off. Either way, it wasn't working that well.

"Eli, do you have your keys on you?"

"I do," he said, pulling them out of his pocket and handing them to her. "Do you want me to go get Leslie's jacket so you can sit down?"

Breanna smiled as she shook her head. "I'm okay, blue eyes. I need the fresh air, anyway."

"Alright, Bree," he replied, staring into her eyes. "As soon as Leslie is done trying on her dress, I'm taking you back home ASAP."

"Eli, seriously, I'm okay."

"And have the mother of my second child passing out on me, I don't think so."

"You know I like it when you take charge like that."

He took a deep breath. "My God, woman. You're making it difficult for me to wait until our wedding night."

"I know," she said, walking away from him. She watched him smile at her until she exited the building and stood on the sidewalk. Her heart pounded against her chest as she stepped onto the pavement and walked toward Eli's truck.

You're okay, Breanna. Nathaniel isn't out here. Just calm down.

As she opened the truck's passenger door and grabbed Leslie's jacket, Breanna turned around and stared Nathaniel square in the eyes. This couldn't have been happening again.

"You've been hiding from me, huh, Beautiful?"

Breanna swallowed hard as she stared into Nathaniel's cognac eyes. "How did you find me?"

"I've got good people who support me, Breanna."

This was Momma's doing. With Tessa in jail and Howard no longer in her contact log, she was the only person she thought would pull a stunt like this.

"What do you want from me, Nathaniel?"

"That tight little pussy of yours," he said. A smirk pulled on his lips. "You owe me that. Remember?"

"I don't owe you anything, Nathaniel." Breanna held a hand in front of him, keeping him at a distance. With her other hand in her back pocket, she pulled her cellphone out and woke it, hoping he wouldn't hear it.

"You know," Nathaniel said, yanking her other hand in front of her. "You keep thinking that I'm stupid, Bree. I wish you wouldn't do that."

She struggled to pull the arm he broke from his grasp. "I don't think you're stupid. I think you're fucking insane."

"Bitch got jokes." He laughed. "Too bad she ain't smart like her mother."

He gripped her throat and squeezed it. The smirk on his face was just as devious as the first time he tried to rape her in Soul Bistro's parking lot. She squirmed, fighting to get out of his grasp. Breanna glanced at his legs, noticing how far apart they were from each other. She only had one shot at getting herself out of this mess.

Focus, Bree, and remember what Elijah taught you.

Kicking him with as much force as she could, Nathaniel loosened his grip from around her throat. Breanna ran from him, hoping he wouldn't follow her. His coughs and grunts alerted her he was only down for a few moments, but it was now or never to get away from him.

Breanna ran through the parking lot and hid behind a blue pickup truck. Her hands shook as she dialed Elijah's number.

"Breanna," he answered, listening to her staggered breathing. "Babe, are you okay?"

"He's out here."

"Nathaniel?"

418

Breanna trembled as she listened to his footsteps near her. "Yes."

"I'm on my way, Bree. Stay where you are, okay."

She nodded. Her hands trembled as she tried to keep the phone steady in her hands. "Okay."

"Breanna," Nathaniel yelled. "Come out from where you are. I won't hurt you."

She covered her mouth, trying to keep herself from whimpering too loud. She closed her eyes tight and prayed. His footsteps grew closer to her as she breathed harder. This was her fault, for sure. But by no means did she expect Nathaniel to take his lust for her body this far. He needed help.

"There she is," he said. Nathaniel grabbed a hand full of her hair and yanked her to her feet. "Since you didn't obey like a good little bitch, you're going to have to pay the price."

The sound of a cocking gun stopped them both.

"Let her go, Nathaniel, and I'll stand down."

"Ole dude," he said, turning toward Elijah. "You came to save this bitch."

"That woman," Elijah said, stepping closer to him slowly. "Means more to me than you could ever fathom."

"She ain't nothing but a hoe, Elijah. Hoes get what they deserve in the end, man. Just save yourself and walk away."

"Let her go, Nathaniel. Think about yourself."

"Come on, Elijah." Nathaniel laughed. "You're honestly going to shoot me for her."

"For the mother of my children, I wouldn't hesitate."

"Children?" He stared at Breanna with squinted eyes, then chuckled. "It doesn't surprise ole dude knocked you up again. That's all yo' ass did was fuck him when you should have been giving that pussy to me."

Nathaniel pulled a knife from his pocket and placed the blade's sharp edge at Breanna's throat. "I'm going to make you regret you ever went back to white boy."

"You hurt her, Nathaniel, and I'm going to make sure you use a wheelchair for the rest of your life."

Nathaniel laughed. "You're as dumb as they come for letting this bitch ruin your life."

"Just let her go, Nathaniel."

"Why are you even wasting your breath, Elijah? Let her come to where she belongs. With me."

Nathaniel gripped her hair tighter as the loud, whirring police siren drew closer to them. Her breathing labored as she kept eye contact with Elijah. His steel-blue eyes seemed so dark; they seemed almost malicious.

419

She struggled against Nathaniel's hold, only to be yanked closer to him.

"Keep moving bitch, and I'll write your name on the ground with your own blood."

"Nathaniel!"

"Let me go, Nathaniel. You're hurting me."

He gripped her cheeks and forced her head in his direction. Nathaniel stared into her eyes. "Ya' think white boy here is going to save you now." He hissed, pressing the knife's blade further into her neck. A drop of blood slid down her neck. "Go ahead, white boy. Try to save your bitch now."

Breanna stared into Elijah's eyes still. A tear slid down her cheek. If this would be the last time she ever laid eyes on the man she loved, she wanted to remember him at his happiest.

"I'm so sorry I dragged you into this, Eli," Breanna sobbed. "I love you."

"Bree," Elijah said, focusing his attention on Nathaniel. "You're going to be okay."

"Put the gun on the ground, Elijah," Detective Bradford yelled.

"That's right, white boy. Do what the officer told you to do."

Breanna watched Elijah slowly place his gun on the ground and hold his hands up. She breathed deeper, feeling Nathaniel press the blade's edge further into her skin. She closed her eyes and whimpered.

"That's right, my guy. Be a good little bitch and back away."

"Let go of my wife, Nathaniel."

"Damn, bruh! You're full of surprises, aren't you?"

"Let her go, Nathaniel," Elijah growled.

"Nathaniel," Detective Bradford spoke. He stepped closer toward the three of them. "Let go of Mrs. Bryson and walk away from this."

"Sounds like you ain't never been screwed over by a woman before, detective?"

"I have, Nathaniel," Detective Bradford replied. "I just knew when to walk away from her."

Breanna swallowed hard, feeling the knife tear into more of her skin. She glanced around at the onlookers. Several of them covered their mouths and pointed in their direction while others had their phones out, recording her imminent demise.

"Please, let me go, Nathaniel," she cried. "Please."

"It's going to be okay, Bree."

"I love you, Elijah."

Nathaniel twisted his neck from side to side before glaring at her. Sweat rolled into his furrowed eyebrows and down the sides of his face. "You love ole dude more than me?"

420

"Yes."

"Would you die for him?" He removed the knife from her throat, then yanked her head back and smirked. "Answer me, Breanna!"

"Yes," she cried out, fighting against his hold. "I would die for him."

"Let go of Mrs. Bryson, Nathaniel," Detective Bradford yelled once more.

"Don't struggle, Breanna. I need you to stay calm, okay."

Nathaniel chuckled. His smirk never left his face. "How about I take the one thing you love the most away from you so you can see what you've done to me."

"Don't you hurt her, Nathaniel!"

"Shanking her ass first won't solve my problems, bruh." Nathaniel laughed. "But taking yo' ass first will."

He shoved Breanna into Detective Bradford, forcing him to lower his gun. Nathaniel ran toward Elijah and lunged at him, knocking him to the ground. She watched her husband struggle against Nathaniel's hold as they rolled around on the ground. Elijah jabbed him in the side three times before Nathaniel came back with his own left hook to her husband's eye.

Breanna held onto Detective Bradford as he pulled her away from the two men.

"Stay with me, Mrs. Bryson."

"He's hurting him," she yelled. Breanna watched as Elijah pushed Nathaniel off him and landed two punches to his eye and jaw. Nathaniel shoved her husband to the ground once more and lunged for his gun. Elijah sprang to his feet and lunged at Nathaniel. She watched the two men wrestle over the weapon between them.

"Control, this is Detective Bradford. I need backup and two buses ASAP!" he demanded. "I've got an innocent in my custody and a fight ensuing before me."

"Copy that, Detective," a woman's voice said over the radio. "Backup's en route."

She watched Nathaniel hit Elijah in the face with the butt end of the gun before her husband grabbed it. As they struggled to get control of the weapon, the deafening sounds of two gunshots reverberated in the atmosphere. Screams lingered in the background as people ran from where they were. The whirring of another police siren and two ambulances blared in her ears as they neared their location.

Elijah stood to his feet, breathing deeply. Nathaniel grunted through coughs as blood began pooling around his body. Nathaniel struggled to speak as blood trickled down the side of his mouth. He stared at Breanna as he rested his head on the ground and closed his eyes.

421

Breanna ran toward Elijah and wrapped her arms around his neck. He wrapped his arms around her body, holding her tight in his embrace.

"Are you okay, Eli?"

"I'm okay, Bree," he said, burying his head into her shoulder.

Her tears greeted his black shirt as she cried. She grabbed onto the back of his shirt and held it tight. "I love you, Eli."

"I love you too, Bree."

"Mr. Bryson," Detective Malone said, walking toward her partner. "We need to let the paramedics checkout that gash over your eye."

He stared into her eyes, then placed his hand on her stomach. "You should probably check my wife out first. She's two weeks pregnant."

Breanna stared into his eyes, trying to muster a smile. "I'm okay, Blue Eyes. You need to get that looked at."

He nodded. "Okay."

"Right this way, Mr. Bryson," Detective Malone said, escorting Elijah to the ambulance.

"You should tell your husband he should consider joining the force, Mrs. Bryson." Detective Bradford said before walking over to Nathaniel's body.

"Detective, I know my husband," Breanna said. "He's happy throwing old tubs and toilets out of windows."

Detective Bradford nodded, then chuckled. "Maybe I should give him a call one of these days."

Breanna looked at Elijah sitting in the back of the ambulance and smiled. "You should, Detective."

Breanna watched two paramedics hoist Nathaniel's limp body onto the gurney and strap him down before loading him up into the other ambulance. She scowled. For everything he'd done to her, she forgave him. He didn't deserve to be lying in a pool of his own blood. But for every ill intention he had in store for her, Breanna wanted him to rot where he laid. Even dirt was too good for his body.

Chapter Sixty-Three

B reanna sat in front of the mirror, took a deep breath, and smiled. Today was finally here. Of all the arguments and bullshit she and Elijah put themselves through, there was nothing better than knowing she could stand on her own two feet, admit she was wrong, and love the person who stared back at her in the mirror.

Breanna held her stomach for a moment. A twinge of nausea toyed with her, forcing her to take another deep breath. "Alright little one, be easy on Mommy today. Please."

"I used to tell Katrina the same thing when I was pregnant with her." Mrs. Lori stood behind and smiled before embracing her. Her white and marigold floral patterned tea length dress meshed with the embroidery in her veil. "You are so beautiful, sweetheart."

"Thank you, Mrs. Lori," she said. She stood to her feet and adjusted her white dress. The floor length trained flowed over her white peep toe pumps, mingling with the single-tier veil Grandma Zora styled in her side swept curls.

"Breanna." Mrs. Lori took her hands. "Sweetheart, I can't tell you how long I've been waiting for this day. I'm so happy my son chose you. I love you so much."

"I love you too, Mrs. Lori."

"Bree," Amber said, peeping her head inside the dressing room. "Mom and Dad have already gotten Isabella fitted in her dress, have been to the ice cream parlor, and are on their way to take pictures."

"That little girl doesn't like waiting long for nothing at all."

"She gets it from her momma, little sis."

"Whatever, Amber." Breanna smiled. "Just wait until you and Leilani decide to have kids. I'm going to be at your door counting down the minutes you sleep."

"Until Leilani decides she wants to go down that route, I'll be getting my beauty sleep," she said, sticking her tongue out at her before scampering away in laughter.

"Mmm-hmm," Breanna said, folding her arms across her chest. "I wouldn't give it two months after they get married that Leilani's going to want kids."

Mrs. Lori shook her head as she laughed. "I'm so happy to see you two talking to each other again."

"To be honest with you, Mrs. Lori." Breanna smiled. "I wouldn't be here right now had it not been for my big sister. I'm grateful for her, my mom, and my daddy."

"What about Ms. Gwendolyn?"

Breanna looked away from Mrs. Lori and sat in front of the mirror. She'd spent the last several hours trying to convince Momma to come to the wedding. She even disregarded the fact Momma told Nathaniel where she was. Breanna wanted to share this moment with her. But all she did was blame her for the coma Nathaniel fell into after suffering two gunshot wounds to the hip and chest.

To Momma, Elijah should have been the one lying in that hospital bed. Not Nathaniel. Elijah should have been the one near death. Yet Momma refused to see that Nathaniel did the same thing to her that Peter did. Momma just told her to pull up her panties like a big girl and apologize to the man.

Though Breanna knew it was wrong, Momma was better off not knowing she was pregnant again. "Momma doesn't want to be here."

"Did you try to talk to her, sweetheart?"

"I did, Mrs. Lori," Breanna said. "But as she told me time and time again, she didn't want to have anything to do with this shit show."

A tear slid down Breanna's cheek. The one person who she thought would support her denied her with every chance she got.

"Please don't cry, Breanna." Mrs. Lori pulled her into her embrace and kissed her cheek. "This is you and your soon-to-be husband's special day. The only tears there should be are happy ones."

"Mom," Kat said, poking her head inside the dressing room. "Are you in here?"

"Yes, honey. I am."

"Oh, thank God." Kat stepped inside and closed the door behind her. Her marigold dress accentuated her slender yet hippy curves well. "Dad said that Mr. Marvin and Mrs. Regina are only ten minutes out.

The guy at Izzy's photoshoot had another client to call him, so they're leaving the studio earlier than we hoped for."

"Crap," Mrs. Lori said under her breath. "Have they already taken her to the Build-A-Bear Workshop yet?"

"I'm not sure."

"If they haven't, that will buy us about twenty more minutes until the musicians get here and set up their band. If not, then we've only got fifteen minutes until showtime."

"Do you need me to do anything, Mrs. Lori?" Breanna stared into her ocean blue eyes.

"No, sweetheart. All you need to do is sit here and wait for your groom to meet you at the altar in the next fifteen minutes."

Breanna nodded. Hearing those words made another tear slide down her cheek. She swatted it away quickly, trying to maintain the exquisite application of makeup Grandma Zora applied to her face.

Kat pranced toward her and kissed her on the cheek. "I can't wait to officially call you my real sister."

"Kat," Breanna said. "Now, you know I have always considered you to be my sister from another mother, anyway."

Kat smiled. "Bree, please don't make me cry. I don't want to ruin my makeup before Miguel sees me."

"There you go again, Katrina." Mrs. Lori shook her head. "He's going to think you're beautiful regardless of how you look."

"I don't need to be a hot mess walking down the aisle, Mom." Kat opened the door and beckoned for Mrs. Lori to follow her.

"We'll see you in another fourteen minutes, okay."

Watching them leave out the room, Breanna turned toward the mirror and took another deep breath. Only fourteen minutes left until she became Mrs. Bryson. She pinched her skin, hoping this day wasn't a dream. Breanna glanced in the mirror once more and smiled. She heard her phone vibrate on the vanity's countertop and stared at it. She smiled. He must have been anxious too.

"Eli," Breanna answered. "You know Mrs. Lori would have a fit if she knew you called me."

"What she doesn't know won't hurt her. Besides, she doesn't even know where I am right now."

Breanna furrowed an eyebrow. "Where are you, anyway?"

"I'm close by."

The rhythmic sounds of knuckles against wood made Breanna furrow her eyebrows. She walked to the door and opened it. Elijah smiled at her as he held the phone to his ear. The black and white pinstripe tux he wore fit his slender, muscular build just right. His black tie sat snuggly over the buttons of his white dress shirt, and the marigold vest he wore made her bite her bottom lip. God, she wanted to tear each piece of clothing off him where he stood, but if she didn't want to risk getting caught by his mother, Breanna had to remain calm and copacetic.

He stepped inside the room and pulled her into his embrace. Elijah cupped her chin and kissed her lips. "God, I can't wait to marry you, Mrs. Bryson."

"I can't wait to marry you too, Mr. Bryson." She kissed his lips once more.

"When I was sneaking my way to come see you, I saw the musicians setting up their equipment."

"They're finally here."

Elijah nodded. "And Kat told me that Shortcake will be here with your parents in another two minutes since the shop closed earlier than they expected."

"Do you have the birthday card we bought her?"

"It's inside my suit jacket pocket," he answered, patting it.

He stared at his phone as it vibrated in his hand. "I better get going. My dad is covering for me."

Breanna kissed him one last time before he left out the door. She smiled, watching him strut before he turned around and smiled at her again. Everything she wanted couldn't compare to the things she needed around her. And for that, she was so thankful. Now, she could say she was blessed.

The sounds of piano keys and a woman's smooth alto-like melodies harmonized from a distance. Breanna hummed along with the tunes, then sang the lyrics to Izzy's favorite song, Brand New, by Mac Ayres. She wiped away another tear. In less than eight minutes, she was about to make her family whole.

"I wish you were here to see this Grandma Isabella and Aunt Aubrey, but I know that you're standing right here with me." She sniffled, wiping away another fleeting tear. Breanna placed her hand on her stomach and smiled. "I love you so much, Cameron."

She sat back down at the vanity and stared in the mirror one last time. Six months ago, she went in search of a want that nearly left her dead in a parking lot. But when she realized what she needed outweighed what she wanted, Breanna was grateful her path took the direction it did.

"Bree," Mom said, knocking on the door. She stepped inside and smiled at her. Water played at her tear ducts. "Oh, my baby. You are so beautiful."

"Thank you, Mom."

"Not to turn this day sour, but did you ever get in touch with your mother?"

"She never answered, Mom."

"Are you going to be okay?"

Another tear slid down her cheek as she nodded. "I have my mom in front of me."

Mom pulled her into her embrace and kissed her cheek. "I love you so much, my baby."

"I love you too, Mom."

"Hey, my beautiful ladies," Daddy said, stepping inside the room. "The coordinator said that we're ready to march."

Breanna smiled. She stared at Mom and Daddy and wiped away another tear. This was the very moment she prayed for, and God didn't fall short on his promise to her. Though Momma had nothing else to do with her, she still had room in her heart for her to come back in.

"Now, are you sure you're able to sing this song without feeling out of breath?" Daddy took her by the arm and led her out the room.

"I think I'll be okay," Breanna said. "I sang a lot during my pregnancy with Isabella. Hopefully, this little guy or gal will let me sing too."

"I hope so." Mom closed the door behind them and took Breanna by the other arm. "Isabella's going to burst into tears when she hears you singing her other favorite song."

As they walked outside the building, Breanna peered at the outdoor venue. White, light green, yellow, and pink flowers sat decoratively across several arches throughout the garden.

"Is Izzy wearing the white dress Eli and I picked out for her?"

"She sure is," Mom said. "And she looks so gorgeous in it."

"I wonder if she asked any questions about Grandma Zora doing her hair."

"Nope. She's been living the fabulous life, honey," Mom answered. "Your father put his shades on her, and she thought she was Doug E Fresh for a moment."

Breanna giggled. That was Elijah through and through.

"Alright, Ms. Isabella," the woman said over the microphone. "Your Mommy and Daddy have a big surprise for you today. Are you ready to see what that surprise is?"

"Un-huh," Isabella said.

"So, before we bring them out to give you your birthday gift, could you remind everyone sitting out here with you what you wanted for your birthday."

"I want my mommy and daddy to get married today."

"That's some birthday wish, Izzy," the woman said. "I'm not sure if I can make that happen with the snap of my fingers, but I bet if you closed your eyes really tight and wished upon that evening star, I know it's bound to come true."

Hearing the piano play its melody, Breanna watched Amber take Grandma Zora by the arm and walk down the runner leading to the large arch erected before the park's waterfall. Breanna took a deep breath and wiped away another tear as she watched Leslie and AJ walk down the aisle together. Kat and Miguel followed behind them.

She noticed Elijah standing between Mrs. Lori and Mr. Jonah as they walked down the aisle after Kat and Miguel.

"Are you ready, my baby?" Mom smiled at her, kissing her on the cheek one last time.

Breanna nodded. "I'm ready, Mom."

As she stepped out into the sunlight with Mom and Daddy by her side, Breanna belted out every melody to Exclusively by Tiana Major9 as they made their way down the aisle. She watched Isabella wipe her eyes with the backs of her hands. She was so pretty in her white laced flower dress. Yellow, green, and white flowers sat in her curly hair. She held onto her Tiana Princess doll as she cried.

Breanna stood before Elijah and took both of his hands as she sang until the other musician took over. He smiled. A fleeting tear slid down his cheek. She watched the pastor come before them. The smile on his face reminded her of Granddaddy Edwards.

"Before we begin this ceremony, the bride and groom want to share a little news with their daughter first."

Breanna beckoned for her to come toward them. Elijah held his hand out to her and picked her up with one arm.

"Shortcake," Breanna said, smiling. "Daddy and I want you to know that we love you so much. We couldn't let this moment pass us by."

"And shortcake," Elijah said, kissing her on the cheek. "Mommy and I want you to know that you're going to be the best big sister your future little brother or sister will ever have."

Breanna watched Isabella's eyes and smile widen before she pouted and cried once more.

"I love you two so much, Mommy and Daddy."

"We love you too, Shortcake," Breanna and Elijah said together.

Breanna smiled at the people standing before her as she wiped away more tears. They were the happiness her soul craved for; they were the warmth her heart longed for. This was what she wanted for so long. No. This was what she needed.

Epilogue

Breanna patted Cameron's little back as she rocked and hummed with him in her arms. He wiggled in them every time he fussed. She kissed his forehead and continued to hum. Just two months ago, this little angel came wailing and shivering into the world. The only feature of Breanna he had was her hair. From his ears to his nose and even his tiny fingers, Cameron was Elijah's replica, through and through.

And when he opened his beautiful steel-blue eyes to her and Elijah for the first time, Breanna knew they outnumbered her. She kissed his forehead, hearing him coo before he fell asleep for the night.

Unlike his big sister, Isabella, Cameron would sleep soundly through the night. Then again, he hardly gave her any trouble when she was pregnant with him, she thought.

Elijah stepped into the nursery and smiled. He wrapped his arms around Breanna's waist and kissed the side of her forehead.

"Is my little man finally asleep?" he whispered against her ear.

She nodded. "Is K.O. good enough for an answer for you?"

He kissed her forehead again and smiled. "He's mine for sure."

Breanna laid Cameron in his cradle and placed her hand on his stomach for a moment. His little eyebrows furrowed as he moved his head to the side. He yawned, then nuzzled his head against the mattress before breathing deeply.

"Mommy and Daddy love you, Cameron," Breanna said. She took Elijah by the hand and closed the door behind her as he led her out of the room.

"Is Shortcake still watching the movie?"

"I'm not sure," he said, shrugging his shoulders. "The last time I checked, she was falling asleep too."

"It's beginning to sound like a date night, Mr. Bryson."

Elijah smiled as he pulled her into his embrace. "I concur, Mrs. Bryson. What do you suggest we do?"

"Well," Breanna said, smiling as she stared into his eyes. "Since Dr. Harrison gave me the all-clear two weeks ago to return my normal, I think a little fun wouldn't hurt."

"I like the sound of that," he said, kissing her lips. "I'm going to get Shortcake and put her to bed."

"Okay," she said, watching him walk down the stairs. Her phone vibrated in her pants pocket as she walked into the bedroom. Pulling the device out of her pocket, she frowned at the screen. Why in the hell was Detective Bradford calling her at nine o'clock at night.

"Hello."

"Mrs. Bryson," Detective Bradford said. "I hope I'm not disturbing your family, but I wanted to talk to you about something Detective Malone and I recently discovered."

"Okay." Breanna sat on the bed and wrapped one of her arms around her waist. Her heart pounded against her chest like a hard drumbeat.

"My partner and I reopened Aubrey Marshall's murder case a few weeks ago, after we received a phone call from a Makayla Oswald. Do you know of her?"

She stared at Elijah with a raised eyebrow and shook her head. "The name doesn't sound familiar to me, Detective Bradford."

Elijah sat on the bed next to her with furrowed eyebrows and took her hand in his. Breanna tapped the speaker button on her phone and held it between her and her husband.

"Well, Ms. Oswald named you and your sister, Amber Ellis, as people she knew."

"Detective, I don't know of her."

"She knows you."

Breanna's frown deepened. "How?"

"Ms. Oswald brought forward the person who murdered Aubrey Marshall and her partner back in 1995."

Breanna placed her hand over her heart as it beat hard against it. "Detective, who murdered my Aunt Aubrey?"

"Pauline Marshall," Detective Bradford answered. "Ms. Oswald found the missing bent blood-stained license plate that was originally reported at the scene of the crime."

"Oh my God." Breanna stared at Elijah with wide eyes. "Has she been arrested yet?"

430

"She has, Mrs. Bryson, but theirs one other suspect we're still looking for."

"Who is it?"

"Peter Oswald."

Breanna shook her head as she breathed deeply. Peter was the very man Momma cheated on Daddy with. He nearly killed her. He almost ruined—Momma lied to her and Amber. She frowned. How many false truths and honest lies had Momma told them?

Made in the USA
Columbia, SC
25 March 2022